I0726752

All rights reserved. No part of this publication may be reproduced, distributed, or transmitted in any form or by any means, including photocopying, recording, or other electronic or mechanical methods, without the prior written permission of the publisher, except in the case of brief quotations embodied in critical reviews and certain other noncommercial uses permitted by copyright law.

This publication includes new works of fiction as well as those in the public domain.
Any resemblance to actual events or persons, living or dead, is entirely coincidental.

COPYRIGHT© 2025, OFFBEAT PUBLISHING, LLC

ISBN: (PAPERBACK) 978-1-950464-83-8
ISBN: (EBOOK) 978-1-950464-86-9

FALL 2025

ISSUE #17

WHAT

WHERE

IN EVERY ISSUE OF ADV, WE MAKE *NOSTALGIA* A THEME, BUT THIS FALL WE'RE taking it a step further. In addition to our usual segments - Southwest Scenarios, Snapshot in Time, old ads and more - in issue No. 17 we're introducing Retro Rewind and re-introducing classic character Rocky Fortune.

In "Mermaid Show," an original story by Evan Purcell - who is the son of Darryle, writer of the above-mentioned Southwest Scenarios - a character from an old radio show is resurrected. We get into the history of Rocky Fortune in the foreword to the story, so we'll just say here that he was a fun character voiced by none other than Frank Sinatra.

Starting in this issue, we're also going to bring you reviews of classic books and movies. The brains behind ADV all love reading and watching the classics, and we thought we'd share that enjoyment and let you know how these works stand up all these years later.

For the inaugural entry, we've chosen "Psycho." We review the book that started it all, and also review the original movie, directed by the great Alfred Hitchcock. We already have plans for what we'll be reviewing for the next edition of ADV, but if you have any suggestions, please email us and let us know!

We also have plenty of other stories in this edition that you'll enjoy, including works by Charles Dickens and Virginia Woolf. And because this is fall, we have included a seriously spooky story - "Carmilla" by Joseph Sheridan Le Fanu. It's one of the earliest vampire stories in all of literature, even predating Bram Stoker's "Dracula."

(By the way, if you're interested in vampires, be sure to check out our special collection of early vampire works. You can see those on our website.)

As always, thanks for joining us on another adventure!

Michael Brian

Michael Brian

Letters to the editor:
Comments/Questions accepted.
Put *Letter to Editor* in Subject
and send to:
AdventuresBookzine@proton.me
*Name and Email content could
be published in a future Issue.

VINTAGE & Velvet
CLOTHING
Style from the Past for the Woman of Today
www.vintageandvelvetclothing.com

The following ballad is a medieval Swedish ballad.

It is translated from a 1673 manuscript, the earliest recorded source.

Ingmar Bergman partly based his 1960 film, *The Virgin Spring*, on this
ballad.

Töres döttrar i Wänge

("Per Tyrsson's daughters in Vänge")

Cold was their forest
While the forest bloomed with leaves

The daughters of Per Tyrsson in Vänge,
Cold was their forest,
They slept a sleep too long.
While the forest bloomed with leaves

The youngest woke first,
Cold was their forest,
And so she roused her sisters.
While the forest bloomed with leaves

They sat upon their bedstead,
Braided each other's locks,
Put on their silken dresses,
And set off for the church.

But when they reached Vänge hill,
Three highwaymen they met.
"Will you be wives to robbers,
Or lose your youthful lives?"

"We'll not be wives to robbers,
We'd rather lose our lives."
They struck their heads on birch logs,
And three wells sprang up there.

Their bodies they buried in mire,
Their clothes they bore to town.
When they came to Vänge farm,
Lady Karin stood in the yard.

"Will you buy silken shirts,
Knitted and stitched by nine maidens?"
"Untie your sacks, let me see,
Perhaps I know all three."

Lady Karin struck her breast,
Sought Per Tyrsson in haste.
"Three highwaymen are in our yard,
They've slain our daughters dear."

Per Tyrsson seized his sword,
Struck dead the eldest two.
The third he left alive,
And asked him who he was.

"Who is your father, your mother?"
"Our father, Per Tyrsson in Vänge,
Our mother, Karin in Stränge."
Per Tyrsson went to the forge,
Had iron forged round his waist.

"What shall we do for our sins?"
"We'll build a church of lime and stone,
The church shall be called Kärna,
And we'll build it with zeal."
Cold was their forest
While the forest bloomed with leaves

Southwest Scenarios

COMMENTARIES FROM RURAL ARIZONA
BY DARRYLE PURCELL

Some of my columns, like the one which follows, may cause readers to think I am not very conservative and am picking on Republicans a little too much. Most elected officials in Mohave County are Republicans. In the most recent election (2020), 75 percent of county voters chose the Republican candidate over that other guy. So suck it up, buttercup.
(Printed in the paper Aug. 14, 1998)

News scoops pigeon poop problem

THE *MOHAVE VALLEY DAILY NEWS* HAS COVERED SOME INTERESTING TOPICS IN the last couple of weeks including killer bees, poopy pigeons and snotty Republicans.

Supervisors have decided that pigeons with loose bowels have become a deadly menace for Mohave County. They contend that these winged pariahs have not only reached critical mass population-wise, but are now hell-bent on a rampage of destruction through aerial poopy bombardment of civilian and government rooftops. And, unlike killer bees, they cannot be scooped up in a vacuum cleaner.

Therefore, county residents have been saddled with the draconian rule now commonly known as "feed a pigeon, go to jail."

Already, I understand, there has been a backlash to this law, which has created a whole new category of criminal. It may only be a rumor, but an unnamed informant has told me that a new category of criminal gang has been created in reaction to the ruling. The gang, known as the Pigeon Putsch, is made up of elderly ladies, many who fought in the underground during the big war, who hang around parks and street corners flaunting their distaste for the law. They can be recognized by their black leather jackets with pictures of a Walter Lanz' cartoon character, Homer Pigeon, painted on the backs. They carry large bags of contraband popcorn that they criminally disperse to the feathered manure spreaders. It's said they are armed with bird-head topped canes. (One has a bird-head topped walker.)

Certainly there must be some more-reasonable reaction available to our county leaders in dealing with our feathered friends' potty problems. Possibly, the county could allow the feeding of pigeons as long as the popcorn is laced with Kaopectate. This would allow the birds to pucker up and clean up their act, and, as a possible side benefit, improve their image among other birds. (This may help the above-mentioned Republicans as well.)

Another possible cure for the problem would be to tie a hungry coyote on the top of every roof in the county. It has been found that rubber snakes and owls do not scare pigeons. They make nests on the snakes and I can't tell you (in a family newspaper) what they do with the owls. But hungry coyotes are another matter. I guarantee that no pigeon would roost on a roof protected by a hungry coyote. Of course there probably would be a slight problem of what to do with the piles of coyote poop that would end up on the roofs.

Then, of course, the county could follow the example of Bullhead City's pet ordinance, and make it a law that all pigeons should be licensed. People would have to license the pigeons they wanted to keep and all unlicensed pigeons would be taken to the fowl pound to wait for adoption.

If this last example is successful, it may also work on killer bees and snotty Republicans.

Southwest Scenarios

The commentaries here and in future issues were originally published by *The Mohave Valley Daily News between 1993 & 2013--and* in many ways they apply to today. We are grateful to republish these commentaries written by Darryle Purcell in full and unedited. His own brand of humor and style can deliver insight, provoke thought, and even boil blood.

HISTORICAL EMPORIUM

Est. 2003

Buy at... HISTORICAL EMPORIUM

Whose **REPUTATION** is *celebrated* world-wide as the pre-eminent clothing source for the **ADVENTUROUS** and *Fashionable*.

We are...

REVERED
by our customers

REVILED
by our competitors

RESPECTED
by all who know us

NO LOCAL DEALER CAN COMPETE WITH OUR QUALITY, VARIETY AND INCOMPARIBLE CUSTOMER SERVICE!

ACCEPT NO SUBSTITUTE!
If you require **clothing and supplies** as stylish and **stout-hearted** as you, contact us immediately to be outfitted.

800-997-4311

HistoricalEmporium.com

FROM 1913: HELEN MAYRE, WITH HER 3 WHEELS AND FOUR LEGS.

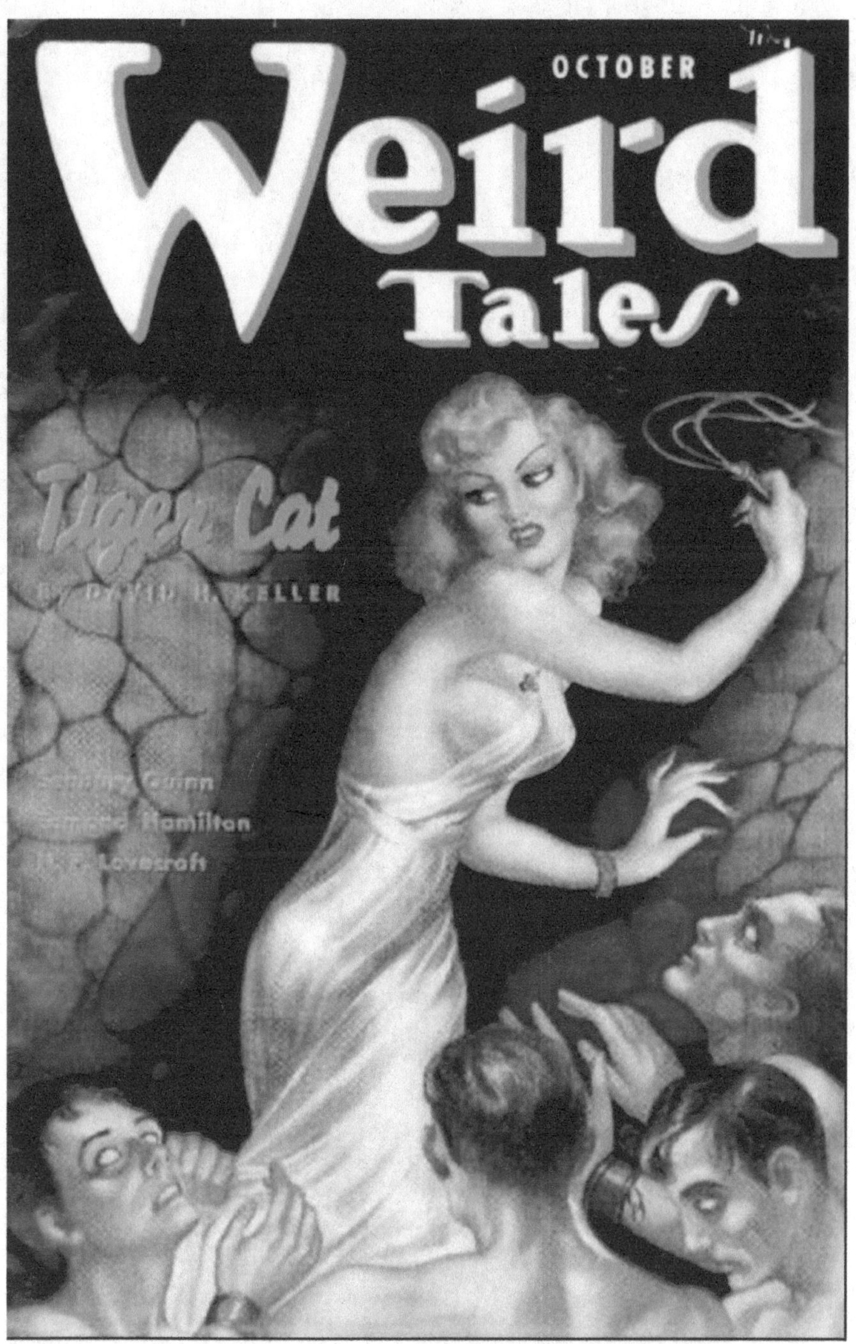

The following story was originally published in this 1937 issue of *Weird Tales*.

PLEDGED TO THE DEAD

BY SEABURY QUINN

A tale of a lover who was pledged to a sweetheart who had been in her grave for more than a century, and of the striking death that menaced him—a story of Jules de Grandin

The autumn dusk had stained the sky with shadows and orange oblongs traced the windows in my neighbors' homes as Jules de Grandin and I sat sipping kaiserschmarrn and coffee in the study after dinner. "*Mon Dieu*," the little Frenchman sighed, "I have the *mal du pays*, my friend. The little children run and play along the roadways at Saint Cloud, and on the Ile de France the pastry cooks set up their booths. *Corbleu*, it takes the strength of character not to stop and buy those cakes of so much taste and fancy! The Napoléons, they are crisp and fragile as a coquette's promise, the éclairs filled with cool, sweet cream, the cream-puffs all aglow with cherries. Just to see them is to love life better. They —"

The shrilling of the door-bell startled me. The pressure on the button must have been that of one who leant against it. "Doctor Trowbridge; I must see him right away!" a woman's voice demanded as Nora McGinnis, my household factotum, grudgingly responded to the hail.

"Th' docthor's offiss hours is over, ma'am," Nora answered frigidly. "Ha'f past nine ter eleven in th' marnin', an' two ter four in th' afthernoon is when he sees his patients. If it's an urgent case ye have there's lots o' good young docthors in th' neighborhood, but Docthor Trowbridge —"

"Is he here?" the visitor demanded sharply.

"He is, an' he's afther digestin' his dinner—an' an illigant dinner it wuz, though I do say so as shouldn't—an' he can't be disturbed —"

"He'll see me, all right. Tell him it's Nella Bentley, and I've *got* to talk to him!"

De Grandin raised an eyebrow eloquently. "The fish at the aquarium have greater privacy than we, my friend," he murmured, but broke off as the visitor came clacking down the hall on high French heels and rushed into the study half a dozen paces in advance of my thoroughly disapproving and more than semi-scandalized Nora.

"Doctor Trowbridge, won't you help me?" cried the girl as she fairly leaped across the study and flung her arms about my shoulders. "I can't tell Dad or Mother, they wouldn't understand; so you're the only one—oh, excuse me, I thought you were alone!" Her face went crimson as she saw de Grandin standing by the fire.

"It's quite all right, my dear," I soothed, freeing myself from her almost hysterical clutch. "This is Doctor de Grandin, with whom I've been associated many times; I'd be glad to have the benefit of his advice, if you don't mind."

She gave him her hand and a wan smile as I performed the introduction, but her eyes warmed quickly as he raised her fingers to his lips with a soft "*Enchanté, Mademoiselle.*" Women, animals and children took instinctively to Jules de Grandin.

Nella dropped her coat of silky shaven lamb and sank down on the study couch, her slim young figure molded in her knitted dress of coral rayon as revealingly as though she had been cased in plastic cellulose. She has long, violet eyes and a long mouth; smooth, dark hair parted in the middle; a small straight nose, and a small pointed chin. Every line of her is long, but definitely feminine; breasts and hips and throat and legs all delicately curved, without a hint of angularity.

"I've come to see you about Ned," she volunteered as de Grandin lit her cigarette and she sent a nervous smoke-stream gushing from between red, trembling lips. "He—he's trying to run out on me!"

"You mean Ned Minton?" I asked, wondering what a middle-aged physician could prescribe for wandering Romeos.

"I certainly do mean Ned Minton," she replied, "and I mean business, too. The darn, romantic fool!"

De Grandin's slender brows arched upward till they nearly met the beige-blond hair that slanted sleekly backward from his forehead. "*Pardonnez-moi,*" he murmured. "Did I understand correctly, *Mademoiselle?* Your *amoureux*—how do you say him?—sweetheart?—has shown a disposition toward unfaithfulness, yet you accuse him of romanticism?"

"He's not unfaithful, that's the worst of it. He's faithful as Tristan and the chevalier Bayard lumped together, *sans peur et sans reproche*, you know. Says we can't get married, 'cause —"

"Just a moment, dear," I interrupted as I felt my indignation mounting. "D'ye mean the miserable young puppy cheated, and now wants to welch —"

HER BLUE EYES WIDENED, THEN THE LITTLE LAUGHTER-WRINKLES FORMED around them. "You dear old mid-Victorian!" she broke in. "No, he ain't done wrong by our Nell, and I'm not asking you to take your shotgun down and force him to make me an honest woman. Suppose we start at the beginning: then we'll get things straight.

"You assisted at both our débuts, I've been told; you've known Ned and me since we were a second old apiece, haven't you?"

I nodded.

"Know we've always been crazy about each other, too; in grammar school, high school and college, don't you?"

"Yes," I agreed.

"All right. We've been engaged ever since our freshman year at Beaver. Ned just had his frat pin long enough to pin it on my shoulder-strap at the first freshman dance. Everything was set for us to stand up in the chancel and say 'I do' this June; then Ned's company sent him to New Orleans last December." She paused, drew deeply at her cigarette, crushed its fire out in an ash-tray, and set a fresh one glowing.

"That started it. While he was down there it seemed that he got playful. Mixed up with some glamorous Creole gal." Once more she lapsed into silence and I could see the heartbreak showing through the armor of her flippant manner.

"You mean he fell in love —"

"I certainly do *not*! If he had, I'd have handed back his ring and said 'Bless you, me children', even if I had to bite my heart in two to do it; but this is no case of a new love crowding out the old. Ned still loves me; never stopped loving me. That's what makes it all seem crazy as a hashish-eater's dream. He was on the loose in New Orleans, doing the town with a crowd of local boys, and prob'bly had too many Ramos fizzes. Then he barged into this Creole dame's place, and —" she broke off with a gallant effort at a smile. "I guess young fellows aren't so different nowadays than they were when you were growing up, sir. Only today we don't believe in sprinkling perfume in the family cesspool. Ned cheated, that's the bald truth of it; he didn't stop loving me, and he hasn't stopped now, but I wasn't there and that other girl was, and there were no conventions to be recognized. Now he's fairly melting with remorse, says he's not worthy of me—wants to break off our engagement, while he spends a lifetime doing penance for a moment's folly."

"But good heavens," I expostulated, "if you're willing to forgive —"

"You're telling me!" she answered bitterly. "We've been over it a hundred times. This isn't 1892; even nice girls know the facts of life today, and while I'm no more anxious than the next one to put through a deal in shopworn goods, I still love Ned, and I don't intend to let a single indiscretion rob us of our happiness. I —" the hard exterior veneer of modernism melted from her like an autumn ice-glaze melting in the warm October sun, and the tears coursed down her cheeks, cutting little valleys in her carefully-applied make-up. "He's my man, Doctor," she sobbed bitterly. "I've loved him since we made mud-pies together; I'm hungry, thirsty for him. He's everything to me, and if he follows out this fool renunciation he seems set on, it'll kill me!"

De Grandin tweaked a waxed mustache-end thoughtfully. "You exemplify the practicality of woman, *Mademoiselle*; I applaud your sound, hard common sense," he told her. "Bring this silly young romantic foolish one to me. I will tell him —"

"But he won't come," I interrupted. "I know these hard-minded young asses. When a lad is set on being stubborn —"

"Will you go to work on him if I can get him here?" interjected Nella.

"Of a certitude, *Mademoiselle*."

"You won't think me forward or unmaidenly?"

"This is a medical consultation, *Mademoiselle*."

"All right; be in the office this time tomorrow night. I'll have my wandering boy friend here if I have to bring him in an ambulance."

HER PERFORMANCE MATCHED HER PROMISE ALMOST TOO CLOSELY FOR OUR comfort. We had just finished dinner next night when the frenzied shriek of tortured brakes, followed by a crash and the tinkling spatter of smashed glass, sounded in the street before the house, and in a moment feet dragged heavily across the porch. We were at the door before the bell could buzz, and in the disk of brightness sent down by the porch light saw Nella bent half double, stumbling forward with a man's arm draped across her shoulders. His feet scuffed blindly on the boards, as though they had forgot the trick of walking, or as if all strength had left his knees. His head hung forward, lolling drunkenly; a spate of blood ran down his face and smeared his collar.

"Good Lord!" I gasped. "What —"

"Get him in the surgery—quick!" the girl commanded in a whisper. "I'm afraid I rather overdid it."

Examination showed the cut across Ned's forehead was more bloody than extensive, while the scalp-wound which plowed backward from his hairline needed but a few quick stitches.

Nella whispered to us as we worked. "I got him to go riding with me in my runabout. Just as we got here I let out a scream and swung the wheel hard over to the right. I was braced for it, but Ned was unprepared, and went right through the windshield when I ran the car into the curb. Lord, I thought I'd killed him when I saw the blood—you do think he'll come through all right, don't you, Doctor?"

"No thanks to you if he does, you little ninny!" I retorted angrily. "You might have cut his jugular with your confounded foolishness. If —"

"*S-s-sh*, he's coming out of it!" she warned. "Start talking to him like a Dutch uncle; I'll be waiting in the study if you want me," and with a tattoo of high heels she left us with our patient.

"Nella! Is she all right?" Ned cried as he half roused from the surgery table. "We had an accident —"

"But certainly, *Monsieur*," de Grandin soothed. "You were driving past our house when a child ran out before your car and *Mademoiselle* was forced to swerve aside to keep from hitting it. You were cut about the face, but she escaped all injury. Here"—he raised a glass of brandy to the patient's lips—"drink this. Ah, so. That is better, *n'est-ce-pas?*"

For a moment he regarded Ned in silence, then, abruptly: "You are distrait, *Monsieur*. When we brought you in we were forced to give you a small whiff of ether while we patched your cuts, and in your delirium you said —"

The color which had come into Ned's cheeks as the fiery cognac warmed his veins drained out again, leaving him as ghastly as a corpse. "Did Nella hear me?" he asked hoarsely. "Did I blab —"

"Compose yourself, *Monsieur*," de Grandin bade. "She heard nothing, but it would be well if we heard more. I think I understand your difficulty. I am a physician and a Frenchman and no prude. This renunciation which you make is but the noble gesture. You have been unfortunate, and now you fear. Have courage; no infection is so bad there is no remedy —"

Ned's laugh was hard and brittle as the tinkle of a breaking glass. "I only wish it were the thing you think," he interrupted. "I'd have you give me salvarsan and see what happened; but there isn't any treatment I can take for this. I'm not delirious, and I'm not crazy, gentlemen; I know just what I'm saying. Insane as it may sound, I'm pledged to the dead, and there isn't any way to bail me out."

"*Eh*, what is it you say?" de Grandin's small blue eyes were gleaming with the light of battle as he caught the occult implication in Ned's declaration. "Pledged to the dead? *Comment cela?*"

NED RAISED HIMSELF UNSTEADILY AND BALANCED ON THE TABLE EDGE.

"It happened in New Orleans last winter," he answered. "I'd finished up my business and was on the loose, and thought I'd walk alone through the *Vieux Carré*—the old French Quarter. I'd had dinner at Antoine's and stopped around at the Old Absinthe House for a few drinks, then strolled down to the French Market for a cup of chicory coffee and some doughnuts. Finally I walked down Royal Street to look at Madame Lalaurie's old mansion; that's the famous haunted house, you know. I wanted to see if I could find a ghost. Good Lord, I *wanted* to!

"The moon was full that night, but the house was still as old Saint Denis Cemetery, so after peering through the iron grilles that shut the courtyard from the street for half an hour or so, I started back toward Canal Street.

"I'd almost reached Bienville Street when just as I passed one of those funny two-storied iron-grilled balconies so many of the old houses have I heard something drop on the sidewalk at my feet. It was a japonica, one of those rose-like flowers they grow in the courtyard gardens down there. When I looked up, a girl was laughing at me from the second story of the balcony. '*Mon fleuron, monsieur, s'il vous plait,*' she called, stretching down a white arm for the bloom.

"The moonlight hung about her like a veil of silver tissue, and I could see her plainly as though it had been noon. Most New Orleans girls are dark. She was fair, her hair was very fine and silky and about the color of a frosted chestnut-burr. She wore it in a long bob with curls around her face and neck, and I knew without being told that those ringlets weren't put in with a hot iron. Her face was pale, colorless and fine-textured as a magnolia petal, but her lips were brilliant crimson. There was something reminiscent of those ladies you see pictured in Directoire prints about her; small, regular features, straight, white, high-waisted gown tied with a wide girdle underneath her bosom, low, round-cut neck and tiny, ball-puff sleeves that left her lovely arms uncovered to the shoulder. She was like Rose Beauharnais or Madame de Fontenay, except for her fair hair, and her eyes. Her eyes were like an Eastern slave's, languishing and passionate, even when she laughed. And she was laughing then, with a throaty, almost caressing laugh as I tossed the flower up to her and she leant across the iron railing, snatching at it futilely as it fell just short of reach.

"'*C'est sans profit,*' she laughed at last. 'Your skill is too small or my arm too short, *m'sieur*. Bring it up to me.'

"'You mean for me to come up there?' I asked.

"'But certainly. I have teeth, but will not bite you—maybe.'

"The street door to the house was open; I pushed it back, groped my way along a narrow hall and climbed a flight of winding stairs. She was waiting for me on the balcony, lovelier, close up, if that were possible, than when I'd seen her from the sidewalk. Her gown was China silk, so sheer and clinging that the shadow of her charming figure showed against its rippling folds like a lovely silhouette; the sash which bound it was a six-foot length of rainbow ribbon tied coquettishly beneath her shoulders and trailing in fringed ends almost to her dress-hem at the back; her feet were stockingless and shod with sandals fastened with cross-straps of purple grosgrain laced about the ankles. Save for the small gold rings that scintillated in her ears, she wore no ornaments of any kind.

"'*Mon fleur, m'sieur,*' she ordered haughtily, stretching out her hand; then her eyes lighted with sudden laughter and she turned her back to me, bending her head forward. 'But no, it fell into your hands; it is that you must put in its place again,' she ordered, pointing to a curl where she wished the flower set. 'Come, *m'sieur*, I wait upon you.'

"On the settee by the wall a guitar lay. She picked it up and ran her slim, pale fingers twice across the strings, sounding a soft, melancholy chord. When she began to sing, her words were slurred and languorous, and I had trouble understanding them; for the song was ancient when Bienville turned the first spadeful of earth that marked the ramparts of New Orleans:

O knights of gay Toulouse
And sweet Beaucaire,
Greet me my own true love
And speak him fair....

"Her voice had the throaty, velvety quality one hears in people of the Southern countries, and the words of the song seemed fairly to yearn with the sadness and passionate longing of the love-bereft. But she smiled as she put by her instrument, a curious smile, which heightened the mystery of her face, and her wide eyes seemed suddenly half questing, half drowsy, as she asked, 'Would you ride off upon your grim, pale horse and leave poor little Julie d'Ayen famishing for love, *m'sieur?*'

"'Ride off from you?' I answered gallantly. 'How can you ask?' A verse from Burns came to me:

Then fare thee well, my bonny lass,
And fare thee well awhile,
And I will come to thee again
An it were ten thousand mile.

"There was something avid in the look she gave me. Something more than mere gratified vanity shone in her eyes as she turned her face up to me in the moonlight. 'You mean it?' she demanded in a quivering, breathless voice.

"'Of course,' I bantered. 'How could you doubt it?'

"'Then swear it—seal the oath with blood!'

"Her eyes were almost closed, and her lips were lightly parted as she leant toward me. I could see the thin, white line of tiny, gleaming teeth behind the lush red of her lips; the tip of a pink tongue swept across her mouth, leaving it warmer, moister, redder than before; in her throat a small pulse throbbed palpitatingly. Her lips were smooth and soft as the flower-petals in her hair, but as they crushed on mine they seemed to creep about them as though endowed with a volition of their own. I could feel them gliding almost stealthily, searching greedily, it seemed, until they covered my entire mouth. Then came a sudden searing burn of pain which passed as quickly as it flashed across my lips, and she seemed inhaling deeply, desperately, as though to pump the last faint gasp of breath up from my lungs. A humming sounded in my ears; everything went dark around me as if I had been plunged in some abysmal flood; a spell of dreamy lassitude was stealing over me when she pushed me from her so abruptly that I staggered back against the iron railing of the gallery.

I GASPED AND FOUGHT FOR BREATH LIKE A WINDED SWIMMER COMING FROM the water, but the half-recaptured breath seemed suddenly to catch itself unbidden in my throat, and a tingling chill went rippling up my spine. The girl had dropped down to her knees, staring at the door which let into the house, and as I looked I saw a shadow writhe across the little pool of moonlight which lay upon the sill. Three feet or so in length it was, thick through as a man's wrist, the faint light shining dully on its scaly armor and disclosing the forked lightning of its darting tongue. It was a cotton-mouth—a water moccasin—deadly as a rattlesnake, but more dangerous, for it sounds no warning before striking, and can strike when only half coiled. How it came there on the second-story gallery of a house so far from any swampland I had no means of knowing, but there it lay, bent in the design of a double S, its wedge-shaped head swaying on up-reared neck a scant six inches from the girl's soft bosom, its forked tongue darting deathly menace. Half paralyzed with fear and loathing, I stood there in a perfect ecstasy of horror, not daring to move hand or foot lest I aggravate the reptile into striking. But my terror changed to stark amazement as my senses slowly registered the scene. The girl was talking to the snake and—it listened as a person might have done!

"'*Non, non, grand'tante; halte là!*' she whispered. '*Cela est à moi—il est dévoué!*'

"The serpent seemed to pause uncertainly, grudgingly, as though but half convinced, then shook its head from side to side, much as an aged person might when only half persuaded by a youngster's argument. Finally, silently as a shadow, it slithered back again into the darkness of the house.

"Julie bounded to her feet and put her hands upon my shoulders.

"'You mus' go, my friend,' she whispered fiercely. 'Quickly, ere she comes again. It was not easy to convince her; she is old and very doubting. O, I am afraid—afraid!'

"She hid her face against my arm, and I could feel the throbbing of her heart against me. Her hands stole upward to my cheeks and pressed them between palms as cold as graveyard clay as she whispered, 'Look at me, *mon beau*.' Her eyes were closed, her lips were slightly parted, and beneath the arc of her long lashes I could see the glimmer of fast-forming tears. '*Embrasse moi*', she commanded in a trembling breath. 'Kiss me and go quickly, but *O mon chèr*, do not forget poor little foolish Julie d'Ayen who has put her trust in you. Come to me again tomorrow night!'

"I was reeling as from vertigo as I walked back to the Greenwald, and the bartender looked at me suspiciously when I ordered a sazarac. They've a strict rule against serving drunken men at that hotel. The liquor stung my lips like liquid flame, and I put the cocktail down half finished. When I set the fan to going and switched the light on in my room I looked into the mirror and saw two little beads of fresh, bright blood upon my lips. 'Good Lord!' I murmured stupidly as I brushed the blood away; 'she bit me!'

"It all seemed so incredible that if I had not seen the blood upon my mouth I'd have thought I suffered from some lunatic hallucination, or one too many frappés at the Absinthe House. Julie was as quaint and out of time as a Directoire print, even in a city where time stands still as it does in old New Orleans. Her costume, her half-shy boldness, her—this was simply madness, nothing less!—her conversation with that snake!

"What was it she had said? My French was none too good, and in the circumstances it was hardly possible to pay attention to her words, but if I'd understood her, she'd declared, 'He's mine; he has dedicated himself to me!' And she'd addressed that crawling horror as '*grand'tante*—great-aunt!'

"'Feller, you're as crazy as a cockroach!' I admonished my reflection in the mirror. 'But I know what'll cure you. You're taking the first train north tomorrow morning, and if I ever catch you in the *Vieux Carré* again, I'll —'

"A sibilating hiss, no louder than the noise made by steam escaping from a kettle-spout, sounded close beside my foot. There on the rug, coiled in readiness to strike, was a three-foot cottonmouth, head swaying viciously from side to side, wicked eyes shining in the bright light from the chandelier. I saw the muscles in the creature's fore-part swell, and in a sort of horror-trance I watched its head dart forward, but, miraculously, it stopped its stroke half-way, and drew its head back, turning to glance menacingly at me first from one eye, then the other. Somehow, it seemed to me, the thing was playing with me as a cat might play a mouse, threatening, intimidating, letting me know it was master of the situation and could kill me any time it wished, but deliberately refraining from the death-stroke.

"With one leap I was in the middle of my bed, and when a squad of bellboys came running in response to the frantic call for help I telephoned, they found me crouched against the headboard, almost wild with fear.

"They turned the room completely inside out, rolling back the rugs, probing into chairs and sofa, emptying the bureau drawers, even taking down the towels from the bathroom rack, but nowhere was there any sign of the water moccasin that had terrified me. At the end of fifteen minutes' search they accepted half a dollar each and went grinning from the room. I knew it would be useless to appeal for help again, for I heard one whisper to another as they paused outside my door: 'It ain't right to let them Yankees loose in N'Orleans; they don't know how to hold their licker.'

I DIDN'T TAKE A TRAIN NEXT MORNING. SOMEHOW, I'D AN IDEA—CRAZY AS IT seemed—that my promise to myself and the sudden, inexplicable appearance of the snake beside my foot were related in some way. Just after luncheon I thought I'd put the theory to a test.

"'Well,' I said aloud, 'I guess I might as well start packing. Don't want to let the sun go down and find me here —'

"My theory was right. I hadn't finished speaking when I heard the warning hiss, and there, poised ready for the stroke, the snake was coiled before the door. And it was no phantom, either, no figment of an overwrought imagination. It lay upon a rug the hotel management had placed before the door to take the wear of constant passage from the carpet, and I could see the high pile of the rug crushed down beneath its weight. It was flesh and scales—and fangs!—and it coiled and threatened me in my twelfth-floor room in the bright sunlight of the afternoon.

"Little chills of terror chased each other up my back, and I could feel the short hairs on my neck grow stiff and scratch against my collar, but I kept myself in hand. Pretending to ignore the loathsome thing, I flung myself upon the bed.

"'Oh, well,' I said aloud, 'there really isn't any need of hurrying. I promised Julie that I'd come to her tonight, and I mustn't disappoint her."

Half a minute later I roused myself upon my elbow and glanced toward the door. The snake was gone.

"'Here's a letter for you, Mr. Minton,' said the desk clerk as I paused to leave my key. The note was on gray paper edged with silver-gilt, and very highly scented. The penmanship was tiny, stilted and ill-formed, as though the author were unused to writing, but I could make it out:

Adoré
Meet me in St. Denis Cemetery at sunset
À vous de coeur pour l'éternité
Julie

"I stuffed the note back in my pocket. The more I thought about the whole affair the less I liked it. The flirtation had begun harmlessly enough, and Julie was as lovely and appealing as a figure in a fairy-tale, but there are unpleasant aspects to most fairy-tales, and this was no exception. That scene last night when she had seemed to argue with a full-grown cottonmouth, and the mysterious appearance of the snake whenever I spoke of breaking my promise to go back to her—there was something too much like black magic in it. Now she addressed me as her adored and signed herself for eternity; finally named a graveyard as our rendezvous. Things had become a little bit too thick.

"I was standing at the corner of Canal and Baronne Streets, and crowds of office workers and late shoppers elbowed past me. 'I'll be damned if I'll meet her in a cemetery, or anywhere else,' I muttered. 'I've had enough of all this nonsense —'

"A woman's shrill scream, echoed by a man's hoarse shout of terror, interrupted me. On the marble pavement of Canal Street, with half a thousand people bustling by, lay coiled a three-foot water moccasin. Here was proof. I'd seen it twice in my room at the hotel, but I'd been alone each time. Some form of weird hypnosis might have made me think I saw it, but the screaming woman and the shouting man, these panic-stricken people in Canal Street, couldn't all be victims of a spell which had been cast on me. 'All right, I'll go,' I almost shouted, and instantly, as though it been but a puff of smoke, the snake was gone, the half-fainting woman and a crowd of curious bystanders asking what was wrong left to prove I had not been the victim of some strange delusion.

Old Saint Denis Cemetery lay drowsing in the blue, faint twilight. It has no graves as we know them, for when the city was laid out it was below sea-level and bodies were stored away in crypts set row on row like lines of pigeon-holes in walls as thick as those of mediæval castles. Grass-grown aisles run between the rows of vaults, and the effect is a true city of the dead with narrow streets shut in by close-set houses. The rattle of a trolley car in Rampart Street came to me faintly as I walked between the rows of tombs; from the river came the mellow-throated bellow of a steamer's whistle, but both sounds were muted as though heard from a great distance. The tomb-lined bastions of Saint Denis hold the present out as firmly as they hold the memories of the past within.

"Down one aisle and up another I walked, the close-clipped turf deadening my footfalls so I might have been a ghost come back to haunt the ancient burial ground, but nowhere was there sign or trace of Julie. I made the circuit of the labyrinth and finally paused before one of the more pretentious tombs.

"'Looks as if she'd stood me up,' I murmured. 'If she has, I have a good excuse to —'

"'But *non, mon coeur*, I have not disappointed you!' a soft voice whispered in my ear. 'See, I am here.'

"I think I must have jumped at sound of her greeting, for she clapped her hands delightedly before she put them on my shoulders and turned her face up for a kiss. 'Silly one,' she chided, 'did you think your Julie was unfaithful?'

"I put her hands away as gently as I could, for her utter self-surrender was embarrassing. 'Where were you?' I asked, striving to make neutral conversation. 'I've been prowling round this graveyard for the last half-hour, and came through this aisle not a minute ago, but I didn't see you —'

"'Ah, but I saw you, *chéri*; I have watched you as you made your solemn rounds like a watchman of the night. *Ohé*, but it was hard to wait until the sun went down to greet you, *mon petit*!'

"She laughed again, and her mirth was mellowly musical as the gurgle of cool water poured from a silver vase.

"'How could you have seen me?' I demanded. 'Where were you all this time?'

"'But here, of course,' she answered naïvely, resting one hand against the graystone slab that sealed the tomb.

"I shook my head bewilderedly. The tomb, like all the others in the deeply recessed wall, was of rough cement incrusted with small seashells, and its sides were straight and blank without a spear of ivy clinging to them. A sparrow could not have found cover there, yet....

"Julie raised herself on tiptoe and stretched her arms out right and left while she looked at me through half-closed, smiling eyes. '*Je suis engourdie*—I am stiff with sleep,' she told me, stifling a yawn. 'But now that you are come, *mon cher*, I am wakeful as the pussy-cat that rouses at the scampering of the mouse. Come, let us walk in this garden of mine.' She linked her arm through mine and started down the grassy, grave-lined path.

"Tiny shivers—not of cold—were flickering through my cheeks and down my neck beneath my ears. I *had* to have an explanation ... the snake, her declaration that she watched me as I searched the cemetery—and from a tomb where a beetle could not have found a hiding-place—her announcement she was still stiff from sleeping, now her reference to a half-forgotten graveyard as her garden.

"'See here, I want to know —' I started, but she laid her hand across my lips.

"'Do not ask to know too soon, *mon coeur*,' she bade. 'Look at me, am I not veritably *élégante*?' She stood back a step, gathered up her skirts and swept me a deep curtsy.

"There was no denying she was beautiful. Her tightly curling hair had been combed high and tied back with a fillet of bright violet tissue which bound her brows like a diadem and at the front of which an aigret plume was set. In her ears were hung two beautifully matched cameos, outlined in gold and seed-pearls, and almost large as silver dollars; a necklace of antique dull-gold hung round her throat, and its pendant was a duplicate of her ear-cameos, while a bracelet of matt-gold set with a fourth matched anaglyph was clasped about her left arm just above the elbow. Her gown was sheer white muslin, low cut at front and back, with little puff-sleeves at the shoulders, fitted tightly at the bodice and flaring sharply from a high-set waist. Over it she wore a narrow scarf of violet silk, hung behind her neck and dropping down on either side in front like a clergyman's stole. Her sandals were gilt leather, heel-less as a ballet dancer's shoes and laced with violet ribbons. Her lovely, pearl-white hands were bare of rings, but on the second toe of her right foot there showed a little cameo which matched the others which she wore.

"I could feel my heart begin to pound and my breath come quicker as I looked at her, but:

"'You look as if you're going to a masquerade,' I said.

"A look of hurt surprize showed in her eyes. 'A masquerade?' she echoed. 'But no, it is my best, my very finest, that I wear for you tonight, *mon adoré*. Do not you like it; do you not love me, Édouard?'

"'No,' I answered shortly, 'I do not. We might as well understand each other, Julie. I'm not in love with you and I never was. It's been a pretty flirtation, nothing more. I'm going home tomorrow, and —'

"'But you will come again? Surely you will come again?' she pleaded, 'You cannot mean it when you say you do not love me, Édouard. Tell me that you spoke so but to tease me —'

"A warning hiss sounded in the grass beside my foot, but I was too angry to be frightened. 'Go ahead, set your devilish snake on me,' I taunted. 'Let it bite me. I'd as soon be dead as —'

"The snake was quick, but Julie quicker. In the split-second required for the thing to drive at me she leaped across the grass-grown aisle and pushed me back. So violent was the shove she gave me that I fell against the tomb, struck my head against a small projecting stone and stumbled to my knees. As I fought for footing on the slippery grass I saw the deadly, wedge-shaped head strike full against the girl's bare ankle and heard her gasp with pain. The snake recoiled and swung its head toward me, but Julie dropped down to her knees and spread her arms protectingly about me.

"'*Non, non, grand'tante!*' she screamed; 'not this one! Let me —' Her voice broke on a little gasp and with a retching hiccup she sank limply to the grass.

"I tried to rise, but my foot slipped on the grass and I fell back heavily against the tomb, crashing my brow against its shell-set cement wall. I saw Julie lying in a little huddled heap of white against the blackness of the sward, and, shadowy but clearly visible, an aged, wrinkled Negress with turbaned head and cambric apron bending over her, nursing her head against her bosom and rocking back and forth grotesquely while she crooned a wordless threnody. Where had she come from? I wondered idly. Where had the snake gone? Why did the moonlight seem to fade and flicker like a dying lamp? Once more I tried to rise, but slipped back to the grass before the tomb as everything went black before me.

"The lavender light of early morning was streaming over the tomb-walls of the cemetery when I waked. I lay quiet for a little while, wondering sleepily how I came there. Then, just as the first rays of the sun shot through the thinning shadows, I remembered. Julie! The snake had bitten her when she flung herself before me. She was gone; the old Negress—where had *she* come from?—was gone, too, and I was utterly alone in the old graveyard.

"Stiff from lying on the ground, I got myself up awkwardly, grasping at the flower-shelf projecting from the tomb. As my eyes came level with the slab that sealed the crypt I felt the breath catch in my throat. The crypt, like all its fellows, looked for all the world like an old oven let into a brick wall overlaid with peeling plaster. The sealing-stone was probably once white, but years had stained it to a dirty gray, and time had all but rubbed its legend out. Still, I could see the faint inscription carved in quaint, old-fashioned letters, and disbelief gave way to incredulity, which was replaced by panic terror as I read:

> *Ici repose malheureusement*
> *Julie Amelie Marie d'Ayen*
> *Nationale de Paris France*
> *Née le 29 Aout 1788*
> *Décédée a la N O le 2 Juillet 1807*

"Julie! Little Julie whom I'd held in my arms, whose mouth had lain on mine in eager kisses, was a corpse! Dead and in her grave more than a century!"

THE SILENCE LENGTHENED. NED STARED MISERABLY BEFORE HIM, HIS OUTward eyes unseeing, but his mind's eye turned upon that scene in old Saint Denis Cemetery. De Grandin tugged and tugged again at the ends of his mustache till I thought he'd drag the hairs out by the roots. I could think of nothing which might ease the tension till:

"Of course, the name cut on the tombstone was a piece of pure coincidence," I hazarded. "Most likely the young woman deliberately assumed it to mislead you —"

"And the snake which threatened our young friend, he was an assumption, also, one infers?" de Grandin interrupted.

"N-o, but it could have been a trick. Ned saw an aged Negress in the cemetery, and those old Southern darkies have strange powers —"

"I damn think that you hit the thumb upon the nail that time, my friend," the little Frenchman nodded, "though you do not realize how accurate your diagnosis is." To Ned:

"Have you seen this snake again since coming North?"

"Yes," Ned replied. "I have. I was too stunned to speak when I read the epitaph, and I wandered back to the hotel in a sort of daze and packed my bags in silence. Possibly that's why there was no further visitation there. I don't know. I do know nothing further happened, though, and when several months had passed with nothing but my memories to remind me of the incident, I began to think I'd suffered from some sort of walking nightmare. Nella and I went ahead with preparations for our wedding, but three weeks ago the postman brought me this —"

He reached into an inner pocket and drew out an envelope. It was of soft gray paper, edged with silver-gilt, and the address was in tiny, almost unreadable script:

M. Édouard Minton,
30 Rue Carteret 30,
Harrisonville, N. J.

"U'm?" de Grandin commented as he inspected it. "It is addressed à la française. And the letter, may one read it?"

"Of course," Ned answered. "I'd like you to."

Across de Grandin's shoulder I made out the hastily-scrawled missive:

Adoré
Remember your promise and the kiss of blood that sealed it.
Soon I shall call and you must come.
Pour le temps et pour l'éternité,
Julie.

"You recognize the writing?" de Grandin asked. "It is —"

"Oh, yes," Ned answered bitterly, "I recognize it; it's the same the other note was written in."

"And then?"

The boy smiled bleakly. "I crushed the thing into a ball and threw it on the floor and stamped on it. Swore I'd die before I'd keep another rendezvous with her, and —" He broke off, and put trembling hands up to his face.

"The so mysterious serpent came again, one may assume?" de Grandin prompted.

"But it's only a phantom snake," I interjected. "At worst it's nothing more than a terrifying vision —"

"Think so?" Ned broke in. "D'ye remember Rowdy, my airedale terrier?"

I nodded.

"He was in the room when I opened this letter, and when the cottonmouth appeared beside me on the floor he made a dash for it. Whether it would have struck me I don't know, but it struck at him as he leaped and caught him squarely in the throat. He thrashed and fought, and the thing held on with locked jaws till I grabbed a fire-shovel and made for it; then, before I could strike, it vanished.

"But its venom didn't. Poor old Rowdy was dead before I could get him out of the house, but I took his corpse to Doctor Kirchoff, the veterinary, and told him Rowdy died suddenly and I wanted him to make an autopsy. He went back to his operating-room and stayed there half an hour. When he came back to the office he was wiping his glasses and wore the most astonished look I've ever seen on a human face. 'You say your dog died suddenly—in the house?' he asked.

"'Yes,' I told him; 'just rolled over and died.'

"'Well, bless my soul, that's the most amazing thing I ever heard!' he answered. 'I can't account for it. That dog died from snake-bite; copperhead, I'd say, and the marks of the fangs show plainly on his throat.'"

"But I thought you said it was a water moccasin," I objected. "Now Doctor Kirchoff says it was a copperhead —"

"*Ah hah!*" de Grandin laughed a thought unpleasantly. "Did no one ever tell you that the copperhead and moccasin are of close kind, my friend? Have not you heard some ophiologists maintain the moccasin is but a dark variety of copperhead?" He did not pause for my reply, but turned again to Ned:

"One understands your chivalry, *Monsieur*. For yourself you have no fear, since after all at times life can be bought too dearly, but the death of your small dog has put a different aspect on the matter. If this never-to-be-sufficiently-anathematized serpent which comes and goes like the *boîte à surprise*—the how do you call him? Jack from the box?—is enough a ghost thing to appear at any time and place it wills, but sufficiently physical to exude venom which will kill a strong and healthy terrier, you have the fear for Mademoiselle Nella, *n'est-ce-pas*?"

"Precisely, you —"

"And you are well advised to have the caution, my young friend. We face a serious condition."

"What do you advise?"

The Frenchman teased his needlepoint mustache-tip with a thoughtful thumb and forefinger. "For the present, nothing," he replied at length. "Let me look this situation over; let me view it from all angles. Whatever I might tell you now would probably be wrong. Suppose we meet again one week from now. By that time I should have my data well in hand."

"And in the meantime —"

"Continue to be coy with Mademoiselle Nella. Perhaps it would be well if you recalled important business which requires that you leave town till you hear from me again. There is no need to put her life in peril at this time."

IF IT WEREN'T FOR KIRCHOFF'S TESTIMONY I'D SAY NED MINTON HAD GONE raving crazy," I declared as the door closed on our visitors. "The whole thing's wilder than an opium smoker's dream—that meeting with the girl in New Orleans, the snake that comes and disappears, the assignation in the cemetery—it's all too preposterous. But I know Kirchoff. He's as un-imaginative as a side of sole-leather, and as efficient as he is unimaginative. If he says Minton's dog died of snake-bite that's what it died of, but the whole affair's so utterly fantastic —"

"Agreed," de Grandin nodded; "but what is fantasy but the appearance of mental images as such, severed from ordinary relations? The 'ordinary relations' of images are those to which we are accustomed, which conform to our experience. The wider that experience, the more ordinary will we find extraordinary relations. By example, take yourself: You sit in a dark auditorium and see a railway train come rushing at you. Now, it is not at all in ordinary experience for a locomotive to come dashing in a theater filled with people, it is quite otherwise; but you keep your seat, you do not flinch, you are not frightened. It is nothing but a motion picture, which you understand. But if you were a savage from New Guinea you would rise and fly in panic from this steaming, shrieking iron monster which bears down on you. *Tiens*, it is a matter of experience, you see. To you it is an everyday event, to the savage it would be a new and terrifying thing.

"Or, perhaps, you are at the hospital. You place a patient between you and the Crookes' tube of an X-ray, you turn on the current, you observe him through the fluoroscope and *pouf!* his flesh all melts away and his bones spring out in sharp relief. Three hundred years ago you would have howled like a stoned dog at the sight, and prayed to be delivered from the witchcraft which produced it. Today you curse and swear like twenty drunken pirates if the Röntgenologist is but thirty seconds late in setting up the apparatus. These things are 'scientific,' you understand their underlying formulæ, therefore they seem natural. But mention what you please to call the occult, and you scoff, and that is but admitting that you are opposed to something which you do not understand. The credible and believable is that to which we are accustomed, the fantastic and incredible is what we cannot explain in terms of previous experience. *Voilà, c'est très simple, n'est-ce-pas?*"

"You mean to say you understand all this?"

"Not at all by any means; I am clever, me, but not that clever. No, my friend, I am as much in the dark as you, only I do not refuse to credit what our young friend tells us. I believe the things he has related happened, exactly as he has recounted them. I do not understand, but I believe. Accordingly, I must probe, I must sift, I must examine this matter. We see it now as a group of unrelated and irrelevant occurrences, but somewhere lies the key which will enable us to make harmony from this discord, to gather these stray, tangled threads into an ordered pattern. I go to seek that key."

"Where?"

"To New Orleans, of course. Tonight I pack my portmanteaux, tomorrow I entrain. Just now"—he smothered a tremendous yawn—"now I do what every wise man does as often as he can. I take a drink."

SEVEN EVENINGS LATER WE GATHERED IN MY STUDY, DE GRANDIN, NED AND I, and from the little Frenchman's shining eyes I knew his quest had been productive of results.

"My friends," he told us solemnly, "I am a clever person, and a lucky one, as well. The morning after my arrival at New Orleans I enjoyed three Ramos fizzes, then went to sit in City Park by the old Dueling-Oak and wished with all my heart that I had taken four. And while I sat in self-reproachful thought, sorrowing for the drink that I had missed, behold, one passed by whom I recognized. He was my old schoolfellow, Paul Dubois, now a priest in holy orders and attached to the Cathedral of Saint Louis.

"He took me to his quarters, that good, pious man, and gave me luncheon. It was Friday and a fast day, so we fasted. *Mon Dieu*, but we did fast! On créole gumbo and oysters à la Rockefeller, and baked pompano and little shrimp fried crisp in olive oil and chicory salad and seven different kinds of cheese and wine. When we were so filled with fasting that we could not eat another morsel my old friend took me to another priest, a native of New Orleans whose stock of local lore was second only to his marvelous capacity for fine champagne. *Morbleu*, how I admire that one! And now, attend me very carefully, my friends. What he disclosed to me makes many hidden mysteries all clear:

"In New Orleans there lived a wealthy family named d'Ayen. They possessed much gold and land, a thousand slaves or more, and one fair daughter by the name of Julie. When this country bought the Louisiana Territory from Napoléon and your army came to occupy the forts, this young girl fell in love with a young officer, a Lieutenant Philip Merriwell. *Tenez*, army love in those times was no different than it is today, it seems. This gay young lieutenant, he came, he wooed, he won, he rode away, and little Julie wept and sighed and finally died of heartbreak. In her lovesick illness she had for constant company a slave, an old mulatress known to most as Maman Dragonne, but to Julie simply as *grand'tante*, great-aunt. She had nursed our little Julie at the breast, and all her life she fostered and attended her. To her little white '*mamselle*' she was all gentleness and kindness, but to others she was fierce and frightful, for she was a 'conjon woman,' adept at obeah, the black magic of the Congo, and among the blacks she ruled as queen by force of fear, while the whites were wont to treat her with respect and, it was more than merely whispered, retain her services upon occasion. She could sell protection to the duelist, and he who bore her charm would surely conquer on the field of honor; she brewed love-drafts which turned the hearts and heads of the most capricious coquettes or the most constant wives, as occasion warranted; by merely staring fixedly at someone she could cause him to take sick and die, and— here we commence to tread upon our own terrain—she was said to have the power of changing to a snake at will.

"Very good. You follow? When poor young Julie died of heartbreak it was old Maman Dragonne—the little white one's *grand'tante*—who watched beside her bed. It is said she stood beside her mistress' coffin and called a curse upon the fickle lover; swore he would come back and die beside the body of the sweetheart he deserted. She also made a prophecy. Julie should have many loves, but her body should not know corruption nor her spirit rest until she could find one to keep his promise and return to her with words of love upon his lips. Those who failed her should die horribly, but he who kept his pledge would bring her rest and peace. This augury she made while she stood beside her mistress' coffin just before they sealed it in the tomb in old Saint Denis Cemetery. Then she disappeared."

"You mean she ran away?" I asked.

"I mean she disappeared, vanished, evanesced, evaporated. She was never seen again, not even by the people who stood next to her when she pronounced her prophecy."

"But —"

"No buts, my friend, if you will be so kind. Years later, when the British stormed New Orleans, Lieutenant Merriwell was there with General Andrew Jackson. He survived the battle like a man whose life is charmed, though all around him comrades fell and three horses were shot under him. Then, when the strife was done, he went to the grand banquet tendered to the victors. While gayety was at its height he abruptly left the table. Next morning he was found upon the grass before the tomb of Julie d'Ayen. He was dead. He died from snake-bite.

"The years marched on and stories spread about the town, stories of a strange and lovely *belle dame sans merci,* a modern Circe who lured young gallants to their doom. Time and again some gay young blade of New Orleans would boast a conquest. Passing late at night through Royal Street, he would have a flower dropped to him as he walked underneath a balcony. He would meet a lovely girl dressed in the early Empire style, and be surprized at the ease with which he pushed his suit; then—upon the trees in Chartres Street appeared his funeral notices. He was dead, invariably he was dead of snake-bite. *Parbleu,* it got to be a saying that he who died mysteriously must have met the Lady of the Moonlight as he walked through Royal Street!"

He paused and poured a thimbleful of brandy in his coffee. "You see?" he asked.

"No, I'm shot if I do!" I answered. "I can't see the connection between —"

"Night and breaking dawn, perhaps?" he asked sarcastically. "If two and two make four, my friend, and even you will not deny they do, then these things I have told you give an explanation of our young friend's trouble. This girl he met was most indubitably Julie, poor little Julie d'Ayen on whose tombstone it is carved: '*Ici repose malheureusement*—here lies unhappily.' The so mysterious snake which menaces young Monsieur Minton is none other than the aged Maman Dragonne—*grand'tante,* as Julie called her."

"But Ned's already failed to keep his tryst," I objected. "Why didn't this snake-woman sting him in the hotel, or —"

"Do you recall what Julie said when first the snake appeared?" he interrupted. "'Not this one, *grand'tante!*' And again, in the old cemetery when the serpent actually struck at him, she threw herself before him and received the blow. It could not permanently injure her; to earthly injuries the dead are proof, but the shock of it caused her to swoon, it seems. *Monsieur,*" he bowed to Ned, "you are more fortunate than any of those others. Several times you have been close to death, but each time you escaped. You have been given chance and chance again to keep your pledged word to the dead, a thing no other faithless lover of the little Julie ever had. It seems, Monsieur, this dead girl truly loves you."

"How horrible!" I muttered.

"You said it, Doctor Trowbridge!" Ned seconded. "It looks as if I'm in a spot, all right."

"*Mais non*," de Grandin contradicted. "Escape is obvious, my friend."

"How, in heaven's name?"

"Keep your promised word; go back to her."

"Good Lord, I can't do that! Go back to a corpse, take her in my arms—kiss her?"

"*Certainement*, why not?"

"Why—why, she's *dead*!"

"Is she not beautiful?"

"She's lovely and alluring as a siren's song. I think she's the most exquisite thing I've ever seen, but —" he rose and walked unsteadily across the room. "If it weren't for Nella," he said slowly, "I might not find it hard to follow your advice. Julie's sweet and beautiful, and artless and affectionate as a child; kind, too, the way she stood between me and that awful snake-thing, but—oh, it's out of the question!"

"Then we must expand the question to accommodate it, my friend. For the safety of the living—for Mademoiselle Nella's sake—and for the repose of the dead, you must keep the oath you swore to little Julie d'Ayen. You must go back to New Orleans and keep your rendezvous."

THE DEAD OF OLD SAINT DENIS LAY IN DREAMLESS SLEEP BENEATH THE PALELY argent rays of the fast-waxing moon. The oven-like tombs were gay with hardly-wilted flowers; for two days before was All Saints' Day, and no grave in all New Orleans is so lowly, no dead so long interred, that pious hands do not bear blossoms of remembrance to them on that feast of memories.

De Grandin had been busily engaged all afternoon, making mysterious trips to the old Negro quarter in company with a patriarchal scion of Indian and Negro ancestry who professed ability to guide him to the city's foremost practitioner of voodoo; returning to the hotel only to dash out again to consult his friend at the Cathedral; coming back to stare with thoughtful eyes upon the changing panorama of Canal Street while Ned, nervous as a race-horse at the barrier, tramped up and down the room lighting cigarette from cigarette and drinking absinthe frappés alternating with sharp, bitter sazarac cocktails till I wondered that he did not fall in utter alcoholic collapse. By evening I had that eery feeling that the sane experience when alone with mad folk. I was ready to shriek at any unexpected noise or turn and run at sight of a strange shadow.

"My friend," de Grandin ordered as we reached the grass-paved corridor of tombs where Ned had told us the d'Ayen vaults were, "I suggest that you drink this." From an inner pocket he drew out a tiny flask of ruby glass and snapped its stopper loose. A strong and slightly acrid scent came to me, sweet and spicy, faintly reminiscent of the odor of the aromatic herbs one smells about a mummy's wrappings.

"Thanks, I've had enough to drink already," Ned said shortly.

"You are informing me, *mon vieux*?" the little Frenchman answered with a smile. "It is for that I brought this draft along. It will help you draw yourself together. You have need of all your faculties this time, believe me."

Ned put the bottle to his lips, drained its contents, hiccuped lightly, then braced his shoulders. "That *is* a pick-up," he complimented. "Too bad you didn't let me have it sooner, sir. I think I can go through the ordeal now."

"One is sure you can," the Frenchman answered confidently. "Walk slowly toward the spot where you last saw Julie, if you please. We shall await you here, in easy call if we are needed."

The aisle of tombs was empty as Ned left us. The turf had been fresh-mown for the day of visitation and was as smooth and short as a lawn tennis court. A field-mouse could not have run across the pathway without our seeing it. This much I noticed idly as Ned trudged away from us, walking more like a man on his way to the gallows than one who went to keep a lovers' rendezvous ... and suddenly he was not alone. There was another with him, a girl dressed in a clinging robe of sheer white muslin cut in the charming fashion of the First Empire, girdled high beneath the bosom with a sash of light-blue ribbon. A wreath of pale gardenias lay upon her bright, fair hair; her slender arms were pearl-white in the moonlight. As she stepped toward Ned I thought involuntarily of a line from Sir John Suckling:

"Her feet ... like little mice stole in and out."

"*Édouard, chêri! O, coeur de mon coeur, c'est véritablement toi?* Thou hast come willingly, unasked, *petit amant?*"

"I'm here," Ned answered steadily, "but only —" He paused and drew a sudden gasping breath, as though a hand had been laid on his throat.

"*Chèri,*" the girl asked in a trembling voice, "you are cold to me; do not you love me, then—you are not here because your heart heard my heart calling? O heart of my heart's heart, if you but knew how I have longed and waited! It has been *triste, mon Édouard,* lying in my narrow bed alone while winter rains and summer suns beat down, listening for your footfall. I could have gone out at my pleasure whenever moonlight made the nights all bright with silver; I could have sought for other lovers, but I would not. You held release for me within your hands, and if I might not have it from you I would forfeit it for ever. Do not you bring release for me, my Édouard? Say that it is so!"

An odd look came into the boy's face. He might have seen her for the first time, and been dazzled by her beauty and the winsome sweetness of her voice.

"Julie!" he whispered softly. "Poor, patient, faithful little Julie!"

In a single stride he crossed the intervening turf and was on his knees before her, kissing her hands, the hem of her gown, her sandaled feet, and babbling half-coherent, broken words of love.

She put her hands upon his head as if in benediction, then turned them, holding them palm-forward to his lips, finally crooked her fingers underneath his chin and raised his face. "Nay, love, sweet love, art thou a worshipper and I a saint that thou should kneel to me?" she asked him tenderly. "See, my lips are famishing for thine, and wilt thou waste thy kisses on my hands and feet and garment? Make haste, my heart, we have but little time, and I would know the kisses of redemption ere —"

They clung together in the moonlight, her white-robed, lissome form and his somberly-clad body seemed to melt and merge in one while her hands reached up to clasp his cheeks and draw his face down to her yearning, scarlet mouth.

De Grandin was reciting something in a mumbling monotone; his words were scarcely audible, but I caught a phrase occasionally: "... rest eternal grant to her, O Lord ... let light eternal shine upon her ... from the gates of hell her soul deliver.... *Kyrie eleison....*"

"Julie!" we heard Ned's despairing cry, and:

"*Ha*, it comes, it has begun; it finishes!" de Grandin whispered gratingly.

The girl had sunk down to the grass as though she swooned; one arm had fallen limply from Ned's shoulder, but the other still was clasped about his neck as we raced toward them. "*Adieu, mon amoureux; adieu pour ce monde, adieu pour l'autre; adieu pour l'éternité!*" we heard her sob. When we reached him, Ned knelt empty-armed before the tomb. Of Julie there was neither sign nor trace.

"So, assist him, if you will, my friend," de Grandin bade, motioning me to take Ned's elbow. "Help him to the gate. I follow quickly, but first I have a task to do."

As I led Ned, staggering like a drunken man, toward the cemetery exit, I heard the clang of metal striking metal at the tomb behind us.

WHAT DID YOU STOP BEHIND TO DO?" I ASKED AS WE PREPARED FOR BED AT THE hotel.

He flashed his quick, infectious smile at me, and tweaked his mustache ends, for all the world like a self-satisfied tomcat furbishing his whiskers after finishing a bowl of cream. "There was an alteration to that epitaph I had to make. You recall it read, '*Ici repose malheureusement*—here lies unhappily Julie d'Ayen'? That is no longer true. I chiseled off the *malheureusement*. Thanks to Monsieur Édouard's courage and my cleverness the old one's prophecy was fulfilled tonight; and poor, small Julie has found rest at last. Tomorrow morning they celebrate the first of a series of masses I have arranged for her at the Cathedral."

"What was that drink you gave Ned just before he left us?" I asked curiously. "It smelled like —"

"*Le bon Dieu* and the devil know—not I," he answered with a grin. "It was a voodoo love-potion. I found the realization that she had been dead a century and more so greatly troubled our young friend that he swore he could not be affectionate to our poor Julie; so I went down to the Negro quarter in the afternoon and arranged to have a philtre brewed. *Eh bien*, that aged black one who concocted it assured me that she could inspire love for the image of a crocodile in the heart of anyone who looked upon it after taking but a drop of her decoction, and she charged me twenty dollars for it. But I think I had my money's worth. Did it not work marvelously?"

"Then Julie's really gone? Ned's coming back released her from the spell—"

"Not wholly gone," he corrected. "Her little body now is but a small handful of dust, her spirit is no longer earth-bound, and the familiar demon who in life was old Maman Dragonne has left the earth with her, as well. No longer will she metamorphosize into a snake and kill the faithless ones who kiss her little mistress and then forswear their troth, but—*non*, my friend, Julie is not gone entirely, I think. In the years to come when Ned and Nella have long been joined in wedded bliss, there will be minutes when Julie's face and Julie's voice and the touch of Julie's little hands will haunt his memory. There will always be one little corner of his heart which never will belong to Madame Nella Minton, for it will be for ever Julie's. Yes, I think that it is so."

Slowly, deliberately, almost ritualistically, he poured a glass of wine and raised it. "To you, my little poor one," he said softly as he looked across the sleeping city toward old Saint Denis Cemetery. "You quit earth with a kiss upon your lips; may you sleep serene in Paradise until another kiss shall waken you."

THE END.

ACTRESS TALLULAH BANKHEAD, FROM 1931

A CALL TO SERVE

AN ORIGINAL STORY

BY JOHN LEAHY

Note: A short glossary of terms used in this story is printed for easy reference in the back of this issue.

H e'd explored almost every corner of Monsiel and had enjoyed the experience but he absolutely hated wet-soil environments. Swamps, marshes, bogs…curse them all. His appetite for knowledge of the world's various creatures and plants had pushed him all over the continent. He'd climbed to the top of treacherous, icy mountains and had dived down to the beds of rivers and bays. Dangerous ventures all, but none as sapping, and spirit-draining as wading through miles of rushes, muck, and water-pools. Pools which were often quite deceiving, of course. What often looked like maybe a few inches of water could sometimes turn out to be maybe a foot and a half deep. A foolishly trusting step into one of these beasts and one ended up moving forward in misery after water had flooded over the top of one's boot and down inside.

He looked at the boy walking a little ahead of him. Of course the boy never blundered into a deep pool. He seemed to have an almost supernatural sense regarding them – he only stood in ones that actually were as shallow as they looked.

"It's not much further now" the boy said.

HE'D MET THE BOY IN A TINY VILLAGE ON THE PATCH OF LAND BETWEEN THE Toliad mountains and the bog itself. He'd been passing through the village when a gaggle of children, poorly-attired barefoot urchins, had gathered around him, walking beside him as he made his way onward. To get rid of them he threw some coins to his left and right and sped up his progress as they scattered to retrieve the money. He was almost clear of the village when he saw an older boy up ahead, standing outside a hut. The boy was watching him intently as he approached and fell in beside him as he walked by.

"You're a soldier" the boy said.

"Amongst other things" the traveller responded.

"What other things might these be?"

The traveller had looked down at the boy upon hearing this. Usually when boys saw a sword at a man's side it was the only thing about that man that they remained interested in. He'd decided to humour the boy.

"I study things. Nature. The world around us. Animals and plants, mainly."

"I can show you a very special plant. A tree. A tree the likes of which you've never seen."

"I've been all over this continent, boy. I've seen every type of tree it has to offer."

"Have you ever been to the heart of the Yexan bog?"

"No."

"Then you haven't seen this tree. And there's four of them. In a little grove."

They were clear of the village now and the traveller stopped walking. He looked the boy in the eye, testing his mettle. The boy returned his gaze, unflinching. There was intelligence there, and strength. Not your average, timid village child.

"Describe this tree."

"Black. Leafless branches. Strange, gold-coloured flowers sprouting from some of the branches." The boy paused. "Over a hundred feet high. Thorns over a foot long."

The traveller remained silent as he tried to see such a tree in his mind. It sounded like a drunkard's dream.

"The thorns are alive" the boy continued.

"What do you mean?" the traveller asked, his brow furrowing in irritation. Was this boy perhaps some sort of mentally unwell fantasist? A foolish poetic dreamer of a sort?

"I've seen them killing fairies."

"Killing *fairies*?"

"Yes. By stabbing them and sucking their blood."

"Really."

"Yes. I swear it. I'll take you to the grove for ten gold coins."

The traveller snorted. "Ten gold coins?"

The boy's eyes dropped to the traveller's sidearm. "That's not the sword of a poor man."

The traveller smiled humourlessly.

"How far is this grove from here?"

"About a day and a half's walk. If we leave now we'd be there tomorrow evening."

Part of the traveller was frustrated that he was even entertaining this story, while another part was intrigued by it. He knew a little about small carnivorous plants that inhabited bogs. Due to the poor nutritional content of the soil in bogs, some of the plants that grew in them derived their food from insects, which they trapped and digested. These he found interesting enough, but a carnivorous *tree*! And one that got its sustenance from *fairies*!

"I'll give you five coins now, and five when I see these trees in front of me."

"Alright." The boy extended his palm.

The traveller began depositing coins in the boy's hand. As soon as the fifth coin jangled against the others the boy's hand closed and disappeared inside his pocket.

The traveller cocked his head back in the direction of the village.

"Get yourself some bedding and some food. Meet me back here."

THE GROVE GREW CLEARER IN THE FOG AS THEY APPROACHED.

The boy's definition of the trees had flattered them – they were eerie, unpleasant-looking things, like frightening elements that a writer would use to darken a child's fairy-tale, except they were very real, towering before them. They were taller than the boy had said – the traveller estimated their heights to be close to a hundred and fifty feet. And their jet-black colour was terribly strange. As they drew closer, the bizarre, pretty flowers that sprouted mysteriously from various branches came into sharper relief. They were at odds with the black branches and the brutal, queer thorns that protruded viciously from them. The traveller walked from tree to tree, marvelling at their monstrousness. How were these things growing here at all? They were completely out of kilter with their surroundings. The largest plant that he had come across in the bog had been a heather shrub about two feet high.

"We'd better get out of sight" the boy said.

"Why?"

"The fairies won't come if they see us. I presume you want to see the thorns at work."

"Yes" the traveller said, lowering his head. In his wonder, he'd forgotten about this element of the story.

"Let's hide behind that rock" the boy said, pointing beyond the grove.

When they were behind the rock the boy extended his palm. The traveller gave him the remainder of his payment.

THE LIGHT WAS GROWING DIM WHEN THE BOY WHISPERED TO HIS COMPANION.

"Look."

The traveller, who had just been about to empty his loaded bladder, shifted his gaze toward where the boy was pointing. He stared, rapt, at a fairy as it alighted on a tree branch, its wings coming to rest behind its back. The traveller had only seen a fairy once, in a forest, when he'd been a child. The one he'd seen had been tiny, and had had no wings. This one before him now he guessed was about twice the size of that one in the forest, and its skin was an eerie, pale grey. It walked along the branch and stopped by one of the flowers protruding from it. It knelt down and dipped its hands inside its petals. The fairy's hands re-emerged in the shape of a bowl, and it raised them to its mouth. When the fairy had finished drinking whatever fluid they had held, it flew down to the base of the tree and sat down. After a while its upper body began to sway uncertainly from side to side and the soft smile of a simpleton appeared on its features. Eventually its head drooped to its chest and it fell sideways to the ground. The traveller kept his eyes on the unmoving form. Obviously the fluid in the flower had acted as some sort of pleasure-drug on the fairy. Movement at the top of his vision caught his attention and he looked up to see a thorn on the branch immediately above the fairy begin to elongate in the direction of the inert form beneath it. As it lengthened, it became translucent. It entered the fairy's upturned side and the traveller saw a line of red ascend through the almost see-through pipe. Gradually the flow of blood began to lessen before stopping completely. The sucking pipe withdrew and began to shrink back upward. Eventually nothing of its existence remained except the black, angry thorn that it had begun as.

Stunned, it was a while before the traveller moved. Eventually he emerged from behind the rock and walked slowly toward the inert form of the fairy. Its body was now diminished in size and its skin was heavily wrinkled, giving the creature an ancient, wizened look. There was a hole in its clothing where the thorn had pierced it.

When the traveller reached the fairy he looked up at the thorn. It pointed down at him menacingly. He waited for it to begin its descent toward him, but it never came. The boy had said that the trees drained the blood of fairies – obviously they consumed from fairies only, given that he was standing right beneath a thorn and it was showing no interest in feeding from him. The traveller moved to the tree's trunk and placed his hand on it, studying the strange, black bark. He noticed thin lines of what appeared to be sap running down in grooves along its length. He extended his forefinger and touched the sap. He rubbed the pad of his finger against his thumb. The clear fluid was greasy, its texture like that of a thin oil.

He stared wonderingly at the sap, pondering. His heart began to beat a little faster as he contemplated what properties the liquid might have. The tree lived on fairy blood, and fairy blood was an amazing substance. There were various types of fairies all over the continent of Monsiel – forest fairies, city fairies, underground fairies, cave fairies, and many others. The blood of the various groups had different properties – the traveller couldn't recall exact specifics but he'd heard that certain fairy blood was explosive, some was highly flammable, some made excellent fertiliser. The drinking of one type of fairy blood could help people to see in the dark. Various types could cure certain illnesses. Despite these valuable qualities, the drinking of fairy blood was frowned upon in most parts of Monsiel as fairies were seen as eerie, magical creatures that few people knew much about.

Before his nerve failed him, the traveller put his finger in his mouth. Not noticing any taste from the sap, he swallowed.

PORT OF DEMNOIN, NORTHERN AMADAST

VOLGAN SAT DOWN ON THE EDGE OF HIS BED AND WIPED SWEAT FROM HIS FOREHEAD. He drank some water from the cup on the chair before him. A bed and chair. That was the extent of the furniture in his quarters. Ha. Quarters. His "quarters" consisted of nothing more than a tiny room. A far cry from his tower in the castle back home in Drenkat. And a lot less peaceful. Sleep was hard to come by in this place. When the men came back after their days of mapping, tree-felling and vegetation-clearing, they drank and whored until late in the night. In the morning Volgan would hear them vomiting in their rooms before they staggered out into a new day to repeat the process.

It was Volgan's fourth day in Demnoin, a tiny port that was expanding with each passing day. Boats of every shape and size were constantly arriving, disgorging pilgrims and adventurers, eager to begin a new life in this virgin kingdom – Amadast, as it had been named by its discoverer, Kanreth Shacken, a female Euramdianese explorer.

Demnoin was the most easterly settlement in this new land. Nearly a hundred miles to the southwest, on the Chalzer inlet, lay the burgeoning port of Prasta. There were four more settlements west of Prasta - Treng, Akandrul, Shmax and Yabastio. Volgan intended to visit them all. This was his fourth night in Demnoin. In the morning he would leave for Prasta. The town was situated at the mouth of the Wosoleg river, a body of water that Volgan was looking forward to seeing. It was said that the distance from one side of the river's mouth to the other was over twenty miles. The mouth of the Eretwel, the longest river in all of Monsiel was barely over half that width.

Volgan ran his hand all the way from his face back along his bald head to the nape of his neck, feeling a layer of sweat all the way. Up to two weeks ago he'd always had hair. He was hairless as part of a change of appearance, the other part of which was the rich beard he now sported – which he'd never had before leaving Drenkat. He hadn't wanted to run the risk of being spotted and questioned by agents of Nedeman Shorc, the Dullun of Euramdian. So far he hadn't attracted any suspicious glances. In his current, roughly-clothed state, he looked like many of the other settlers – mildly villainous and a little the worse for wear.

The noise in the tavern below him was building – soon the glass-breaking and fighting would begin. After that the racket would transfer to the rooms on either side of him as the sex took over. The heat in his room was simply stifling. He decided to head outside for some air. He left the room and went down to the tavern, the smell of farts, ale and sweat growing stronger as he made his way down the flimsy staircase. He went through the crowd, being jostled by revellers as they danced to the drunken efforts of a group of musicians. A whore put her hand on his arm as he made his way to the door, her alcohol-flooded eyes full of promise. Volgan gently removed it and left the tavern. The air was not much cooler than that inside the tavern, but it was cleansed by the smell of the sea. Volgan looked at the water which began about fifty yards ahead of him.

The sea of Euramdian. About four hundred miles away, across the water, lay the city of Ansidiu in south-eastern Euramdian. To the east of Ansidiu lay the city of Jast-Monmeth. It was these two cities and the dry, poor farmlands behind them that were adding to the population of Demnoin each day.

Volgan turned to his left and began walking along the crude dirt-road that served as a street. The businesses he passed were a collection of taverns, whorehouses, food parlours and tool shops.

"My Lord."

Volgan stopped walking, but did not turn around to face the speaker.

"Who are you?" he asked. "Speak quietly lest anyone hear."

"My name is Sir Ilick Wildris. I am serving under King Alwil at Masraff. He sent me to you."

Volgan turned around. Before him stood a slight, well-tailored young man.

"How did he find me?"

"The king has his ways."

"What did he send you here for?"

"To offer you a position at his court."

"Hmm. And what might this position be?"

Wildris moved a little closer.

"The king is setting up a special unit. To protect him and to investigate crimes against the throne."

"And he wants me to join this unit."

"He wants you to be its leader."

Volgan looked out at the water. The moon had emerged from behind a cloud and was spilling light over its shimmering surface.

"He said you wouldn't say no to an old friend" Wildris added.

Volgan sighed. It looked like his little reconnaissance mission was at an end.

As they passed the dusty, unpopulated Cape Posnas which marked the south-eastern extremity of Monsiel, Volgan found it difficult to imagine the carnage that had taken place further inland a few months earlier. The "war of the unwilling" as it had become known, had been the most catastrophic in the continent's history. Alwil Treggessun, the Jakeram of Zorran and the King of Monsiel, had fought off an invasion by Queen Kinsen Helinter of Chadriac. Four other sedrens had reluctantly allowed themselves to be sucked into the conflict as it had worn on. These were Kantuo and Quobia who had joined with Zorran, and Maxan and Imgoll who had allied themselves with Chadriac. Two sedrens had remained neutral, Belchar – Volgan's homeland, and Euramdian. The war had only lasted a year and a half but the fighting had been ferocious. An uneasy peace – now in its third month – had descended after Queen Kinsen had withdrawn her forces inside her borders. Nearly a million souls had perished in the conflict. Villages and towns in the main theatres of combat – south-western Maxan, north-eastern Zorran and southern Imgoll – had been devastated. Thousands of acres of fertile farmland had been torn up. The recovery from the conflict would take an age.

They were making good time on their voyage, the winds being in their favour. Their destination was Pidostaca, a port in Belchar which Volgan estimated they would reach in five days. From there they would journey to Drenkat, Belchar's capital. There Volgan, at King Alwil's request, would select four of the finest soldiers in his father's army to accompany him to Masraff in Zorran where they would be part of the Throne Hammer, which was the title that Alwil had given to the new unit he was setting up. Kantuo, Quobia and Euramdian had also been invited to contribute five soldiers each to the force. The core of the force would consist of ten Zorranese warriors, bringing the total number of personnel to thirty. Volgan's current sailing companion, Ilick Wildris, was one of the contingent from Kantuo.

Volgan looked to his right. Ilick Wildris had joined him in his study of the barren Cape.

"Tell me, Sir Ilick" Volgan said. "How is our King? How are his spirits?"

"As well as can be expected, given the circumstances" came the response. Alwil had suffered two grievous wounds during the war – his left arm had been so badly burned in a shaitfish attack that it had had to be amputated, and his right leg had been gored by a spear which meant he would walk with a limp for the rest of his days. Added to this, his wife, Queen Anrys, had died in childbirth during the war, along with the infant.

"What do you think of war, Wildris?"

"War is…inevitable. There is only so much that can be done to avoid it. But in the end it always comes. The best we can do is…try to be prepared for it."

"Did you do much fighting?"

"I had my share."

"Did you kill any men?"

"I killed men and women."

"Had you killed anybody before the war?"

"No."

"You would have been a boy when I killed my first man" Volgan said. "In the Mezprutian invasion of Prackus. I was thrown from my horse and fell into a stream. A soldier was running toward me, his sword raised, meaning to cut me to pieces. I barely got my sword out in time to block his blow. Such was the force of his strike that my blade fell from my grasp. He raised his sword for the fatal blow but I was lucky that he was old and I was young. I was faster than him. I whipped my dagger out and lashed it into his leg. He fell on his backside and let his sword drop. He lay there screaming, holding his leg. I jumped at him, not thinking about his sword. If I'd had more presence of mind I'd have ran him through with it and given him a quick death. But I didn't. I put my hands under his old neck and pushed him backward until his head went under the water. He was a strong old bull and came up three times before his strength left him and he stayed under." Volgan went silent for a while. "The musicians sang songs about me after that war. The young hero who had beaten the Euramdianese out of our most fertile lands. Of course they don't mention that for my first kill I drowned an old man."

"They wouldn't sing about my first kill, either" Wildris said. "During the siege of Tengelm castle I cut a catapult rope with my sword and a huge baslin bomb went in over the walls. After that we had no further attacks on our battering ram and we were able to get inside." Ildris went silent for a moment. "I poisoned twelve men when I cut that rope. That was my first kill."

Volgan decided to change the subject.

"Tell me about your homeland. Tell me about your strong."

"My father owns about twelve hundred acres northwest of Antost. Some if it is desert. As my brothers and I fought for the King in the war, Alwil is lending my father money at a very favourable rate. My father plans to buy better lands to the south now, along the banks of the Zimhox river." He paused. "On a fine evening there's a beautiful view from the parapet of my father's castle. You can see for miles out over the Kantish sea, the sun setting on the horizon. I haven't seen that view in a long time."

"There's a pleasing enough view from the battlements of Masraff" Volgan said. "The peaks of the Jadnynes…the Olbosh weaving its way through the valley below."

"Yes, it soothes the eye" Ildris said. "I fear we may not see much of it, my Lord."

"Why do you say that?"

"There is an air of unease in Masraff. I am only a young man…but I can sense it. There is discontent bubbling under the surface."

"So you think we will be busy men."

"Yes, my lord."

AFTER ARRIVING IN PIDOSTACA, IT TOOK THEM THREE DAYS ON HORSEBACK TO reach Drenkat. When Volgan and Wildris entered the throne room of Havar Borinth's castle, the Halisant of Belchar was cutting an apple into pieces on a plate by his side. He greeted his son with a scowl. Volgan had gone on his excursion to the Amadast against his father's will and he hadn't expected to be welcomed back.

"Ah!" Havar exclaimed. "The wanderer returns! So what brings you back? You miss your soft bed? Your wardrobe of silks?"

"I've been summoned to Masraff by the King-."

"Oh!" Havar interjected. "Well, I should have known that it wasn't for me you returned. My heir heads off against my wishes, risking his life on a tour of an untamed new land but comes running back when our crippled king clicks his fingers!". Havar looked at Volgan's companion. "What's your name, boy?"

"Sir Ilick Wildris, my lord."

"Your *highness*, boy."

"Forgive me, your highness."

"Tell me, boy – have you ever disobeyed your father?"

Wildris hesitated, uncomfortable for a moment. "No, your highness."

Havar pointed at Wildris and looked at Volgan.

"You should take a leaf out of *his* book" Havar said. "Learn some respect." He put down his knife and began to eat the apple he had cut up.

"Alwil is setting up a new force, father" Volgan said. "And he wants me in charge of it."

"Hmm" Havar said, continuing with his apple. "And what is the function of this…force?"

"To protect the king and to investigate crimes against the throne."

Havar munched noisily, still not looking at his son. "Soldiering and detective work. That's a lot of responsibility."

"I'm to bring four men with me."

"Four of *my* men, you mean."

"Yes."

When Havar made no response to this, Volgan spoke again.

"I'd like to take Vusel Amanthing, Markian Drookus, Fenhus Manthelm and Greck."

"You did not say you wanted four of my best" Havar said, gesturing to a servant to come and take his plate away.

"It would be prudent, father."

"Hmm. Maybe I should give you the dregs. Teach you not to go running off into the wild again."

Volgan remained silent.

"You can have the first three. But not Greck."

"I need brains as well as brawn, father-."

"DO NOT CHALLENGE ME!!!" Havar shouted. "I have had enough of your impudence!"

For a few seconds not a sound could be heard in the room. The silence was eventually broken by a knock on the door.

"Come!" Havar barked.

A servant boy entered tentatively, carrying a tray on which there was a flask of wine and a goblet. He made his way to the throne where he placed the tray by Havar's side and filled the goblet. Then he hurriedly left.

"I presume you're leaving in the morning" Havar said, raising the goblet to his mouth.

"Yes, father."

"Well then you'd better get some rest. And wash yourselves, too. I can smell you up here."

AFTER A LONG BATH, AN EXHAUSTED VOLGAN MADE HIS WAY BACK TO HIS room. When he entered it, he found his father sitting in a chair in the corner.

"Sit down."

Wearing only a towel, Volgan sat on the edge of his bed.

"Alwil cannot last long" Havar said.

"Father-."

"He is broken. He has suffered too much. They say he drinks too much now, and he is not as even-tempered as he used to be-."

Volgan raised a hand. He knew where the discussion was heading and he wanted no part of it.

"Father, no, I am not-."

"I know he is you friend, Volgan. I know that one time he had it in him to be king but that time is gone. The war has taken too much from him."

"Yes he is my friend, Father, but that is not why I am going to him. I am going to him because I believe in him. Alwil was always popular and a good diplomat. He was fair, level-headed and firm. I refuse to believe that the war has taken all of that from him." Volgan paused. "He's the best man for the job" he added softly.

His father sniffed. "Alright. Say he does have some of his old self left. Will he have the strength to cope with what lies ahead? Will he be able to prevent hostilities from breaking out again? What about Euramdian? They had no part in the war, their armies are intact. They could decide to march on Masraff any day. I'm no supporter of Alwil Treggessun but I'd prefer his small toe to a Euramdianese King. We had enough of those over the centuries and every single one was a tyrant."

"Nedeman Shorc is not a tyrant."

"Maybe not now, but the throne of Monsiel changes men."

"I don't think Nedeman has any interest in the throne. I think he's more interested in consolidating his position in the Amadast."

"And you know this, how? Do you have spies in Miambech?"

"No, but I've seen what's going on in Nedeman's new world. Every day more and more people flock to the Amadast seeking to build a new life. The land is fertile, the jungle along the coast is rich with timbers of the highest quality and the rivers are full of fish. Gold, silver, copper, tin and lead have all been found. Nedeman will take a royalty on the gains from all of this. He is actively encouraging people from the poorer parts of his kingdom to settle there. That means he has less poverty on his own doorstep and tax coming in from the emigrants when they gain a foothold in their new lives. I think we should be doing the same with our poorer folk – encourage them to seek their fortune in the lands east of the Euramdianese settlements-."

"Enough about the Amadast!" Havar snapped. "Monsiel is our immediate problem! The land we *live* in! A weak king is at the helm. And weakness invites challenge. We need someone strong on the throne."

"And that someone is you, father."

They had gotten to the heart of the issue.

"Yes" Havar said after a few seconds of silence. "I can bring a long-lasting peace to the continent. But you have our army's heart, Volgan. They will follow the hero of Prackus with greater zeal than they will follow me."

"You would risk our army against Alwil's? The strongest in Monsiel?"

"Zorran is exhausted. Chadriac gave them much more of a fight than they'd bargained for." Havar paused. He leaned forward in his chair, his right hand curling into a fist. "Volgan…the throne is there for the taking."

"Oh. A while ago it was the welfare of Monsiel you were concerned about."

Havar's fist unclenched and he slowly sat back, his face full of sullen anger.

"You would throw away this golden opportunity to see the first Belcharan in history on the throne of Monsiel? To see our strong rule over the entire continent? To see the name of Borinth in the Tome of Monarchs?"

"I do not wish to continue this treasonous conversation any further, father."

"It's only treason when you *lose*, boy," Havar said in a low, menacing voice. "And we wouldn't lose."

"I'm tired, father. I wish to sleep."

Both men held the other's eyes. Volgan could see the sullen, almost childish petulance in his father's. It was the look that rendered Havar Borinth unpopular amongst his nobility and people. There was something else in the visage before him now, though – Volgan realised that it was a tinge of hatred. Havar Borinth hated the fact that his son was liked more than he was.

Havar rose and left the room. Volgan dressed and laid down to sleep, savouring the feel of the luxurious bedclothes and mattress. His father had been right about one thing. He had indeed missed his bed.

He woke in the morning feeling refreshed and ready for the long road to Masraff. As he ate breakfast there was a knock at the door.

"Come."

The door opened and his old friend Greck Manru walked in. Greck opened his arms bombastically.

"No sooner does he return than he departs again!"

Volgan smiled as he chewed a piece of bread.

"I met your new friend Ilick Wilris on the way in," Greck added. "A rather serious chap." He sat down across the table from Volgan.

"So you know where I am bound? Volgan asked.

"Your father told me. He also told me that you asked could I be part of your group and he refused. He didn't give me a reason, of course. I think he's worried that if I left my laboratory might explode and poison the entire castle." As well as being a capable soldier and intelligent courtier, Greck was also a keen natural historian, and his laboratory near his quarters was packed with insects, creatures and plants from all over the continent. He did a little work with toxins, and sometimes Havar would remark on this with a little concern. He never ordered Greck to cease this work though, as Greck's father was Lothind Manru, a powerful lord and one of Havar's staunchest allies.

Volgan chuckled.

"So" Greck said. "Tell me about the Amadast."

"Singing. Drinking. Whoring."

"Ah. Do you need an ointment before you go? You've a long time in the saddle ahead of you."

Volgan laughed. It was a pity Greck wasn't coming with him. He could use his friend's humour on the journey.

"We need to get some colonists out there" Volgan said. "If we don't, we're going to get left behind. All our neighbours are prospering in this age of exploration. Zorran gets money from Madgans, Chadriac from Hondrint and now Euramdian has part of the Amadast. We need to get people on the lands east of the Euramdianese settlements. We need to stake our claim." He paused. "Not that my father agrees with me."

"What does he think of your new position?"

"He voiced no opinion on it."

"I'd imagine he's at least some bit impressed. Chief of the Throne Hammer. It's quite the title. The highest servant of the throne in the land."

"I don't think he sees it that way. He can't get beyond the man who's actually *sitting* on the throne."

"It's hard to blame him, Volgan. Alwil is a damaged man."

"He fought off a serious challenge to his reign, Greck. People should give him the benefit of the doubt."

Greck didn't respond and Volgan knew that his friend didn't really agree with the sentiment. He decided to change the subject.

"So who has my father given me in your stead?"

"Gostan Lumgight."

Volgan nodded. A political decision on Havar's part. Lumgight was a reasonable warrior, but was by no means intelligent. His parents were powerful though, and Havar would endear himself to them by bestowing this honour upon their son.

"Are all the men here?"

"Yes. Amanthing and Drookus are a little the worse for wear. They went out celebrating their appointments last night. Your father has given you a ten-man guard for the journey, by the way."

"Good." Volgan rose. "Well. Best be shortening the road."

"I'll walk down with you."

When they walked out onto the bailey, the four men that Havar had given him greeted Volgan and thanked him for the privilege of serving the crown.

"The king has honoured us greatly by giving us this commission" Volgan said, looking at the men. "Now let us honour him and Belchar by giving selflessly and bravely in our duties. Let us rise to the challenge and embrace it."

"For the king and Belchar!" Vusel Amanthing said. Volgan could smell the drink from him. The rest of the group echoed Amanthing's call.

Volgan mounted his horse and looked around.

"Well" he said to Greck. "Looks like my father won't be wishing us farewell."

Greck smiled wanly. "Take care on the road" he said. "And take care of the king."

THEY MADE GOOD TIME ON THE ROAD AS FAR AS THE BORDER, BUT NOT LONG after they crossed into Ansedo, the southernmost sond of Maxan, their progress slowed. Here the biggest engagements of the war had taken place and the sod had been broken up by the activity of hooves, feet and wheels. Some of the villages they passed through were shattered and deserted. In others, the few people that remained watched with barren stares as Volgan's mounted procession made its way past them. Starving souls wandered aimlessly through the streets of half-destroyed towns. Volgan counted twelve large forts that had been reduced to blackened rubble.

As they passed by yet another blasted town, Fenhus Manthelm shook his head.

"How on earth is Ansedo going to recover from this? There is no way Piragem can afford to rebuild the region." Piragem was the capital of

Maxan. "It's a task that even Zorran or Chadriac would struggle with. Not to mind a poor backwater like Maxan."

"Indeed" Markian Drookus said. "Solbiun Dronda has a lot to answer for. He should never have dragged Maxan into the war. He should have known that most of the fighting would take place on his lands. I mean, the sedren is situated right between the main combatants! What an idiot."

"It's difficult to say no when a powerful neighbour expects your help" Gostan Lumgight said. "Most of Maxan's produce goes to Chadriac. If Solbiun had turned down Kinsen, she could have blocked Maxanese goods from entering her lands and that would have made them poorer than they already are."

"Maybe they would have been better off" Vusel Amanthing growled, looking around him. "At least then one of their sonds wouldn't be left in ruins."

"Some say that Solbiun cares little for Ansedo" Ilick Wildris said. "Most of the support for his reign lies in Hondel and Megansas. He has difficulty collecting taxes from the Ansedans. Solbiun may see the destruction wrought here as a fitting punishment for their defiance."

They rode on in silence for a while.

"Perhaps we should have entered the war" Vusel Amanthing said, looking at Volgan. "We could have tipped the scales in Alwil's favour and blasted that Helinter bitch from the face of Monsiel. "

"I'm glad we didn't. If we had then maybe Bastoleg would look like this."

Volgan's father had wanted to enter the war on Zorran's side. Havar had felt the same as Amanthing – that the Belcharan army could have been a deciding force in the war. In the victorious aftermath, Alwil would reward Belchar with some of Chadriac's territory. Volgan had quickly put paid to that notion by refusing to lead the army into a war that he felt had nothing to do with Belchar. To him, the army was there to defend the people of Belchar, nothing more. It was not a force to be risked for conquest. That engagement with his father, over a year earlier, had soured their relationship permanently. Their bond, although never very strong to begin with, had never recovered afterward.

On the seventh day of their journey, they encountered the Olbosh river where it veered westward toward Masraff. At this point, at the foot of the Jadnyne mountains, it was only about twenty feet wide. It was a far cry from the waterway it would later become, the wide and powerful beast that flowed through the Ostigal plain and meandered through the Yesetoot marsh in southern Euramdian as the second longest river in Monsiel.

Eventually the spires of Masraff came into view.

"It's not much compared to Monja, is it?" Amanthing remarked as they drew closer.

Masraff was more of a large town than a city. And now it was to be the seat of the throne of Monsiel. Immediately after the truce, Alwil had moved the continent's capital from Monja, the largest city in Zorran, four hundred miles to the east to Masraff. He'd done this to be physically closer to both Imgoll and Maxan. He wanted to foster closer relations with them going forward, and to keep them away from Chadriac.

Upon reaching the bridge that would take them across the Olbosh to the city gate, they bade goodbye to the escort that Havar had given them. After the escort had departed, Volgan and his group crossed the river. Upon admitting them to the city, the gate-master informed them that they were the last members of Alwil's new force to arrive.

They made their way along the streets toward the city's castle. People stood outside shops and taverns, watching them as they passed by. For the most part the citizens were modestly dressed. It was a far cry from the ostentatious attire of the rich merchants and large business owners of Monja, and other large Zorranese cities like Imeljepon.

The streets began to slope upward and eventually they found themselves before the gate of the castle. Once inside, they were greeted with the sight of knights sparring amidst the other activities of the bailey. As they progressed onward, Volgan saw the crests of some of the other sedrens on the chests of the warriors. Some of them looked up at the new arrivals and nodded a greeting, Volgan and his companions returning the courtesy. Volgan observed some women in the cohort.

Two soldiers and some stable-hands approached them. The stable-hands took their horses away and the soldiers led them to the throne room. They waited before an empty throne while the two soldiers went to a door to the left of the room. One of them knocked on it and a small, fat, elderly man opened it. Volgan recognised him as Lord Sonrel Gonthigae, who had once been a senior general in the Zorranese army and was now one of Alwil's advisers. Gonthigae looked behind him, and said something that Volgan couldn't hear. A few seconds later the door swung back and the king himself emerged, with another man behind him, the tall, bald Lord Geram Yecka, another adviser. Alwil walked toward his guests, the soldiers flanking him, one at either side. He smiled broadly upon seeing Volgan, and opened his arms.

"The Belcharan contingent!" Alwil declared. "Led by the noble Lord Volgan Borinth! Welcome!"

Volgan managed a smile in return, but it was difficult to maintain. He was shocked at his friend's appearance. The last time Volgan had seen his old friend had been a few months before the war had started. Then, Alwil had been hale and hearty. Now he was pale, with heavy bags under his eyes, his hair greasy and a little unkempt. He had lost a lot of weight. Then there were the injuries that he had sustained in the war – the absence of his left arm and the limp in his right leg. As he drew closer, Volgan could see the alcohol in his friend's eyes.

"Hello, old friend" Alwil said, and embraced Volgan. As he returned the greeting, Volgan could feel his friend's thin, bony form beneath his clothes. The smell of wine from him was strong.

"It's good to see you again, my king" Volgan said.

After they parted, Alwil looked to Volgan's right.

"Good to have you back with us, Sir Ilick."

Wildris bowed. "Your highness."

Alwil turned his attention to the three other Belcharans in the group.

"My king, may I present Fenhus Manthelm, Vusel Amanthing, Gostan Lumgight and Markian Drookus" Volgan said, gesturing to each soldier in turn.

Each man bowed, uttering "your highness" as they were introduced.

"Welcome to Masraff" Alwil said to them collectively. "Monsiel is at a critical juncture in its history. I need its best warriors around me at this time. You must be tired after your long journey. Show these men to their quarters" he said to his guards. "Lord Volgan, I would speak with you privately."

"Yes, your highness."

As the guards led the Belcharans and Wildris from the throne room, Alwil swept a hand in the direction of the two men beside him.

"My two most trusted advisers, Lord Sonrel Gonthigae and Lord Geram Yecka."

Volgan and the advisers exchanged greetings.

"Gentlemen" Alwil said to Gonthigae and Yecka, "you have before you Lord Volgan Borinth, heir to the throne of Belchar, commander-in-chief of her armies, and hero of the Prackus war."

Volgan smiled. "You do me great honour with such an introduction, my king."

"I have stated no inaccuracies" Alwil said.

"How was your journey, Lord Volgan?" Yecka asked.

"Uneventful…but trying. The desolation of Ansedo was difficult to witness."

"Indeed. The sond has suffered greatly."

"They will have difficulty rising from it. They will need all the help they can get."

"And they will have it from *me*" Alwil said. "Ansedo answered Solbiun Dronda's call to arms with great reluctance. Of her fighters who did go to battle, many of them ended up switching to our side." Alwil clapped his hands together. "And now let us continue our conversation in the high chamber, Lord Volgan." He looked at Gonthigae and Yecka. "Gentlemen, that will be all. We will speak again on the morrow." The two men bowed and left.

When Alwil looked at him again, Volgan could see that the formality was gone from the king's eyes. He gestured toward the room he had emerged from earlier. The two men went inside, where Alwil went to the head of a large table. There was a jug of wine there with a goblet beside it.

"Drink?" Alwil asked.

"No thank you, your highness."

As he went to lift the jug of wine, Alwil fixed his company with a look of mild admonishment.

"I don't want to hear "your highness" when we're on our own, Volgan."

He filled his goblet almost to the brim and sat down with a loud release of breath. Volgan sat to his left.

"So how was your time in the Amadast?"

"Brief."

"My apologies" Alwil said, and took a large gulp of wine. "But I had to have you here. I need people around me who I can trust. Now more than ever."

Volgan nodded.

"What does your father think of you being here?"

"He doesn't like it."

"Because you're serving weakness."

Volgan said nothing. Alwil had always been very direct.

Alwil smiled wanly. "It's alright. I know what people are thinking. The cripple with the limp, haunted by the death of his wife and child. How can he keep a continent at peace?" He took another drink. "I'd probably even think it myself if it was someone else."

"Alwil…the losses that you've endured…I'm truly sorry."

Alwil's eyes fell to the table. "Thank you" he said. "I was at the front when the news of Anrys and the child came to me. I was in my tent, planning with my generals. We'd had a good day, having succeeded in pushing the Chadriacans back by about half a mile. After the rider delivered his message, I was like a wraith for days. I didn't know if I was dead or alive. I was only returning to my old, full self when I lost my arm." He paused, after which he lifted his eyes to Volgan's. "Have you ever seen a shaitfish?"

"No. I'd never even heard of them until after what happened to you."

"They're nothing remarkable to look at. About the size of an average brown trout. A bit darker in colour with large black spots. We'd taken a fort outside a village called Yilemal in central Ansedo and had come under a heavy counterattack. The Chadriacans were firing every type of thing in on top of us from their catapults – rocks, timber, rubbish, even dead animals. And then a fish landed right in front of me! Me and some of the other men laughed. I mean, have you ever had a *fish* catapulted at you? Then its body started to swell, as though it were filling up with air, and its skin began to bubble. Someone cried "it's a shaitfish. Run!" Something told me to listen to that voice and I turned and fled, though I knew not what the threat was. The six men who had remained staring at the thing were killed when it exploded. Its flesh struck their heads and torsos, burning through their armour and bodies in seconds. I was lucky. Only my left arm was hit. The pain was…beyond describing. When the surgeons saw the wounds, they were alarmed, for a strange, rapid necrosis was spreading toward my shoulder. They counselled an immediate amputation. And so it was."

He paused before resuming.

"About a week later we captured one of their generals. She told us that shaitfish were rare, only to be found in the Zarapent sea north of the Smiriang peninsula. Their bodies become extremely corrosive when exposed to direct air and direct sunlight. They swell up and explode, scattering their lethal flesh everywhere."

"And they brought these things hundreds of miles to the front?" Volgan asked. "How do they keep them from rotting?"

"They don't have to. Shaitfish eat sea fairies. That has the effect of their bodies remaining preserved for a year after they die."

Volgan snorted in amazement. "Incredible."

"They used another poison weapon – the bark of the blenhing tree, which only grows in the valleys of the Rantenth range. When a flame is put to it, it does not burn but smoulders, giving off a thick orange smoke that if breathed in can cause a disabling dizziness that can last for nearly a day. The first time they used that, they killed nearly two hundred Quobians. They catapulted about thirty pieces of smouldering timber into the Quobian ranks and had them on the ground coughing in no time. Then when the smoke cleared, the Chadriacans walked among them, slaughtering them as they tried and failed repeatedly to get to their feet. The survivors – those who hadn't breathed in much of the smoke and managed to stagger away – said it was terrible to behold. Some men were so disoriented that they could not even raise a sword to defend themselves. Others couldn't even crawl."

He paused briefly, studying a point on the table. He took a drink and continued.

"I cannot say that *we* were pure in our warfare. We used our own cruelties. I had ten barrels of baslin grains shipped to the front from Madgans. We killed thousands of them with it."

"There's no such thing as decency in war" Alwil said. "It's just an ideal. There's only winning and losing."

"We didn't win it. I ensured that by accepting the truce."

"You brought peace, Alwil. An end to the killing."

"Some of the generals strongly opposed the truce. We were slowly pushing them back when Kinsen made the offer. The generals wanted to push on, all the way to Gendesun if necessary." Gendesun was the capital of Chadriac. "They wanted to destroy the Chadriacan army and to cripple their war-making ability for decades. But we were paying too much for our gains on the field. Every step forward we took cost us so much in blood. I didn't want to be walking through the ruins of Gendesun with three quarters of my army lost along the way."

"You did the right thing, Alwil. I would have done the same."

"The generals are sore about it. I have to look upon their bitter faces every day."

"Let them to their bitterness" Volgan said. "Which generals are these by the way?"

"Varm…Yormith…Manshareck."

Volgan snorted and smiled emptily. "All rich landowners. No doubt they'd hoped to add to their lands with some estates in the Anchipt plain." The Anchipt plain contained Chadriac's most productive land.

Alwil didn't respond for a while.

"Many are unhappy with my moving of the capital here" he eventually said. "Some in Monja are upset about their city's loss of status. Many here are uneasy about the increased military presence on their streets." He took a deep drink of wine. "Then there is the refugee situation to consider. I am allowing tens of thousands of Ansedans to enter eastern Zorran – many of them are homeless and many others fear reprisals from Solbiun Dronda after they refused to fight against us. I'm letting many Imgollans enter Jeroso. Thousands of them are starving after the tearing up of their land and the burning of their crops. The large estates of the Feltind plain have been ordered to feed them."

"A noble gesture" Volgan said. "Some of your own people will be unsettled by it."

"I know. They won't be happy with a sudden influx of poor, starving foreigners. But they'll warm to the idea over time. It will enable them to one day look back with pride at something good that they've done."

"The real danger is-."

"The bad elements that might come in with the refugees."

"Yes. Destabilising elements that might seek to stir up unrest inside your borders. Embittered hard-line military personnel, religious fundamentalists…assassins."

Alwil nodded. A grin full of false cheer appeared on his face.

"So you can see why you're here! And why the Throne Hammer has come about."

Volgan nodded. "If you're assassinated there will be chaos."

"Yes. The fact that I have no male heir would create a vacuum of confusion. The generals might decide to create a military dictatorship. Civil war might break out between the powerful strongs of Zorran over the throne. Not to mention the anti-foreigner attacks that might befall the refugees. Chadriac might decide to re-invade amidst the chaos!"

Volgan exhaled loudly. He stood and fetched himself a glass. He sat back down and reached for the jug of wine at Alwil's elbow. "I will have some of that after all" he said.

AS HE WAITED FOR SLEEP TO TAKE HIM, VOLGAN COULDN'T HELP BUT DIGEST the contents of his meeting with Alwil. Even in his exhausted state this caused him to feel discomfort – there was so much to actually digest. Disgruntled generals, citizens of Masraff irritated with their city's new status as capital, powerful elements of the previous capital Monja angered at their city's loss of status, refugees pouring into Zorran from the north and east…and Chadriac, of course. Volgan didn't think there was much danger there – Queen Kinsen's armies had suffered badly in the conflict, losing a significant number of personnel on the battlefield. It would be years before they regained their strength to wage an offensive war again – if they ever found the courage to do so.

He found himself focusing on Chadriac's problem - its constantly rising population. The thing was, only part of the sedren was very densely populated – the north-east coast. The five large cities there – Jadanch, Iklikat, Moslinth, Holmiens and the capital Gendesun along with numerous large towns constituted a region of huge economic power that attracted migrants from not only the poorer parts of Chadriac, but from all over the continent. These urban centres were growing in size all the time and the cities were bursting at the seams. The Angasing islands off the coast had provided a release valve for a decade but then they passed the point of overload and the newly discovered land of Hondrint to the north-east of the islands began to be settled. But since the mysterious Spoiling of the Beboltain peninsula in southern Hondrint, emigration to this fertile, resource-rich land had stopped completely. People worried that the Spoil would spread north to the rest of Hondrint.

The people of northeastern Chadriac and the Angasings were fed by the fertile lands of the Anchipt plain in central Chadriac. But the inexorable population rise was putting pressure on the food production capacity of the Anchipt. This was why Kinsen had gone to war. She had wanted more fertile land to feed her people. So she had marched her armies across Maxan toward eastern Zorran and south through Imgoll toward central Zorran with the goal of driving the farmers there from their lands and replacing them with her own. With the help of Imgoll and Maxan she had sought to break the Zorranese army in the process and take the throne of Monsiel from Alwil. But she hadn't been strong enough to achieve this end.

So what would Chadriac do now? Volgan could see no quick solution. But that was Kinsen Helinter's problem, not his. His problems were more immediate and close by. For the wounds of war to close, Alwil had to be kept alive. And the simple fact was that the steps he'd taken to heal the wounds had made him some enemies.

Volgan's mind switched its focus to what lay ahead in the morning. After breakfast he would be addressing the other twenty-nine members of the Throne Hammer. There would be a lot of strong personalities in the cohort, men and women who had fought heroically in the war, sons and daughters of powerful strongs. To get their respect he would have to get off to a good start with them and lay down the law. *His* law.

Eventually sleep came.

AFTER BREAKFASTING WITH ALWIL, VOLGAN MADE HIS WAY TO THE CASTLE'S main hall where the twenty-nine warriors awaited him. When he entered the hall, the buzz of conversation stopped and all eyes focused on him. He ordered the soldiers into four rows and stood before them in silence. He placed his hands behind his back, resting one in the other. He scanned the faces before him. Some, he knew.

Towering over all the warriors was the menacing, blonde-haired figure of Jurbel Vidaker, a knight from the service of Derenom Gostrage, a sea lord, whose large fleet ran most of the trade in the gulf of Zorran between the cities of Ater-Venchario and Siakanem. Vidaker was not far off seven feet tall, barrel-chested and with a neck like a tree trunk. He had a patch over one eye and a long burn scar stretched from the bottom of his nose back along the right-hand side of his face. He had picked up these injuries after having been taken captive by pirates during a raid on a ship that he had been protecting. The pirates had slaughtered every soul on the ship except for Vidaker. The only reason they had left him alive was because he had killed half of their number in the struggle, some with his hands and feet after his sword had been knocked from his grasp. They took him on board their own vessel where they tortured him, rendering his right eye useless with a hot poker and burning his face. Despite the grievances inflicted upon him, Vidaker had managed to free himself from his bonds and murdered every single remaining pirate with the poker they had burned him with. In the recent war he had earned the nickname Sir Monster, after having dispatched a huge number of opponents from life, some in brutal fashion.

There was Treyadour Hota, another great Zorranese warrior. Almost as tall as Vidaker but much less broad, Hota was a master with the sword and spear. He also had a keen brain, and had risen from the rank of sergeant to commander during the war.

Then there were the women. Volgan walked down between the first and second rows of soldiers before him. Halfway down the second row was the diminutive figure of Shoonsa Hurian, who was probably the most famous female warrior in all of Monsiel. The young major, widely tipped to one day become Quobia's first female general, had commanded a unit in a Quobian force which had performed heroics on the battlefield to halt a joint Chadriacan-Imgollan rush toward the Zorranese border in the early days of the war. Stopping this advance in its tracks had given Zorran time to get its troops across the border with Imgoll and to meet the enemy force head on. The successful Quobian interception of the attempted invasion had ensured that this second front of the war never touched Zorranese soil. It was fought entirely in southern Imgoll, in the sonds of Menoxa and Xanquil, saving the villages and rich croplands of central Zorran from destruction.

Volgan rounded the end of the second row of warriors. The first soldier he passed in the third row was Antal Hijitun, the only other female in the assembly. The dark-skinned, muscled soldier was a captain in the service of Lady Dalquen Hariganch, whose lands encompassed the entirety of the Chobisal peninsula north of the Efol desert in Kantuo. She was a lethal swordswoman and hand-to-hand dagger-fighter.

When Volgan reached the top of the row, he turned and stopped.

"My fellow warriors" he said. "This commission is a great honour for us all. We have been tasked with a duty of the highest importance – the protection of our king. If a move is made against our ruler we must be swift in dealing with it. Our ultimate goal of course must be the prevention of any such actions. As well as our strength, we must also use our intelligence." He paused. "I look around and I see some warriors of high status. I see faces from rich and powerful strongs. Make no mistake. Your fame or your wealth will entitle you to nothing here. I will not have politics in this force. If you prove weak in your duty or behave in an unprofessional manner I will send you home and replace you. I will not care for bruised egos or feelings of being slighted. This is a crucial time for Monsiel. We are rebuilding after war and this can only be achieved in an atmosphere of security and stability. *We* are that security and stability." He paused, looking around the room. "The king needs us…and we need him".

IN THE WEEKS THAT FOLLOWED, VOLGAN GOT HIS RECRUITS TO MOVE IN EVeryday clothes about the city and listen to the citizens on the streets. They left no part of the city unvisited, spending time in every tavern, shop, square and marketplace in Masraff. Outside of grumblings from farmers and landowners about the number of refugees entering eastern Zorran from the war-torn lands of Ansedo, the members of the Throne Hammer heard no serious complaints against the King. Some of the refugees made their way to Masraff, where they were housed in apartment buildings all over the city, the majority ending up in Lamothint, an area in the west.

The Throne Hammer kept a close eye on the new arrivals, watching out for any subversive elements that might be amongst them.

A month after Volgan's arrival in Masraff, Alwil announced a royal procession through the new capital.

"It's time that I showed my face in the streets" Alwil said in the high chamber, to his advisers and Volgan. "It'll be a good opportunity to welcome the refugees, to bring them and the citizens closer together."

Sonrel Gonthigae and Geram Yecka looked at each other. Yecka was the first to nod his approval. "Yes, your highness, that's a good idea."

Alwil looked at Volgan.

"I would suggest the use of a strong palanquin, my king" Volgan said.

"A palanquin?" Alwil asked, a little perturbed. "For my first meeting with the people of the city? I've never used a palanquin in my life! I'm not going to start now! Palanquins make you aloof, like you think the people are…dirty, almost. No. I'll be on foot, same as I used to do in Monja."

"Just for this occasion, your highness, I would urge caution. Next time you could consider going on-."

"There will be no palanquin, Lord Volgan" Alwil said, quietly and firmly.

"Your highness-."

"You've told me that you've encountered no elements of a plot against me. No potential subversive movements of any kind."

"No, your highness."

"Do you have reason to expect an attack on my person in the near future?"

Volgan didn't answer immediately, but he knew it was pointless. He was being pushed toward one specific answer. One that suited the king.

"No, my King, but the Throne Hammer has only been in operation for barely a month-."

"And I am satisfied with the chief's intelligence report" Alwil said, holding Volgan's eyes. "I see no reason not to hold a foot procession…a week from today."

Volgan nodded. "Yes, your highness."

"Very good. I will have the protection of you and your agents, Lord Volgan. I know I couldn't be in better hands." Alwil clapped his hands together. "My first meeting with the good folk of our new capital! I can see it being a special day indeed!

THE EVENING BEFORE THE PROCESSION, VOLGAN STOOD AT THE CASTLE BAT-tlements, looking out at the city. From where he stood, he couldn't see the streets, only the rooftops. It was almost as though the roads, lanes and walkways beneath didn't exist. The illusion was almost comforting. But of course it wasn't long before reality once more came crashing home and Volgan saw himself walking on the cobbles ahead of the king, studying the thousands of pairs of eyes all around the procession, waiting for a threat to reveal itself in a look or a stare. *This time tomorrow it'll all be over* he thought to himself.

Movement caught the corner of his eye and he looked to his left to see the hulking form of Jurbel Vidaker approaching him. Vidaker nodded a greeting.

"Chief."

"Sir Jurbel" Volgan said.

Vidaker snorted. "Sir Jurbel. I haven't been called that in a long time."

"Would you prefer if I called you by your other title?"

"Suit yourself" Vidaker said, and joined Volgan in his study of the city beyond.

"Over seven thousand arrived today alone" Vidaker said. "Nearly every soul from the neighbouring towns and villages is here. Midkun, Belve, Japter, Tansally…Gospat…they're all empty. Every tavern, rooming house and apartment building in the city is full. The damn place is close to bursting."

"Make no mistake" Volgan said. "We'll need our wits about us."

"Your exploits in the war for Prackus precede you" Vidaker said. "It is said by some that you are the finest warrior in Monsiel."

Volgan smiled. "And you made quite a name for yourself in the war just past."

"I killed seventy-five men and thirteen women. With every manner of weapon under the sun. Sword, spear, dagger, mace, hatchet, war-hammer, arrow…I even beat a man to death with a bow. Another I smashed to a pulp with the severed leg of his dead colleague. I'm not sure if that man died…he certainly wasn't moving when I left him." Vidaker paused. "How many did you kill in Prackus?"

"Enough. Certainly not that many."

"Let's hope we won't have to use our skills tomorrow."

"Yes."

THE FOLLOWING MORNING VOLGAN SENT ILICK WILDRIS AND ANTAL HIJITUN on a plainclothes patrol covering the route that the procession would take. The two returned to the castle reporting no visible threats or unusual behaviour on the streets. When the procession left the castle a faint mist was beginning to fall. As the procession made its way through the streets the mist slowly grew heavier. Not that Volgan noticed. His focus was on the multitudes to his left and right and watching from the rooftops overhead. The atmosphere for the most part was a positive one – most of the onlookers had smiles on their faces, with plenty cheering and clapping as Alwil made his way past. Outside taverns, drinkers raised their tankards when Alwil waved at them.

Volgan was at the head of the procession, immediately in front of Alwil, who was flanked on either side by Jurbel Vidaker to his left and Shoonsa Hurian to his right. Behind them, the rest of the Throne Hammer followed in three lines.

About three quarters of the way along their route they came to Lamothint, in the west of the city. By now the mist was turning to rain. Refugees from the war in the east clapped and waved at the king, who smiled back at them, not letting the rain dampen his spirits. Some of the refugees bore war injuries – there were missing limbs, patches over eyes, hideous burn-scars.

They were passing a tavern called *The Fallen Goose* when a group of people – a mix of men and women – rushed at the procession, shrieking and roaring, teeth bared in ferocity, their eyes blazing. Some of them were armed with daggers. They slashed at Volgan and he parried their blows with his shield. He could hear some of his colleagues shouting behind him as they too were assaulted.

"Protect the king!" he roared as dagger blades rained against his shield.

When one of Volgan's assailants saw that he was getting nowhere, he grabbed the top edge of Volgan's shield, seeking to tear it away from him. The man was small and thin and Volgan thought that he would have no trouble preventing the man from taking his shield as he was a powerfully built man. A ball of alarm mushroomed in Volgan's gut as he felt the shield inching away from him, despite the fact that he was using every bit of his strength to pull it toward him. A woman joined the man in his struggle against Volgan, placing her hands at the top of the shield. When it began to move quickly away from him, Volgan raised his sword and brought it down on one set of the woman's fingers. There was a shriek as the severed fingers dropped to the ground. The bleeding stumps that remained at the top of the shield disappeared, along with the woman's remaining unharmed hand. Volgan slashed again and there was another cry of pain, this time from the man. Four more fingers fell to the cobbles and then Volgan's shield was free.

Two more assailants lunged toward him. Volgan was taken aback by the iron looks of sheer fearlessness in their eyes. Volgan thrusted his sword into the chest of one of them and the man slumped down. Volgan had no time to remove his blade from the man's body to meet the attack of his companion. Volgan grabbed his dagger from his belt and rammed it into the man's gut. He withdrew his weapons and let the two dead bodies fall to the ground. Seeing that he was momentarily devoid of any more potential attackers, he looked behind him.

Jurbel Vidaker was trying to fend off four attackers. Two more were lying dead at his feet. Vidaker was badly wounded – he had been stabbed twice in the chest and there was a deep gash in his neck also. Between him and Shoonsa Hurian stood Alwil, his eyes wide but unafraid, his sword raised and ready. Beside him, Hurian held her ground against two assailants, blood streaming from a vicious-looking wound in her right arm. Her left shoulder was also torn open. Behind her lay the dead form of Markian Drookus, his unseeing eyes staring at Volgan's boots. A pool of blood lay beneath his shredded throat.

On both sides of the street, people were fleeing the scene. The din was terrible – a mix of bellowing and screeching from the frenzied attackers, cries of fear from those running from the carnage and exclamations of exertion from Volgan's colleagues as they struggled against the intensity of the assault. He saw one of his comrades - a Euramdianese warrior, being forced backward under a furious onslaught from a man and a woman - trip over the felled form of one of the attackers. He tumbled to the ground and the duo were upon him instantly, plunging their daggers into him repeatedly.

Volgan's eyes came back to Alwil. The king was looking around him frantically, on guard. Behind him, another member of the Throne Hammer slumped to the ground, holding his guts in his hands and his attacker ran past him toward Alwil.

"Your highness!" Volgan shouted, looking in the direction of the approaching man.

Alwil turned just in time to ram his sword into the assailant's midriff.

We have to get out of here Volgan thought. *Now.*

"Back to the castle!" he shouted into the melee. He looked at Alwil. "Your highness, we need to run!" Alwil nodded.

Shoonsa Hurian finished off one of the demented mob with a blow of her sword that cleaved halfway through her opponent's neck, then she threw her shield to the ground and grabbed Alwil by his right arm. She pulled him toward Volgan. Volgan looked at Vidaker just in time to see a screaming woman thrust a dagger into his side. Vidaker rammed his huge sword into the woman's belly, lifted her clear from the ground and flung her still flailing form into two of her fellow attackers, sending them tumbling to the ground. Vidaker lurched toward Alwil and grabbed the king's free arm, moving forward quickly with Hurian. How Vidaker was still standing, Volgan did not know. Blood was pouring from his wounds and the dagger that had just been stuck in his side was buried up to the hilt.

"Come on!" Volgan shouted, and began running. The three behind him did likewise, the rain coming down heavily by this stage. Volgan ran a little ahead of the king, shielding him at the front, while Hurian and Vidaker protected him from the sides. Volgan glanced behind him and was relieved to see Treyadour Hota and two more warriors, Lembel Oswig and Hostaes Alnatry running beside him, providing protection at the rear. But his relief turned to alarm when he saw three men disengage from the fracas and begin to give chase. Their speed and the determined look on their faces was terrifying. They rapidly began to close the gap on the departing septet.

"Hota!" Volgan called. "Oswig, Alnatry! Hold them off!"

The three soldiers turned and engaged with the attackers.

With a grunt of exertion Vidaker collapsed to the street. Volgan took his place at Alwil's side and the trio ran on through the downpour.

VOLGAN WATCHED AS ALWIL LIFTED THE FULL-TO-THE-BRIM GOBLET WITH A trembling hand to his mouth. He drank it greedily, a thin rivulet of wine running down his chin and onto his neck. When he was finished he beckoned his servant boy to fill up the goblet again.

"My first walk amongst the people and I come within a hair's breadth of being chopped to pieces" Alwil said as he watched the servant boy pour. "Thank the gods you were there, Volgan."

As soon as the boy was finished pouring, Alwil lifted the goblet quickly and drained half of it.

"How is Hurian?" he asked.

"She'll be alright."

"She fought bravely" Alwil said. "So tell me. How many did we lose?"

"Six. Drookus…Shart…Vaul…Zostas…Alnatry…and Vidaker."

Alwil shook his head slowly. "One fifth of the Throne Hammer lost in one day. The mighty Jurbel Vidaker slain. Our enemies, whoever they are, were unsuccessful today but they will take heart in the killing of one of the continent's most powerful warriors." He raised his eyes to Volgan's. "They will try again."

"I fear they may" Volgan agreed.

"They didn't even look like warriors, Volgan!" Alwil said in an incredulous tone. "They were just ordinary folk who decided to kill a king! And did you see the courage in their eyes? The conviction? They were completely without fear! They went up against the mightiest warriors in the continent…and their *strength*! It was terrifying!"

A worm of unease coiled in Volgan's gut as he recalled the strength of the man and woman who had almost succeeded in pulling his shield away from him. Their physical power had been completely out of proportion to their physiques. The words that the king had just uttered rang in his ear: *ordinary folk who decided to kill a king* The prospect of this being true was actually more troubling than the thought of trained, skilled assassins. You could expect highly-paid killers to have demonstrated such might and will. But to have witnessed these traits in the common-looking folk who had attacked them earlier was quite a sinister experience.

"There will be trouble tonight" Alwil said. "Yobs will get drunk and decide to become vigilantes. They'll go into Lamothint and take their anger out on the refugees."

"Gonthigae predicted that" Volgan said. "He's swearing in extra lawfolk. They'll be in Lamothint by the evening."

Alwil nodded. "Good. The last thing we need is civil war on the streets."

WHEN ALWIL DECIDED TO GO TO HIS ROOM AND GET SOME REST, VOLGAN tripled the guard at his door from two members of the Throne Hammer to six. He went to the infirmary to check on Shoonsa Hurian. When she saw him, she smiled faintly, a peaceful glaze in her eyes.

"First time getting jolip sap, Lord Volgan" she said from her bed. "It's good."

Volgan was glad she'd taken the pain reliever from the medicine men. By the time they'd gotten Alwil to safety inside the castle gates she'd been clenching her teeth in agony, and had lost a lot of blood. She looked comfortable now, the colour returning to her face. The dreadful wounds in her arm and shoulder had been cleaned and dressed. Volgan smiled and sat in the chair by her bed.

"How is the king?" she asked, her words slow.

"Resting. And well. Thanks to you."

"Not thanks to me. I'm still alive. Thanks to the ones who died."

"He commended your bravery."

She closed her eyes. When Volgan wondered if maybe she was dropping off to sleep, she opened them again.

"I've been thinking about what happened today." She paused. "And…I can't think of any way to explain how those people behaved…how they inflicted such damage upon us. There was nothing *natural* about it." She paused again. "I guess that only leaves one possibility."

"What's that?"

"Magic."

THE CASTLE'S DUNGEON WAS NO LONGER IN USE SO GERAM YECKA HAD THE bodies of the eighteen attackers brought there, and placed in two rows in the largest cell. Volgan walked slowly amidst the wrecked corpses, counting thirteen men and five women. One man and one woman looked as though they'd been at least in their seventh decade of life, their faces being wrinkled and their bodies frail.

"Fourteen refugees" Yecka said.

Volgan sighed inwardly. With this fact, there would undoubtedly be trouble on the streets later.

"I'll have the bodies stripped and examined for lodge tattoos" Yecka said. Volgan nodded. There were numerous groups, or lodges, of assassins throughout Monsiel. Each lodge had its own unique tattoo.

"Tell me what you find" Volgan said as he left the cell, knowing that Yecka would find nothing.

AS NIGHT FELL, VOLGAN STOOD AT THE WINDOW IN HIS ROOM. LOOKING IN the direction of Lamothint, he sipped some wine from the goblet in his hand. He was struggling and failing to keep an image from his mind – an image where the rooftops about half a mile away had flames rising from them into the dark sky. So far these flames didn't exist in reality and he was relieved. *There's a long night to go yet*, a voice inside him said.

There was a quiet knock on his door. He went to it and opened it. He found himself looking at Shoonsa Hurian. Gone was the faint smile that had bedecked her lips when he had visited her earlier. The face before him now was serious, the eyes clear, the jolip sap having worn off. Her face was pale again and Volgan had no doubt that she was in considerable pain.

"I need to speak with you, Lord Volgan" she said. "It's…important."

Seeing as she had seen fit not to sup any more jolip sap, Volgan had no doubt that it was.

"Come in" he said, standing back to let her pass.

He closed the door behind her and fetched her a chair. She sat down and he offered her some wine.

"Please" she said.

He filled a goblet for her and placed it in her hand. He sat down opposite her. She drank some wine and spoke.

"What I said to you earlier…about there being magic involved in the attack."

"Yes."

"It wasn't just the jolip sap talking. I meant it. I really believe that there was…a powerful spell of some sort involved. Those people had to be under the influence of something extraordinary. They weren't assassins. None of them were."

"I agree with you. After I went to see the bodies in the dungeon I was even more convinced of it."

"Perhaps…someone was using them. Controlling them."

Volgan made no response. His heart began to beat a little faster. They were venturing down a dark road now and Volgan did not like to think where it might lead them. But he had to admit that Hurian's thinking made sense. "Perhaps" he said eventually.

She took a deep breath as though she were worried about something. "If that is what actually happened…then I may be able to help."

"How?"

"I may be able to find out what spell was involved. What substances were used."

"And how would you do that?"

"Because I know some magic myself."

"You know some magic?"

"Yes."

"Are you a mage?"

She shook her head.

Volgan remained silent. He held Hurian's eyes. She didn't drop hers, but he could see concern in her gaze. Spell-casting by anyone other than an anointed mage was a crime throughout the continent. She was taking a serious risk sharing this information with him.

"Five years ago" she said, "when I was a lieutenant, I was approached by a Captain Gulkamin in the intelligence wing of the Quobian army. Work had just started on the Mapenholom tunnel." This was a tunnel through the expansive Pilezur mountain range which lay in north-eastern Quobia, extending across the border into north-western Imgoll. The tunnel was a major trade route between the two regions. "Gulkamin told me that there was a shulring living in the Pilezurs who was conjuring up demons and using them to terrorize the tunnel-diggers." A shulring was what Quobians called a mage. "He didn't want the tunnel to be built and was determined to stop it at all costs. They had tried to have him arrested but he'd simply used his demons on the soldiers who'd approached his mountain-dwelling. They changed tactics then and offered him a chest of gold. He had his demons lift the chest and fling it over a cliff. They decided to change strategy once more. My commanding officer had told Gulkamin that I was an effective stealth fighter and he asked me would I be interested in a special assignment. I said yes. So I sneaked my way into the shulring's cave and before he had a chance to summon his demons I killed him." She paused. "Before I left, I took one of his spell-books."

Volgan smiled slightly. He'd probably have done the same thing. There was something deeply intoxicating about magic.

"Do you know what the penalty for possession of something like that is here in Zorran?" he asked her.

"Five years in prison."

"Did you bring it here with you?"

"Yes. I take it everywhere."

"And you think there's a spell in it that could help us?"

"Yes. Two of them. The first is an identifier spell. Right now, the blood in the attacker's bodies will still contain a trace of whatever spell – if any – was cast upon them. I'll extract some blood from them and cast the identifier upon it. The identifier will tell me the type of spell that was cast. Right now, I'm presuming that two spells were cast upon them – a mind-control spell and a strength-giver." Hurian paused. "And I'd have to cast the identifier tonight. By morning whatever spells were used will be completely gone."

Volgan drew in a deep breath and exhaled loudly. What Hurian was suggesting they do was a serious crime. He wondered should he mention it to Alwil. He knew that Alwil would let them go ahead – he desperately wanted to find out more about the attack. The simple fact was – Volgan couldn't see any other way to get to the bottom of it. Deep in his heart he knew there had been magic involved. And magic could only be defeated by magic. He decided not to involve Alwil. At least then, if he – Volgan - and

Hurian were discovered and their actions exposed, Alwil could claim that he knew nothing of what they had done. If he knew about it and the spell-casting was uncovered, he would be irreparably scandalized. The king of Monsiel authorizing the head of his personal guard and his underling to cast a spell on dead people! Alwil's detractors could use it as grounds to launch a challenge to his reign and civil war could ensue. No – there was no way Alwil could be allowed to know.

"Where's the spell-book?" Volgan asked Hurian.

"In my room."

"Let's get it and head to the dungeon."

WHEN THEY GOT TO THE DUNGEON DOOR, VOLGAN WAS SURPRISED TO FIND no guard on duty. They went inside and made their way to the cell containing the bodies of the attackers. When he saw that the cell was empty, Volgan froze. He stared for a moment at the bare floor before turning and hurrying back the way they had come, Hurian rushing behind him.

Where had the confounded bodies disappeared to? Volgan asked himself as he went up the stairs to the dungeon door. *Who had taken them?* In the hallway beyond the door he stopped walking, as he realized that he had no idea where he was going. He needed to think. He paced about slowly, wondering who would have had the bodies moved. Alwil? One of his advisers – Yecka, or Gonthigae? Movement caught the corner of his eye and he saw Treyadour Hota walking toward him along the hallway. As Hota was nodding a salute to his superior, Volgan spoke.

"Hota – did you see who took the bodies of the attackers?"

"Sir Ilick, my lord-."

"Wildris?" Volgan cut across him, surprised.

"Yes, my lord."

"Why did he take them? And where has he taken them?"

"He's burying them. In the foothills of the mountains."

AS THEY GALLOPED ON HORSEBACK IN THE GATHERING DUSK, VOLGAN FOUGHT hard to force down the rage he was feeling. That little whelp! What arrogance! To think that the boy had come along and given the order to have the bodies taken away without consulting his superior!

As they crested a small hill, three carts came into sight. Ahead of the carts, five men on horseback led the way. Volgan spurred his horse onward. When he felt they were within earshot of the caravan, he called out.

"Halt!"

The caravan kept moving.

"Halt!!!" Volgan called again, louder.

This time he got a reaction. The men on horseback turned around.

As he drew closer, the face of Ilick Wildris grew clearer. The four men with him were soldiers of Alwil's.

"Lord Volgan" Wildris said to his approaching commander. "I took it upon myself to organize the burial of this scum quickly. Lest word get out that the bodies were in the castle and mobs came storming in to defile them-."

Volgan slapped him across the face so hard that Wildris almost fell from his horse.

"Boy" Volgan said to the youth. "It is not your place to *take things upon yourself*. How dare you act without my authorization!" He saw anger flush in Wildris' face which took a while to be replaced by a wounded calm. "Get these bodies back to the dungeon immediately" Volgan said. He turned and headed back toward the castle, Hurian following him. Behind them, Wildris barked the order at the carts.

With the castle asleep above them, Hurian set about extracting blood from the bodies. When she had eighteen vials filled, she placed her forefinger into the first vial, submerging her fingertip in the blood it contained. She began reading from the spell-book beside her. Exhausted after the long day's events, Volgan watched her from outside the cell, where he sat on a stool. The words that she chanted were strange and frightened him a little. It was said that magic had been created by demons, and had never been intended for the human world. Humans, according to legend, had heard demons speaking magic words and had written them down. As Hurian went from vial to vial, repeating the same spell, Volgan's fear began to lessen.

He studied Hurian as she worked. For the first time, he noticed her good looks. There was a scar beneath her left eye but to Volgan it merely gave her character. Most warriors had scars. It was a testament to her bravery.

He had to admire her. Here she was, in the middle of the night, carrying battle wounds, taking a big risk to help the king. She could have simply kept the fact of the spell-book to herself and never mentioned it at all. Right now she could be lying in bed asleep instead of chanting over dead bodies. His eyelids growing heavy, Volgan found himself thinking of the women that his father had introduced him to over the years, in a bid to get him married and to secure the Borinth name into the next generation. Like Alwil, Volgan was an only child, and a lot of responsibility rested on his shoulders. His father had been pushing girls before him since his seventeenth birthday. All well-bred ladies of noble birth, Volgan had politely rejected each one. After spurning the seventh woman, a daughter of a powerful lord in Rinchar, a Chadriacan sedren to the north of Belchar, Havar had asked his son if he was homosexual. Volgan had calmly told him that he wasn't and that he would marry when he was ready. That had been three years ago, when Volgan had been twenty-seven years old. Since then, his father hadn't presented him with any more women. Others still tried their luck, however. Senior generals in the Belcharan army had introduced him to their daughters, as had Euramdianese and Maxanese lords. All seeking to enhance their positions by marrying into high royalty. Volgan knew he was one of the most eligible bachelors in the continent – the heir to the throne of Belchar, commander of its armies and a soldier of high repute. Having been made the Chief of the Throne Hammer had added to his standing. It was only a matter of time before approaches came his way from the most powerful men in the continent – the Zorranese lords who owned huge estates in the most fertile areas of Monsiel and fed Alwil's army with thousands of soldiers. The women that had been put before Volgan in the past had all been decent, impeccably mannered, some quite beautiful…but they'd been *lacking*. Lacking in what Volgan saw before him now, in Hurian. They'd all been too sheltered, growing up in privilege. Not that it was their fault - it was what their rich fathers had wanted for them. They'd never done anything like what Hurian was doing now before him. They'd never *risked* themselves. *Sacrificed* themselves.

Realizing that he was still looking at Hurian, Volgan averted his gaze, embarrassed. He let his head rest against the bars of the cell and closed his eyes. By now the eerie words that Hurian was reciting over each body were no longer unsettling. Sleep came quickly.

He woke to Hurian tapping his arm.

"Lord Volgan."

He opened his eyes which were heavy with sleep and sat up.

"Lord Volgan, I've finished with the bodies. I found only one spell – a mind-controller."

"So what gave them the strength?"

Hurian didn't answer immediately. Her face was deadly serious, Volgan noticed.

"Fairy blood" she eventually said.

"Fairy blood" he repeated.

Hurian nodded.

"You're absolutely certain?"

"Yes. Whoever used it went to great lengths to conceal it, too. They used a barrier spell. The first identifier spell I cast couldn't break through it so I had to use a more powerful one." She looked inside the cell. Volgan followed her gaze to the eighteen corked vials of blood. "We have to bury those. Just to be safe. We can't just toss them idly away or pour them into the sewers. The spells will die away but the fairy blood…" She trailed off.

He nodded. "Alright."

Hurian led them into a wooded ravine in the foothills of the Jultinth mountains. They went all the way to the bottom of the ravine, where Hurian eventually stopped.

"Here will do" she said.

They began digging. The moonlight shone down between the trees, illuminating their labors, and they made quick progress in the soft ground. When they had reached a little over a foot in depth, Volgan stopped.

"That should be enough" he said.

"We should go a little deeper" Hurian said, still shovelling.

I can't accuse her of not being cautious, Volgan said to himself, and rejoined her.

They were nearly three feet down before Hurian eventually put her shovel aside. She removed some of the blood-vials from the satchel she had put them in and placed them gently in the hole. When all of the vials were in the ground they refilled the hole and scattered leaves and some stones over the replaced earth. They climbed out of the ravine and galloped back to the castle.

WITH THE FIRST HINTS OF DAWN BEGINNING TO APPEAR IN THE SKY OUTSIDE HIS bedroom window, Volgan lay unable to sleep, despite never having been so tired in his life.

Mind-control spells. Fairy blood. Assassination by proxy.

A knot tightened in his stomach as he thought of the eighteen attackers. They had been nothing more than unwitting puppets. He wondered what it must have been like, to have had been used in such a deadly manner? What had it been like, to have had their minds hijacked? Had their consciousnesses been wiped out and replace by the homicidal will of the killer (or killers) or had the poor individuals simply had their personalities pushed to the side while the invader took over the controls, relegating the personalities to the role of observer as they helplessly watched their bodies attempt to hack their way through the Throne Hammer in a mad bid to slaughter their ruler?

It was a pity that none of the attackers had been taken alive. Such was the frenzied and determined nature of their assault that they had had to be killed in order to eliminate their threat. If one of them had survived and the Throne Hammer had been able to keep the attacker securely in chains until the mind-control spell had worn off, then perhaps they'd have gotten some information.

And then there was the fairy blood. Volgan knew even less about this than he did about magic. Hurian's knowledge of the substance was at the same level as his – she was familiar with the same tales about fairy blood that he was – a certain type of fairy blood could bring down a fever, another could accelerate healing, another could be used as a plant fertilizer. He'd heard that the drinking of fairy blood had been reasonably acceptable in certain parts of Monsiel up until ninety years before. Then Manrel Magatoyce, the mad son of a Zorranese lord had drunk the blood of the rare gold-flesh fairy which had given him the power to control the minds of all living things, bar humans. Magatoyce had acquired a large amount of gold-flesh fairy blood by hijacking the minds of some mosquitos and getting them to seek out more gold-flesh fairies. The mosquitoes would suck blood from the fairies and travel back to Magatoyce, who would promptly put the mosquitoes in his mouth and devour them. Magatoyce had used the power to control an army of mansind spiders and had marched them – riding atop the largest – to the Zorranese capital, Monja. When the city's defenders had seen the terrifying force thudding its way toward them in the distance, they had thrown down their weapons and had fled, the king with them. Upon arriving in the capital, Magatoyce had walked through the empty city streets toward the royal palace, the smaller mansinds following behind him. The terrified populace watched the shocking procession through cracks in doorways, some of them soiling themselves as spiders the size of cattle passed by outside. Magatoyce had left the largest spiders – ten great mansinds the size of houses – outside the city gates to patrol its perimeter. Upon entering the abandoned palace, Magatoyce had crowned himself the new Jakeram of Zorran and King of Monsiel. His reign had lasted fifty-seven days. The mosquitoes he sent out had been too greedy and had sucked so much blood from the fairies they encountered that they had died, resulting in a rapid depletion in their number. It grew progressively more difficult for the mosquitoes to find more fairies and eventually they could find none at all. Not having any blood to consume meant the loss of Magatoyce's power over the mansinds, and they left him, heading back east where Magatoyce had found them. Magatoyce's father, the octogenarian Potrian Magatoyce, had then entered Monja with his army and made his way to the palace, where he found his son dead on the throne by his own hand, having driven a dagger into his stomach. Not being content with this, Potrian had driven his own dagger into his son's body five times, his rage at his son's shameful actions growing with each thrust.

Since this bizarre episode in Monsiel's history, fairies were rarely spoken of in the continent, and the consumption of their blood was a taboo subject. Now someone had discovered a fairy blood that made people fearless and incredibly strong, and had used it in an attempt on the king's life. Volgan drew a deep breath.

Who was the mastermind behind the attack? Kinsen Helinter? Solbiun Dronda? Swalthus Verg, the Shulmik of Imgoll? These, the leaders of the sedrens that had gone to war with Alwil were who immediately came to mind. And then of course there were the entities that Alwil had mentioned in their conversation in the high chamber the day Volgan had arrived – the generals who were upset at the truce that Alwil had signed with Chadriac… the rich merchants of Monja who were unhappy with the moving of the capital to Masraff…the Zorranese who were unhappy with all the refugees that Alwil had allowed in from the warzones…dangerous elements within the refugees themselves…

There were so many depressing possibilities. Volgan tried to purge all thought from his mind in a bid to get some sleep. It was difficult but eventually he succeeded.

In the morning he had breakfast with Hurian.

"So what are we doing today?" she asked as they ate.

"We're going to Lamothint" Volgan said. "We question people."

They spent the day questioning the relatives, friends and associates of the eighteen attackers. None of their interviews yielded any information that painted the attackers as being anti-king or anti-Zorran militants or having any affiliations in those spheres. The only crimes they discovered in the histories of the attackers had been two drunken assault offences and one jewellery theft offence. The one thing that the entire eighteen had in common was that they drank regularly in *The Fallen Goose*, the tavern outside which the attack had taken place.

The tavern was lively when Volgan and Hurian entered. Dressed in simple tunics like the locals, they attracted no attention. It was early evening time and most of those present were eating after a hard day's work, but a few patrons were already loud with liquor, occasionally shouting and laughing bawdily. A man and woman were behind the counter while a boy and a girl busily tended to tables. It was easy to ascertain that the youngsters were children of the two adults as they had their features. Volgan and Hurian approached the counter, where they were met by the man there.

"Good evening, sir" the man greeted as he wiped a tankard. "What can I get for you?"

"My name is Volgan Borinth. I'm chief of the Throne Hammer." He gestured to his companion. "This is Major Shoonsa Hurian. We would have a word in private with you."

The man stopped wiping, a worried look appearing on his features. The look quickly changed to one of resignation, making it obvious that he had been expecting this visit. He nodded. The woman arrived at his side. She had sensed something regarding the visitors and there was a look of concern on her face.

"Greetings, sir" she said. She looked at Hurian. "Madam."

"This gentleman and his associate are with the king's personal guard, my dear" the man said. "I need to speak with them."

The woman looked at Volgan. "About yesterday?" she asked.

"Yes."

The woman shook her head sorrowfully. "A dreadful day" she said. "Thank the broken the king was not harmed. And condolences on the loss of your brave colleagues."

"Thank you, Madam."

The man emerged from behind the counter and moved toward a door at the side of the room.

"We can talk in the back" he said, and opened the door.

Beyond was a short hallway. The man led them to its end, where there was a staircase on the left and a door to the right. The man opened the door and went inside. He stood back to allow Volgan and Hurian to pass, then he closed the door.

They were in a kitchen which had at its centre a table with four chairs around it. The man gestured to the table.

"Please" he said.

He sat at the head of the table. Volgan sat at his left and Hurian at his right.

"My name is Zosar Lantash, by the way" the man said. "You've met my wife, Xintimas" he said, cocking his head vaguely in the direction of the tavern room. "My son Belmens and daughter Oleran are tending the tables."

"Are you aware that all eighteen of yesterday's attackers were customers of yours?" Volgan asked.

Lantash nodded sorrowfully. "Yes."

"Have any of them engaged in violent behaviour previously?"

Lantash snorted. "Outside of a few pushes and shoves on festival days…no. Four or five of them I knew quite well. They've been coming here for years. What happened yesterday…" He trailed off, shaking his head, uncomprehending. "It's just so damned *bizarre*…"

"What about the refugees?" Hurian asked. "How well did you know them?"

Lantash shook his head. "I didn't really know them. None of them have been coming here for more than a month. But none of them have ever caused trouble. Never seen any one of them drunk. Never heard them insulting the king, or Zorran."

"Were you very busy yesterday?" Volgan asked.

"Yes. Busier than we've been in years. A lot of faces that I've never laid eyes on. Everybody was in good form, eager to see the king."

"Did you see anyone behaving in a strange manner?" Hurian asked.

"No. But I was run off my feet all day. I hardly got a chance to look at anyone for any decent length of time."

Volgan nodded. "Send in your wife, please. We'd like to speak with her too."

Lantash rose and left the kitchen. His wife entered a moment later. They asked her the same questions that they had asked her husband, but they learned nothing new. Xintimas Lantash left and then it was the turn of the youngsters, Belmens and Oleran. Their father remained in the kitchen during their questioning. With the interviews yielding no valuable information, Volgan and Hurian made their goodbyes and left. As they made their way along the street, Volgan saw Hurian wince in pain. He had to marvel at her strength – she was carrying two battle-wounds and had spent the day on her feet with him, going from here to there questioning people. Most men in her position would have spent the day recuperating.

"I think maybe it's time you called it a day, Major. You should be in bed with a saucer of jolip sap beside you."

"I'll be alright. I could use a drink, though."

They went into the next tavern they encountered. It was quiet. They sat down in a corner and when the barmaid came to their table they ordered two goblets of wine. While they waited for their drinks, Volgan decided to put the horror and pressures of the previous two days out of his mind by getting to know a little about his companion.

"So tell me, Major. What was the war like for you?"

Hurian drew a deep breath. "Dreadful. And glorious. I lost some good friends. But Quobia made its mark. We won many battles where we were outnumbered by larger forces. We've a lot to be proud of."

"Indeed. I've heard it said that each Quobian proved to be worth four Imgollans, and two Chadriacans."

"It'll give the Kantuoans something to think about in the future in case they ever get… *interested* in our land again."

Volgan chuckled. Quobia had a scrappy history with its larger neighbour to the west. Every now and then a powerful lord in eastern Kantuo would get greedy and go on a territorial raid in the fertile lands of southern Quobia. The Quobians would eventually succeed in either beating or buying the invaders out, but always at enormous cost. The current strong state of the Quobian army would indeed prove an effective deterrent to any future potential invasions.

"Do you come from a military background?" Volgan asked.

"No. My family have been farmers and fishermen for as far back as my father can remember. We have some land by the sea, north of Julsend. When I was little, every now and then our part of the coast was raided by Kantish pirates. They'd come ashore, smash up a few houses, take some of our harvest and some of our animals. Sometimes the people would put up a fight, and even though the pirates were undisciplined and unconditioned fighters, our peaceful, simple folk were no match for them. Eventually the seecher listened to our pleas to have a military garrison installed in the area. I remember the day the soldiers arrived…thirty of them…marching in formation, ten rows of three…I'd never seen anything so amazing in all my life. About a month after they arrived, two pirate ships attacked us. Arrows rained down on the pirates as they waded ashore. The survivors rowed as fast as they could back to their ships. That was the day I decided that I wanted to be a soldier. I didn't want to grow up meek, dependant upon the protection of others. I wanted to *be* the protector."

The barmaid came with their wine. Hurian lifted her goblet and drank.

"What do you think of Monsiel's current situation?" Volgan asked.

Hurian put her drink down.

"I think we'll definitely have peace for a while. Hopefully for a long time. Chadriac has learned its lesson. Maxan and Imgoll have taken such beatings that I doubt they'll ever ally with Chadriac again. Even though it was costly for Quobia, we came through for the Zorranese, and I'm glad we did. We have a powerful ally who owes us a favour now. And it was the first time we ever allied with Kantuo, and fought side by side with them. It can only be good for relations between our two sedrens going forward."

Volgan smiled. "That's quite an astute analysis. A soldier *and* a diplomat. Two very impressive skills."

Hurian smiled in return. The expression faded slowly into contemplation. "I really admire what King Alwil is doing. Moving the capital here was a big sacrifice to make. But it was the right thing to do to bring Zorran closer to Maxan and Imgoll. And taking in refugees from those two sedrens…that's a powerful goodwill gesture that will pay off in the future." She paused. "All these things might cost Alwil some old friendships, but…he's thinking of the greater good. And I really respect him for it." She lifted her eyes to Volgan's. "I'm not just protecting him because it's my job. I'm protecting him because I *believe* in him."

"So do I" Volgan said. He drank some wine.

"Now, my lord" Hurian said. "You know a little about me. Would you care to return the favour?"

"What would you like to know?"

"What every commoner wishes to know about being noble born. What's it like?"

Volgan didn't answer immediately.

"Delicate" he eventually responded. "That's the best way I can describe it."

"Do you…think about being the Halisant much? About one day taking your father's place, and being master of all you survey?"

An image flashed in Volgan's mind – he saw himself sitting on his father's throne, the jewelled sceptre of Belchar in his hand. A shiver of excitement coursed through him, the same as it always did when he thought of being ruler. He pushed the feeling aside as quickly as he could. He was afraid of that feeling – it was why he thought of being Halisant as little as possible.

Before he could answer Hurian, he became aware of movement at the corner of his eye. He turned to see the boy Belmens Lantash approaching the table tentatively. He looked worried.

"Chief…major…" he greeted each of them in turn, in a tone that was bordering on fearful.

"Don't be afraid, boy" Volgan said softly. "Speak."

This reassured the youth somewhat but there was still a troubled look on his face.

"I'm sorry to interrupt your leisure" he said, with a little more confidence in his tone now. "But I'm afraid I have a confession to make. You see…I wasn't…fully honest with you earlier." He paused. He was clearly having difficulty with his admission.

"If you lied, it's in the past" Volgan said. "Just be honest with us now."

"I wanted to tell you, but with my father in the room…I didn't want to worry him…"

"It's alright, Belmens" Hurian said. "We understand. No-one's going to punish you for that."

The youth nodded slightly and took a deep breath.

"I told you that I didn't see anything suspicious yesterday. Well…I saw something that was *more* than suspicious. It was scary. And what happened after that…well, it was even scarier. I hardly slept last night at all."

"What happened?"

"It was a fluke that I saw it at all, the place was so busy. I was cleaning off a table and I just happened to glance up and…I saw a jug of wine that I had just placed on a nearby table, and over the jug was a hand holding a…vial of some sort. There was a pale red fluid in it. The hand poured a few drops of the fluid into the jug and then it was gone. Lost in the crowd. This all happened in a heartbeat. No-one at the table must have noticed it because I didn't hear anyone complaining or shouting at whoever had poured in the fluid. I froze. I didn't know what to do. Eventually I headed for the table, as quickly as I could. Something told me that whatever had gone into that jug wasn't good. Between me and the table was thick with bodies. I was pushing my way through when suddenly my tunic was grabbed from behind and I was pulled back. Then I felt something sharp against my back. A threatening male voice spoke in my ear, telling me not to move. He told me not to even think of taking the jug from the table. If

I did, he'd come back that night while my family and I were asleep and he'd kill us in our beds. Then he'd burn the place to the ground." The boy paused and swallowed. "He pushed the sharp thing harder against my back – I presume it was a knife – and he asked me to nod if I'd heard what he'd just said and I did. Then the knife was gone. For a few seconds I couldn't move. I felt sick. I felt something trickling down my leg and I thought for a second that I had wet myself. I looked down and I saw a line of blood going down my leg below my tunic. And I saw something else." The boy put a hand in his pocket and it re-emerged holding a tiny pearl. "I don't know if the person who threatened me dropped this…but maybe he did." The boy extended his hand toward Volgan, who took the pearl and studied it.

"Thank you, Belmens" Volgan said, not taking his eyes from the pearl. "You can go."

"It took a lot of courage to come here" Hurian said to the boy. "Well done."

"I just know that what that man put in the wine had something to do with what happened yesterday" Belmens said, his voice quivering, not far from tears. "I hope you catch him".

"I hope so too" Volgan said.

HURIAN HELD THE PEARL BEFORE HER AS THEY WALKED ALONG THE STREET.

"It's well-crafted. Perfectly spherical." She paused. "Beautiful. This would probably get you a good stallion in a trade." She handed it back to Volgan, who put it in his pocket. As they neared the hill that would take them up to the castle gate, Volgan wondered about the pearl. If it had belonged to the man who had poured the fluid into the jug, had it been payment for the act? Assassins mostly took cash only for their services, but some of the older killers still accepted jewels. At the sound of shouting and clattering up ahead of them, Volgan turned his head toward the source of the commotion, a tavern to their right.

Six men reeled out the door toward them, divided into three fighting duos. A crowd of spectators spilled out after them, egging on the scrappers.

"Filthy foreigner!" one bearded man growled as he struggled with his opponent, a bald, dark-skinned individual.

One man lost his footing and fell backward. His opponent was down on him in a flash doing his best to whack the man beneath him about the face. The felled man did his best to block the blows. The man doing the punching had a lot of support from the crowd and this caused his punches to increase in ferocity.

"Stop!" Volgan called loudly, walking toward the melee.

No one paid him any heed.

"STOP!" he declared, and forcefully separated the bearded man from his opponent.

There was a strong smell of drink. Volgan looked forcefully from one fighter to the other. The noise from the crowd diminished as they pondered the interruption to their entertainment. The two remaining pairs of combatants also ceased their hostilities.

"Get off of him" Hurian said to the fighter who was straddling the man who had fallen.

"Why should I?" the man said with a sneer, his eyes full of liquor.

Hurian pulled back her tunic to reveal her sword. "Because I'm an agent of the Throne Hammer, and you will do as I say. Now…*get up*."

Not taking his eyes from Hurian, the man got to his feet. His opponent also erected himself.

"What's this dispute about?" Volgan asked.

The dark-skinned man that Volgan had separated from the bearded fighter spoke up. "Me, this man and this man are refugees from Ansedo" the dark-skinned man said, pointing to two other men. "We were enjoying ourselves when this man and his friends started to harass us" he said, looking at the bearded man beside him. "They told us that we shouldn't be allowed to drink in a tavern with civilised people. And that we should be out in the alleys drinking with the dogs."

"I was being unkind to the dogs" the bearded man smiled drunkenly.

"You insolent…pig" the dark-skinned man said, moving toward the bearded man, his eyes afire with anger.

"Back!" Volgan said, blocking the man's path with his arm.

"How dare you talk to me in such a manner!" the dark-skinned man shouted at his adversary. "I was a trader with lands before the war! I could have bought and sold you!"

"And now you're here with us, living on the king's charity!"

"Only because he laid waste to my homeland with his armies!"

"Well, Maxan shouldn't have sided with that Helinter bitch, should they? What do you expect when your sedren invades its neighbour? Did you expect us to just send you politely back across the border without teaching you a little bit of a lesson?"

"I was no supporter of Solbiun Dronda, or Kinsen Helinter! I didn't agree with their land grab!"

"Well, you're lucky that the king is merciful, and that he has put a roof over your head."

"Merciful? He owed it to me! His baslin bombs destroyed and poisoned my lands!"

"You sound really bitter, my friend" the bearded man said in a soft, menacing tone. "I'll bet you're sorry that no harm came to the king yesterday. I'll bet you even sympathize with the scum that attacked him!"

"I most certainly DO NOT!" the dark-skinned man railed.

"Enough!" Volgan said, unsheathing his sword. Hurian did likewise. "I will not have this incendiary talk! This is a delicate time. You are all citizens of the city, equal in status." He looked from the groups of combatants to the general crowd as he spoke. "You *will* live in harmony with each other. The Throne Hammer must protect the king and we must prove the provenance of yesterday's attack. We cannot do this if the city is at war with itself!"

This was met with a reluctant but respectful silence.

"You" Volgan said to the bearded man. "Gather your friends and go home."

The man held Volgan's gaze for a while, a look of mild challenge in his eyes. Then he turned and cocked his head in a beckoning gesture. His comrades joined him and they moved off down the street. Two lawfolk passed by them, a look of concern on their faces as they approached the scene of the altercation.

"Everything alright, my lord?" one of them asked Volgan.

"It is now" Volgan said. After telling the newcomers what had happened, he gestured to the dark-skinned man who had been involved. "Hold this man and his friends here for a while before you send them home. I don't want them bumping into the other gang on their way."

"Yes, my lord."

"Major" Volgan said to Hurian. Hurian went to him and they resumed their progress toward the castle.

"We're sitting on a powder-keg" Hurian said.

"Yes."

As night fell, clouds began to gather. When it began to rain, Volgan's nerves settled somewhat. Rioters were less inclined to go about their unwanted business in inclement weather. He was in the depths of a refreshing, deep sleep when there was a knock on his door.

"'Who is it?" he asked with as much energy as he could muster.

"Amanthing, my lord."

"This had better be important, Amanthing."

"There's rioting in Lamothint, my lord. The lawfolk are overwhelmed."

Volgan sat on the edge of his bed. He looked out his window and his stomach rolled in dismay when he saw the red glows in the distance. Three of them. Fires in Lamothint.

"Assemble the Hammer in the hall" he instructed Amanthing. "Except for the ones guarding the king."

"Yes, my lord."

Volgan got dressed as quickly as he could and rushed down to the hall. He addressed the Hammer.

"I'll keep this short" he said. "Have any of you dealt with a riot before?"

A few hands went up. Volgan nodded.

"For those of you new to the situation – it is not war. Our role is threefold – disperse, disarm, disable – in that order of necessity. Protection of persons and property and restoration of the peace – these are our goals. We will not use force unless we absolutely have to. That's all. Follow me."

The Hammer fell into formation behind him. This consisted of three columns – one behind Treyadour Hota, another behind Shoonsa Hurian and the third behind Vusel Amanthing. Volgan got moving and they made their way from the castle. They descended quickly toward the city, the sky open above them, the moonlight aiding their progress. The smell of burning timber began to grow steadily as they made their way through the streets. Eventually the sound of screaming and shouting reached their ears.

They came to Q'onsel square in the heart of Lamothint and Volgan raised his fist. The Hammer came to an instant halt behind him. There were three streets ahead of them – two to their left and one directly ahead. Volgan pointed at the one furthest to the left. He looked behind him.

"Hota" he said. "Take Chelmesh street."

Hota began moving, his column following him.

"Amanthing – take Gunch."

Amanthing nodded and began marching.

Volgan continued onto the street that lay directly before him and the remaining column of soldiers. There was a shriek followed by a thud and Volgan looked behind him to see the motionless form of a man on the cobbles, a halo of blood growing about his head. Volgan looked up as did the other soldiers and studied the rooftop ledge overhead. There was no-one to be seen. Volgan looked back down at the man on the street. One of the Hammer, Solon Bachtra, was on one knee, his fingers to the fallen man's neck. Bachtra looked up at Volgan.

"He's dead, my lord."

"Let's move on" Volgan said.

They had only taken a few steps when a little way up ahead of them a man and woman leaped from the smashed window of a shop onto the street. Their hands were bulging with jewellery.

"Stop! Stop, thieves!" an elderly voice could be heard from inside the shop.

"HALT!" Volgan commanded the duo, his hand going to his sword-hilt.

The thieves turned and stared wide-eyed at Volgan and the Hammer. The owner of the shop emerged from the shattered window onto the street and the two thieves bolted down an alley. Volgan turned.

"Bachtra, Siegas – after them."

The two soldiers immediately gave chase after the thieves.

A moment later Volgan and the three remaining soldiers came to another square, this one smaller than the previous one. Near a burnt-out shop, three lawfolk were dealing with eight rioters. All eight of the rioters were facing a wall, their hands behind them. Two of the lawfolk had their swords drawn and were pointing them in the direction of the rioters. The third member of the lawfolk – a woman – was putting chains on the hands of the rioters. The two lawfolk with their swords drawn looked a little uneasy with the situation – Volgan could sympathise with them. They were a little understaffed for the task. As he was thinking this, the fifth rioter who was about to receive his chains jabbed an elbow behind him, catching his captor squarely in the gut. With a winded cry she staggered sideways and the rioter seized his chance, dashing down a side-street. One of the lawfolk shot off after him.

"Varnack!" his deserted companion called after him. "Varnack, get back here!"

"Hurian…Sarth" Volgan said. "Help him".

Hurian and her comrade went quickly to the lawman's side.

"Nobody move!" Hurian shouted at the rioters, her sword before her. "Keep your face to the wall!"

Volgan could see the relief on the lawman's face. The lawman looked at him, nodding his thanks. Volgan returned the gesture. He was about to move on with his sole remaining soldier, Ilick Wildris, when Wildris suddenly shouted "Stop! You there, I said stop!" Before Volgan could do anything, Wildris raced off down an alley to their right. He vanished around a bend, leaving Volgan conflicted. He was reluctant to leave the square in case there was any more trouble with the rioters nearby, but he was also concerned about the hot-headed boy that had just galloped off on his own in pursuit of heroism.

He went after Wildris. As he tore around the bend, he almost collided with a couple having sex up against the wall to his left. He raced on, his heart pounding in his chest. He heard a cry of pain in the distance and his alarm grew. The alley narrowed a little and curved to the right. When it straightened again he saw Wildris up ahead, sliding down along a wall in a little alcove off the alleyway. He was holding his right side with his hand, which there was blood on. Volgan could see the grimace of pain on the boy's face in the moonlight. On the ground before Wildris was a cloaked, unmoving form.

"I'm sorry I went after him without your permission, my Lord" Wildris said, clenching his teeth in pain, still sliding toward the ground. Eventually he made contact with it. "But he had that dagger in his hand when I saw him, and there was blood on it. I thought he'd used it on someone."

Volgan looked down at the cloaked figure. There was a bloodied dagger with a simple black handle by the individual's hand. Buried almost to the hilt in the victim's chest was a dagger with an ornate handle, undoubtedly Wildris's. Volgan went to Wildris's side and got down on his haunches.

"Let me see" he said.

Wildris lifted a trembling hand from his side.

There was an ugly wound there, not very deep but enough to keep the youth out of action for a while.

"Oh, by the broken!" Volgan heard a female voice exclaim worriedly. He looked up and saw a heavyset woman leaning out of a window, her hand to her mouth. "What happened? Are you men alright?"

"The king's business, madam" Volgan said. "This man is injured. Can you bring us a cloth for his wound?"

"Of course, of course" she said quickly, and left the window. "Oh, by the broken!" Volgan heard her exclaim as she puttered about her apartment. While they waited for the woman to bring the cloth, Volgan went to the dead body beside them.

"When I caught up with him he started slashing that thing about like a madman" Wildris said, looking at the dagger by the form's hand. "I'm lucky he didn't put a lot more holes in me."

Volgan pulled the hood back from the body's face and his stomach rolled unpleasantly. The moonlight spilled on the face below him, illuminating the visage of Belmens Lantash.

With the aid of Vusel Amanthing, Volgan helped Wildris back to the square. As he was in no shape to walk any further, or to even ride a horse back to the castle, they acquired a horse and cart and loaded Wildris into the back of it. With the wounded knight on his way, Volgan and Hurian headed to *The Fallen Goose*, Volgan not relishing the sobering prospect of informing young Belmens' parents of the death of their son. Mercifully there was no rioting on their way to the tavern and their journey was un-impeded.

They informed the Lantashs of their bereavement in the kitchen where they had questioned them on the previous day. Xintimas Lantash howled with grief, her daughter Oleran gripping her by the shoulders in a bid to comfort her as she bawled herself. Xintimas's anguish was such that Oleran decided to take her mother from the kitchen to her bedroom.

Even when there were two doors between them, Volgan could still hear the heart-rending sobs of the woman. Before him, Zosar Lantash stared at the table between them, his eyes glassy with tears of sorrow and bitterness.

"I gave him that dagger myself, a few days ago" Lantash said. "My father gave it to me when I was about the same age. This is a tough part of town. He has a…" Lantash swallowed as he realized his mistake. "*Had* a girl who lived where the riots broke out. He'd been seeing her for nearly a year. He was besotted with her. When the rioting started, he begged me to let him go to her apartment – she lived with her mother and her father was dead so Belmens felt it was up to him to protect them. I said he could go – I knew he'd go anyway even if I refused." Lantash broke off, putting a hand to his mouth. He shook his head. When he removed his hand, his mouth was quivering with emotion. "He was a good boy" he managed, the utterance sounding almost like a gasp. He lifted his eyes to Volgan's. "I can assure you my lord, that if there was blood on his dagger like your man says – it only came about as a result of my son defending himself. He would not have set out to deliberately harm anyone unless he had been attacked. He just wasn't that kind of boy."

Lantash's eyes were full of earnestness but then they flickered uncertainly and dropped. Volgan remained silent. He knew what Lantash was thinking. He was pondering the same question himself. If Belmens had had blood on his dagger as Wildris had said – and he'd harmed someone in self-defence – then why had he ran?

As the night wore on, the rioters began to drift from the streets little by little. This helped the lawfolk and Throne Hammer to gain the upper hand and they drove the rest home before them with threats and a show of bared weapons. Thankfully they didn't have to resort to violence to secure their end. Back in his room at the castle, Volgan sat on his bed, still fully dressed, looking out the window at the growing dawn. He was utterly exhausted but his mind wouldn't let him lie down to sleep. There was something at the back of his mind regarding Wildris and Lantash that was trying to bare itself, trying to make itself known to him…but it was maddeningly eluding him. What was he missing? Damn, but it was vexing!

In his mind's eye he saw Wildris sliding down along the wall…the body before him…

The body. Something about the body.

But what? He pondered the clothes Belmens Lantash had been wearing – the cloak, the jerkin over a simple tunic, an unremarkable pair of boots… no – no clues there. The boy's weapon? A cheaply forged blade attached to a simple hilt. Nothing there either. Volgan drew a deep breath and rose to his feet. He walked to the window and looked out over the city. In the brightening sky he could see smoke still rising languidly from the buildings that had been burned in the rioting.

After a while he turned and headed back to his bed. Halfway across the floor he froze. In his mind's eye he saw himself pulling Wildris's dagger from the body of Belmens Lantash and handing it back to the knight. *Wildris took it and wiped the blood from it. As he did so, a beam of moonlight illuminated the ornate hilt, with its beautiful designs and embellishments. The dagger of a rich man of noble birth. A jewel-encrusted dagger.*

Volgan left his room and walked quickly to the infirmary. Upon arriving there he found himself looking at Wildris' sleeping form. The knight's clothes were draped over a chair by his bed. Volgan quietly searched his clothes and came upon the dagger that Wildris had killed Belmens Lantash with. He took it from its holster and studied it. What he discovered made his heart beat a little faster.

"Sir Ilick" he said.

Nothing.

"Sir Ilick."

Wildris's eyes opened slowly. Volgan could see the glaze of jolip sap in them.

"My lord" the knight said hoarsely.

Volgan held Wildris' dagger in front of him. He took the pearl that Belmens Lantash had given him the previous day from his pocket and placed it in an ornate hole in the hilt of the dagger. It fitted perfectly.

"Belmens Lantash gave me that" Volgan said, pointing at the pearl. "The youngster you killed last night."

A look of concern appeared on Wildris' features.

"Here's the interesting part" Volgan said. "Lantash gave me this yesterday, and he told me that he'd found it the day before that, after someone had threatened him outside his family's tavern. The same someone that he suspected of spiking a jug of wine with some sort of potion. *A jug that ended up at the table of the men and women who ended up killing five members of the throne hammer and nearly succeeding in killing the king.*"

Wildris blinked, but Volgan didn't see any fear appear in the young man's eyes. He was tough – Volgan had to give him that much.

"The men and women who YOU tried to bury without my permission" Volgan went on. "Now why would you do that, hmmm?"

Silence. Still, Volgan didn't see Wildris's eyes widening. The only ground the young knight conceded was the sight of his throat working as he swallowed.

"I'll tell you why" Volgan growled. "You wanted them buried because their blood was filled with spells!!! Spells that *you* administered through your potion. And you *did it when I sent you out on patrol to scout the procession route!!!* "

His anger overwhelming him, Volgan put his hands beneath Wildris's bed, gripped it and lifted. His side of the bed rose into the air, spilling Wildris onto the ground in a tangle of bedclothes. Volgan pushed the simple bed aside and pulled the bedclothes from Wildris, who was wearing nothing but a loincloth and a heavy bandage about his midsection, covering his wound.

"Spotting Belmens Lantash on the street last night was a nice little stroke of luck for you, wasn't it?" Volgan said. "You knew he'd run when he heard your voice. The voice that had threatened to kill him and his family and burn their house down if he took that spiked wine-jug from the table. You saw your chance to close that loop once and for all and you took it. To make it look more believable you slashed yourself with his dagger, didn't you?"

When Wildris gave no response, Volgan kicked him right where he knew the knight's wound was. Wildris shrieked in pain and the sound gave Volgan a bitter satisfaction. Wildris curled up in a protective ball and Volgan kicked his exposed rump, hard. Wildris cried out again.

"WHO ARE YOU WORKING FOR, WILDRIS?" Volgan roared. When he got no answer he kicked the knight again, this time in the small of his back. Wildris barked in pain.

"WHO ARE YOU WORKING FOR???"

"YOUR FATHER! I'M WORKING FOR YOUR FATHER!"

Volgan stared down at the crumpled form of the knight who was breathing hard through his pain. Wildris put a quivering hand around a bloodstain on his bandage where his wound was. The bloodstain hadn't been there before Volgan had kicked him. Volgan turned and went to the infirmary door. He locked it and returned to Wildris. He took his sword from its sheath and put it to the knight's neck.

"If you're lying" he said softly, "I'll kill you."

"I'm not lying" Wildris said in a voice that was little more than an agonised gasp. "He wants Alwil dead and the throne for himself. He promised my family lands if I agreed to help him."

"You betrayed the king's trust just like that after fighting for him in the war."

"Your father believes that Alwil is too weak to hold the continent together. To keep the peace. He's right. Alwil has suffered too many blows. He's damaged beyond repair. If he stays on the throne it's only a matter of time before there's another war. Alwil's enemies smell his weakness. It's only a matter of time before one of them strikes. Your father is the strongest of them. My family wants to be on the side of the winner when the smoke clears."

Volgan took a deep breath.

"That potion you put in the wine-jug" he said. "Who concocted it for him?"

"Your friend. Greck Manru."

Volgan's stomach rolled. He'd been shocked (but not terribly surprised) at the revelation that his father had been behind the assassination attempt on the king, but he was massively taken aback upon hearing that his lifelong friend had provided the weapon for the deed.

"Hadn't been expecting that, had you..my lord?"

Volgan clenched his teeth at Wildris' comment and moved the tip of his sword south to the bloodstain on Wildris's bandage. He pressed down a little until he saw fresh pain appear on Wildris's now sweating face.

"Do not try me, boy" he said. "Or I'll make this hole in you a lot bigger than it is. Tell me about the potion."

"While you were in Amadast, Manru was travelling. In Rinchar. In the Yexan bog he came across a tree that somehow sucked the blood of a previously undiscovered type of fairy. Greck had the idea that the sap of the tree might contain some special properties. So he drank some of it." Wilidris paused to grimace in pain. "He was right. For about half a day the sap gave him enormous bravery and strength. He told your father about it and they came up with the idea of mixing it with a mind-control spell."

"And who came up with the idea of using it on innocent bystanders in the procession?"

Wildris held Volgan's eyes. "I did."

Volgan kicked they boy's face, hard. The young knight's eyes closed as he was knocked unconscious. Volgan made his way quickly to the castle stables where he mounted his horse and rose hard into the dawn.

A WEEK LATER, THE DOOR TO THE BATTLEMENTS OF HAVAR BORINTH'S CASTLE at Drenkat opened and Volgan appeared. Havar was speaking with three men – Volgan recognised them all – they were three of his father's most powerful under-lords. Volgan approached the quartet, his eyes fixed on his father.

"My lords" he said, his gaze not leaving Havar. "My father and I wish to have some words. Please forgive us."

Havar's three companions, clearly realising that this was not a conversation for them, curtsied their goodbyes and left quickly.

"Wildris told me everything" Volgan said.

Havar smiled humourlessly. "So what do you think of it?"

"What do I think of what?"

"Greck's little mixture. It wasn't successful…but that was its first time being used in the field. It came close, though. From what I heard, if you hadn't been there -."

In fury, Volgan grabbed his father by the collar. In all his life it had been the first time he had ever laid a hand on him.

"You tried to kill the king of Monsiel!" Volgan said through gritted teeth. "My friend! The man I pledged to protect! *Five* of my men died! *I* could have been one of them!"

Havar swatted Volgan's arm away angrily.

"And I'm *sorry* you were!" Havar said. "But it was a risk I was prepared to take! I knew a soldier of your might and skill would have as good a chance as any of prevailing against a bunch of super-strong peasants. And you did! Unfortunately so did Alwil -.”

“Unfortunately!!!” Volgan declared in a tone of incredulity. “Father… you truly are unbelievable. You are the greatest snake I have ever met!!!”

“Shut your mouth, you moral FOOL!!!” Havar spat. “Open your eyes! Wildris did, why can’t you? *Think* for once with that sentimental brain of yours!” He paused before continuing. “Alwil is frail. His armies are tired. Zorran might still be strong but beneath the surface it is divided. If someone strong marches against Alwil, not all of his lords will give him their men.” He paused again, and when he resumed it was in a soft, resolute tone. “Now is our chance to take the throne, my son. Our army is fresh, intact… and you saw what Greck’s potion can do. If we give it to our men…we’ll cut through Alwil’s forces like a knife through butter. When they see our men coming at them, roaring, their eyes afraid of nothing…there may not even be a battle. We might get to Masraff without spilling any blood at all.”

Neither man said anything for a while. It was Havar who finally broke the silence.

“So. What do you think, my son? Will you march with me on Masraff, and propel our family to greatness?”

“No” Volgan said abruptly. “I’m going to arrest Greck and take him back to Masraff. And if he ever makes a drop of that potion again it’ll be for Alwil.”

Volgan put his sword back in its scabbard and turned to leave. He heard an enraged roar from behind him and turned to see his father coming at him with his teeth bared, a dagger in his hand.

“You wretched, cowardly -!”

Volgan interrupted him by deflecting his father’s weapon-bearing arm and grabbing him about the throat. He walked his father’s thin, light form two steps to the battlements and flung him between two merlons. Havar made no sound as he fell through the air to the hard, stone bailey below.

Volgan looked down and studied his father’s dead form, the dagger he had intended to kill his son with by his side, a halo of blood slowly growing around his head.

MASRAFF, ONE MONTH LATER

When Volgan finished his story, Alwil clapped emptily.

"You played it masterfully" he said. "Using your father's petulance against him. You knew that he was liable to react like that after you let him down for a second time. You baited him…and he took it."

"I didn't want to do it" Volgan said heavily. "But it had to be done. He was just too dangerous. Too unpredictable."

"I was waiting for him to make a move against me" Alwil said. "I never thought it would be *you* that did the deed." He paused, holding Volgan's eyes firmly. "We were friends, Volgan. You were always honourable. And then you marched your…*drugged* armies against me. Against your *king*."

"I had to do it, Alwil" Volgan said. "It was the wisest course of action. I hate to admit it…but I came around to my father's way of thinking. He was right – your position was weak. It was only a matter of time before someone rose against you! What if it had been one of the lesser lords? And it had turned out to be an even match between you and them? The conflict could have gone on for years! Tens of thousands could have died! At least it was quick between your forces and mine! Greck Manru's potion was…a blessing of a sort."

Alwil snorted derisively. "Tell that to the four hundred of my men who were slaughtered by your super-charged monsters that afternoon on the battlefield!"

"I'm sorry about them!" Volgan said. "But the remaining twenty-thousand survived, didn't they? Because they knew it was pointless and they ran! Would they have survived a long, protracted struggle? I don't think so."

Alwil remained silent.

"With me on the throne backed by my army and Greck's…*drug*, as you might call it, no-one will dare rise against the crown. The continent will have the peace it needs to heal and recover from the war."

Alwil considered this. Eventually he spoke.

"Volgan…why am I here? You exile me…then your men seize me and bring me back here under cover of darkness. How come you haven't just killed me?"

"Because you're a good man. And more importantly – a wise one."

Alwil chucked cynically. "Volgan…perhaps you should read the history of Monsiel in more detail. Being good and wise have rarely preserved a man's life when his back is to the wall."

"Those qualities will matter on this occasion" Volgan said. "You performed admirably during a very difficult period in Monsiel's history, Alwil." He paused. "I would like you to be my counsel on occasion."

"Your counsel?"

"You've been the king of Monsiel for eight years. You're an effective thinker and a good handler of people. You're a diplomat." Volgan paused. "And your letting of refugees from the warzones into Zorran…it was truly human of you."

Alwil studied his new master, an expression of sarcastic amusement on his face.

"You want me to be your…counsel…from *here*?" Alwil lifted his arms, looking around him at the room they were in. It was a sizeable room, its furniture and dressings luxurious but it was not much more than a bedroom on one side with a study area on the other. It was the top room in an old, disused tower in the castle grounds. The room of someone who was not meant to be found.

"Yes" Volgan said. "Most of my under-lords felt that I should kill you. But I interceded for you – I pointed out the good things that you'd done during your reign. Grudgingly, they acceded to my proposal to force you into exile."

"Which was your plan all along, I presume."

"Yes."

"What if they had really pushed for my death, Volgan? Would you have given it to them?"

Volgan made no response.

Alwil nodded, looking away from his former friend, knowing what the silence meant.

"You'll want for nothing" Volgan resumed, referring to Alwil's prospective future in his current location. "You'll have the best of food and clothing. Women when you want them – but you'll have to wear a mask during their visits."

Alwil, pacing his room, snorted in disdain.

"I never saw myself on the throne, Alwil" Volgan said. "I never *wanted* it. Both of us are in positions that we don't relish."

"Oh, I would imagine that you're happier in yours than I am in mine".

"Perhaps. But we are both men of the realm. We put the continent's needs before our own desires. Fate has placed us in positions where we can better the future of Monsiel, if we work together." Volgan paused. "So" he said, watching Alwil walk toward his window. "Are you a man of the realm, Alwil? Will you help me? Be my counsel?"

Alwil turned and looked at the man who had been his friend since their boyhood years. Volgan extended his hand.

"I won't help *you*" Alwil said. "But I will help Monsiel."

Seeing that Alwil would not take his proferred hand, Volgan withdrew it. He nodded and left the room. Alwil listened to the sound of a guard locking the door followed by Volgan's footsteps as he walked away. Eventually there was only silence.

THE END

JOHN LEAHY HAS HAD THREE NOVELS PUBLISHED - HARVEST, CROGIAN, AND Unity. His story *The Tale In The Attic* attained an honorable mention in L Ron Hubbard's Writers Of The Future Contest. His short story *Singers* has been included in Flame Tree Publishing's 2017 Pirates and Ghosts anthology, alongside tales by literary greats such as Homer, Joseph Conrad, Rudyard Kipling, Arthur Conan Doyle, Robert Louis Stevenson, H.P. Lovecraft, and H.G. Wells. When not writing he spends his time teaching and performing music, working out, and keeping abreast of the stock market and current affairs. He lives in Killarney, Ireland.

WELCOME TO **RETRO REWIND**, A NEW SECTION IN ADV IN WHICH WE TAKE a look back at classic works. We want to see if some of our nostalgic favorites hold up today; if they're worth revisiting, or for some of you, worth encountering for the first time. We plan to feature one book and one movie each time. This inaugural feature focuses on "Psycho" the book and "Psycho" the movie, but we won't necessarily tie them together every time. We'll try to avoid major spoilers, but seeing as how these works are 50-plus years old, sometimes that won't be possible. We hope you enjoy **Retro Rewind** and that you find some new old stories to check out!

REREAD
"PSYCHO" BY ROBERT BLOCH, 1959

I CAN'T REMEMBER A TIME WHEN I DIDN'T KNOW ABOUT NORMAN BATES AND his mother. I can't even remember if I saw the Hitchcock movie or read the Bloch book first. Or maybe it was a pop culture reference that introduced me. Any one of those could be true, because "Psycho" - as with stories such as "The Shining" or "Dracula" - is one of those literature-and-film works that has so deeply embedded itself in the cultural zeitgeist, you feel you were born knowing about it.

So the question then becomes: Does knowing the plot twist - one of the most shocking, original twists ever conceived - ruin the book? Can you go back and read it again knowing what happens?

I'll answer with a definitive YES and say that knowing the twist actually makes it a freakier story. (But at the same time, boy do I envy those of you who know nothing of the plot!)

It helps, too, that Bloch - who was a highly successful pulp fiction writer before he wrote his magnum opus - is a master story-teller; "Psycho" is a fast-paced, almost modern novel. You can read this entire book over the course of a rainy day or a stormy night.

To return to my first point, I'm sure you, dear reader, know the twist in the story, but I'll refrain from spoiling it just in case there IS that envious someone out there who is ignorant of the plot.

For that person, and for those who need a reminder, here's the setup:

Norman Bates, an "odd" middle-age man who still is psychologically dominated by his mother, runs a motel that no longer receives many visitors because the town moved its main road elsewhere. People do still come to Bates Motel, but very few - there's no chance the sign will ever read "No vacancy."

One night a young woman shows up needing a room. She's on the lam after stealing $40,000 from her workplace (the equivalent of $440,000 today) and deciding if she wants to go through with her ill-conceived, spur-of-the-moment theft. But unfortunately she stops at Bates Motel.

Now comes one of the most famous cinematic moments of all time, a scene so iconic it infiltrates the source material. The "shower scene." In the book, the scene takes place over a few short paragraphs, but you're bound to "see" it happen as it did in the movie(s) or in the many pop culture parodies. The woman, Mary, is killed by Norman Bates' mom, who doesn't want her "pure" boy (he's definitely not as pure as she thinks) tainted by this "bitch."

The rest of the book is half a mystery story, as the victim's sister, boyfriend, private detective, and sheriff try to find out what happened to Mary, who disappeared after taking the money. Did she run away to start a new life? We know the answer of course, but it's enjoyable to watch them try to crack the case. It's also half about Norman and his mother's creepy relationship and how they deal with the murders. (Yes, there are two, but I won't spoil what the second one is.)

Some classics can be rather dull, but that is certainly NOT the case with "Psycho." It is eminently readable, and aside from some minor outdated references,

PUBLIC STILL: ANTHONY PERKINS

it holds up very well. I have some quibbles with some of the closing scenes, but it didn't affect my overall impression of the novel.

REWATCH
"PSYCHO" BY ALFRED HITCHCOCK, 1960

Only a year after "Psycho" the novel was published, the great director Alfred Hitchcock put the story on film and released what would ultimately turn out to be his most famous movie.

The film pushed the boundaries of what movies could be, and while critics initially were divided on its impact, audiences LOVED it. "Psycho" was creepy, had psychological depth, featured an unforgettable scene (the "shower scene," of course), and, did I mention, was creepy?

Does it hold up for the modern movie reviewer? Yes and no.

If you were to put this in theaters nowadays and show it to a young audience with no knowledge of cinematic history, the majority of the audience likely would find it a bit too slow and unintentionally funny at times (the second murder, for example).

But despite that, it still does hold up fairly well.

JANET LEIGH, FROM PSYCHO

I find the slower pace and more traditional scores of old movies comforting. And to me, it works well here in establishing tension. I will say, this movie would benefit more than the book by not knowing anything before going into it; it's one of those rare times I would recommend watching the movie first. Knowing the plot does rob the film of some of the tension, but not completely. It's still worth a watch.

As far as comparing the book to the movie, Hitchcock followed the novel rather closely, mainly changing things for the sake of expediency. (And they Hollywooded-up Norman Bates, changing him from an overweight weirdo to a handsome, skinny weirdo.) I had some minor issues with some differences, like why did Hitchcock change what happens to the money? It served no real purpose. And I think he made the movie version of Mary - here known as Marion, for some reason - not as smart as the book version. But again, those are minor issues, and if one is not comparing the film to the book, they aren't issues anyway.

One fun change to note is that the film alters the most famous quote (spoken by Norman Bates). I would say this one is definitely for the better - the movie version is pithier and more quotable.

Book version: "I think perhaps all of us go a little crazy at times."

Movie version: "We all go a little mad sometimes."

I didn't really love Janet Leigh's overall acting in the movie, but my goodness, she nails the shower scene. There's a reason Leigh is known as one of the best "scream queens" of all time!

Anthony Perkins is suitably strange and does a good job creating the first on-screen Norman Bates. In the book I think Norman came off creepier, but Perkins was great nonetheless.

Since this 1960 film, there have been sequels and remakes and prequels (including the fairly recent "Bates Motel" TV show), but if you're going to watch a version, I would start with Hitchcock's classic.

-Michael Toeset

THE SIGNAL-MAN

BY CHARLES DICKENS

"**H**ALLOA! Below there!"

When he heard a voice thus calling to him, he was standing at the door of his box, with a flag in his hand, furled round its short pole. One would have thought, considering the nature of the ground, that he could not have doubted from what quarter the voice came; but instead of looking up to where I stood on the top of the steep cutting nearly over his head, he turned himself about, and looked down the Line. There was something remarkable in his manner of doing so, though I could not have said for my life what. But I know it was remarkable enough to attract my notice, even though his figure was foreshortened and shadowed, down in the deep trench, and mine was high above him, so steeped in the glow of an angry sunset, that I had shaded my eyes with my hand before I saw him at all.

"Halloa! Below!"

From looking down the Line, he turned himself about again, and, raising his eyes, saw my figure high above him.

"Is there any path by which I can come down and speak to you?"

He looked up at me without replying, and I looked down at him without pressing him too soon with a repetition of my idle question. Just then there came a vague vibration in the earth and air, quickly changing into a violent pulsation, and an oncoming rush that caused me to start back, as though it had force to draw me down. When such vapour as rose to my height from this rapid train had passed me, and was skimming away over the landscape, I looked down again, and saw him refurling the flag he had shown while the train went by.

I repeated my inquiry. After a pause, during which he seemed to regard me with fixed attention, he motioned with his rolled-up flag towards a point on my level, some two or three hundred yards distant. I called down to him, "All right!" and made for that point. There, by dint of looking closely about me, I found a rough zigzag descending path notched out, which I followed.

The cutting was extremely deep, and unusually precipitate. It was made through a clammy stone, that became oozier and wetter as I went down. For these reasons, I found the way long enough to give me time to recall a singular air of reluctance or compulsion with which he had pointed out the path.

When I came down low enough upon the zigzag descent to see him again, I saw that he was standing between the rails on the way by which the train had lately passed, in an attitude as if he were waiting for me to appear. He had his left hand at his chin, and that left elbow rested on his right hand, crossed over his breast. His attitude was one of such expectation and watchfulness that I stopped a moment, wondering at it.

I resumed my downward way, and stepping out upon the level of the railroad, and drawing nearer to him, saw that he was a dark, sallow man, with a dark beard and rather heavy eyebrows. His post was in as solitary and dismal a place as ever I saw. On either side, a dripping-wet wall of jagged stone, excluding all view but a strip of sky; the perspective one way only a crooked prolongation of this great dungeon; the shorter perspective in the other direction terminating in a gloomy red light, and the gloomier entrance to a black tunnel, in whose massive architecture there was a barbarous, depressing, and forbidding air. So little sunlight ever found its way to this spot, that it had an earthy, deadly smell; and so much cold wind rushed through it, that it struck chill to me, as if I had left the natural world.

Before he stirred, I was near enough to him to have touched him. Not even then removing his eyes from mine, he stepped back one step, and lifted his hand.

This was a lonesome post to occupy (I said), and it had riveted my attention when I looked down from up yonder. A visitor was a rarity, I should suppose; not an unwelcome rarity, I hoped? In me, he merely saw a man who had been shut up within narrow limits all his life, and who, being at last set free, had a newly-awakened interest in these great works. To such purpose I spoke to him; but I am far from sure of the terms I used; for, besides that I am not happy in opening any conversation, there was something in the man that daunted me.

He directed a most curious look towards the red light near the tunnel's mouth, and looked all about it, as if something were missing from it, and then looked at me.

That light was part of his charge? Was it not?

He answered in a low voice,—"Don't you know it is?"

The monstrous thought came into my mind, as I perused the fixed eyes and the saturnine face, that this was a spirit, not a man. I have speculated since, whether there may have been infection in his mind.

In my turn, I stepped back. But in making the action, I detected in his eyes some latent fear of me. This put the monstrous thought to flight.

"You look at me," I said, forcing a smile, "as if you had a dread of me."

"I was doubtful," he returned, "whether I had seen you before."

"Where?"

He pointed to the red light he had looked at.

"There?" I said.

Intently watchful of me, he replied (but without sound), "Yes."

"My good fellow, what should I do there? However, be that as it may, I never was there, you may swear."

"I think I may," he rejoined. "Yes; I am sure I may."

His manner cleared, like my own. He replied to my remarks with readiness, and in well-chosen words. Had he much to do there? Yes; that was to say, he had enough responsibility to bear; but exactness and watchfulness were what was required of him, and of actual work—manual labour—he had next to none. To change that signal, to trim those lights, and to turn this iron handle now and then, was all he had to do under that head. Regarding those many long and lonely hours of which I seemed to make so much, he could only say that the routine of his life had shaped itself into that form, and he had grown used to it. He had taught himself a language down here,—if only to know it by sight, and to have formed his own crude ideas of its pronunciation, could be called learning it. He had also worked at fractions and decimals, and tried a little algebra; but he was, and had been as a boy, a poor hand at figures. Was it necessary for him when on duty always to remain in that channel of damp air, and could he never rise into the sunshine from between those high stone walls? Why, that depended upon times and circumstances. Under some conditions there would be less upon the Line than under others, and the same held good as to certain hours of the day and night. In bright weather, he did choose occasions for getting a little above these lower shadows; but, being at all times liable to be called by his electric bell, and at such times listening for it with redoubled anxiety, the relief was less than I would suppose.

He took me into his box, where there was a fire, a desk for an official book in which he had to make certain entries, a telegraphic instrument with its dial, face, and needles, and the little bell of which he had spoken. On my trusting that he would excuse the remark that he had been well educated, and (I hoped I might say without offence) perhaps educated above that station, he observed that instances of slight incongruity in such wise would rarely be found wanting among large bodies of men; that he had heard it was so in workhouses, in the police force, even in that last desperate resource, the army; and that he knew it was so, more or less, in any great railway staff. He had been, when young (if I could believe it, sitting in that hut,—he scarcely could), a student of natural philosophy, and had attended lectures; but he had run wild, misused his opportunities, gone down, and never risen again. He had no complaint to offer about that. He had made his bed, and he lay upon it. It was far too late to make another.

All that I have here condensed he said in a quiet manner, with his grave, dark regards divided between me and the fire. He threw in the word, "Sir," from time to time, and especially when he referred to his youth,—as though to request me to understand that he claimed to be nothing but what I found him. He was several times interrupted by the little bell, and had to read off messages, and send replies. Once he had to stand without the door, and display a flag as a train passed, and make some verbal communication to the driver. In the discharge of his duties, I observed him to be remarkably exact and vigilant, breaking off his discourse at a syllable, and remaining silent until what he had to do was done.

In a word, I should have set this man down as one of the safest of men to be employed in that capacity, but for the circumstance that while he was speaking to me he twice broke off with a fallen colour, turned his face towards the little bell when it did NOT ring, opened the door of the hut (which was kept shut to exclude the unhealthy damp), and looked out towards the red light near the mouth of the tunnel. On both of those occasions, he came back to the fire with the inexplicable air upon him which I had remarked, without being able to define, when we were so far asunder.

Said I, when I rose to leave him, "You almost make me think that I have met with a contented man."

(I am afraid I must acknowledge that I said it to lead him on.)

"I believe I used to be so," he rejoined, in the low voice in which he had first spoken; "but I am troubled, sir, I am troubled."

He would have recalled the words if he could. He had said them, however, and I took them up quickly.

"With what? What is your trouble?"

"It is very difficult to impart, sir. It is very, very difficult to speak of. If ever you make me another visit, I will try to tell you."

"But I expressly intend to make you another visit. Say, when shall it be?"

"I go off early in the morning, and I shall be on again at ten to-morrow night, sir."

"I will come at eleven."

He thanked me, and went out at the door with me. "I'll show my white light, sir," he said, in his peculiar low voice, "till you have found the way up. When you have found it, don't call out! And when you are at the top, don't call out!"

His manner seemed to make the place strike colder to me, but I said no more than, "Very well."

"And when you come down to-morrow night, don't call out! Let me ask you a parting question. What made you cry, 'Halloa! Below there!' to-night?"

"Heaven knows," said I. "I cried something to that effect—"

"Not to that effect, sir. Those were the very words. I know them well."

"Admit those were the very words. I said them, no doubt, because I saw you below."

"For no other reason?"

"What other reason could I possibly have?"

"You had no feeling that they were conveyed to you in any supernatural way?"

"No."

He wished me good-night, and held up his light. I walked by the side of the down Line of rails (with a very disagreeable sensation of a train coming behind me) until I found the path. It was easier to mount than to descend, and I got back to my inn without any adventure.

Punctual to my appointment, I placed my foot on the first notch of the zigzag next night, as the distant clocks were striking eleven. He was waiting for me at the bottom, with his white light on. "I have not called out," I said, when we came close together; "may I speak now?" "By all means, sir." "Good-night, then, and here's my hand." "Good-night, sir, and here's mine." With that we walked side by side to his box, entered it, closed the door, and sat down by the fire.

"I have made up my mind, sir," he began, bending forward as soon as we were seated, and speaking in a tone but a little above a whisper, "that you shall not have to ask me twice what troubles me. I took you for some one else yesterday evening. That troubles me."

"That mistake?"

"No. That some one else."

"Who is it?"

"I don't know."

"Like me?"

"I don't know. I never saw the face. The left arm is across the face, and the right arm is waved,—violently waved. This way."

I followed his action with my eyes, and it was the action of an arm gesticulating, with the utmost passion and vehemence, "For God's sake, clear the way!"

"One moonlight night," said the man, "I was sitting here, when I heard a voice cry, 'Halloa! Below there!' I started up, looked from that door, and saw this Some one else standing by the red light near the tunnel, waving as I just now showed you. The voice seemed hoarse with shouting, and it cried, 'Look out! Look out!' And then again, 'Halloa! Below there! Look out!' I caught up my lamp, turned it on red, and ran towards the figure, calling, 'What's wrong? What has happened? Where?' It stood just outside the blackness of the tunnel. I advanced so close upon it that I wondered at its keeping the sleeve across its eyes. I ran right up at it, and had my hand stretched out to pull the sleeve away, when it was gone."

"Into the tunnel?" said I.

"No. I ran on into the tunnel, five hundred yards. I stopped, and held my lamp above my head, and saw the figures of the measured distance, and saw the wet stains stealing down the walls and trickling through the arch. I ran out again faster than I had run in (for I had a mortal abhorrence of the place upon me), and I looked all round the red light with my own red light, and I went up the iron ladder to the gallery atop of it, and I came down again, and ran back here. I telegraphed both ways, 'An alarm has been given. Is anything wrong?' The answer came back, both ways, 'All well.'"

Resisting the slow touch of a frozen finger tracing out my spine, I showed him how that this figure must be a deception of his sense of sight; and how that figures, originating in disease of the delicate nerves that minister to the functions of the eye, were known to have often troubled patients, some of whom had become conscious of the nature of their affliction, and had even proved it by experiments upon themselves. "As to an imaginary cry," said I, "do but listen for a moment to the wind in this unnatural valley while we speak so low, and to the wild harp it makes of the telegraph wires."

That was all very well, he returned, after we had sat listening for a while, and he ought to know something of the wind and the wires,—he who so often passed long winter nights there, alone and watching. But he would beg to remark that he had not finished.

I asked his pardon, and he slowly added these words, touching my arm,—

"Within six hours after the Appearance, the memorable accident on this Line happened, and within ten hours the dead and wounded were brought along through the tunnel over the spot where the figure had stood."

A disagreeable shudder crept over me, but I did my best against it. It was not to be denied, I rejoined, that this was a remarkable coincidence, calculated deeply to impress his mind. But it was unquestionable that remarkable coincidences did continually occur, and they must be taken into account in dealing with such a subject. Though to be sure I must admit, I added (for I thought I saw that he was going to bring the objection to bear upon me), men of common sense did not allow much for coincidences in making the ordinary calculations of life.

He again begged to remark that he had not finished.

I again begged his pardon for being betrayed into interruptions.

"This," he said, again laying his hand upon my arm, and glancing over his shoulder with hollow eyes, "was just a year ago. Six or seven months passed, and I had recovered from the surprise and shock, when one morning, as the day was breaking, I, standing at the door, looked towards the red light, and saw the spectre again." He stopped, with a fixed look at me.

"Did it cry out?"

"No. It was silent."

"Did it wave its arm?"

"No. It leaned against the shaft of the light, with both hands before the face. Like this."

Once more I followed his action with my eyes. It was an action of mourning. I have seen such an attitude in stone figures on tombs.

"Did you go up to it?"

"I came in and sat down, partly to collect my thoughts, partly because it had turned me faint. When I went to the door again, daylight was above me, and the ghost was gone."

"But nothing followed? Nothing came of this?"

He touched me on the arm with his forefinger twice or thrice giving a ghastly nod each time:—

"That very day, as a train came out of the tunnel, I noticed, at a carriage window on my side, what looked like a confusion of hands and heads, and something waved. I saw it just in time to signal the driver, Stop! He shut off, and put his brake on, but the train drifted past here a hundred and fifty yards or more. I ran after it, and, as I went along, heard terrible screams and cries. A beautiful young lady had died instantaneously in one of the compartments, and was brought in here, and laid down on this floor between us."

Involuntarily I pushed my chair back, as I looked from the boards at which he pointed to himself.

"True, sir. True. Precisely as it happened, so I tell it you."

I could think of nothing to say, to any purpose, and my mouth was very dry. The wind and the wires took up the story with a long lamenting wail.

He resumed. "Now, sir, mark this, and judge how my mind is troubled. The spectre came back a week ago. Ever since, it has been there, now and again, by fits and starts."

"At the light?"

"At the Danger-light."

"What does it seem to do?"

He repeated, if possible with increased passion and vehemence, that former gesticulation of, "For God's sake, clear the way!"

Then he went on. "I have no peace or rest for it. It calls to me, for many minutes together, in an agonised manner, 'Below there! Look out! Look out!' It stands waving to me. It rings my little bell——"

I caught at that. "Did it ring your bell yesterday evening when I was here, and you went to the door?"

"Twice."

"Why, see," said I, "how your imagination misleads you. My eyes were on the bell, and my ears were open to the bell, and if I am a living man, it did NOT ring at those times. No, nor at any other time, except when it was rung in the natural course of physical things by the station communicating with you."

He shook his head. "I have never made a mistake as to that yet, sir. I have never confused the spectre's ring with the man's. The ghost's ring is a strange vibration in the bell that it derives from nothing else, and I have not asserted that the bell stirs to the eye. I don't wonder that you failed to hear it. But _I_ heard it."

"And did the spectre seem to be there, when you looked out?"

"It WAS there."

"Both times?"

He repeated firmly: "Both times."

"Will you come to the door with me, and look for it now?"

He bit his under lip as though he were somewhat unwilling, but arose. I opened the door, and stood on the step, while he stood in the doorway. There was the Danger-light. There was the dismal mouth of the tunnel. There were the high, wet stone walls of the cutting. There were the stars above them.

"Do you see it?" I asked him, taking particular note of his face. His eyes were prominent and strained, but not very much more so, perhaps, than my own had been when I had directed them earnestly towards the same spot.

"No," he answered. "It is not there."

"Agreed," said I.

We went in again, shut the door, and resumed our seats. I was thinking how best to improve this advantage, if it might be called one, when he took up the conversation in such a matter-of-course way, so assuming that there could be no serious question of fact between us, that I felt myself placed in the weakest of positions.

"By this time you will fully understand, sir," he said, "that what troubles me so dreadfully is the question, What does the spectre mean?"

I was not sure, I told him, that I did fully understand.

"What is its warning against?" he said, ruminating, with his eyes on the fire, and only by times turning them on me. "What is the danger? Where is the danger? There is danger overhanging somewhere on the Line. Some dreadful calamity will happen. It is not to be doubted this third time, after what has gone before. But surely this is a cruel haunting of me. What can I do?"

He pulled out his handkerchief, and wiped the drops from his heated forehead.

"If I telegraph Danger, on either side of me, or on both, I can give no reason for it," he went on, wiping the palms of his hands. "I should get into trouble, and do no good. They would think I was mad. This is the way it would work,—Message: 'Danger! Take care!' Answer: 'What Danger? Where?' Message: 'Don't know. But, for God's sake, take care!' They would displace me. What else could they do?"

His pain of mind was most pitiable to see. It was the mental torture of a conscientious man, oppressed beyond endurance by an unintelligible responsibility involving life.

"When it first stood under the Danger-light," he went on, putting his dark hair back from his head, and drawing his hands outward across and across his temples in an extremity of feverish distress, "why not tell me where that accident was to happen,—if it must happen? Why not tell me how it could be averted,—if it could have been averted? When on its second coming it hid its face, why not tell me, instead, 'She is going to die. Let them keep her at home'? If it came, on those two occasions, only to show me that its warnings were true, and so to prepare me for the third, why not warn me plainly now? And I, Lord help me! A mere poor signal-man on this solitary station! Why not go to somebody with credit to be believed, and power to act?"

When I saw him in this state, I saw that for the poor man's sake, as well as for the public safety, what I had to do for the time was to compose his mind. Therefore, setting aside all question of reality or unreality between us, I represented to him that whoever thoroughly discharged his duty must do well, and that at least it was his comfort that he understood his duty, though he did not understand these confounding Appearances. In this effort I succeeded far better than in the attempt to reason him out of his conviction. He became calm; the occupations incidental to his post as the night advanced began to make larger demands on his attention: and I left him at two in the morning. I had offered to stay through the night, but he would not hear of it.

That I more than once looked back at the red light as I ascended the pathway, that I did not like the red light, and that I should have slept but poorly if my bed had been under it, I see no reason to conceal. Nor did I like the two sequences of the accident and the dead girl. I see no reason to conceal that either.

But what ran most in my thoughts was the consideration how ought I to act, having become the recipient of this disclosure? I had proved the man to be intelligent, vigilant, painstaking, and exact; but how long might he remain so, in his state of mind? Though in a subordinate position, still he held a most important trust, and would I (for instance) like to stake my own life on the chances of his continuing to execute it with precision?

Unable to overcome a feeling that there would be something treacherous in my communicating what he had told me to his superiors in the Company, without first being plain with himself and proposing a middle course to him, I ultimately resolved to offer to accompany him (otherwise keeping his secret for the present) to the wisest medical practitioner we could hear of in those parts, and to take his opinion. A change in his time of duty would come round next night, he had apprised me, and he would be off an hour or two after sunrise, and on again soon after sunset. I had appointed to return accordingly.

Next evening was a lovely evening, and I walked out early to enjoy it. The sun was not yet quite down when I traversed the field-path near the top of the deep cutting. I would extend my walk for an hour, I said to myself, half an hour on and half an hour back, and it would then be time to go to my signal-man's box.

Before pursuing my stroll, I stepped to the brink, and mechanically looked down, from the point from which I had first seen him. I cannot describe the thrill that seized upon me, when, close at the mouth of the tunnel, I saw the appearance of a man, with his left sleeve across his eyes, passionately waving his right arm.

The nameless horror that oppressed me passed in a moment, for in a moment I saw that this appearance of a man was a man indeed, and that there was a little group of other men, standing at a short distance, to whom he seemed to be rehearsing the gesture he made. The Danger-light was not yet lighted. Against its shaft, a little low hut, entirely new to me, had been made of some wooden supports and tarpaulin. It looked no bigger than a bed.

With an irresistible sense that something was wrong,—with a flashing self-reproachful fear that fatal mischief had come of my leaving the man there, and causing no one to be sent to overlook or correct what he did,—I descended the notched path with all the speed I could make.

"What is the matter?" I asked the men.

"Signal-man killed this morning, sir."

"Not the man belonging to that box?"

"Yes, sir."

"Not the man I know?"

"You will recognise him, sir, if you knew him," said the man who spoke for the others, solemnly uncovering his own head, and raising an end of the tarpaulin, "for his face is quite composed."

"O, how did this happen, how did this happen?" I asked, turning from one to another as the hut closed in again.

"He was cut down by an engine, sir. No man in England knew his work better. But somehow he was not clear of the outer rail. It was just at broad day. He had struck the light, and had the lamp in his hand. As the engine came out of the tunnel, his back was towards her, and she cut him down. That man drove her, and was showing how it happened. Show the gentleman, Tom."

The man, who wore a rough dark dress, stepped back to his former place at the mouth of the tunnel.

"Coming round the curve in the tunnel, sir," he said, "I saw him at the end, like as if I saw him down a perspective-glass. There was no time to check speed, and I knew him to be very careful. As he didn't seem to take heed of the whistle, I shut it off when we were running down upon him, and called to him as loud as I could call."

"What did you say?"

"I said, 'Below there! Look out! Look out! For God's sake, clear the way!'"

I started.

"Ah! it was a dreadful time, sir. I never left off calling to him. I put this arm before my eyes not to see, and I waved this arm to the last; but it was no use."

WITHOUT PROLONGING THE NARRATIVE TO DWELL ON ANY ONE OF ITS CURIOUS circumstances more than on any other, I may, in closing it, point out the coincidence that the warning of the Engine-Driver included, not only the words which the unfortunate Signal-man had repeated to me as haunting him, but also the words which I myself—not he—had attached, and that only in my own mind, to the gesticulation he had imitated.

THE END

AN EDISON KINETOGRAM CATALOGUE FROM 1910
FEATURING THE FILM FRANKENSTEIN.

THE BURIAL OF THE DEAD

BY T.S. ELIOT

April is the cruellest month, breeding
Lilacs out of the dead land, mixing
Memory and desire, stirring
Dull roots with spring rain.
Winter kept us warm, covering
Earth in forgetful snow, feeding
A little life with dried tubers.
Summer surprised us, coming over the Starnbergersee
With a shower of rain; we stopped in the colonnade,
And went on in sunlight, into the Hofgarten,
And drank coffee, and talked for an hour.
Bin gar keine Russin, stamm' aus Litauen, echt deutsch.
And when we were children, staying at the archduke's,
My cousin's, he took me out on a sled,
And I was frightened. He said, Marie,
Marie, hold on tight. And down we went.
In the mountains, there you feel free.
I read, much of the night, and go south in the winter.

What are the roots that clutch, what branches grow
Out of this stony rubbish? Son of man,
You cannot say, or guess, for you know only
A heap of broken images, where the sun beats,

And the dead tree gives no shelter, the cricket no relief,
And the dry stone no sound of water. Only
There is shadow under this red rock,
(Come in under the shadow of this red rock),
And I will show you something different from either
Your shadow at morning striding behind you
Or your shadow at evening rising to meet you;
I will show you fear in a handful of dust.

Frisch weht der Wind
Der Heimat zu
Mein Irisch Kind,
Wo weilest du?

"You gave me hyacinths first a year ago;
"They called me the hyacinth girl."
—Yet when we came back, late, from the Hyacinth garden,
Your arms full, and your hair wet, I could not
Speak, and my eyes failed, I was neither
Living nor dead, and I knew nothing,
Looking into the heart of light, the silence.
Oed' und leer das Meer.

Madame Sosostris, famous clairvoyante,
Had a bad cold, nevertheless
Is known to be the wisest woman in Europe,
With a wicked pack of cards. Here, said she,
Is your card, the drowned Phoenician Sailor,
(Those are pearls that were his eyes. Look!)
Here is Belladonna, the Lady of the Rocks,
The lady of situations.
Here is the man with three staves, and here the Wheel,
And here is the one-eyed merchant, and this card,
Which is blank, is something he carries on his back,
Which I am forbidden to see. I do not find
The Hanged Man. Fear death by water.

I see crowds of people, walking round in a ring.
Thank you. If you see dear Mrs. Equitone,
Tell her I bring the horoscope myself:
One must be so careful these days.

Unreal City,
Under the brown fog of a winter dawn,
A crowd flowed over London Bridge, so many,
I had not thought death had undone so many.
Sighs, short and infrequent, were exhaled,
And each man fixed his eyes before his feet.
Flowed up the hill and down King William Street,
To where Saint Mary Woolnoth kept the hours
With a dead sound on the final stroke of nine.
There I saw one I knew, and stopped him, crying "Stetson!
"You who were with me in the ships at Mylae!
"That corpse you planted last year in your garden,
"Has it begun to sprout? Will it bloom this year?
"Or has the sudden frost disturbed its bed?
"Oh keep the Dog far hence, that's friend to men,
"Or with his nails he'll dig it up again!
"You! hypocrite lecteur!—mon semblable,—mon frère!"

READING BREAK!!!

> "Without freedom of thought there can be no such thing as wisdom, and no such thing as public liberty, without freedom of speech."
> —Benjamin Franklin

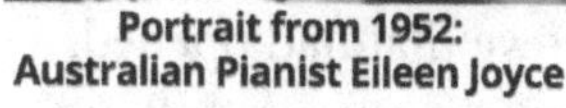

Portrait from 1952: Australian Pianist Eileen Joyce

Want your short story published in *Adventures*?
Email your entire story, with "Submission" in Subject to:
AdventuresBookzine@pm.me

R. RIVETER
AMERICAN ★ HANDMADE

Explore the Books at
flick-it-books.com
Small Independant Publishing House

SUDOKU

				7	8			
						5	6	9
	4			5	6			2
	3			7				
6	2		9		4			
	9		2				1	
						8	4	1
2	8				5			

(Medium Difficulty; Answers in back of book.)

THE FASCINATING STRANGER

BY BOOTH TARKINGTON

MR. GEORGE TUTTLE, reclining at ease in his limousine, opened one eye just enough to perceive that daylight had reached his part of the world, then closed that eye, and murmured languidly. What he said, however, was not, "Home, Parker," or "To the club, Eugene;" this murmur of his was not only languid but plaintive. A tear appeared upon the lower lid of the eye that had opened, for it was a weak and drowsy eye, and after hours of solid darkness the light fretted it. Moreover, the tear, as a greeting to the new day, harmonized perfectly with Mr. Tuttle's murmur, which was so little more than a husky breathing that only an acute ear close by could have caught it: "Oh, Gosh!" Then he turned partly over, shifting his body so as to lie upon his left side among the shavings that made his limousine such a comfortable bedroom.

After thousands of years of wrangling, economists still murder one another to emphasize varying ideas of what constitutes the ownership of anything; and some people (the most emphatic of all) maintain that everybody owns everything, which is obviously the same as saying that nobody owns anything, especially his own right hand. So it may be a little hasty to speak of this limousine, in which Mr. Tuttle lay finishing his night's sleep, as belonging to him in particular; but he was certainly the only person who had the use of it, and no other person in the world believed himself to be its owner. A doubt better founded may rest upon a definition of the word "limousine;" for Mr. Tuttle's limousine was not an automobile; it had no engine, no wheels, no steering-gear; neither had it cushions nor glass; yet Mr. Tuttle thought of it and spoke of it as his limousine, and took some pleasure in such thinking and speaking.

Definitely, it was what is known as a "limousine body" in an extreme but permanent state of incompletion. That is to say, the wooden parts of a "limousine body" had been set up, put together on a "buck," or trestle, and then abandoned with apparently the same abruptness and finality that marked the departure of the Pompeiian baker who hurried out of his bakery and left his bread two thousand years in the oven. So sharply the "post-war industrial depression" had struck the factory, that the workmen seemed to have run for their lives from the place, leaving everything behind them just as it happened to be at the moment of panic. And then, one cold evening, eighteen months afterward, the excavator, Tuttle, having dug within the neighbouring city dump-heap to no profitable result, went to explore the desert spaces where once had been the bustling industries, and found this body of a limousine, just as it had been abandoned by the workmen fleeing from ruin. He furnished it plainly with simple shavings and thus made a home.

His shelter was double, for this little house of his itself stood indoors, under a roof that covered acres. When the watery eye of Mr. Tuttle opened, it beheld a room vaster than any palace hall, and so littered with unaccountable other automobile bodies in embryo that their shapes grew vague and small in the distance. But nothing living was here except himself; what leather had been in the great place was long since devoured, and the rats had departed. A night-watchman, paid by the receiver-in-bankruptcy, walked through the long shops once or twice a night, swinging a flashlight; but he was unaware of the tenant, and usually Mr. Tuttle, in slumber, was unaware of him.

The watery eye, having partly opened and then wholly closed, remained closed for another hour. All round about, inside and outside the great room, there was silence; for beyond these shops there were only other shops and others and others, covering square miles, and all as still as a village midnight. They were as quiet as that every day in the week; but on weekdays the cautious Tuttle usually went out rather early, because sometimes a clerk from the receiver's office dawdled about the place with a notebook. To-day was Sunday; no one would come; so he slept as long as he could.

His reasons were excellent as reasons, though immoral at the source;— that is to say, he should not have had such reasons. He was not well, and sleep is healing; his reasons for sleeping were therefore good: but he should not have been unwell; his indisposition was produced by sin; he had broken the laws of his country and had drunk of illegal liquor, atrocious in quality; his reasons for sleeping were therefore bad. His sleep was not a good sleep.

From time to time little manifestations proved its gross character; he lay among the shavings like a fat grampus basking in sea-foam, and he breathed like one; but sometimes his mouth would be pushed upward in misdirected expansions; his cheeks would distend, and then suddenly collapse, after explosion. Lamentable sounds came from within his corrugated throat, and from deeper tubes; a shoulder now and then jumped suddenly; and his upper ear, long and soiled, frequently twitched enough to move the curl of shaving that lay upon it. For a time one of his legs trembled violently; then of its own free will and without waking him, it bent and straightened repeatedly, using the motions of a leg that is walking and confident that it is going somewhere. Having arrived at its destination, it rested; whereupon its owner shivered, and, thinking he pulled a blanket higher about his shoulders, raked a few more shavings upon him. Finally, he woke, and, still keeping his eyes closed, stroked his beard.

It was about six weeks old and no uncommon ornament with Mr. Tuttle; for usually he wore either a beard or something on the way to become one; he was indifferent which, though he might have taken pride in so much originality in an over-razored age. His round and somewhat oily head, decorated with this beard upon a face a little blurred by puffiness, was a relic; the last survival of a type of head long ago gloriously portrayed and set before a happy public by that adept in the most perishable of the arts, William Hoey. Mr. Tuttle was heavier in body than the blithe comedian's creation, it is true; he was incomparably slower in wit and lower in spirits, yet he might well enough have sat for the portrait of an older brother of Mr. Hoey's masterpiece, "Old Hoss."

Having stroked his beard with a fat and dingy hand, he uttered detached guttural complaints in Elizabethan monosyllables, followed these with sighing noises; then, at the instigation of some abdominal feeling of horror, shuddered excessively, opened his eyes to a startled wideness and abruptly sat up in his bed. To the interior of his bosky ear, just then, was borne the faint religious sound of church bells chiming in a steeple miles away in the centre of the city, and he was not pleased. An expression of disfavour slightly altered the contours of his face; he muttered defiantly, and decided to rise and go forth.

Nothing could have been simpler. The April night had been chilly, and he had worn his shoes; no nightgear had to be exchanged for other garments;—in fact no more was to be done than to step out of the limousine. He did so, taking his greenish and too plastic "Derby" hat with him; and immediately he stood forth upon the factory floor as well equipped to face the public as ever. Thus, except for several safety-pins, glinting too brightly where they might least have been expected, he was a most excellent specimen of the protective coloration exhibited by man; for man has this instinct, undoubtedly. On the bright beaches by the sea, how gaily he conforms is to be noted by the dullest observer; in the autumnal woods man goes dull green and dead leaf brown; and in the smoky city all men, inside and out, are the colour of smoke. Mr. Tuttle stood forth, the colour of the grimy asphalt streets on which he lived; and if at any time he had chosen to rest in a gutter, no extraneous tint would have hinted of his presence.

Not far from him was a faucet over a sink; and he went to it, but not for the purpose of altering his appearance. Lacking more stimulating liquid, it was the inner man that wanted water; and he set his mouth to the faucet, drinking long, but not joyously. Then he went out to the sunshine of that spring morning, with the whole world before him, and his the choice of what to do with it.

He chose to walk toward the middle part of the city, the centre of banking and trade; but he went slowly, his eye wandering over the pavement; and so, before long, he decided to smoke. He was near the great building of the railway station at the time, and, lighting what was now his cigarette (for he had a match of his own) he leaned back against a stone pilaster, smoked and gazed unfavourably upon the taxicabs in the open square before the station.

As he stood thus, easing his weight against the stone and musing, he was hailed by an acquaintance, a tall negro, unusually limber at the knees and naïvely shabby in dress, but of amiable expression and soothing manners.

"How do, Mist' Tuttle," he said genially, in a light tenor voice. "How the worl' treatin' you vese days, Mist' Tuttle? I hope evathing movin' the ri' way to please you nicely."

Mr. Tuttle shook his head. "Yeh!" he returned sarcastically. "Seems like it, don't it! Look at 'em, I jest ast you! *Look* at 'em!"

"Look at who?"

"At them taxicabs," Mr. Tuttle replied, with sudden heat. "That's a nice sight fer decent people to haf to look at!" And he added, with rancour: "On a Sunday, too!"

"Well, you take them taxicabs now," the negro said, mildly argumentative, "an' what hurt they doin' to nobody to jes' look at 'em, Mist' Tuttle? I fine myse'f in some difficulty to git the point of what you was a-settin' you'se'f to point out, Mist' Tuttle. What make you so industrious 'gains' them taxicabs?"

"I'll tell you soon enough," Mr. Tuttle said ominously. "I reckon if they's a man alive in this here world to-day, I'm the one 't can tell you jest exackly what I got against them taxicabs. In the first place, take and look where the United States stood twenty years ago, when they wasn't any o' them things, and then take and look where the United States stands to-day, when it's full of 'em! I don't ast you to take my word fer it; I only ast you to use your own eyes and take and look around you and see where the United States stands to-day and what it's comin' to!"

But the coloured man's perplexity was not dispelled; he pushed back his ancient soft hat in order to assist his brain, but found the organ still unstimulated after adjacent friction, and said plaintively: "I cain' seem to grasp jes' whur you aiminin' at. What you say the United States comin' to?"

"Why, nowhere at all!" Mr. Tuttle replied grimly. "This country's be'n all ruined up. You take and look at what's left of it, and what's the use of it? I jest ast you the one simple question: What's the use of it? Just tell me that, Bojus."

"You got me, Cap'n!" Bojus admitted. "I doe' know what you aiminin' to say 't all! What *do* all them taxicabs do?"

"Do?" his friend repeated hotly. "Wha'd they do? You take and look at this city. You know how many people it's got in it?"

"No, I don't, Mist' Tuttle. Heap of 'em, though!"

"Heap? I sh'd say they was! They's hunderds and hunderds and hunderds o' thousands o' men, women and chuldern in this city; you know that as well as I do, Bojus. Well, with all the hunderds o' thousands o' men, women and chuldern in this city, I ast you, how many livery-stables has this city got in it?"

"Livvy-stables, Mist' Tuttle? Lemme see. I ain't made the observation of no livvy-stable fer long time."

Tuttle shook a soiled forefinger at him severely. "You ain't answered my question. Didn't you hear me? I ast you the simple question: How many livery-stables is they?"

"Well, I ain't *see* none lately; I guess I doe' know, Cap'n."

"Then I'll tell you," said Tuttle fiercely. "They ain't *any*! What's more, I'll bet twenty thousand dollars they ain't five livery-stables left in the whole United States! That's a nice thing, ain't it!"

Bojus looked at him inquiringly, still rather puzzled. "You interust you'se'f in livvy-stables, Mist' Tuttle?"

At this Mr. Tuttle looked deeply annoyed; then he thought better of it and smiled tolerantly. "Listen here," he said. "You listen, my friend, and I'll tell you something 't's worth any man's while to try and understand the this-and-that of it. I grew up in the livery-stable business, and I guess if they's a man alive to-day, why, I know more about the livery-stable business than all the rest the men, women and chuldern in this city put together."

"Yes, suh. You own a livvy-stable one time, Mist' Tuttle?"

"I didn't exackly own one," said the truthful Tuttle, "but that's the business I grew up in. I'm a horse man, and I like to sleep around a horse. I drove a hack for the old B. P. Thomas Livery and Feed Company more than twenty years, off and on;—off and on, I did. I was a horse man all my life and I was in the horse business. I could go anywhere in the United States and I didn't haf to carry no money with me when I travelled; I could go into any town on the map and make all the money I'd care to handle. I'd never go to a boarding-house. What's the use of a hired room and all the useless fixin's in it they stick you fer? No man that's got the gumption of a man wants to waste his money like that when they's a whole nice livery-stable to sleep in. You take some people—women, most likely!—and they git finicky and say it makes you kind of smell. 'Oh, don't come near *me*!' they'll say. Now, what kind of talk is that? You take me, why, I *like* to smell like a horse."

"Yes, suh," said Bojus. "Hoss smell ri' pleasan' smell."

"Well, I should *say* it is!" Mr. Tuttle agreed emphatically. "But you take a taxicab, all you ever git a chance to smell, it's burnt grease and gasoline. Yes, sir, that's what you got to smell of if you run one o' them things. Nice fer a man to carry around on him, ain't it?" He laughed briefly, in bitterness; and continued: "No, sir; the first time I ever laid eyes on one, I hollered, 'Git a horse!' but if you was to holler that at one of 'em to-day, the feller'd prob'ly answer, 'Where'm I goin' to git one?' I ain't seen a horse I'd be willin' to *call* a horse, not fer I don't know how long!"

"No, suh," Bojus assented. "I guess so. Man go look fer good hoss he fine mighty fewness of 'em. I guess automobile put hoss out o' business— an' hoss man, too, Mist' Tuttle."

"Yes, sir, I guess it did! First four five years, when them things come in, why, us men in the livery-stable business, we jest laughed at 'em. Then, by and by, one or two stables begun keepin' a few of 'em to hire. Perty soon after that they all wanted 'em, and a man had to learn to run one of 'em or he was liable to lose his livin'. They kep' gittin' worse and worse—and then, my goodness! didn't even the undertakers go and git 'em? 'Well,' I says, 'I give up! *I* give up!' I says. 'Men in this business that's young enough and ornery enough,' I says, 'why, they can go ahead and learn to run them things. I can git along nice with a horse,' I says. 'A horse knows what you say to him, but I ain't goin' to try and talk to no engine!' "

He paused, frowning, and applied the flame of a match to the half-inch of cigarette that still remained to him. "Them things ought to be throwed in the ocean," he said. "That's what *I'd* do with 'em!"

"You doe' like no automobile?" Bojus inquired. "You take you' enjoyment some way else, I guess, Mist' Tuttle."

"There's jest one simple question I want to ast you," Mr. Tuttle said. "S'pose a man's been drinkin' a little; well, he can git along with a horse all right—like as not a horse'll take him right on back home to the stable—but where's one o' *them* things liable to take him?"

"Jail," Bojus suggested.

"Yes, sir, or right over the bank into some creek, maybe. I don't want nothin' to do with 'em, and that's what I says from the first. I don't want nothin' to do with 'em, I says, and I've stuck to it." Here he was interrupted by a demand upon his attention, for his cigarette had become too short to be held with the fingers; he inhaled a final breath of smoke and tossed the tiny fragment away. "I own one of 'em, though," he said lightly.

At this the eyes of Bojus widened. "You own automobile, Mist' Tuttle?"

"Yes, I got a limousine."

"What!" Bojus cried, and stared the more incredulously. "You got a limousine? Whur you got it?"

"I got it," Mr. Tuttle replied coldly. "That's enough fer me. I got it, but I don't go around in it none."

"What you *do* do with it?"

"I use it," said Tuttle, with an air of reticence. "I got my own use fer it. I don't go showin' off like some men."

Bojus was doubtful, yet somewhat impressed, and his incredulous expression lapsed to a vagueness. "No," he said. "Mighty nice to ride roun' in, though. I doe' know where evabody git all the money. Money ain't come knockin' on Bojus' do' beggin' 'Lemme in, honey!' No, suh; the way money act with me, it act like it think I ain' goin' use it right. Money act like I ain't its lovin' frien'!"

He laughed, and Mr. Tuttle smiled condescendingly. "Money don't amount to so much, Bojus," he said. "Anybody can make money!"

"They *kin*?"

"Why, you take a thousand dollars," said Tuttle; "and you take and put it out at compound interest; jest leave it lay and go on about your business—why, it'll pile up and pile up, you can't stop it. You know how much it'd amount to in twenty-five years? More than a million dollars."

"Whur all that million dolluhs come from?"

"It comes from the poor," said Mr. Tuttle solemnly. "That's the way all them rich men git their money, gougin' the poor."

"Well, suh," Bojus inquired reasonably, "what about me? I like git rich, too. Whur's some poor I kin go gouge? I'm willin' to do the gougin' if I kin git the money."

"Money ain't everything," his friend reminded him. "Some day the people o' this country's goin' to raise and take all that money away from them rich robbers. What *right* they got to it? That's what I want to know. We're goin' to take it and divide it among the people that need it."

Bojus laughed cheerfully. "Tell Bojus when you goin' begin dividin'! *He* be on han'!"

"Why, anybody could have all the money he wants, any time," Tuttle continued, rather inconsistently. "Anybody could."

"How anybody goin' git it?"

"I didn't say anybody *was* goin' to; I said anybody *could*."

"How could?"

"Well, you take me," said Tuttle. "John Rockafeller could drive right up here now, if he wanted to. S'pose he did; s'pose he was to drive right up to that curbstone there and s'pose he was to lean out and say, 'Howdy do, Mr. Tuttle. Git right in and set down, and let's take a drive. Now, how much money would you like me to hand you, Mr. Tuttle?' "

"Hoo-*oo*!" cried Bojus in high pleasure, for the sketch seemed beautiful to him; so he amplified it. " 'How much money you be so kine as to invite me to p'litely han' ovuh to you?' *Hoo!* Jom B. Rockfelluh take an' ast *me*, I tell 'im, 'Well, jes han' me out six, sevvum, eight, nine hunnud dolluhs; that'll do fer *this* week, but you come 'roun' *nex'* Sunday an' ast me same. Don't let me ketch you not comin' roun' every Sunday, now!' *Hoo!* I go Mist' Rockfelluh's house to dinnuh; he say, 'What dish I serve you p'litely, Mist' Bojus?' I say, 'Please pass me that big gol' dish o' money an' a scoop, so's I kin fill my soup-plate!' Hoo-*oo*!" He laughed joyously; and then, with some abruptness descended from these roseate heights and looked upon the actual earth. "I reckon Jom B. Rockfelluh ain' stedyin' about how much money you and me like to use, Mist' Tuttle," he concluded. "He ain' comin' roun' *this* Sunday, nohow!"

"No, and I didn't say he was," Mr. Tuttle protested. "I says he *could*, and you certainly know enough to know he *could*, don't you, Bojus?"

"Well," said Bojus, "whyn't he go on ahead an' do it, then? If he kin do it as well as not, what make him all time decide fer *not*? Res' of us willin'!"

"That's jest the trouble," Tuttle complained, with an air of reproof. "You're willin' but you don't use your brains."

"Brains?" said Bojus, and laughed. "Brains ain' goin' make Bojus no money. What I need is a good lawn-mo'. If I could take an' buy me a nice good lawn-mo', I could make all the money I'm a-goin' a need the live-long summuh."

"Lawn-mower?" his friend inquired. "You ain't got no house and lot, have you? What you want of a lawn-mower?"

"I awready got a rake," Bojus explained. "If I had a lawn-mo' I could make th'ee, fo', fi' dolluhs a day. See that spring sun settin' up there a-gittin' ready to shine so hot? She's goin' to bring up the grass knee-high, honey, 'less somebody take a lawn-mo' an' cut it down. I kin take a lawn-mo' an' walk 'long all vese resident'al streets; git a dozen jobs a day if I kin do 'em. I truly would like to git me a nice good lawn-mo', but I ain' got no money. I got a diamon' ring, though. I give a diamon' ring fer a good lawn-mo'."

"Diamon' ring?" Mr. Tuttle inquired with some interest. "Le'ss see it."

"Gran' big diamon' ring," Bojus said, and held forth his right hand for inspection. Upon the little finger appeared a gem of notable dimensions, for it was a full quarter of an inch in width, but no one could have called it lustrous; it sparkled not at all. Yet its dimness might have been a temporary condition that cleaning would relieve, and what struck Mr. Tuttle most unfavourably was the fact that it was set in a metal of light colour.

"Why, it ain't even gold," he said. "That's a perty pore sample of a diamon' ring I expect, Bojus. Nobody'd want to wear a diamon' ring with the ring part made o' silver. Truth is, I never see no diamon' ring jest made o' silver, before. Where'd you git it?"

"Al Joles."

"Wha'd you give Al Joles fer it?"

"Nothin'," said Bojus, and laughed. "Al Joles, he come to where my cousin Mamie live, las' Feb'uary an 'bo'de with 'er week or so, 'cause he tryin' keep 'way f'm jail. One day he say this city too hot; he got to leave, an' Mamie tuck an' clean up after him an' she foun' this ring in a crack behine the washstan'. Al Joles drop it an' fergit it, I reckon. He had *plenty* rings!"

"I reckon!"

"Al Joles show Mamie fo' watches an' a whole big han'ful o' diamon' pins and rings an' chains. Say he got 'em in Chicago an' he tuck 'em all with him when he lit out. Mamie she say this ring worf fi', six thousan' dolluhs."

"Then what fer'd she take and give it to you, Bojus?"

"She di'n'," said Bojus. "She tuck an' try to sell it to Hillum's secon' han' joolry sto' an' Hillum say he won' bargain fer it 'count its bein' silvuh. So she trade it to me fer a nice watch chain. I like silvuh ring well as gol' ring. 'S the diamon' counts: diamon' worf fi', six thousan' dolluhs, I ain' carin' what jes' the *ring* part is."

"Well, it's right perty," Tuttle observed, glancing at it with some favour. "I don't hardly expect you could trade it fer no lawn-mower, though. I expect ——" But at this moment a symptom of his indisposition interrupted his remarks. A slight internal convulsion caused him to shudder heavily; he fanned his suddenly bedewed forehead with his hat, and seemed to eat an impalpable but distasteful food.

"You feel sick, Mist' Tuttle?" Bojus inquired sympathetically, for his companion's appearance was a little disquieting. "You feel bad?"

"Well, I do," Tuttle admitted feebly. "I eat a hambone yestiddy that up and disagreed on me. I ain't be'n feelin' none too well all morning, if the truth must be told. The fact is, what I need right now—and I need it right bad," he added—"it's a little liquor."

"Yes, suh; I guess so," his friend agreed. "That's somep'n ain' goin' hurt nobody. I be willin' use a little myse'f."

"You know where any is?"

"Don't I!" the negro exclaimed. "I know whur plenty *is*, but the trouble is: How you an' me goin' git it?"

"Where is it?"

"Ri' dow' my cousin Mamie' celluh. My cousin Mamie' celluh plum full o' Whi' Mule. Man say he goin' buy it off her but ain' show up with no money. Early 's mawn' I say, 'Mamie, gi' me little nice smell o' you' nice whisky?' No, suh! Take an' fretten me with a brade-knife! Mad 'cause man ain' paid 'er, I reckon."

"Le'ss go on up there and ast her again," Tuttle suggested. "She might be feelin' in a nicer temper by this time. Me bein' sick, and it's Sunday and all, why, she ought to show some decency about it. Anyways, it wouldn't hurt anything to jest try."

"No, suh, tha's so, Mist' Tuttle," the negro agreed with ready hopefulness. "If she say no, she say no; but if she say yes, we all fix fine! Le'ss go!"

They went up the street, walking rather slowly, as Mr. Tuttle, though eager, found his indisposition increased with any rapidity of movement; then they turned down an alley, followed it to another alley, and at the intersection of that with another, entered a smoke-coloured cottage of small pretensions, though it still displayed in a front window the card of a Red Cross subscriber to the "drive" of 1918.

"Mamie!" Bojus called, when they had closed the door behind them. "Mamie!"

Then, as they heard the response to this call, both of them had the warming sense of sunshine rushing over them: the world grew light and bright and they perceived that luck did not always run against worthy people. Mamie's answer was not in words, yet it was a vocal sound and human: somewhere within her something quickened to the call and endeavoured to speak. Silently they opened the door of her bedroom and looked upon her where she reposed.

She had consoled herself for her disappointment; she was peaceful indeed; and the callers at once understood that for several hours, at least, she could deny them nothing they would ask. They paused but a moment to gaze, and then, without a word of comment upon their incredible good fortune, they exchanged a single hurried glance, and forthwith descended to the cellar.

An hour later they were singing there, in that cool dimness. They sang of romantic love, of maternal sacrifices, of friendship; and this last theme held them longest, for Tuttle prevailed upon his companion to join him many, many times in a nineteenth century tribute to brotherly affection. With their hands resting fondly upon each other's shoulders, they sang over and over:

Comrades, comrades, *ev*-er since we was boys,
Sharing each other's sorrows, sharing each other's joys,
Comrades when manhood was *daw*-ning —

Our own, our native land, somewhat generally lawless in mood of late, has produced few illegal commodities more effective than the ferocious liquid rich in fusel oil and known as White Mule. Given out of the imaginative heart of a race that has a genius for naming things, this perfect name tells everything of the pale liquor it so precisely labels. The silence of the mule is there, the sinister inertia of his apparent complete placidity as he stands in an interval of seeming patience;—for this is the liquor as it rests in the bottle. And the mule's sudden utter violence is there, with a hospital cot as a never-remote contingency for those who misunderstand.

Over-confidence in himself was not a failing of the experienced Tuttle; and he well knew the potencies of the volcanic stuff with which he dealt. His sincere desire was but to rid himself of the indisposition and nervousness that depressed him, and he indulged himself to-day with a lighter hand than usual. He wished to be at ease in body and mind, to be happy and to remain happy; therefore he stopped at the convivial, checking himself firmly, and took a little water. Not so the less calculating Bojus who had nothing of the epicure about him. Half an hour after the two friends had begun to sing "Comrades," Bojus became unmusical in execution, though his impression was that he still sang; and a little later Mr. Tuttle found himself alone, so far as song, conversation and companionship were concerned. Bojus still lived, but had no animation.

His more cautious friend, on the contrary, felt life freshening within him; his physical uncertainties had disappeared from his active consciousness; he was a new man, and said so. "Hah!" he said with great satisfaction and in a much stronger voice than he had dared to use earlier in the day. "I'm a new man!" And he slapped himself on the chest, repeatedly. Optimism came to him; he began to believe that he was at the end of all his troubles, and he decided to return to the fresh air, the sunshine and an interesting world. "Le'ss git outdoors and see what all's goin' *on!*" he said heartily.

But first he took some precautions for the sake of friendship. Fearing that all might not go well with Bojus if Mamie were the first to be stirring and happened to look into her cellar, he went to the top of the stairs and locked the door there upon the inside. Then he came down again and once more proved his moderation by placing only one flask of Mamie's distillation in his pocket. He could have taken much more if he wished, but he sometimes knew when to say no. In fact, he now said it aloud and praised himself a little. "No! No, sir!" he said to some applicant within him. "I know what's good fer you and what ain't. If you take any more you're liable to go make a hog of yourself again. Why, jest look how you felt when you woke up this morning! I'm the man that knows and I'm perty smart, too, if you ever happen to notice! You take and let well enough alone."

He gave a last glance at Bojus, a glance that lingered with some interest upon the peculiar diamond ring; but he decided not to carry it away with him, because Bojus might be overwhelmingly suspicious later. "No, sir," he said. "You come along now and let well enough alone. We want to git out and see what's goin' on all over town!"

The inward pleader consented, he placed a box against the wall, mounted it and showed a fine persistence in overcoming what appeared to be impossibilities as he contrived to wriggle himself through a window narrower than he was. Then, emerging worm-like upon a dirty brick path beside the cottage, he arose brightly and went forth from that quarter of the city.

It suited his new mood to associate himself now with all that was most brilliant and prosperous; and so, at a briskish saunter he walked those streets where stood fine houses in brave lawns. It was now an hour and more after noon, the air was lively yet temperate in the sunshine, and the wealth he saw in calm display about him invigorated him. Shining cars passed by, proud ladies at ease within them; rich little children played about neat nursemaids as they strolled the cement pavements; haughty young men strode along, flashing their walking-sticks; noble big dogs with sparkling collars galloped over the bright grass under tall trees; and with all of this, Tuttle now felt himself congenial, and even intimate. Moreover, he had the conviction that some charming and dramatic adventure was about to befall him; it seemed to be just ahead.

The precise nature of this adventure remained indefinite in his imagination for a time, but gradually the thought of eating (abhorrent to him earlier in the day) again became pleasant, and he sketched some little scenes climaxing in banquets. "One these here millionaires could do it easy as not," he said, speaking only in fancy and not vocally. "One of 'em might jest as well as not look out his big window, see me, and come down his walk and say, 'Step right in, Mr. Tuttle. We got quite a dinner-party to-day, but they's always room fer you, Mr. Tuttle. Now what'd you like to have to eat? Liver and chili and baked beans and ham and eggs and a couple of ice-cold muskmelons? We can open three or four cans o' sardines fer you, too, if you'd like to have 'em. You only got to say the word, Mr. Tuttle.' "

He began to regret Bojus's diamond ring a little; perhaps he could have traded it for a can of sardines at a negro restaurant he knew; but the regret was a slight one; he worried himself little about obtaining food, for people will always give it. However, he did not ask for it among the millionaires, whose servants are sometimes cold-hearted; but turned into an unpretentious cross-street and walked a little more slowly, estimating the houses. He had not gone far when he began to smell his dinner.

The odour came from the open front door of a neat white frame house in a yard of fair size; and here, near the steps of the small veranda, a man of sixty and his wife were discussing the progress of a row of tulips about to bloom. Their clothes new-looking, decorous and worn with a little unfamiliarity, told everybody that this man and his wife had been to church; that they dined at two o'clock on Sunday, owned their house, owned a burial lot in the cemetery, paid their bills, and had something comfortable in a safety deposit box. Tuttle immediately walked into the yard, took off his hat and addressed the wife.

"Lady," he said, in a voice hoarser from too much singing than he would have liked to make it, "Lady, I be'n out o' work fer some time back. I took sick, too, and I be'n in the hospital. What I reely wish to ast fer is work, but the state of unemployment in this city is awful bad. I don't ast fer no money; all I want is a chance to work."

"On Sunday?" she said reprovingly. "Of course there isn't any work on Sunday."

Tuttle stepped a little closer to her—a mistake—and looked appealing. "Then how'm I a-goin' to git no nourishment?" he asked. "If you can't give me no work, I ain't eat nothin' at all since day before yestiddy and I'd be truly thankful if you felt you could spare me a little nourishment."

But she moved back from him, her nostrils dilating slightly and her expression unfavourable. "I'd be glad to give you all you want to eat," she said coldly, "but I think you'd better sign the pledge first."

"Ma'am?" said Tuttle in plaintive astonishment.

"I think you've been drinking."

"No, lady! No!"

"I'm sure you have. I don't believe in doing anything for people that drink; it doesn't do them any good."

"Lady —" Tuttle began, and he was about to continue his protest to her, when her husband interfered.

"Run along!" he said, and tossed the applicant for nourishment a dime.

Tuttle looked sadly at the little round disk of silver as it lay shining in his asphalt coloured palm; then he looked at the donor and murmured: "I ast fer bread—and they give me a stone!"

"Go along!" said the man.

Tuttle went slowly, seeming to be bowed in thoughtful melancholy; he went the more reluctantly because there was a hint of fried chicken on the air; and before he reached the pavement a buxom fair woman, readily guessed to be of Scandinavian descent, appeared in the doorway. "Dinner's served, Mrs. Pinney," she called briskly.

Tuttle turned and looked at Mrs. Pinney with eloquence, but she shook her head disapprovingly. "You ought to sign the pledge!" she said.

"Yes, lady," he said, and abruptly turned away. He walked out into the street, where a trolley car at that moment happened to stop for another passenger, jumped on the step, waved his hand cordially, and continued to wave it as the car went down the street.

"Well of *all*!" Mrs. Pinney exclaimed, dumfounded, but her husband laughed aloud.

"That's a good one!" he said. "Begged for 'nourishment' and when I gave him a dime went off for a street-car ride! Come on in to dinner, ma; I guess he's passed out of our lives!"

Nothing was further from Mr. Tuttle's purpose, however; and Mr. and Mrs. Pinney had not finished their dinner, half an hour later, when he pushed the bell-button in their small vestibule, and the buxom woman opened the door, but not invitingly, for she made the aperture a narrow one when she saw who stood before her.

"Howdydo," he said affably. "Ole lady still here, isn't she?"

"What you want?" the woman inquired.

"Jest ast her to look this over," he said, and proffered a small paper-bound Bible, open, with a card between the leaves. "I'll wait here," he added serenely, as she closed the door.

She took the Bible to the dining-room, and handed it to Mrs. Pinney, remarking, "That tramp's back. He says to give you this. He's waitin'."

The Bible was marked with a rubber stamp: "Presented by Door of Hope Rescue Mission 337 South Maryland Street," and the card was a solemn oath and pledge to refrain from intoxicants, thenceforth and forever. It was dated that day, and signed, in ink still almost wet, "Arthur T. De Morris."

Mrs. Pinney stared at the pledge, at first frowningly, then with a tendency toward a slight emotion; and without speaking she passed it to her husband for inspection, whereupon he became incredulous enough to laugh.

"That's about the suddenest conversion on record, I guess!" he said. "Used the dime to get down to the Door of Hope and back before our dinner was over. It beats all!"

"You don't think it could be genuine, Henry?"

"Well, no; not in twenty minutes."

"It *could* be—just possibly," she said gently. "We never know when the right word *may* touch some poor fellow's heart."

"Now, ma," he remonstrated, "don't you go and get one of your spells of religious vanity. That was about as tough an old soak as I ever saw, and I'm afraid it'll take more than one of your 'right words' to convert him."

"Still —" she said, and a gentle pride showed in her expression. "We can't tell. It seems a little quick, of course, but he may have been just at the spiritual point for the right word to reach him. Anyhow, he did go right away and get a pledge and sign it—and got a Bible, too. It might be—I don't say it probably is, but it just might be the beginning of a new life for him, and it wouldn't be right to discourage him. Besides he must really be hungry: he's proved that, anyhow." She turned to the woman in waiting. "Give him back the Bible and his card, Tilly," she said, "and take him out in the kitchen and let him have all he wants to eat. Tell him to wait when he gets through; and you let me know; I'll come and talk to him. His name's Mr. De Morris, Tilly, when you speak to him."

Tilly's expression was not enthusiastic, but she obeyed the order, conducted the convert to the kitchen and set excellent food before him in great plenty; whereupon Mr. Tuttle, being not without gallantry, put his hat on the floor beside his chair, and thanked her warmly before he sat down. His appetite was now vigorous, and at first he gave all his attention to the fried chicken, but before long he began to glance appreciatively, now and then, at the handmaiden who had served him. She was a well-shaped blonde person of thirty-five or so, tall, comely, reliable looking, visibly energetic, and, like her kitchen, incredibly clean. His glances failed to interest her, if she took note of them; and presently she made evident her sense of a social gulf. She prepared a plate for herself, placed it upon a table across the room from him and sat there, with her profile toward him, apparently unconscious of his presence.

"Plenty room at my table," he suggested hospitably. "*I* jest as soon you eat over here."

"No," she said discouragingly.

Not abashed, but diplomatic, he was silent for a time, then he inquired casually, "Do all the work here?"

"Yep."

"Well, well," he said. "You look too young fer sech a rough job. Don't they have nobody 'tend the furnace and cut the grass?"

"Did," said Tilly. "Died last week."

"Well, ain't that too bad! Nice pleasant feller was he?"

"Coloured man," said Tilly.

"You Swedish?" Tuttle inquired.

"No. My folks was."

"Well sir, that's funny," Tuttle said genially, "I knowed they was *some*p'n Swedish about you, because I always did like Swedish people. I don't know why, but I always did taken a kind o' likin' to Swedish people, and Swedish people always taken kind of a likin' to me. My ways always seem to suit Swedish people—after we git well acquainted I mean. The better Swedish people git acquainted with me the more they always seem to taken a likin' to me. I ast a Swedish man oncet why it was he taken sech a likin' to me and he says it was my ways. 'It's jest your ways, George,' he says. 'It's because Swedish people like them ways you got, George,' he says." Here Tuttle laughed deprecatingly and added, "I guess he must 'a' be'n right, though."

Tilly made no response; she did not even glance at him, but continued gravely to eat her dinner. Then, presently, she said, without any emphasis: "I thought your name was Arthur."

"What?"

"That pledge you signed," Tilly said, still not looking at him, but going on with her dinner;—"ain't it signed Arthur T. De Morris?"

For the moment Mr. Tuttle was a little demoralized, but he recovered himself, coughed, and explained. "Yes, that's my *name*," he said. "But you take the name George, now, it's more kind of a nickname I have when anybody gits real well acquainted with me like this Swedish man I was tellin' you about; and besides that, it was up in *Dee*-troit. Most everybody I knowed up in *Dee*-troit, they most always called me George fer a nickname like. You know anybody in *Dee*-troit?"

"No."

"Married?" Tuttle inquired.

"No."

"Never be'n?" he said.

"No."

"Well, now, that's too bad," he said sympathetically. "It ain't the right way to live. I'm a widower myself, and I ain't never be'n the same man since I lost my first wife. She was an Irish lady from Chicago." He sighed; finished the slice of lemon pie Tilly had given him, and drank what was left of his large cup of coffee, holding the protruding spoon between two fingers to keep it out of his eye. He set the cup down, gazed upon it with melancholy, then looked again at the unresponsive Tilly.

She had charm for him; and his expression, not wholly lacking a kind of wistfulness, left no doubt of it. No doubt, too, there fluttered a wing of fancy somewhere in his head: some picture of what might-have-been trembled across his mind's-eye's field of vision. For an instant he may have imagined a fireside, with such a competent fair creature upon one side of it, himself on the other, and merry children on the hearth-rug between. Certainly he had a moment of sentiment and sweet longing.

"You ever think about gittin' married again?" he said, rather unfortunately.

"I told you I ain't been married."

"Excuse *me*!" he hastened to say. "I was thinkin' about myself. I mean when I says 'again' I was thinkin' about myself. I mean I was astin' you: You think about gittin' married at all?"

"No."

"I s'pose not," he assented regretfully; and added in a gentle tone: "Well, you're a mighty fine-lookin' woman; I never see no better build than what you got on you."

Tilly went out and came back with Mrs. Pinney, who mystified him with her first words. "Well, De Morris?" she said.

"What?" he returned blankly, then luckily remembered, and said, "Oh, yes, ma'am?"

"I *hope* you meant it when you signed that pledge, De Morris."

"Why, lady, of course I did," he assured her warmly. "If the truth must be told, I don't never drink hardly at all, anyways. Now we got prohibition you take a poor man out o' work, why where's *he* goin' to git any liquor, lady? It's only rich people that's usually able to git any reel good stew on, these days, if I'm allowable to used the expression, so to speak. But that's the unfairness of it, and it makes poor people ready to break out most anytime. Not that it concerns me, because I put all that behind me when I signed the pledge like you told me to. If the truth must be told, I was goin' to sign the pledge some time back, but I kep' kind o' puttin' it off. Well, lady, it's done now, and I'm thankful fer it."

"I do hope so, I'm sure," Mrs. Pinney said earnestly. "And I want to help you; I'll be glad to. You said you wanted some work."

"Yes'm," he said promptly, and if apprehension rose within him he kept it from appearing upon the surface. Behind Mrs. Pinney stood Tilly, looking straight at him with a frigid skepticism of which he was fully conscious. "Yes'm. Any honest work I can turn my hand to, that's all I ast of anybody. I'd be glad to help wash the dishes if it's what you had in your mind, lady."

"No. But if you'll come back to-morrow morning about nine or ten o'clock, I'll give you two dollars for cutting the grass. It isn't a *very* large yard, and you can get through by evening."

"I ain't got no lawn-mower, lady."

"We have one in the cellar," said Mrs. Pinney. "If you come back, Tilly'll have it on the back porch for you. That's all to-day, De Morris."

"All right, lady. I thank you for your hospitillity and I'll be back in the morning," he said, and as he turned toward the door he glanced aside at Tilly and saw that her mouth quivered into the shape of a slight smile—a knowing smile. "I will!" he said defiantly. "I'll be back here at ten o'clock to-morrow morning. You'll see!"

But when the door closed behind him, Tilly laughed aloud—and was at once reproved by her mistress. "We always ought to have faith that the better side of people will conquer, Tilly. I really think he'll come."

"Yes'm, like that last one 't said he was comin' back, and stole the knife and fork he ate with," said Tilly, laughing again.

"But this one didn't steal anything."

"No'm, but he'll never come back, to *work*," said Tilly. "He said 'You'll see,' and you will, but you won't see *him*!"

They had a mild argument upon the point, and then Mrs. Pinney returned to her husband, who was waiting for her to put on her Sunday wrap and hat, and go with him to spend their weekly afternoon among the babies at their son's house. She found her husband to be strongly of Tilly's opinion, and when they came home that evening, she renewed the argument with both of them; so that this mild and orderly little household was slightly disturbed (a most uncommon thing in its even life) over the question of the vagrant's return. Thus, Mrs. Pinney prepared a little triumph for herself;—at ten o'clock the next morning Tuttle opened the door of Tilly's bright kitchen and inquired:

"Where's that lawn-mower?"

He was there. He had defeated the skeptic and proved himself a worthy man, but at a price; for again he was far from well, and every movement he made increased well-founded inward doubts of his constitution. Unfortunately, he had taken his flask of White Mule to bed with him in his limousine, and in that comfortable security moderation had seemed useless to the verge of absurdity. The point of knowing when to say no rests in the "when;" and when a man is already at home and safe in bed, "Why, my Glory!" he had reasoned it, "Why, if they ever *is* a time to say yes, it must be then!" So he had said "Yes," to the White Mule and in the morning awoke feeling most perishable. Even then, as in the night, from time to time he had vagrant thoughts of Tilly and her noble build, of the white and shining kitchen, and of those disbelieving cool blue eyes that seemed to triumph over him and indict him, accusing him of things she appeared to think he would do if he had the chance. There was something in her look that provoked him, as if she would stir his conscience, and though his conscience disturbed him no more than a baby's disturbs a baby, he was indeed somewhat disquieted by that cold look of hers. And so, when he had collected his mind a little, upon waking, he muttered feebly. "I'll show her!" Something strange and forgotten worked faintly within him, fluttered a little; and so, walking carefully, he kept his word and came to her door.

She looked at him in a startled way. Unquestionably he caused her to feel something like an emotion, and she said not a word, but went straightway and brought him the lawn-mower. He looked in her eyes as he took it from her hand.

"You thought I wouldn't come," he said.

"Yes," she admitted gravely.

"Well," he said, and smiled affably, "you certainly got a fine build on you!" And with that, pushing the lawn-mower before him, he went out to his work, leaving her visibly not offended.

"You showed her!" he said to himself.

In the yard he looked thoughtfully upon the grass, which was rather long and had not been cut since the spring had enlivened it to a new growing. The lot seemed longer than it had the day before; he saw that it must be two hundred feet from the street on which it fronted to the alley in the rear; it was a hundred feet wide, at least, and except for the area occupied by the house, which was of modest proportions, all of this was grass. He sighed profoundly: "Oh, Gosh!" he mourned. But he meant to do the work, and began it manfully.

With the mower rolling before him, reversed, the knives upward, he went to the extreme front of the lot, turned the machine over, and, surveying the prospect, decided to attack the lawn with long straight swathes, running from the front clear through to the alley—though, even before he began, the alley seemed far, far away. However, he turned up the sleeves of his ancient coat an inch or two, and went at his task with a good heart. That is to say, he started with a good heart, but the lawn-mower was neither new nor sharp; the grass was tough, the sun hot, and his sense of unwellness formidable. When he had gone ten feet, he paused, wiped his forehead with a sleeve, and leaned upon the handle of the mower in an attitude not devoid of pathos. But he was yet determined; he thought of the blue eyes in the kitchen and resolved that they should not grow scornful again. Once more he set the mower in motion.

Mrs. Pinney heard the sound of it in her room upstairs, looked from the window, and with earnest pleasure beheld the workman at his toil. Her heart rejoiced her to have been the cause of a reformation, and presently she went down to the kitchen to gloat gently over a defeated antagonist in argument.

"Yes'm," Tilly admitted meekly. "He fooled me."

"You see I was right, Tilly. We always ought to have faith that the best part of our natures will conquer."

"Yes'm; it looks so."

"Have we some buttermilk in the refrigerator, Tilly?"

"Yes'm."

"Then I think you might have some ready for him, if he gets too hot. I don't think he looks very well and you might ask him if he'd like some. You might ask him now, Tilly."

"Now?" Tilly asked, and coloured a little. "You mean right now, Mrs. Pinney?"

"Yes. It might do him good and help keep him strong for his work."

"All right," Tilly said, and turned toward the ice-box; but at a thought she paused. "I don't hear the lawn-mower," she said. "It seems to me I ain't heard it since we began talking."

"Perhaps he's resting," Mrs. Pinney suggested, but her voice trembled a little with foreboding. "We might just go out and see."

They went out and saw. Down the full length of the yard, from the street to the alley, there was one long swathe of mowed grass; and but one, though it was perfect. Particularly as the trail of a fugitive it was perfect, and led straight to the alley, which, being paved with brick, offered to the searchers the complete bafflement of a creek to the bloodhound. A brick alley shows no trace of a reversed lawn-mower hurrying over it—yet nothing was clearer than that such a hurrying must have taken place. For Arthur T. De Morris was gone, and so was the lawn-mower.

"Mr. Pinney'll laugh at me I guess, too!" Mrs. Pinney said, swallowing, as she stood with Tilly, staring at the complete vacancy of the brick alley.

"Yes'm, he will," said Tilly, and laughed again, a little harshly.

THE FUGITIVE, ALREADY SOME BLOCKS DISTANT, PROPELLED THE RAVISHED mower before him, and went so openly through the streets in the likeness of an honest toiler seeking lawns to mow that he had to pause and decline several offers, on his hurried way. He took note of these opportunities, however, remembering the friend he was on his way to see, and, after some difficulty, finding him in a negro pool-room, proffered him the lawn-mower in exchange for five dollars, spot cash.

"I ain' got it," replied Bojus, flaccid upon a bench. "I ain' feelin' like cuttin' nobody's grass to-day, nohow, an' besides I'm goin' stay right here till coas' clear. Mamie ain' foun' out who make all her trouble, 'cause I clim' out the window whiles she was engage' kickin' on celluh do'; but neighbours say she mighty s'picious who 'twas. I don' need no lawn-mo' in a pool-room."

"Well, you ain't goin' to stay in no pool-room forever; you got to git out and earn your livin' some time," Tuttle urged him. "Every man that's got the gumption of a man, he's got to do that!" And upon Bojus's lifeless admission of the truth of this statement, the bargaining began. It ended with Bojus's becoming the proprietor of the lawn-mower and Tuttle's leaving the pool-room after taking possession of everything in the world that Bojus owned except a hat, a coat, a pair of trousers, a shirt, two old shoes and four safety-pins. The spoil consisted of seventy-eight cents in money, half of a package of bent cigarettes, a pair of dice, a "mouth-organ" and the peculiar diamond ring.

This latter Mr. Tuttle placed upon his little finger, and as he walked along he regarded it with some pleasure; but he decided to part with it, and carried it to a pawn-shop he knew, having had some acquaintance with the proprietor in happier days.

He entered the place with a polite air, removing his hat and bowing, for the shop was a prosperous one.

"Golly!" said the proprietor, who happened to be behind a counter, instructing a new clerk. "I believe it's old George the hackman."

"That's who, Mr. Breitman," Tuttle responded. "Many's the cold night I yousta drive you all over town and —"

"Never mind, George," the pawnbroker interrupted crisply. "You payin' me just a social call, or you got some business you want to do?"

"Business," said Tuttle. "If the truth must be told, Mr. Breitman, I got a diamon' ring worth somewheres along about five or six thousand dollars, I don't know which."

Breitman laughed, "Oh, you got a ring worth either five or six thousand, you don't know which, and you come in to ask me to settle it. Is that it?"

"Yes. I don't want to hock her; I jest want to git a notion if I ever do decide to sell her." He set the ring upon the glass counter before Breitman. "Ain't she a beauty?"

Breitman glanced at the ring and laughed, upon which the owner hastily protested: "Oh, I know the ring part ain't gold: you needn't think I don't know that much! It's the diamon' I'm talkin' about. Jest set your eye on her."

The pawnbroker set his eye on her—that is, he put on a pair of spectacles, picked up the ring and looked at it carelessly, but after his first glance his expression became more attentive. "So you say I needn't think you don't know the 'ring part' ain't gold, George? So you knew it was platinum, did you?"

"Of course, I knowed it was plapmun," Tuttle said promptly, rising to the occasion, though he had never before heard of this metal. "I reckon I know plapmun when I see it."

"I think it's worth about ten or twelve dollars," Breitman said. "I'll give you twelve if you want to sell it."

Eager acceptance rushed to Tuttle's lips, but hung there unspoken as caution checked him. He drew a deep breath and said huskily, "Why, you can't fool me on this here ring, Mr. Breitman. I ain't worryin' about what I can git fer the plapmun part; all I want to know is how much I ought ast fer the diamon'. I ain't fixin' to sell it to you; I'm fixin' to sell it to somebody else."

"Oh, so that's it," said Breitman, still looking at the ring. "Where'd you get it?"

Tuttle laughed ingratiatingly. "It's kind of funny," he said, "how I got that ring. Yet it's all open and above-board, too. If the truth must be told, it belonged to a lady-cousin o' mine in Auburndale, Wisconsin, and her aunt-by-marriage left it to her. Well, this here lady-cousin o' mine, I was visitin' her last summer, and she found I had a good claim on the house and lot she was livin' in, account of my never havin' knowed that my grandfather—he was her grandfather, too—well, he never left no will, and this house and lot come down to her, but I never made no claim on it because I thought it had be'n willed to her till I found out it hadn't, when I went up there. Well, the long and short of it come out like this: the house and lot's worth about nine or ten thousand dollars, but she didn't have no money, so she handed me over this ring to settle my claim. Name's Mrs. Moscoe, Mrs. Wilbur N. Moscoe, three-thirty-two South Liberty Street, Auburndale, Wisconsin."

"I see," Breitman said absently. "Just wait here a minute, George; I ain't going to steal it." And, taking the ring with him, he went into a room behind the shop, remaining there closeted long enough for Tuttle to grow a little uneasy.

"Hay!" he called. "You ain't tryin' to eat that plapmun ring are you, Mr. Breitman?"

Breitman appeared in the doorway. There was a glow in his eyes, and although he concealed all other traces of a considerable excitement, somehow Tuttle caught a vibration out of the air, and began to feel the presence of Fortune. "Step in here and sit down, George," the pawnbroker said. "I wanted to look at this stone a little closer, and of course I had to go over my lists and see if it was on any of 'em."

"What lists?" Tuttle asked as he took a chair.

"From the police. Stolen goods."

"Looky here! I told you how that ring come to me. My cousin ain't no crook. Her name's Mrs. Wilbur N. Moscoe, South Liberty Street, Auburnd —"

"Never mind," Breitman interrupted. "*I* ain't sayin' it ain't so. Anyway, this ring ain't on any of the lists and —"

"I should say it ain't!"

"Well, don't get excited. Now look here, George"—Breitman seated himself close to his client and spoke in a confidential tone—"George, you know I always took a kind of interest in you, and I want to tell you what you need. You ought to go get yourself all fixed up. You ought to go to a barber's and get your hair cut and your whiskers trimmed. Don't go to no cheap barber's; go to a good one, and tell 'em to fix your whiskers so's you'll have a Van Dyke —"

"A what?"

"A Van Dyke beard. It's swell," said Breitman. "Then you go get you a fine pearl-gray Fedora hat, with a black band around it, and a light overcoat, and some gray gloves with black stitching, and a nice cane and a nobby suit o' clo'es and some fancy top shoes —"

"Listen here!" Tuttle said hoarsely, and he set a shaking hand on the other's knee, "how much you willin' to bid on my plapmun ring?"

"Don't go so fast!" Breitman said, but his eyes were becoming more and more luminous. He had the hope of a great bargain; yet feared that Tuttle might have a fairly accurate idea of the value of the diamond. "Hold your hosses a little, George! You don't need so awful much to go and get yourself fixed up like I'm tellin' you, and you'll have a lot o' money left to go around and see high life with. I'll send right over to the bank and let you have it in cash, too, if you meet my views."

"How much?" Tuttle gasped. "How much?"

Breitman looked at him shrewdly. "Well, I'm takin' chances: the market on stones is awful down these days, George. Your cousin must have fooled you *bad* when she talked about four or five thousand dollars! That's ridiculous!"

"How *much*?"

"Well, I'll say!—I'll say seven hundred and fifty dollars."

Tuttle's head swam. "Yes!" he gasped.

No doubt as he began that greatest period in his whole career, half an hour later, he thought seriously of a pair of blue eyes in a white kitchen;—seven hundred and fifty dollars, with a competent Swedish wife to take care of it and perhaps set up a little shop that would keep her husband out of mischief and busy — But there the thought stopped short and his expression became one of disillusion: the idea of orderliness and energy and profit was not appetizing. He had seven hundred and fifty dollars in his pocket; and Tuttle knew what romance could come to him instantly at the bidding of this illimitable cash: he knew where the big crap games were; he knew where the gay flats and lively ladies were; he knew where the fine liquor gurgled—not White Mule; he knew how to find the lights, the lights and the music!

Forthwith he approached that imperial orgy of one heaped and glorious week, all of high-lights, that summit of his life to be remembered with never-failing pride when he went back, after it was all over, to his limousine and the shavings.

It was glorious straight through to the end, and the end was its perfect climax: the most dazzling memory of all. He forgave automobiles, on that last day, and in the afternoon he hired a splendid, red new open car, with a curly-haired chauffeur to drive it. Then driving to a large hardware store he spent eighteen dollars, out of his final fifty, upon the best lawn-mower the store could offer him. He had it placed in the car and drove away, smoking a long cigar in a long holder. Such was his remarkable whim; and it marks him as an extraordinary man.

That nothing might be lacking, his destiny arranged that Mrs. Pinney was superintending Tilly in the elimination of dandelions from the front yard when the glittering equipage, to their surprise, stopped at the gate. Seated beside the lawn-mower in the tonneau they beheld a superb stranger, portly and of notable presence. His pearl-gray hat sat amiably upon his head; the sleeves of his fawn-coloured overcoat ran pleasantly down to pearl gloves; his Van Dyke beard, a little grizzled, conveyed an impression of distinction not contradicted by a bagginess of the eyelids; for it is strangely true that dissipation sometimes even adds distinction to certain types of faces. All in all, here was a man who might have recalled to a student of courts some aroma of the entourage of the late King Edward at Hombourg. There was just that about him.

He alighted slowly—he might well have been credited with the gout— and entering the yard, approached with a courteous air, being followed by the chauffeur, who brought the lawn-mower.

"Good afternoon, lady and Tilly," he said, in a voice unfortunately hoarse; and he removed his pearl-gray hat with a dignified gesture.

They stared incredulously, not believing their eyes.

"I had a little trouble with your lawn-mower, so I up and got it fixed," he said. "It's the same one. I took and got it painted up some."

"Oh, me!" Tilly said, in a whisper. "Oh, me!" And she put her hand to her heart.

He perceived that he dazzled her; that she felt deeply; and almost he wished, just for this moment, to be sober. He was not—profoundly not—

yet he maintained his dignity and his balance throughout the interview. "I thought you might need it again some day," he said.

"Mis-ter De *Mor*-ris!" Mrs. Pinney cried, in awed recognition. "Why, what on earth —"

"Nothin'," he returned lightly. "Nothin' at all." He waved his hand to the car. "One o' my little automobiles," he said.

With that he turned, and, preceded by the chauffeur, walked down the path to the gate. Putting his whole mind upon it, he contrived to walk without wavering; and at the gate, he paused and looked wistfully back at Tilly. "You certainly got a good build on you," he said.

Then beautifully and romantically he concluded this magnificent gesture—this unsolvable mystery story that the Pinneys' very grandchildren were to tell in after years, and that kept Tilly a maiden for many months in the hope of the miraculous stranger's return—at least to tell her who and what he was!

He climbed into the car, placed the long holder of the long cigar in his mouth, and, as the silent wheels began to turn, he took off his hat again and waved it to them graciously.

"I kept the pledge!" he said.

We think you'll enjoy this reimagining of a classic character.

THE END

WHO IS ROCKY FORTUNE?

Fictional characters who never truly "die" are a rarity. To gain immortality, one needs to be in a classic story that never gets forgotten (Hamlet, for example), or to be so memorable that they're constantly being reinvented (Sherlock Holmes, for example). But so many others fade into obscurity, often perhaps to our detriment.

Author Evan Purcell (son of Darryle Purcell, ADV author and contributor), is doing his part to keep one old, great character alive. In the following story, Rocky Fortune is officially resurrected.

Rocky was a character on an NBC radio show called "Rocky Fortune," that ran from 1953-1954. Voiced for the airwaves by the legendary Frank Sinatra, Rocky was a "footloose and fancy-free young gentleman" who did odd jobs for "the Agency". His exploits, which found him capturing criminals and rescuing damsels in distress, entertained America for only 25 episodes. His wit and charm, however, made an indelible mark on pop culture.

Now, Evan Purcell revives Rocky Fortune in an original story exclusive to ADV. We think you'll enjoy.

MERMAID SHOW

BY EVAN PURCELL

The Agency has placed me in some pretty fishy situations, but this latest gig really throws me into the deep end.

I get a job at the city's aquarium. Not the finest establishment, I'll admit, but the job seems like smooth sailing… Though I can't shake the feeling that there might be some rough waters ahead.

You've probably been to an aquarium or two, so you know the drill. Fish tanks, koi ponds, and those little food cubes that you can throw at bottom-feeders, just to watch them splash around. Not really my jam.

Our city aquarium was a lot like that, until they decided to do some renovations. Goodbye koi ponds. Hello mermaids.

That's right. About three months ago, our aquarium rebranded itself as a Mermaid Show. Tourists come by the boatful, gather around a giant tank, and watch a dozen women in fake fins do some synchronized swimming routines. The whole thing is modeled after similar shows in Florida and Hawaii. It's the latest thing. Children like it, husbands love it, and wives tolerate it.

In short, this is a low-stakes job with plenty of eye candy. (Along with some actual candy, as the mermaids throw tootsie rolls into the crowd at the end of each show. It's kind of their gimmick.)

Before this morning, the closest I've been to a mermaid is my uncle Monty's fish market, but I know what to expect. Besides, I've heard that the mermaids here put on one hell of a show. Word from the station is that our fearless law-enforcer, Sergeant Hamilton J. Finger, has watched them perform a dozen or so times. Marine enthusiast, I guess. Don't tell his wife.

I report for duty in the early morning, passing by a big, metal gate and a flashing neon sign: "Come sea the wonders of the deep."

Cute.

I don't know the job description yet, but I doubt it's anything I've done before. The Agency has been sending me to some really random places lately, so why not add fish girls to the mix?

Right away, I'm greeted by the park's owner Gus, a guy who's small in every way except his forehead. He wears a sailor cap that makes his large cranium look even larger. Before he took over the business, he was some sort of sea captain, apparently. I guess that explains why he runs the place like a sinking ship.

"Mr. Fortunato," he says. "Welcome to the crew."

He meets me at the entrance, where plastic mermaids smile down at us from pillars on either side. His handshake is wet and clammy, which seems appropriate.

"Glad to be here," I tell him.

He takes me inside and gives me a quick tour of the place. "We run a tight ship around here," he says. (He doesn't mention the "sinking" part.) "And I expect only the best. At first, I wasn't sure about hiring you on, considering your status."

"And what status is that?" I ask him.

"As a card-carrying member of the frequently unemployed."

I don't like the insinuation. I probably have more work experience than all his other employees combined.

"Correction," I say. "I like to refer to myself as frequently employed."

"Touché," he says. "Well, welcome anyway."

We pass through the front courtyard, where one lonely security guard is napping on a stool. I can't tell whether he's dead or just depressingly old. Probably both.

So far, the place doesn't inspire a lot of confidence. Everything is chipped and run-down. I see broken turnstiles, cracks in the concrete, and a wooden cut-out of a cartoon tuna that would look a lot more inviting if it still had its head.

We pass by the food stalls (not very appetizing) and the toilets (even less appetizing) before we get to the main attraction: a huge water tank where the mermaids do their show. Whatever money Gus saves on everything else goes straight into that tank. It's filled with giant clams and pirate chests and other aquarium regulars. No mermaids, though. Not yet.

"Beautiful, yeah?" Gus says. "Just wait 'til you see it in use. My girls put on one hell of a show."

"So I've heard," I tell him. "But you still haven't told me what my job is. I'm not against strapping on some shells and swimming around, but I doubt anyone would pay money to see that."

Gus laughs, the loud, snorting kind. "No, sir. You got too many legs and not enough fins. We have a much less important job for you."

From there, he takes me around the side of the aquarium into an open area with more shopping kiosks. The centerpiece is a gift shop decorated like pirate booty. It has a skull-shaped lock on its front and a roof that looks like a wooden lid. And the gems inside this particular box of treasure: fish toys and fake pearls. Real classy stuff.

"So I'll be selling toys?"

Gus shakes his head. "Not until you've earned a promotion. Right now, we need someone to man the petting zoo."

He takes me past the booty to a dirt square surrounded by a wooden fence. Inside, there are regular farm animals. Pigs, sheep, and a single goat that takes one look at us and charges at the fence.

"Oh," Gus says. "I forgot." He pulls off his sailor's cap and the goat instantly calms down. "That's little Gus Junior. He's a good kid, hence the name, but he has a thing for hats. He doesn't like 'em. Or maybe he likes them too much. He sees a hat, he tries to tear it off your head. Don't know why. I guess he's just particular."

To prove his point, Gus (the human, not the goat) points toward a wooden box at the edge of the animal pen. It's filled with confiscated hats, probably from paying customers who learned the hard way about Gus Junior's aversion to headware.

"So I'm babysitting animals?" I ask.

"You're manning the zoo," Gus corrects me. "Customers come to you, put their nickels in this slot over here, and they get twenty minutes to be one with nature and whatnot. You just stand there to make sure that the customers aren't accidentally trampled and, more importantly, they pay. Got it?"

I glance around the zoo. It's probably the least impressive part of the whole aquarium, and that's including the headless tuna. Who in their right mind would pay five whole cents to see this?

"Seems easy," I say. I reach through the fence to give little Gus Junior a pat on the head, and he slams his horns at me. "More or less."

"Good," Gus says. "The feed boxes are over there. First aid is right behind that. The bandages are for customers only, so if you get hurt, you'll have to fend for yourself. Any questions?"

"Just one, but it might be existential."

"Hit me."

"Why does this exist?"

Gus looks at me funny. He doesn't get the question.

"This is an aquarium, right? People come here for the fish. And the fish-people. So why do you have a pen for farm animals."

"It's a petting zoo, not a pen. Remember that. But it's also a second option for our customers, specifically those whose wives might not want their husbands ogling the mermaids."

I look up at the water tank, which is just feet away. "But they can still see the show from here."

"Exactly. They can still watch our girls and pretend they're not watching. Everyone wins." He pauses. "But don't you watch too much. You're on duty."

"So just for clarity, my job specifics are as follows: Take care of the animals, confiscate hats, and pretend not to watch the mermaids as they swim by."

"You're gonna do just fine." He pats me on the head, which is exactly what I'd done to Gus Junior. Now I know why the goat wanted to ram me. "Oh, and before I forget, we got an all-hands-on-deck policy here. We look out for trouble, so always have your eyes open."

"That won't be a problem," I say. "What do you expect me to look out for? Fish hooks?"

"For danger," he says. He glances back at the empty tank. He gets this far-off look, kinda sad, and says, "We don't want another accident."

Now my ears are burning. If there's some danger going on in this neck of the ocean, I need to know. It'll make my goat-sitting duties much more interesting.

"Look," he says, "I'm gonna tell you something, but it's strictly confidential. You promise to zip your lip?"

"Cross my heart," I say, "but keep your voice down. I think the goat's listening in."

He rolls his eyes. "Two weeks back, we lost a mermaid."

"It's a big ocean."

"We lost her in the floating-belly-up sense," he says. "Tragic. Her name was Pearl, and she used to be the lead performer. In the middle of a show, she… Well, she ain't with us no more. But it happens."

"And you don't suspect foul play?"

He shook his head. "It's a dangerous profession, even with our safety guy Manny watching each performance. But the show must go on. What I'm saying, Fortunato, is… can you please keep an eye on my girls when they're under? You're close enough to see anything fishy when it happens. *If* it happens. I don't expect anything to happen again, but if it does…"

"So I'm not supposed to watch the mermaids, but I should keep an eye on them at all times?" The paradox hurts my brain.

"Pretty much. You can swim, right?"

"More or less."

"Good." He pats my head again, wishes me luck, and then scurries off to greet the mermaids before they change into their fins.

So it looks like I gotta add another job duty to the list. In addition to goat-sitting and the rest, I need to do some light lifeguarding. Maybe this job is harder than I expected.

I'm not complaining, of course, especially not when the first show starts and I get to watch the mermaids do their thing. My little animal paradise gives me a prime view of the mermaid show. And what a show it is. The girls float out on giant plastic clams. Then they dive in and swim around each other for ten full minutes. They do these synchronized figure-eights and other aquatic dance moves, and the whole time, they never go up for air. I don't know how they do it.

Then, for their big finish, they all surface at the same time, reach into these jellyfish-shaped buckets hanging on the edge of the tank, and toss candy at the crowd.

Cheers. Hooting. Standing ovations. You get the idea.

After that, they go off-stage (or off-tank, really), take a thirty-minute break where they can adjust their shells in private, and then come back to do it all again.

I hope I'm not underselling this. It really is amazing. With all the skin and skills on display, the show certainly earns its repeat customers.

And I haven't even mentioned the star performer, a redhaired mermaid in purple shells. She leads all the others in the center of the tank, and each time she swims out, I can't keep my eyes off her. She's the queen of the ocean, a knockout with a body that would raise the Titanic.

I watch for a bit, careful to keep my tongue in my mouth, until I get rudely interrupted by a large man in a striped shirt. He blocks my view, looming over me like a striped gorilla. He doesn't say anything for a while, just stares me down.

"Uh, hello?" I finally say. I'd extend my arm for a handshake but he'd probably rip it off my shoulder.

"What are you lookin' at?" the guy grumbles between chomps of his gum. He sounds pretty much exactly how he looks… i.e. unpleasant.

"Just enjoying the show," I tell him.

"Don't," he said. "And keep your eyes off Coral. That fish is mine." He nods his head toward the redhaired mermaid, which seems a bit hard for him owing to the fact that he doesn't have a neck.

"That's Coral?" I ask. "She's…?"

"My girl," he grumbles. "Off the market."

Coral is in the middle of flipping through the water, fiery hair swaying around her. She's beautiful. The kind of girl to stop boat traffic. This guy, on the other hand, would feel right at home at a museum. The caveman exhibit. She's way out of his league, is all I'm saying. Probably by about 20,000 leagues or so.

"What did I just say?" He grabs my head and twists until I'm no longer facing the tank. Now I'm facing the trash cans, which aren't as fun to look at.

Not every guy resorts to head-twisting before they introduce themselves, so I guess this guy means business.

"Name's Rocky," I say. "Nice to meet you."

"Manny," he mumbles. He lets go of my head and I slowly turn to face him. Never keep your back to wild animals.

"You work here, or are you just on loan from the zoo?" I ask.

"I'm in charge of underwater safety," he explains, patting the snorkel strapped to his belt. "Gotta keep an eye out for my girl. And keep punks like you away from her."

He snaps his gum at me, the most threatening gum-snap you can think of, and then he lumbers back toward the tank.

I've had some difficult coworkers in the past, lotsa lowlifes and thugs, but this guy takes the thug cake.

After that, my first shift wears on without anything to write home about. I only get rammed by Gus Jr. twice, which isn't half bad. It's not half-good, either, considering the goat-horn bruises, but I've had worse jobs. Honestly, Gus Jr. and I are getting kinda close, though I wouldn't invite him to my wedding.

I get eight paying customers that first day. The first two are a young couple who opt for the petting zoo as a way to protest the "unfair treatment and degradation" of the underwater performers. (The girlfriend's words, of course.) They come over and ruffle some fur, with the woman doing most of the ruffling while the boyfriend glances over his shoulder and pretends not to watch the aquatic show.

The third paying customer is a freckle-faced kid of about nine. I confiscate his ball cap (just in case). He seems like a good kid, even though the nickel he sticks in our pay-box is very much a penny.

After that, we have three more kids of varying levels of annoyance and then two old biddies who seem more interested in me than the animals.

Other than that, I'm just waiting for something interesting to happen. And in that waiting, thankfully, I get to watch the next three mermaid shows.

Each time, Coral is by far the star performer. You should see her twirl around and swing that tail. Everything about her is graceful, even her bubbles.

I still mind the animals, giving minimum effort for minimum wage, but I can't stop staring at the Coral. I'm transfixed. The siren's call is real, let me tell you. I gotta be careful, though, because Manny is off to the side of the tank, and throughout the day, I catch him glaring at me and using one finger to draw a line across his throat. Not exactly the universal symbol for friendship.

As I eat my tuna sandwich on my lunch break, Manny comes over to the petting zoo just to growl at me. No words. Just a low throat noise. Then he turns around and leaves, somehow taking my appetite with him.

At the end of my shift, I start to pack up, which basically means shooing the animals into their little hut and gathering the meager cash I've collected. It's been a long, not-so-profitable work day, and I'm ready to head home and rinse off the goat-smell.

Suddenly, I get interrupted by Coral, who walks up to the fence and smiles. She's dry and in regular clothes now, but just as beautiful as before.

"Catch the show?" she asks.

"I did."

"You're new here, huh?"

I look around to see if Manny is nearby. His growl is still ringing in my ears, so I want to make sure that my conversation with Coral is short and professional. I'm definitely not in the mood for a beating. I don't see the goon anywhere, so I relax a little.

"Yeah," I say. "I'm new. Name's Rocky."

"Coral," she says. "Rocky and Coral. Sounds like we can do a comedy act together."

I smile. I like when beautiful women crack jokes, even when they're not particularly funny. Still, with Manny lurking somewhere, so I try to dial back the chemistry. "Sorry," I say. "I'm not a comedian."

She looks at me for a long moment. "Good. Because I don't need a funny person right now." At first, I think she's still flirting, but there's something about her expression. Something dark. She looks around to make sure no one's listening in, and then she whispers, "I think someone wants me dead."

"So there's a fisherman nearby," I joke, but she doesn't smile. "Who wants you dead?"

"I don't know," she answers. "The same person who killed Pearl."

Pearl, the previous head fish, found doing the dead man's stroke last week.

"I'm sorry," I tell her. "She must've been your friend."

"Who? Pearl? Definitely not!" she says. "I hated her guts. She gave mermaids a bad name. But…" Coral slowly exhales. "She was one hell of a swimmer. It just doesn't add up that she'd… die."

"Yeah, that's a little…" I'm going to say "fishy," but I'm already maxed out on ocean puns, so I say "suspicious." I wait for her to continue. I've learned through various workplace exploits that when a beautiful woman asks for help, especially if murder is involved, it's best to just stand and listen.

"I don't have any proof," she says, "but I know that one of her breathing tubes was sabotaged."

"Breathing tubes?"

Coral turns to face the tank. She points toward something small and plastic tucked behind some fake seaweed. "See that? It's connected to our oxygen supply. We have dozens of them hidden throughout the tank. Like what scuba divers use. That's how we stay under for so long."

I squint into the tank, trying to spot more of the breathing tubes. I can't find any.

"But I never see you stop for a breath," I tell her.

She winks at me. "Because we're performers."

"And you think one of those tubes was faulty?"

"Sabotaged," she says again. "We time our breaths down to the second. All it would take is one blocked tube and…"

"You go belly-up," I finish her sentence for her.

She glares at my word choice. "Pearl was performing in the exact center, where I perform now. It was our last show of the day. She was right there, between that patch of seaweed and that pirate chest. Right after her triple-flip/swirl/watusi combo, she used a breathing tube right behind the chest. My best guess is that nothing came out, and instead of immediately swimming to the surface, she kept trying to unblock the tube. The struggle got all her tangled up in seaweed. I knew something was wrong when she didn't come up for our big finish, but by then, it was too late. Pearl was a grade-A diva, but she didn't deserve to die that way."

While she talks, I hop the fence to join her. I don't even realize I'm doing it. "Sorry to ask this," I tell her, "but isn't your boyfriend the guy who makes sure this kind of stuff doesn't happen?" I'm talking about Manny.

She doesn't look at me. "Yes."

"But didn't he—"

"He didn't see anything wrong." She raises her voice. "And after the tank was evacuated, he dove in to check on the breathing tubes. He couldn't find anything. But I know that there was something he missed. And I'm so afraid that… that if it could happen to Pearl, it could happen to me, too."

"And you're telling me this because…?"

"Because, look at you!" she says. "You've spent all day wrangling a goat, you're covered in dirt and bruises, and yet… you still look like some C-list movie detective."

"Thanks," I mutter. I know that's an insult, but I can't argue with it.

"So… You'll figure out what's going on around here?" she pleads. "Before it's too late?"

I can tell that she's dead serious, especially for someone who makes her living decked out in pearls and C-cup seashells. She believes what she's saying, but does that mean that she's right? Or is she just paranoid after swallowing too much seawater?

"Got it, ma'am," I say. "I'll get to the bottom of this."

"You promise?"

I'm about to answer when Manny shows up and ruins the party. He looms over us both, chomping on his gum and flaring his gorilla nostrils in a nice little rhythm. *Chomp-flare-chomp.* "Is there a problem?"

"Besides your chewing," I say, but he doesn't hear me. He's too busy glaring at his girl.

Coral cowers next to him and mutters, "No problem, Manny. I swear."

But there is a problem. Mermaids ain't meant to date gorillas, and someone needs to push this gentleman off the Empire State Building before he causes her any more trouble.

He grabs her by the arm and starts walking her away, glaring at me as he leaves. If I knew what was good for me, I'd stay away from them both. Thankfully, I've never developed that particular brand of self-preservation.

Besides, I promised I'd help her. Or at least I woulda promised that if we weren't so rudely interrupted. And I never go back on my almost-promises.

I watch as the odd couple, mermaid and gorilla, disappear out of the park.

As work starts the next day, and I get back into the routine of goat-sitting, I can't stop thinking about Coral. Dating a neanderthal, mourning a colleague, fearing for her own life... Seems like pretty choppy waters for this mermaid. I meet a couple of her other fish-tailed associates, and they all seem fine. Coral is the only one who suspects foul play, and in my experience, that usually means she's the next target.

Gus (the boss, not the goat) comes over to my area to check on me. It's usually nice when people check on you, unless those people are employers. He asks me the standard new-worker questions. (How's your first week going? Any problems? How many hats have you confiscated? The usual.) He seems friendly enough, especially after I lie to him about how much money I've collected, but then his face gets serious and he says, "So you haven't noticed any... issues, right?"

Issues.

It's a weird word to use. In my book, "issues" means things like pollution or street crime, neither of which seem particularly relevant to an aquatic theme park.

"I don't know what you mean," I tell him.

"Interpersonal issues," he says. "You know, between workers." He seems more nervous than yesterday, but of course he doesn't flat-out tell me why. That would make my job much too easy.

"Between workers, you say." I rub my chin in a *don't-bother-me-while-I'm-thinking* way.

I *could* tell him that Coral is spooked. I could also tell him that her boyfriend is both a threatening goon and a loud gum-chewer. But instead, I say, "Not particularly. Aside from a goat that has given me more bruises than a banana at a farmers' market."

He doesn't get it. That's okay. It's not my best analogy.

He gives me this serious little nod and says, "You know, you came highly recommended at the Agency. And they weren't talking about your animal skills."

"And what *were* they talking about?" I ask. I want to hear him tell me that I'm a known mystery-solver who could possibly help him get to the bottom of his company's little pescacide.

"Never mind," he says and charges off.

As far as conversations go, this one is pretty painless.

I watch Gus walk around the perimeter of the tank, searching for something in the water. I'm not sure I know what he's looking for, but I'm pretty sure that *he* doesn't know what he's looking for, either. It takes a certain type of person to run a business, and on the Venn diagram of life, business people rarely share their circle with the detective side of the diagram. To solve a murder, you gotta have nothing to lose. Like me. It doesn't sound like a positive, but trust me. It is.

Gus looks around the backside of the tank for a while, until he walks head-first into Manny. One of the hazards of keeping your eyes on the ground is that you sometimes run into people. And Manny doesn't look like the kind of person who enjoys being run into. They're too far away for me to hear, but I can see Gus apologizing and Manny glaring. And I can see the two of them disappear around the edge of the tank.

I don't think much about it, though, because the mermaid show has just started again. And with Manny otherwise occupied, I can watch Coral without worrying for my safety.

Once again, the show is hypnotic. This time, though, I'm paying particular attention to how the mermaids take quick breaths from their hidden tubes without drawing any attention to themselves. Coral was right. These mermaids are top-notch professionals, so their oxygen breaks are easy to miss unless you're actively looking for them.

Right before their big finish, I pay special attention to Coral. This is the part where she's floating just above the bed of seaweed, the exact place where Pearl died. As she does a forward flip, I see her reach down and take a gulp of air from her tube. But I see something else, too. Coral's found something at the bottom of the tank, something small and plastic. Without stopping her routine, she scoops up the object and slides it into her seashells.

That's it! That's the evidence she was talking about!

I glance at the audience to see if anyone else noticed, but it doesn't look like they did. The rest of the mermaids' act goes on without a hitch.

They do their final synchronized flips, reach the surface, and then grab handfuls of candy from the baskets at the top of the tank to throw into the audience. It's a nice little gimmick, the tootsie rolls, if you like your candies wet and slimy.

Doesn't matter. The crowd goes wild, like they always do, and the mermaids climb onto their floating clams and disappear into the fake lagoon at the back of the tank. That's where their changing room is.

I check the petting zoo gate, and then rush off. If I'm gonna get some answers, I need to go behind the tank and talk to Coral alone.

I rush past the gift shop and around the corner. I don't hear any thudding footsteps or snapping gum, so I know that Manny isn't around.

When I make it behind the tank, I see Coral wrapped in a towel. She's ditched the fins and letting her hair dry. She's not alone, though.

Gus, in all his nebbish glory, is with her. I can tell that they're arguing, probably about whatever she'd discovered in the tank. Gus does not look happy. Coral doesn't either.

It's a heated conversation, the kind that could burn someone if they get too close. I try to make out what they're saying, but before I can, two big, beefy hands grab me from behind.

That big and beefy combination could only mean one thing: my good friend Manny. He spins me around to face him. We're eye-to-eye, or eye-to-clavicle since he towers over me by about a foot. "Whatcha doing spying on my girl? You remember what I said."

I absolutely remember what he said. And what he growled.

I figure the question is rhetorical, since he punches me before I can answer. I grab onto his striped shirt to stop myself from falling over, and he punches me again. The first punch cleans out my nasal passages. The second relieves me of my consciousness.

By the time I come to, Manny's gone. So are Coral and Gus.

I stop by the gift shop to grab some tissues and an ice pack. They have neither. The saleswoman sees my fresh black eye and offers me a carp from her freezer as a slightly smellier substitute for a frozen steak. I politely decline. I've had so many black eyes in my life that even the worst ones don't last longer than a couple days.

Then I report back to my post, still smarting over my latest concussion. I still don't have any answers. Just a swollen face.

I spend about an hour of quality time with Gus Jr., who seems particularly feisty today. We get three paying customers, adding up to fifteen cents and one more confiscated hat. Business as usual.

As the crowds leave for the day, I notice Manny lumbering toward the exit. He's taking Coral with him, his massive hands pushing her forward. It's clear she does not want to go with him.

It's also clear that she wants to tell me something. She glances at me, her eyes wide. She's the deer and I'm the headlights. Naw, I'm not good at analogies. She's the deer. Manny's the headlights. I'm the traffic cop. Park ranger. Whatever.

They pass by the petting zoo, close enough for me to see her trembling. I know I should stop them. Whatever that brute is planning, it's not gonna be good. And then, without stopping, she fishes a single tootsie roll out of her purse and tosses it to me. Manny doesn't notice.

I shove the snack into my pocket. Clearly, she wants to get my attention. And lucky for her, she's got it.

I ignore my sense of self-preservation, and the throbbing remnants of my Manny-inflicted concussion, and I walk to them. "Hey!" I shout.

Manny doesn't turn. Coral looks over her shoulder.

He's about to pull her away, but she whispers something to him and he loosens his grip. She turns to me, opens her mouth to say something, but Manny grunts in her ear and she stops herself. She knows she can't say too much, not with her boyfriend right there. I can see the wheels turning as she tries to figure out what to say.

I decide to help her. "Thanks for the candy," I say. "What's it for again?"

She smiles, finally figuring out what she's allowed to say. "Nothing special," she answers. "Just a thank you for helping me with that treasure chest."

"Got it," I say. "Any time."

Manny grunts again. He's good at that. Then he yanks on her arm hard enough for me to feel it, and he leads her out the gate. I know she's in danger, but I also know that she doesn't want me to follow her. That's why she gave me the piece of information I need.

The treasure chest. That's her clue.

Well, the only treasure chest I can think of is the one at the bottom of the water tank. Whatever she discovered in the middle of her last show must be stashed there. It's a good place to hide something, since it's under twelve feet of water and all. So at least it's safe from Manny. The bad news is that I gotta take a dip if I want to find out what's in there. Like I told Gus, I'm more-or-less a good swimmer, emphasis on the "less" part, so if it's what I have to do to find out what's going on, then I don't really have a choice.

It's time to go swimming.

Well, it's not exactly the right time, since I gotta keep my little treasure hunt secret. I have to wait until everyone clears out of the place. By now, all the customers are gone, but there are still a few workers packing up.

I wait for about ten more minutes, mainly for the lady at the gift shop to close the lid on her place and leave. Aside from my failed attempt at finding an ice pack, I haven't said one word to her since I started working here, but for some reason, she's chosen tonight of all nights to start off on some small talk. She walks to me and introduces herself. Mary, I think. She doesn't figure much into this story, so I don't quite remember her name. She asks me how I'm doing and all that.

I tell her I'm A-OK, despite the black eye. And the concussion. And the goat bruises.

Then she asks if everything's okay with Coral. This catches me off-guard. Maybe she knows more than she's letting on.

"Honestly, I don't know yet," I tell her. Signs point to no, but I figure it's best to keep this woman out of things.

Mary (or maybe Sherri) says that Coral seemed out-of-sorts today, especially after the last show. I have to agree with that statement. I consider seeing if she has any information that might help, but it seems more like busybody territory than anything else. If anything, she acts like she's trying to get information out of me, not the other way around. I tell her to have a good night, which is the polite way of telling her to go away, and she leaves.

Now I'm finally alone. The lights are off. The buildings are empty. The aquarium is silent. It would be peaceful if there weren't a murder investigation in progress.

I look around once more to check, and yeah. The coast is clear. Just me, some shadows, and that headless tuna. *Now* it's time for a swim.

As soon as I dive in, I regret all my life choices. The water is ice cold. I assume they keep it warm when the mermaids are performing, but an after-hours water tank is not a fun place to be. It's surprisingly dark, too. I shoulda borrowed some gift shop goggles before I jumped in.

I swim around for a bit. Everything is a fuzzy blur. Thankfully, the treasure chest on the bottom still shines in the dim light, so I know where to go. It's like an X on a pirate map. I dive down to the bottom and reach out toward the chest. Long strands of plastic seaweed brush against me, and I have to make sure I don't get tangled up.

I try to pry open the chest, but its lid won't budge. I grab onto it with both hands, pulling and pulling until my lungs scream for air. My only choice is to resurface and try again. I kick off the ground and rise to the surface, where I gulp in as much oxygen as I can.

I'm about to dive back down when something big and heavy floats against me. My first thought is that a shark is attacking. But no, this is something very different: Gus's bloated, dead body. The poor guy is floating face-down in the water, his thin arms and legs spread out like a depressed starfish.

Needless to say, I do the appropriate amount of screaming and then get out of that tank as fast as I can.

After using the security guard's phone to report the body, I find myself in my usual hangout spot: the police station. More specifically, the interrogation room of one Sergeant Finger, the city's finest, a man who wouldn't know a corpse if it died on him.

I sit at the table, which might as well be my personal office for the number of times I have to sit there and describe the latest murder of the week. He's mostly bark with just a little bit of bite, so I figure it's best to wait until he's done shouting.

"Let me get this straight, Fortune," he says. "You got into an altercation. Again. You take an unscheduled dip and wind up finding a stiff. Again. Is that about right?"

"I wouldn't say 'stiff,'" I tell him. "More like water-logged. But otherwise, that's about right."

"Rocky. Rocky. Rocky." He repeats my name whenever he doesn't know what to say. In times like these, it's best to cut to the chase and tell him everything I know.

So I do. I tell him all about my good friend Manny, the least trustworthy man on the seven seas. And I tell him about Pearl. And the evidence that Coral might've found. I'm pretty confident that I've laid everything out in a simple, elementary-school way, but Finger still looks at me like I'm reciting sonnets. In Mandarin.

"I don't get it," he says at that exact same time that I say, "You don't get it."

I gotta back up a bit. "Manny killed Pearl," I say. "He tampered with her breathing tube. Today, Coral finally found the evidence, but she had to hide it in that treasure chest before Manny could see. She tried to tell Gus Senior about it, and Manny offed him."

"Gus Senior?" he asks.

"Yeah. The corpse. Gus Junior is a goat."

"Oh." He nods as if he suddenly understands everything.

It's honestly like talking to a very stupid wall, but I have to continue. "Now it looks like Manny knows people are onto him. And Coral is with him right now. She's in danger!"

I shoulda talked slower, or used smaller words, because Finger keeps staring at me. He gets this blank look sometimes, mouth half-open, eyes blank. Like I said, the city's finest.

"Rocky," he says. "You're not just jumping to conclusions here. You're hopscotching."

"And you're off somewhere playing jump rope," I tell him. "Come on, sergeant. Think about it."

"I'm not gonna think…"

"It's always nice to try something new," I tell him.

He glares. "Try not to insult a man of the law, kid."

"Try not to give me a reason," I say. "Just hear me out. We have to go back there and find what Coral hid in that treasure chest. And then we have to find Manny before he… strikes again."

"Seems believable," Finger says, "except my men searched the whole tank, including the chest, and we didn't find anything."

"But…"

"The chest is one of those decorative thingamabobs. It won't even open."

"Maybe it's under the…"

"We looked everywhere," he insists.

"Your men couldn't find sand in the desert."

The sergeant's face reddens. "Now you're insulting the whole department?"

"It's not their fault," I say. "They're just following your example."

He relaxes for a second, then reddens even more when he realizes I insulted him again. "Okay, Rocky. You figured everything out except motive."

He's right. I normally won't tell him that, but in this case, a little flattery might be helpful. "You're absolutely right," I say. "I have no idea what Manny's motive is. Especially since he's an upstanding citizen with no criminal record."

"Are you kidding?" Finger asks. "The guy's file is a mile long. We brought him in last week for…" His voice trails off.

"A-*ha!*" I shout. "So Manny has a rap sheet. Good to know."

The sergeant freezes, realizing that he's accidentally given away information. We've done this interrogation room dance plenty of times before. He never wants to tell me what I need to know, so I just gotta needle him until the information pops out. It would be fun if it weren't so frustrating.

"Fine," he says. "His name's Manuel Constanza. Manny for short."

"Also known as the Gorilla," I say.

He raises a brow. "That's not on his record."

"Yeah. New alias. I just gave it to him. So tell me what he's been cuffed for. I'm guessing burglary, intimidation, disturbing the peace…"

"Among others," Finger answers. Now that Finger and I have gone past our usual pleasantries, the information comes fast and quick. "He was called into questioning after Pearl's death. Person of interest, of course. A couple of the mermaids caught him threatening her the day before her accident. But we didn't have anything solid to bust him for."

"What kind of threats?"

He sighs. "Pearl was the lead mermaid. Top fish. And Manny didn't like that. He asked Pearl to step down and give Coral the prime spot."

Now it makes sense. "So Manny killed Pearl to help his girlfriend, even though Coral certainly wouldn't have wanted him to resort to pescacide."

"Pescacide?" Finger asked.

"Fish murder," I tell him. "Nice word, huh? So he offed Pearl and now he's just trying to cover his tracks, even if that means silencing Coral. The guy's a real winner, huh?"

Finger crosses his arms. I hate when he does that. "I'm not totally sold on your little theory," he says.

"Because you didn't think of it yourself," I tell him. "But it's gotta be what happened. Now all I need is to find the evidence that Coral hid."

"Incorrect," Finger said.

"Which part?"

"The *I* part," he says. "*You* are going to stay out of this and let us do our jobs. Got it?"

"Loud and clear," I tell him.

He glares at me, not buying it.

"Scout's honor," I promise. Thankfully, I've never been a scout, so he can't hold me to it. I leave before he thinks of another reason to start yelling.

From the station, I catch a cab back to the aquarium. The exact opposite of what I promised.

By now, all the lights are off, even the glowing "Come sea the wonders of the deep" sign. The only light comes from the front office, where our ancient security guard sits behind the desk. He's very much asleep.

No sweat. All I gotta do is sneak past the ninety-year-old guard without waking him. The gates are closed, so I slowly push them open. The rusted metal loudly creaks, and I turn toward the guard to make sure the sound didn't wake him.

He's still snoring.

I continue on my way, happy that I made it through, when I accidentally step on a cardboard Crown of Neptune that someone had dropped on the ground. It makes a tiny crumpling noise, much quieter than the creaking gate, but it's enough to wake up the guard.

"What are you doing?" he shouts at me.

As a young, healthy human being who wasn't alive during the dawn of man, I know that I can outrun this guard without any problems. But he has one weapon I don't: a phone. If I don't placate the cryptkeeper, then he'll call the cops and Sergeant Finger will once again derail my sleuthing.

The meddling arm of the law has gotten in my way before, but twice in one night would be a personal best.

Or worst.

So I turn around and approach the security guard. "Hello, sir. I'm Rocky. I work here, and I just need to pop in for a second. I forgot to bring home my… valuables."

It's a particularly lame excuse, and the guard isn't buying it. He stares and me and reaches for the phone.

I have to convince him to let me through. In a situation like this, all I need is a nice, crisp five-dollar bill to bribe my way in. I search through my pockets, but I'm fresh out of cash. All I have is lint, a driver's license, and a few coins.

Then I notice the tootsie roll that Coral had given me earlier. I know it's a long shot, but I toss him the candy. "Will this buy me five minutes?"

The guard acts like I've just tossed him a gold doubloon. He snatches up the candy and waves for me to go inside. He doesn't have to tell me twice.

I rush through the dark aquarium, past the headless tuna, past the toilets. I'm going straight to the water tank to try again. Just as I'm passing the petting zoo, I hear Manny's voice echoing from the entrance. "Faster!" he says. "Tell me where it is right now!"

I quickly hop the fence and hide behind a pile of hay. Gus Jr. sleeps right behind me. Through the gaps in the fence, I can see Manny lumbering toward me. Coral is at his side, but not by choice. She looks over her shoulder toward the entrance, but Manny shouts, "Don't stop! No one's here to help you."

I guess the security guard isn't there anymore. Strange.

I can't see Manny's gun, but I can see Coral flinch, and I know the specific way people flinch when someone holds a gun to their back. Manny forces Coral forward, muttering at her. I can't hear everything he's saying. Just individual words, like "where's" and "the" and "evidence." Okay, maybe I hear a whole sentence.

By now, they're about ten feet away. I can see the fear on Coral's beautiful face. A single bead of sweat slides down her forehead.

Coral looks around. "I… I don't remember…" she mutters.

Not the right answer. Manny pushes her away from him and raises his gun. He aims it right between her eyes. "It's now or never, babe. You have ten seconds to tell me where you stashed it."

Coral stands frozen. Even at the threat of gunfire, she doesn't want to cooperate. I admire that. Really.

"Ten," Manny grumbles. "Nine. Eight…"

Coral looks around. I can tell she's going to run away, but he's too close. If she makes a break for it, he'll kill her for sure.

When Manny gets to six, I can't wait any longer. Without any plan, I jump out of the shadows and scream, "Wait!"

"You!" Manny shouts. "What are you doing here?"

"Witnessing another crime in progress, I think. Am I right?"

He glares at me, but I still can't see his gun. It's tucked away between Coral's shoulder blades. The only way to protect Coral is to draw Manny's attention away from her and toward me. I still don't have a plan, but that's never stopped me from staring down bullets before.

"No sudden moves," Manny tells me.

I step closer anyway. "It seems to me that your girlfriend came here under duress." I purposely use a word he doesn't know. "And she probably doesn't know your whole story, does she, Mr. Constanza? Because I know everything. I know that you killed Pearl. And Gus. And I know exactly where the evidence is."

Angering an alleged murderer usually isn't an easy path to success, but I accomplish my goal. Manny loosens his grip on Coral and then aims his gun right at me. "The countdown continues, idiot," he says. "Five. Four."

"It's right here!" I scream, pointing toward the edge of the petting zoo.

That's the exact distraction we need. As Manny looks where I'm pointing, Coral runs into the darkness. She's surprisingly fast. Maybe she didn't need me to cook up a distraction after all.

Of course, Manny does not enjoy losing his hostage, or witness, or girlfriend, or whatever she is. He glares at me with pure, animal hatred.

"I can get it for you," I tell him. I start inching away, but he cocks his gun.

"Nope," he says. "*I'll* get it. Just tell me where."

Manny walks closer. He hops over the fence the way a child would hop over a pile of Lincoln Logs. He towers over me, his gun barrel still in my face, and growls, "Where's the evidence?"

Up until this moment, I'm fine without a plan. But right now, I need one. I look around the petting zoo for anything I can use to protect myself. Aside from the sleeping animals, all I have is that stupid hat box. Anything's possible, of course, but I doubt that I can kill him with a Stetson.

I have both my arms raised now. I don't even know when I raised them, but they're up in the air. With my chin, I point toward the little wooden box at the edge of Gus Jr.'s pen. "The hat box," I mutter.

"The hat box?" He raises an eyebrow. "You're not tricking me, are you?"

"You'll find out soon enough," I say. I glance down at Gus Jr. He's still asleep. Very asleep. Counting sheep, if that's something goats do.

Manny walks toward the hat box, but his eyes (and more importantly, his gun) are still on me. With one foot, he kicks open the top of the box.

Behind me, Gus Jr. slowly opens his eyes.

"Where is it?" Manny demands.

"Find the big, flowered hat. The one with the red feather. The evidence is tucked under the ribbon."

He grumbles and starts rifling through the box. By now, Gus Jr. is slowly rising to his hooves.

"This one?" Manny shouts. He holds up the biggest, brightest hat in the box.

I watch Gus Jr.'s reaction like I'm in the audience of a bullfight. Manny, our unwitting matador, holds up the hat. Gus Jr. sniffs the air, and then the goat charges.

Manny does not see it coming. The goat rams into his stomach. The hat flies out of his hands and he skids across the dirt. His gun slides away. And Gus Jr., proud of himself, snatches up the hat midair and starts chewing.

I normally wouldn't last a single round with someone of Manny's species, but Gus Jr. already did most of the work. I kneel over Manny and hold him down. He struggles under me, but I pin him in place. The gun is within arm's reach. I hold the brute down with one hand and reach for the weapon with the other, but before I can grab it...

Sergeant Finger and his men barge in and surround us. Two of them grab Manny and pull him to his feet. Two more look around. And the sergeant comes up to me directly. Lucky me.

"You knew I'd come back, didn't you?" I ask him.

"Yeah," he says. "You're stupid enough. But I didn't think you'd come back *tonight*."

"Then why are you here?"

"Because we got a call." He nods toward someone standing in the distance. It's the security guard, looking more awake than usual.

I still don't understand, until Finger hands me an empty tootsie roll wrapper. It looks normal on one side, but there's a message written on the other: "Manny killed them. Get the police."

I can't believe it. Coral wrote that note. She wrote it for me, and I didn't even open it. If I just had a sweet tooth, I woulda saved myself a lot of trouble.

The cops cuff Manny before he can fight back. They yank him to his feet and start marching him off. His head is hung low, not an easy feat for a man with no neck.

With the gorilla incapacitated, Coral finally steps forward. She's been hiding in the gift shop, Pirate Booty.

I slap my forehead. The gift shop is shaped like a treasure chest! That's where Coral had stashed the evidence all along! It has nothing to do with the chest in the water tank. I feel like a real idiot. Sure, I brought the killer to justice, but I made things much harder than they needed to be.

Coral walks toward me and Finger.

Finger's smiling again. I know that smile. It's the smile of a man who's ready to wrap up a case and take full credit for everything.

"Officer," Coral says and hands him a small plastic tube.

"Hold it up so the whole class can see," I tell him.

Finger shows me the evidence. It's Pearl's sabotaged air tube. It's just a clear piece of plastic, but there's something small and pink jammed in the middle. A piece of Manny's gum.

The smoking gun, more or less. Finger stares at it, and I can tell he doesn't really know what he's looking at. Once again, our brave sergeant needs a little assistance.

"That's how he killed Pearl," I explain. "It's Pearl's oxygen tube from the bottom of the tank. She needed that to breathe, and since it got gummed up, she drowned."

"And after she died, he replaced it with another tube so that he wouldn't get caught," Coral adds. "But he didn't have time to destroy this one, so he hid it amongst the seaweed… Until I found it today."

The sergeant slapped us both on the backs. "Great teamwork, you two."

Coral and I both back away from the overenthusiastic cop. She looks at me, relieved and grateful. "Thank you."

Behind us, Manny starts screaming, "I did it for you! And I'd do it again. It was all for you." Nice to have a bonus confession, just in case the jury needs some extra encouragement before they lock him away.

The officers shove Manny a bit as they take him out of the aquarium.

Finger bags the piece of plastic, gives a quick "thank you" followed by a not-so-quick "If you ever pull a stunt like this again…" lecture, and then he's gone. Good ol' Finger. He'll never change.

Coral and I are alone now. She wraps her arms around me and whispers something into my ear. You probably want to know what she says, but I'd rather keep that private.

And with the mystery finally over, we kiss. Pretty soon, we'll have to give our statements to Finger, and you know what a wonderful meeting-of-the-minds that'll be. But for now, it's just me and my mermaid.

The End

ABOUT THE AUTHOR

Evan Purcell is an author from Arizona who has written novels, podcasts, and feature films. A world traveler, he's lived and worked in Zanzibar, Bhutan, Kazakhstan, and China. Watch out for his upcoming shark attack movie *Above the Break* later this year. You can read more about his travels and projects at EvanPurcell.blogspot.com or follow him on BlueSky @ evancpurcell.

Orchard Corset

OrchardCorset.com

Ph. 1-866-456-7411

★ ★ ★ ★ ★ 04/23/19

Customer service and sizing experts

Customer service and sizing experts are very helpful and responsive. Feeling great about my order!

koma876omen

★ ★ ★ ★ ★ 04/25/19

Very comfortable

Fits like a glove and is super comfortable. Highly recommend for daily use.

Dayna L.

★ ★ ★ ★ ★ 04/24/19

Gorgeous!

I knew I had to get this one when I saw the teaser picture for it. It's even more gorgeous in person. Fits well even though I have...
Read more

Amy H.

Corsets to suit your purpose: waist training, weddings, costumes, back pain relief, or just for fun.

-Sizing Experts Available 7 Days a Week
-Only Steel-Boned Corsets, Never Plastic
-Interest Free Pay Over Time Option!
-Rewards program
-Men's Corsets too

CARMILLA

BY JOSEPH SHERIDAN LE FANU

PROLOGUE

Upon a paper attached to the Narrative which follows, Doctor Hesselius has written a rather elaborate note, which he accompanies with a reference to his Essay on the strange subject which the MS. illuminates.

This mysterious subject he treats, in that Essay, with his usual learning and acumen, and with remarkable directness and condensation. It will form but one volume of the series of that extraordinary man's collected papers.

As I publish the case, in this volume, simply to interest the "laity," I shall forestall the intelligent lady, who relates it, in nothing; and after due consideration, I have determined, therefore, to abstain from presenting any précis of the learned Doctor's reasoning, or extract from his statement on a subject which he describes as "involving, not improbably, some of the profoundest arcana of our dual existence, and its intermediates."

I was anxious on discovering this paper, to reopen the correspondence commenced by Doctor Hesselius, so many years before, with a person so clever and careful as his informant seems to have been. Much to my regret, however, I found that she had died in the interval.

She, probably, could have added little to the Narrative which she communicates in the following pages, with, so far as I can pronounce, such conscientious particularity.

CHAPTER I

AN EARLY FRIGHT

In Styria, we, though by no means magnificent people, inhabit a castle, or schloss. A small income, in that part of the world, goes a great way. Eight or nine hundred a year does wonders. Scantily enough ours would have answered among wealthy people at home. My father is English, and I bear an English name, although I never saw England. But here, in this lonely and primitive place, where everything is so marvelously cheap, I really don't see how ever so much more money would at all materially add to our comforts, or even luxuries.

My father was in the Austrian service, and retired upon a pension and his patrimony, and purchased this feudal residence, and the small estate on which it stands, a bargain.

Nothing can be more picturesque or solitary. It stands on a slight eminence in a forest. The road, very old and narrow, passes in front of its drawbridge, never raised in my time, and its moat, stocked with perch, and sailed over by many swans, and floating on its surface white fleets of water lilies.

Over all this the schloss shows its many-windowed front; its towers, and its Gothic chapel.

The forest opens in an irregular and very picturesque glade before its gate, and at the right a steep Gothic bridge carries the road over a stream that winds in deep shadow through the wood. I have said that this is a very lonely place. Judge whether I say truth. Looking from the hall door towards the road, the forest in which our castle stands extends fifteen miles to the right, and twelve to the left. The nearest inhabited village is about seven of your English miles to the left. The nearest inhabited schloss of any historic associations, is that of old General Spielsdorf, nearly twenty miles away to the right.

I have said "the nearest inhabited village," because there is, only three miles westward, that is to say in the direction of General Spielsdorf's schloss, a ruined village, with its quaint little church, now roofless, in the aisle of which are the moldering tombs of the proud family of Karnstein, now extinct, who once owned the equally desolate chateau which, in the thick of the forest, overlooks the silent ruins of the town.

Respecting the cause of the desertion of this striking and melancholy spot, there is a legend which I shall relate to you another time.

I must tell you now, how very small is the party who constitute the inhabitants of our castle. I don't include servants, or those dependents who occupy rooms in the buildings attached to the schloss. Listen, and wonder! My father, who is the kindest man on earth, but growing old; and I, at the date of my story, only nineteen. Eight years have passed since then.

I and my father constituted the family at the schloss. My mother, a Styrian lady, died in my infancy, but I had a good-natured governess, who had been with me from, I might almost say, my infancy. I could not remember the time when her fat, benignant face was not a familiar picture in my memory.

This was Madame Perrodon, a native of Berne, whose care and good nature now in part supplied to me the loss of my mother, whom I do not even remember, so early I lost her. She made a third at our little dinner party. There was a fourth, Mademoiselle De Lafontaine, a lady such as you term, I believe, a "finishing governess." She spoke French and German, Madame Perrodon French and broken English, to which my father and I added English, which, partly to prevent its becoming a lost language among us, and partly from patriotic motives, we spoke every day. The consequence was a Babel, at which strangers used to laugh, and which I shall make no attempt to reproduce in this narrative. And there were two or three young lady friends besides, pretty nearly of my own age, who were occasional visitors, for longer or shorter terms; and these visits I sometimes returned.

These were our regular social resources; but of course there were chance visits from "neighbors" of only five or six leagues distance. My life was, notwithstanding, rather a solitary one, I can assure you.

My gouvernantes had just so much control over me as you might conjecture such sage persons would have in the case of a rather spoiled girl, whose only parent allowed her pretty nearly her own way in everything.

The first occurrence in my existence, which produced a terrible impression upon my mind, which, in fact, never has been effaced, was one of the very earliest incidents of my life which I can recollect. Some people will think it so trifling that it should not be recorded here. You will see, however, by-and-by, why I mention it. The nursery, as it was called, though I had it all to myself, was a large room in the upper story of the castle, with a steep oak roof. I can't have been more than six years old, when one night I awoke, and looking round the room from my bed, failed to see the nursery maid. Neither was my nurse there; and I thought myself alone. I was not frightened, for I was one of those happy children who are studiously kept in ignorance of ghost stories, of fairy tales, and of all such lore as makes us cover up our heads when the door cracks suddenly, or the flicker of an expiring candle makes the shadow of a bedpost dance upon the wall, nearer to our faces. I was vexed and insulted at finding myself, as I conceived, neglected, and I began to whimper, preparatory to a hearty bout of roaring; when to my surprise, I saw a solemn, but very pretty face looking at me from the side of the bed. It was that of a young lady who was kneeling, with her hands under the coverlet. I looked at her with a kind of pleased wonder, and ceased whimpering. She caressed me with her hands, and lay down beside me on the bed, and drew me towards her, smiling; I felt immediately delightfully soothed, and fell asleep again. I was wakened by a sensation as if two needles ran into my breast very deep at the same moment, and I cried loudly. The lady started back, with her eyes fixed on me, and then slipped down upon the floor, and, as I thought, hid herself under the bed.

I was now for the first time frightened, and I yelled with all my might and main. Nurse, nursery maid, housekeeper, all came running in, and hearing my story, they made light of it, soothing me all they could meanwhile. But, child as I was, I could perceive that their faces were pale with an unwonted look of anxiety, and I saw them look under the bed, and about the room, and peep under tables and pluck open cupboards; and the housekeeper whispered to the nurse: "Lay your hand along that hollow in the bed; someone did lie there, so sure as you did not; the place is still warm."

I remember the nursery maid petting me, and all three examining my chest, where I told them I felt the puncture, and pronouncing that there was no sign visible that any such thing had happened to me.

The housekeeper and the two other servants who were in charge of the nursery, remained sitting up all night; and from that time a servant always sat up in the nursery until I was about fourteen.

I was very nervous for a long time after this. A doctor was called in, he was pallid and elderly. How well I remember his long saturnine face, slightly pitted with smallpox, and his chestnut wig. For a good while, every second day, he came and gave me medicine, which of course I hated.

The morning after I saw this apparition I was in a state of terror, and could not bear to be left alone, daylight though it was, for a moment.

I remember my father coming up and standing at the bedside, and talking cheerfully, and asking the nurse a number of questions, and laughing very heartily at one of the answers; and patting me on the shoulder, and kissing me, and telling me not to be frightened, that it was nothing but a dream and could not hurt me.

But I was not comforted, for I knew the visit of the strange woman was _not_ a dream; and I was _awfully_ frightened.

I was a little consoled by the nursery maid's assuring me that it was she who had come and looked at me, and lain down beside me in the bed, and that I must have been half-dreaming not to have known her face. But this, though supported by the nurse, did not quite satisfy me.

I remembered, in the course of that day, a venerable old man, in a black cassock, coming into the room with the nurse and housekeeper, and talking a little to them, and very kindly to me; his face was very sweet and gentle, and he told me they were going to pray, and joined my hands together, and desired me to say, softly, while they were praying, "Lord hear all good prayers for us, for Jesus' sake." I think these were the very words, for I often repeated them to myself, and my nurse used for years to make me say them in my prayers.

I remembered so well the thoughtful sweet face of that white-haired old man, in his black cassock, as he stood in that rude, lofty, brown room, with the clumsy furniture of a fashion three hundred years old about him, and the scanty light entering its shadowy atmosphere through the small lattice. He kneeled, and the three women with him, and he prayed aloud with an earnest quavering voice for, what appeared to me, a long time. I forget all my life preceding that event, and for some time after it is all obscure also, but the scenes I have just described stand out vivid as the isolated pictures of the phantasmagoria surrounded by darkness.

CHAPTER II
A GUEST

I am now going to tell you something so strange that it will require all your faith in my veracity to believe my story. It is not only true, nevertheless, but truth of which I have been an eyewitness.

It was a sweet summer evening, and my father asked me, as he sometimes did, to take a little ramble with him along that beautiful forest vista which I have mentioned as lying in front of the schloss.

"General Spielsdorf cannot come to us so soon as I had hoped," said my father, as we pursued our walk.

He was to have paid us a visit of some weeks, and we had expected his arrival next day. He was to have brought with him a young lady, his niece and ward, Mademoiselle Rheinfeldt, whom I had never seen, but whom I had heard described as a very charming girl, and in whose society I had promised myself many happy days. I was more disappointed than a young lady living in a town, or a bustling neighborhood can possibly imagine. This visit, and the new acquaintance it promised, had furnished my day dream for many weeks.

"And how soon does he come?" I asked.

"Not till autumn. Not for two months, I dare say," he answered. "And I am very glad now, dear, that you never knew Mademoiselle Rheinfeldt."

"And why?" I asked, both mortified and curious.

"Because the poor young lady is dead," he replied. "I quite forgot I had not told you, but you were not in the room when I received the General's letter this evening."

I was very much shocked. General Spielsdorf had mentioned in his first letter, six or seven weeks before, that she was not so well as he would wish her, but there was nothing to suggest the remotest suspicion of danger.

"Here is the General's letter," he said, handing it to me. "I am afraid he is in great affliction; the letter appears to me to have been written very nearly in distraction."

We sat down on a rude bench, under a group of magnificent lime trees. The sun was setting with all its melancholy splendor behind the sylvan horizon, and the stream that flows beside our home, and passes under the steep old bridge I have mentioned, wound through many a group of noble trees, almost at our feet, reflecting in its current the fading crimson of the sky. General Spielsdorf's letter was so extraordinary, so vehement, and in some places so self-contradictory, that I read it twice over—the second time aloud to my father—and was still unable to account for it, except by supposing that grief had unsettled his mind.

It said "I have lost my darling daughter, for as such I loved her. During the last days of dear Bertha's illness I was not able to write to you.

Before then I had no idea of her danger. I have lost her, and now learn _all_, too late. She died in the peace of innocence, and in the glorious hope of a blessed futurity. The fiend who betrayed our infatuated hospitality has done it all. I thought I was receiving into my house innocence, gaiety, a charming companion for my lost Bertha. Heavens! what a fool have I been!

I thank God my child died without a suspicion of the cause of her sufferings. She is gone without so much as conjecturing the nature of her illness, and the accursed passion of the agent of all this misery. I devote my remaining days to tracking and extinguishing a monster. I am told I may hope to accomplish my righteous and merciful purpose. At present there is scarcely a gleam of light to guide me. I curse my conceited incredulity, my despicable affectation of superiority, my blindness, my obstinacy—all— too late. I cannot write or talk collectedly now. I am distracted. So soon as I shall have a little recovered, I mean to devote myself for a time to enquiry, which may possibly lead me as far as Vienna. Some time in the autumn, two months hence, or earlier if I live, I will see you—that is, if you permit me; I will then tell you all that I scarce dare put upon paper now. Farewell. Pray for me, dear friend."

In these terms ended this strange letter. Though I had never seen Bertha Rheinfeldt my eyes filled with tears at the sudden intelligence; I was startled, as well as profoundly disappointed.

The sun had now set, and it was twilight by the time I had returned the General's letter to my father.

It was a soft clear evening, and we loitered, speculating upon the possible meanings of the violent and incoherent sentences which I had just been reading. We had nearly a mile to walk before reaching the road that passes the schloss in front, and by that time the moon was shining brilliantly. At the drawbridge we met Madame Perrodon and Mademoiselle De Lafontaine, who had come out, without their bonnets, to enjoy the exquisite moonlight.

We heard their voices gabbling in animated dialogue as we approached. We joined them at the drawbridge, and turned about to admire with them the beautiful scene.

The glade through which we had just walked lay before us. At our left the narrow road wound away under clumps of lordly trees, and was lost to sight amid the thickening forest. At the right the same road crosses the steep and picturesque bridge, near which stands a ruined tower which once guarded that pass; and beyond the bridge an abrupt eminence rises, covered with trees, and showing in the shadows some grey ivy-clustered rocks.

Over the sward and low grounds a thin film of mist was stealing like smoke, marking the distances with a transparent veil; and here and there we could see the river faintly flashing in the moonlight.

No softer, sweeter scene could be imagined. The news I had just heard made it melancholy; but nothing could disturb its character of profound serenity, and the enchanted glory and vagueness of the prospect.

My father, who enjoyed the picturesque, and I, stood looking in silence over the expanse beneath us. The two good governesses, standing a little way behind us, discoursed upon the scene, and were eloquent upon the moon.

Madame Perrodon was fat, middle-aged, and romantic, and talked and sighed poetically. Mademoiselle De Lafontaine—in right of her father who was a German, assumed to be psychological, metaphysical, and something of a mystic—now declared that when the moon shone with a light so intense it was well known that it indicated a special spiritual activity. The effect of the full moon in such a state of brilliancy was manifold. It acted on dreams, it acted on lunacy, it acted on nervous people, it had marvelous physical influences connected with life. Mademoiselle related that her cousin, who was mate of a merchant ship, having taken a nap on deck on such a night, lying on his back, with his face full in the light on the moon, had wakened, after a dream of an old woman clawing him by the cheek, with his features horribly drawn to one side; and his countenance had never quite recovered its equilibrium.

"The moon, this night," she said, "is full of idyllic and magnetic influence—and see, when you look behind you at the front of the schloss how all its windows flash and twinkle with that silvery splendor, as if unseen hands had lighted up the rooms to receive fairy guests."

There are indolent styles of the spirits in which, indisposed to talk ourselves, the talk of others is pleasant to our listless ears; and I gazed on, pleased with the tinkle of the ladies' conversation.

"I have got into one of my moping moods tonight," said my father, after a silence, and quoting Shakespeare, whom, by way of keeping up our English, he used to read aloud, he said:

"'In truth I know not why I am so sad. It wearies me: you say it wearies you; But how I got it—came by it.'

"I forget the rest. But I feel as if some great misfortune were hanging over us. I suppose the poor General's afflicted letter has had something to do with it."

At this moment the unwonted sound of carriage wheels and many hoofs upon the road, arrested our attention.

They seemed to be approaching from the high ground overlooking the bridge, and very soon the equipage emerged from that point. Two horsemen first crossed the bridge, then came a carriage drawn by four horses, and two men rode behind.

It seemed to be the traveling carriage of a person of rank; and we were all immediately absorbed in watching that very unusual spectacle. It became, in a few moments, greatly more interesting, for just as the carriage had passed the summit of the steep bridge, one of the leaders, taking fright, communicated his panic to the rest, and after a plunge or two, the whole team broke into a wild gallop together, and dashing between the horsemen who rode in front, came thundering along the road towards us with the speed of a hurricane.

The excitement of the scene was made more painful by the clear, long-drawn screams of a female voice from the carriage window.

We all advanced in curiosity and horror; me rather in silence, the rest with various ejaculations of terror.

Our suspense did not last long. Just before you reach the castle drawbridge, on the route they were coming, there stands by the roadside a magnificent lime tree, on the other stands an ancient stone cross, at sight of which the horses, now going at a pace that was perfectly frightful, swerved so as to bring the wheel over the projecting roots of the tree.

I knew what was coming. I covered my eyes, unable to see it out, and turned my head away; at the same moment I heard a cry from my lady friends, who had gone on a little.

Curiosity opened my eyes, and I saw a scene of utter confusion. Two of the horses were on the ground, the carriage lay upon its side with two wheels in the air; the men were busy removing the traces, and a lady with a commanding air and figure had got out, and stood with clasped hands, raising the handkerchief that was in them every now and then to her eyes.

Through the carriage door was now lifted a young lady, who appeared to be lifeless. My dear old father was already beside the elder lady, with his hat in his hand, evidently tendering his aid and the resources of his schloss. The lady did not appear to hear him, or to have eyes for anything but the slender girl who was being placed against the slope of the bank.

I approached; the young lady was apparently stunned, but she was certainly not dead. My father, who piqued himself on being something of a physician, had just had his fingers on her wrist and assured the lady, who declared herself her mother, that her pulse, though faint and irregular, was undoubtedly still distinguishable. The lady clasped her hands and looked upward, as if in a momentary transport of gratitude; but immediately she broke out again in that theatrical way which is, I believe, natural to some people.

She was what is called a fine looking woman for her time of life, and must have been handsome; she was tall, but not thin, and dressed in black velvet, and looked rather pale, but with a proud and commanding countenance, though now agitated strangely.

"Who was ever being so born to calamity?" I heard her say, with clasped hands, as I came up. "Here am I, on a journey of life and death, in prosecuting which to lose an hour is possibly to lose all. My child will not have recovered sufficiently to resume her route for who can say how long. I must leave her: I cannot, dare not, delay. How far on, sir, can you tell, is the nearest village? I must leave her there; and shall not see my darling, or even hear of her till my return, three months hence."

I plucked my father by the coat, and whispered earnestly in his ear: "Oh! papa, pray ask her to let her stay with us—it would be so delightful. Do, pray."

"If Madame will entrust her child to the care of my daughter, and of her good gouvernante, Madame Perrodon, and permit her to remain as our guest, under my charge, until her return, it will confer a distinction and an obligation upon us, and we shall treat her with all the care and devotion which so sacred a trust deserves."

"I cannot do that, sir, it would be to task your kindness and chivalry too cruelly," said the lady, distractedly.

"It would, on the contrary, be to confer on us a very great kindness at the moment when we most need it. My daughter has just been disappointed by a cruel misfortune, in a visit from which she had long anticipated a great deal of happiness. If you confide this young lady to our care it will be her best consolation. The nearest village on your route is distant, and affords no such inn as you could think of placing your daughter at; you cannot allow her to continue her journey for any considerable distance without danger. If, as you say, you cannot suspend your journey, you must part with her tonight, and nowhere could you do so with more honest assurances of care and tenderness than here."

There was something in this lady's air and appearance so distinguished and even imposing, and in her manner so engaging, as to impress one, quite apart from the dignity of her equipage, with a conviction that she was a person of consequence.

By this time the carriage was replaced in its upright position, and the horses, quite tractable, in the traces again.

The lady threw on her daughter a glance which I fancied was not quite so affectionate as one might have anticipated from the beginning of the scene; then she beckoned slightly to my father, and withdrew two or three steps with him out of hearing; and talked to him with a fixed and stern countenance, not at all like that with which she had hitherto spoken.

I was filled with wonder that my father did not seem to perceive the change, and also unspeakably curious to learn what it could be that she was speaking, almost in his ear, with so much earnestness and rapidity.

Two or three minutes at most I think she remained thus employed, then she turned, and a few steps brought her to where her daughter lay, supported by Madame Perrodon. She kneeled beside her for a moment and whispered, as Madame supposed, a little benediction in her ear; then hastily kissing her she stepped into her carriage, the door was closed, the footmen in stately liveries jumped up behind, the outriders spurred on, the postilions cracked their whips, the horses plunged and broke suddenly into a furious canter that threatened soon again to become a gallop, and the carriage whirled away, followed at the same rapid pace by the two horsemen in the rear.

CHAPTER III

WE COMPARE NOTES

We followed the _cortege_ with our eyes until it was swiftly lost to sight in the misty wood; and the very sound of the hoofs and the wheels died away in the silent night air.

Nothing remained to assure us that the adventure had not been an illusion of a moment but the young lady, who just at that moment opened her eyes. I could not see, for her face was turned from me, but she raised her head, evidently looking about her, and I heard a very sweet voice ask complainingly, "Where is mamma?"

Our good Madame Perrodon answered tenderly, and added some comfortable assurances.

I then heard her ask:

"Where am I? What is this place?" and after that she said, "I don't see the carriage; and Matska, where is she?"

Madame answered all her questions in so far as she understood them; and gradually the young lady remembered how the misadventure came about, and was glad to hear that no one in, or in attendance on, the carriage was hurt; and on learning that her mamma had left her here, till her return in about three months, she wept.

I was going to add my consolations to those of Madame Perrodon when Mademoiselle De Lafontaine placed her hand upon my arm, saying:

"Don't approach, one at a time is as much as she can at present converse with; a very little excitement would possibly overpower her now."

As soon as she is comfortably in bed, I thought, I will run up to her room and see her.

My father in the meantime had sent a servant on horseback for the physician, who lived about two leagues away; and a bedroom was being prepared for the young lady's reception.

The stranger now rose, and leaning on Madame's arm, walked slowly over the drawbridge and into the castle gate.

In the hall, servants waited to receive her, and she was conducted forthwith to her room. The room we usually sat in as our drawing room is long, having four windows, that looked over the moat and drawbridge, upon the forest scene I have just described.

It is furnished in old carved oak, with large carved cabinets, and the chairs are cushioned with crimson Utrecht velvet. The walls are covered with tapestry, and surrounded with great gold frames, the figures being as large as life, in ancient and very curious costume, and the subjects represented are hunting, hawking, and generally festive. It is not too stately to be extremely comfortable; and here we had our tea, for with his usual patriotic leanings he insisted that the national beverage should make its appearance regularly with our coffee and chocolate.

We sat here this night, and with candles lighted, were talking over the adventure of the evening.

Madame Perrodon and Mademoiselle De Lafontaine were both of our party. The young stranger had hardly lain down in her bed when she sank into a deep sleep; and those ladies had left her in the care of a servant.

"How do you like our guest?" I asked, as soon as Madame entered. "Tell me all about her?"

"I like her extremely," answered Madame, "she is, I almost think, the prettiest creature I ever saw; about your age, and so gentle and nice."

"She is absolutely beautiful," threw in Mademoiselle, who had peeped for a moment into the stranger's room.

"And such a sweet voice!" added Madame Perrodon.

"Did you remark a woman in the carriage, after it was set up again, who did not get out," inquired Mademoiselle, "but only looked from the window?"

"No, we had not seen her."

Then she described a hideous black woman, with a sort of colored turban on her head, and who was gazing all the time from the carriage window, nodding and grinning derisively towards the ladies, with gleaming eyes and large white eyeballs, and her teeth set as if in fury.

"Did you remark what an ill-looking pack of men the servants were?" asked Madame.

"Yes," said my father, who had just come in, "ugly, hang-dog looking fellows as ever I beheld in my life. I hope they mayn't rob the poor lady in the forest. They are clever rogues, however; they got everything to rights in a minute."

"I dare say they are worn out with too long traveling," said Madame.

"Besides looking wicked, their faces were so strangely lean, and dark, and sullen. I am very curious, I own; but I dare say the young lady will tell you all about it tomorrow, if she is sufficiently recovered."

"I don't think she will," said my father, with a mysterious smile, and a little nod of his head, as if he knew more about it than he cared to tell us.

This made us all the more inquisitive as to what had passed between him and the lady in the black velvet, in the brief but earnest interview that had immediately preceded her departure.

We were scarcely alone, when I entreated him to tell me. He did not need much pressing.

"There is no particular reason why I should not tell you. She expressed a reluctance to trouble us with the care of her daughter, saying she was in delicate health, and nervous, but not subject to any kind of seizure—she volunteered that—nor to any illusion; being, in fact, perfectly sane."

"How very odd to say all that!" I interpolated. "It was so unnecessary."

"At all events it _was_ said," he laughed, "and as you wish to know all that passed, which was indeed very little, I tell you. She then said, 'I am making a long journey of _vital_ importance—she emphasized the word—rapid and secret; I shall return for my child in three months; in the meantime, she will be silent as to who we are, whence we come, and whither we are traveling.' That is all she said. She spoke very pure French. When she said the word 'secret,' she paused for a few seconds, looking sternly, her eyes fixed on mine. I fancy she makes a great point of that. You saw how quickly she was gone. I hope I have not done a very foolish thing, in taking charge of the young lady."

For my part, I was delighted. I was longing to see and talk to her; and only waiting till the doctor should give me leave. You, who live in towns, can have no idea how great an event the introduction of a new friend is, in such a solitude as surrounded us.

The doctor did not arrive till nearly one o'clock; but I could no more have gone to my bed and slept, than I could have overtaken, on foot, the carriage in which the princess in black velvet had driven away.

When the physician came down to the drawing room, it was to report very favorably upon his patient. She was now sitting up, her pulse quite regular, apparently perfectly well. She had sustained no injury, and the little shock to her nerves had passed away quite harmlessly. There could be no harm certainly in my seeing her, if we both wished it; and, with this permission I sent, forthwith, to know whether she would allow me to visit her for a few minutes in her room.

The servant returned immediately to say that she desired nothing more.

You may be sure I was not long in availing myself of this permission.

Our visitor lay in one of the handsomest rooms in the schloss. It was, perhaps, a little stately. There was a somber piece of tapestry opposite the foot of the bed, representing Cleopatra with the asps to her bosom; and other solemn classic scenes were displayed, a little faded, upon the other walls. But there was gold carving, and rich and varied color enough in the other decorations of the room, to more than redeem the gloom of the old tapestry.

There were candles at the bedside. She was sitting up; her slender pretty figure enveloped in the soft silk dressing gown, embroidered with flowers, and lined with thick quilted silk, which her mother had thrown over her feet as she lay upon the ground.

What was it that, as I reached the bedside and had just begun my little greeting, struck me dumb in a moment, and made me recoil a step or two from before her? I will tell you.

I saw the very face which had visited me in my childhood at night, which remained so fixed in my memory, and on which I had for so many years so often ruminated with horror, when no one suspected of what I was thinking.

It was pretty, even beautiful; and when I first beheld it, wore the same melancholy expression.

But this almost instantly lighted into a strange fixed smile of recognition.

There was a silence of fully a minute, and then at length she spoke; I could not.

"How wonderful!" she exclaimed. "Twelve years ago, I saw your face in a dream, and it has haunted me ever since."

"Wonderful indeed!" I repeated, overcoming with an effort the horror that had for a time suspended my utterances. "Twelve years ago, in vision or reality, I certainly saw you. I could not forget your face. It has remained before my eyes ever since."

Her smile had softened. Whatever I had fancied strange in it, was gone, and it and her dimpling cheeks were now delightfully pretty and intelligent.

I felt reassured, and continued more in the vein which hospitality indicated, to bid her welcome, and to tell her how much pleasure her accidental arrival had given us all, and especially what a happiness it was to me.

I took her hand as I spoke. I was a little shy, as lonely people are, but the situation made me eloquent, and even bold. She pressed my hand, she laid hers upon it, and her eyes glowed, as, looking hastily into mine, she smiled again, and blushed.

She answered my welcome very prettily. I sat down beside her, still wondering; and she said:

"I must tell you my vision about you; it is so very strange that you and I should have had, each of the other so vivid a dream, that each should have seen, I you and you me, looking as we do now, when of course we both were mere children. I was a child, about six years old, and I awoke from a confused and troubled dream, and found myself in a room, unlike my nursery, wainscoted clumsily in some dark wood, and with cupboards and bedsteads, and chairs, and benches placed about it. The beds were, I thought, all empty, and the room itself without anyone but myself in it; and I, after looking about me for some time, and admiring especially an iron candlestick with two branches, which I should certainly know again, crept under one of the beds to reach the window; but as I got from under the bed, I heard someone crying; and looking up, while I was still upon my knees, I saw you—most assuredly you—as I see you now; a beautiful young lady, with golden hair and large blue eyes, and lips—your lips—you as you are here.

"Your looks won me; I climbed on the bed and put my arms about you, and I think we both fell asleep. I was aroused by a scream; you were sitting up screaming. I was frightened, and slipped down upon the ground, and, it seemed to me, lost consciousness for a moment; and when I came to myself, I was again in my nursery at home. Your face I have never forgotten since. I could not be misled by mere resemblance. _You are_ the lady whom I saw then."

It was now my turn to relate my corresponding vision, which I did, to the undisguised wonder of my new acquaintance.

"I don't know which should be most afraid of the other," she said, again smiling—"If you were less pretty I think I should be very much afraid of you, but being as you are, and you and I both so young, I feel only that I have made your acquaintance twelve years ago, and have already a right to your intimacy; at all events it does seem as if we were destined, from our earliest childhood, to be friends. I wonder whether you feel as strangely drawn towards me as I do to you; I have never had a friend—shall I find one now?" She sighed, and her fine dark eyes gazed passionately on me.

Now the truth is, I felt rather unaccountably towards the beautiful stranger. I did feel, as she said, "drawn towards her," but there was also something of repulsion. In this ambiguous feeling, however, the sense of attraction immensely prevailed. She interested and won me; she was so beautiful and so indescribably engaging.

I perceived now something of languor and exhaustion stealing over her, and hastened to bid her good night.

"The doctor thinks," I added, "that you ought to have a maid to sit up with you tonight; one of ours is waiting, and you will find her a very useful and quiet creature."

"How kind of you, but I could not sleep, I never could with an attendant in the room. I shan't require any assistance—and, shall I confess my weakness, I am haunted with a terror of robbers. Our house was robbed once, and two servants murdered, so I always lock my door. It has become a habit—and you look so kind I know you will forgive me. I see there is a key in the lock."

She held me close in her pretty arms for a moment and whispered in my ear, "Good night, darling, it is very hard to part with you, but good night; tomorrow, but not early, I shall see you again."

She sank back on the pillow with a sigh, and her fine eyes followed me with a fond and melancholy gaze, and she murmured again "Good night, dear friend."

Young people like, and even love, on impulse. I was flattered by the evident, though as yet undeserved, fondness she showed me. I liked the confidence with which she at once received me. She was determined that we should be very near friends.

Next day came and we met again. I was delighted with my companion; that is to say, in many respects.

Her looks lost nothing in daylight—she was certainly the most beautiful creature I had ever seen, and the unpleasant remembrance of the face presented in my early dream, had lost the effect of the first unexpected recognition.

She confessed that she had experienced a similar shock on seeing me, and precisely the same faint antipathy that had mingled with my admiration of her. We now laughed together over our momentary horrors.

CHAPTER IV
HER HABITS—A SAUNTER

I told you that I was charmed with her in most particulars.

There were some that did not please me so well.

She was above the middle height of women. I shall begin by describing her.

She was slender, and wonderfully graceful. Except that her movements were languid—very languid—indeed, there was nothing in her appearance to indicate an invalid. Her complexion was rich and brilliant; her features were small and beautifully formed; her eyes large, dark, and lustrous; her hair was quite wonderful, I never saw hair so magnificently thick and long when it was down about her shoulders; I have often placed my hands under it, and laughed with wonder at its weight. It was exquisitely fine and soft, and in color a rich very dark brown, with something of gold. I loved to let it down, tumbling with its own weight, as, in her room, she lay back in her chair talking in her sweet low voice, I used to fold and braid it, and spread it out and play with it. Heavens! If I had but known all!

I said there were particulars which did not please me. I have told you that her confidence won me the first night I saw her; but I found that she exercised with respect to herself, her mother, her history, everything in fact connected with her life, plans, and people, an ever wakeful reserve. I dare say I was unreasonable, perhaps I was wrong; I dare say I ought to have respected the solemn injunction laid upon my father by the stately lady in black velvet. But curiosity is a restless and unscrupulous passion, and no one girl can endure, with patience, that hers should be baffled by another. What harm could it do anyone to tell me what I so ardently desired to know? Had she no trust in my good sense or honor? Why would she not believe me when I assured her, so solemnly, that I would not divulge one syllable of what she told me to any mortal breathing.

There was a coldness, it seemed to me, beyond her years, in her smiling melancholy persistent refusal to afford me the least ray of light.

I cannot say we quarreled upon this point, for she would not quarrel upon any. It was, of course, very unfair of me to press her, very ill-bred, but I really could not help it; and I might just as well have let it alone.

What she did tell me amounted, in my unconscionable estimation—to nothing.

It was all summed up in three very vague disclosures:

First—Her name was Carmilla.

Second—Her family was very ancient and noble.

Third—Her home lay in the direction of the west.

She would not tell me the name of her family, nor their armorial bearings, nor the name of their estate, nor even that of the country they lived in.

You are not to suppose that I worried her incessantly on these subjects. I watched opportunity, and rather insinuated than urged my inquiries. Once or twice, indeed, I did attack her more directly. But no matter what my tactics, utter failure was invariably the result. Reproaches and caresses were all lost upon her. But I must add this, that her evasion was conducted with so pretty a melancholy and deprecation, with so many, and even passionate declarations of her liking for me, and trust in my honor, and with so many promises that I should at last know all, that I could not find it in my heart long to be offended with her.

She used to place her pretty arms about my neck, draw me to her, and laying her cheek to mine, murmur with her lips near my ear, "Dearest, your little heart is wounded; think me not cruel because I obey the irresistible law of my strength and weakness; if your dear heart is wounded, my wild heart bleeds with yours. In the rapture of my enormous humiliation I live in your warm life, and you shall die—die, sweetly die—into mine. I cannot help it; as I draw near to you, you, in your turn, will draw near to others, and learn the rapture of that cruelty, which yet is love; so, for a while, seek to know no more of me and mine, but trust me with all your loving spirit."

And when she had spoken such a rhapsody, she would press me more closely in her trembling embrace, and her lips in soft kisses gently glow upon my cheek.

Her agitations and her language were unintelligible to me.

From these foolish embraces, which were not of very frequent occurrence, I must allow, I used to wish to extricate myself; but my energies seemed to fail me. Her murmured words sounded like a lullaby in my ear, and soothed my resistance into a trance, from which I only seemed to recover myself when she withdrew her arms.

In these mysterious moods I did not like her. I experienced a strange tumultuous excitement that was pleasurable, ever and anon, mingled with a vague sense of fear and disgust. I had no distinct thoughts about her while such scenes lasted, but I was conscious of a love growing into adoration, and also of abhorrence. This I know is paradox, but I can make no other attempt to explain the feeling.

I now write, after an interval of more than ten years, with a trembling hand, with a confused and horrible recollection of certain occurrences and situations, in the ordeal through which I was unconsciously passing; though with a vivid and very sharp remembrance of the main current of my story.

But, I suspect, in all lives there are certain emotional scenes, those in which our passions have been most wildly and terribly roused, that are of all others the most vaguely and dimly remembered.

Sometimes after an hour of apathy, my strange and beautiful companion would take my hand and hold it with a fond pressure, renewed again and again; blushing softly, gazing in my face with languid and burning eyes, and breathing so fast that her dress rose and fell with the tumultuous respiration. It was like the ardor of a lover; it embarrassed me; it was hateful and yet over-powering; and with gloating eyes she drew me to her, and her hot lips traveled along my cheek in kisses; and she would whisper, almost in sobs, "You are mine, you _shall_ be mine, you and I are one for ever." Then she had thrown herself back in her chair, with her small hands over her eyes, leaving me trembling.

"Are we related," I used to ask; "what can you mean by all this? I remind you perhaps of someone whom you love; but you must not, I hate it; I don't know you—I don't know myself when you look so and talk so."

She used to sigh at my vehemence, then turn away and drop my hand.

Respecting these very extraordinary manifestations I strove in vain to form any satisfactory theory—I could not refer them to affectation or trick. It was unmistakably the momentary breaking out of suppressed instinct and emotion. Was she, notwithstanding her mother's volunteered denial, subject to brief visitations of insanity; or was there here a disguise and a romance? I had read in old storybooks of such things. What if a boyish lover had found his way into the house, and sought to prosecute his suit in masquerade, with the assistance of a clever old adventuress. But there were many things against this hypothesis, highly interesting as it was to my vanity.

I could boast of no little attentions such as masculine gallantry delights to offer. Between these passionate moments there were long intervals of commonplace, of gaiety, of brooding melancholy, during which, except that I detected her eyes so full of melancholy fire, following me, at times I might have been as nothing to her. Except in these brief periods of mysterious excitement her ways were girlish; and there was always a languor about her, quite incompatible with a masculine system in a state of health.

In some respects her habits were odd. Perhaps not so singular in the opinion of a town lady like you, as they appeared to us rustic people. She used to come down very late, generally not till one o'clock, she would then take a cup of chocolate, but eat nothing; we then went out for a walk, which was a mere saunter, and she seemed, almost immediately, exhausted, and either returned to the schloss or sat on one of the benches that were placed, here and there, among the trees. This was a bodily languor in which her mind did not sympathize. She was always an animated talker, and very intelligent.

She sometimes alluded for a moment to her own home, or mentioned an adventure or situation, or an early recollection, which indicated a people of strange manners, and described customs of which we knew nothing. I gathered from these chance hints that her native country was much more remote than I had at first fancied.

As we sat thus one afternoon under the trees a funeral passed us by. It was that of a pretty young girl, whom I had often seen, the daughter of one of the rangers of the forest. The poor man was walking behind the coffin of his darling; she was his only child, and he looked quite heartbroken.

Peasants walking two-and-two came behind, they were singing a funeral hymn.

I rose to mark my respect as they passed, and joined in the hymn they were very sweetly singing.

My companion shook me a little roughly, and I turned surprised.

She said brusquely, "Don't you perceive how discordant that is?"

"I think it very sweet, on the contrary," I answered, vexed at the interruption, and very uncomfortable, lest the people who composed the little procession should observe and resent what was passing.

I resumed, therefore, instantly, and was again interrupted. "You pierce my ears," said Carmilla, almost angrily, and stopping her ears with her tiny fingers. "Besides, how can you tell that your religion and mine are the same; your forms wound me, and I hate funerals. What a fuss! Why you must die—_everyone_ must die; and all are happier when they do. Come home."

"My father has gone on with the clergyman to the churchyard. I thought you knew she was to be buried today."

"She? I don't trouble my head about peasants. I don't know who she is," answered Carmilla, with a flash from her fine eyes.

"She is the poor girl who fancied she saw a ghost a fortnight ago, and has been dying ever since, till yesterday, when she expired."

"Tell me nothing about ghosts. I shan't sleep tonight if you do."

"I hope there is no plague or fever coming; all this looks very like it," I continued. "The swineherd's young wife died only a week ago, and she thought something seized her by the throat as she lay in her bed, and nearly strangled her. Papa says such horrible fancies do accompany some forms of fever. She was quite well the day before. She sank afterwards, and died before a week."

"Well, _her_ funeral is over, I hope, and _her_ hymn sung; and our ears shan't be tortured with that discord and jargon. It has made me nervous. Sit down here, beside me; sit close; hold my hand; press it hard-hard-harder."

We had moved a little back, and had come to another seat.

She sat down. Her face underwent a change that alarmed and even terrified me for a moment. It darkened, and became horribly livid; her teeth and hands were clenched, and she frowned and compressed her lips, while she stared down upon the ground at her feet, and trembled all over with a continued shudder as irrepressible as ague. All her energies seemed strained to suppress a fit, with which she was then breathlessly tugging; and at length a low convulsive cry of suffering broke from her, and gradually the hysteria subsided. "There! That comes of strangling people with hymns!" she said at last. "Hold me, hold me still. It is passing away."

And so gradually it did; and perhaps to dissipate the somber impression which the spectacle had left upon me, she became unusually animated and chatty; and so we got home.

This was the first time I had seen her exhibit any definable symptoms of that delicacy of health which her mother had spoken of. It was the first time, also, I had seen her exhibit anything like temper.

Both passed away like a summer cloud; and never but once afterwards did I witness on her part a momentary sign of anger. I will tell you how it happened.

She and I were looking out of one of the long drawing room windows, when there entered the courtyard, over the drawbridge, a figure of a wanderer whom I knew very well. He used to visit the schloss generally twice a year.

It was the figure of a hunchback, with the sharp lean features that generally accompany deformity. He wore a pointed black beard, and he was smiling from ear to ear, showing his white fangs. He was dressed in buff, black, and scarlet, and crossed with more straps and belts than I could count, from which hung all manner of things. Behind, he carried a magic lantern, and two boxes, which I well knew, in one of which was a salamander, and in the other a mandrake. These monsters used to make my father laugh. They were compounded of parts of monkeys, parrots, squirrels, fish, and hedgehogs, dried and stitched together with great neatness and startling effect. He had a fiddle, a box of conjuring apparatus, a pair of foils and masks attached to his belt, several other mysterious cases dangling about him, and a black staff with copper ferrules in his hand. His companion was a rough spare dog, that followed at his heels, but stopped short, suspiciously at the drawbridge, and in a little while began to howl dismally.

In the meantime, the mountebank, standing in the midst of the courtyard, raised his grotesque hat, and made us a very ceremonious bow, paying his compliments very volubly in execrable French, and German not much better.

Then, disengaging his fiddle, he began to scrape a lively air to which he sang with a merry discord, dancing with ludicrous airs and activity, that made me laugh, in spite of the dog's howling.

Then he advanced to the window with many smiles and salutations, and his hat in his left hand, his fiddle under his arm, and with a fluency that never took breath, he gabbled a long advertisement of all his accomplishments, and the resources of the various arts which he placed at our service, and the curiosities and entertainments which it was in his power, at our bidding, to display.

"Will your ladyships be pleased to buy an amulet against the oupire, which is going like the wolf, I hear, through these woods," he said dropping his hat on the pavement. "They are dying of it right and left and here is a charm that never fails; only pinned to the pillow, and you may laugh in his face."

These charms consisted of oblong slips of vellum, with cabalistic ciphers and diagrams upon them.

Carmilla instantly purchased one, and so did I.

He was looking up, and we were smiling down upon him, amused; at least, I can answer for myself. His piercing black eye, as he looked up in our faces, seemed to detect something that fixed for a moment his curiosity.

In an instant he unrolled a leather case, full of all manner of odd little steel instruments.

"See here, my lady," he said, displaying it, and addressing me, "I profess, among other things less useful, the art of dentistry. Plague take the dog!" he interpolated. "Silence, beast! He howls so that your ladyships can scarcely hear a word. Your noble friend, the young lady at your right, has the sharpest tooth,—long, thin, pointed, like an awl, like a needle; ha, ha! With my sharp and long sight, as I look up, I have seen it distinctly; now if it happens to hurt the young lady, and I think it must, here am I, here are my file, my punch, my nippers; I will make it round and blunt, if her ladyship pleases; no longer the tooth of a fish, but of a beautiful young lady as she is. Hey? Is the young lady displeased? Have I been too bold? Have I offended her?"

The young lady, indeed, looked very angry as she drew back from the window.

"How dares that mountebank insult us so? Where is your father? I shall demand redress from him. My father would have had the wretch tied up to the pump, and flogged with a cart whip, and burnt to the bones with the cattle brand!"

She retired from the window a step or two, and sat down, and had hardly lost sight of the offender, when her wrath subsided as suddenly as it had risen, and she gradually recovered her usual tone, and seemed to forget the little hunchback and his follies.

My father was out of spirits that evening. On coming in he told us that there had been another case very similar to the two fatal ones which had lately occurred. The sister of a young peasant on his estate, only a mile away, was very ill, had been, as she described it, attacked very nearly in the same way, and was now slowly but steadily sinking.

"All this," said my father, "is strictly referable to natural causes. These poor people infect one another with their superstitions, and so repeat in imagination the images of terror that have infested their neighbors."

"But that very circumstance frightens one horribly," said Carmilla.

"How so?" inquired my father.

"I am so afraid of fancying I see such things; I think it would be as bad as reality."

"We are in God's hands: nothing can happen without his permission, and all will end well for those who love him. He is our faithful creator; He has made us all, and will take care of us."

"Creator! _Nature!_" said the young lady in answer to my gentle father. "And this disease that invades the country is natural. Nature. All things proceed from Nature—don't they? All things in the heaven, in the earth, and under the earth, act and live as Nature ordains? I think so."

"The doctor said he would come here today," said my father, after a silence. "I want to know what he thinks about it, and what he thinks we had better do."

"Doctors never did me any good," said Carmilla.

"Then you have been ill?" I asked.

"More ill than ever you were," she answered.

"Long ago?"

"Yes, a long time. I suffered from this very illness; but I forget all but my pain and weakness, and they were not so bad as are suffered in other diseases."

"You were very young then?"

"I dare say, let us talk no more of it. You would not wound a friend?"

She looked languidly in my eyes, and passed her arm round my waist lovingly, and led me out of the room. My father was busy over some papers near the window.

"Why does your papa like to frighten us?" said the pretty girl with a sigh and a little shudder.

"He doesn't, dear Carmilla, it is the very furthest thing from his mind."

"Are you afraid, dearest?"

"I should be very much if I fancied there was any real danger of my being attacked as those poor people were."

"You are afraid to die?"

"Yes, every one is."

"But to die as lovers may—to die together, so that they may live together.

Girls are caterpillars while they live in the world, to be finally butterflies when the summer comes; but in the meantime there are grubs and larvae, don't you see—each with their peculiar propensities, necessities and structure. So says Monsieur Buffon, in his big book, in the next room."

Later in the day the doctor came, and was closeted with papa for some time.

He was a skilful man, of sixty and upwards, he wore powder, and shaved his pale face as smooth as a pumpkin. He and papa emerged from the room together, and I heard papa laugh, and say as they came out:

"Well, I do wonder at a wise man like you. What do you say to hippogriffs and dragons?"

The doctor was smiling, and made answer, shaking his head—

"Nevertheless life and death are mysterious states, and we know little of the resources of either."

And so they walked on, and I heard no more. I did not then know what the doctor had been broaching, but I think I guess it now.

CHAPTER V
A WONDERFUL LIKENESS

This evening there arrived from Gratz the grave, dark-faced son of the picture cleaner, with a horse and cart laden with two large packing cases, having many pictures in each. It was a journey of ten leagues, and whenever a messenger arrived at the schloss from our little capital of Gratz, we used to crowd about him in the hall, to hear the news.

This arrival created in our secluded quarters quite a sensation. The cases remained in the hall, and the messenger was taken charge of by the servants till he had eaten his supper. Then with assistants, and armed with hammer, ripping chisel, and turnscrew, he met us in the hall, where we had assembled to witness the unpacking of the cases.

Carmilla sat looking listlessly on, while one after the other the old pictures, nearly all portraits, which had undergone the process of renovation, were brought to light. My mother was of an old Hungarian family, and most of these pictures, which were about to be restored to their places, had come to us through her.

My father had a list in his hand, from which he read, as the artist rummaged out the corresponding numbers. I don't know that the pictures were very good, but they were, undoubtedly, very old, and some of them very curious also. They had, for the most part, the merit of being now seen by me, I may say, for the first time; for the smoke and dust of time had all but obliterated them.

"There is a picture that I have not seen yet," said my father. "In one corner, at the top of it, is the name, as well as I could read, 'Marcia Karnstein,' and the date '1698'; and I am curious to see how it has turned out."

I remembered it; it was a small picture, about a foot and a half high, and nearly square, without a frame; but it was so blackened by age that I could not make it out.

The artist now produced it, with evident pride. It was quite beautiful; it was startling; it seemed to live. It was the effigy of Carmilla!

"Carmilla, dear, here is an absolute miracle. Here you are, living, smiling, ready to speak, in this picture. Isn't it beautiful, Papa? And see, even the little mole on her throat."

My father laughed, and said "Certainly it is a wonderful likeness," but he looked away, and to my surprise seemed but little struck by it, and went on talking to the picture cleaner, who was also something of an artist, and discoursed with intelligence about the portraits or other works, which his art had just brought into light and color, while I was more and more lost in wonder the more I looked at the picture.

"Will you let me hang this picture in my room, papa?" I asked.

"Certainly, dear," said he, smiling, "I'm very glad you think it so like.

It must be prettier even than I thought it, if it is."

The young lady did not acknowledge this pretty speech, did not seem to hear it. She was leaning back in her seat, her fine eyes under their long lashes gazing on me in contemplation, and she smiled in a kind of rapture.

"And now you can read quite plainly the name that is written in the corner.

It is not Marcia; it looks as if it was done in gold. The name is Mircalla, Countess Karnstein, and this is a little coronet over and underneath A.D.

1698. I am descended from the Karnsteins; that is, mamma was."

"Ah!" said the lady, languidly, "so am I, I think, a very long descent, very ancient. Are there any Karnsteins living now?"

"None who bear the name, I believe. The family were ruined, I believe, in some civil wars, long ago, but the ruins of the castle are only about three miles away."

"How interesting!" she said, languidly. "But see what beautiful moonlight!" She glanced through the hall door, which stood a little open. "Suppose you take a little ramble round the court, and look down at the road and river."

"It is so like the night you came to us," I said.

She sighed; smiling.

She rose, and each with her arm about the other's waist, we walked out upon the pavement.

In silence, slowly we walked down to the drawbridge, where the beautiful landscape opened before us.

"And so you were thinking of the night I came here?" she almost whispered.

"Are you glad I came?"

"Delighted, dear Carmilla," I answered.

"And you asked for the picture you think like me, to hang in your room," she murmured with a sigh, as she drew her arm closer about my waist, and let her pretty head sink upon my shoulder. "How romantic you are, Carmilla," I said. "Whenever you tell me your story, it will be made up chiefly of some one great romance."

She kissed me silently.

"I am sure, Carmilla, you have been in love; that there is, at this moment, an affair of the heart going on."

"I have been in love with no one, and never shall," she whispered, "unless it should be with you."

How beautiful she looked in the moonlight!

Shy and strange was the look with which she quickly hid her face in my neck and hair, with tumultuous sighs, that seemed almost to sob, and pressed in mine a hand that trembled.

Her soft cheek was glowing against mine. "Darling, darling," she murmured, "I live in you; and you would die for me, I love you so."

I started from her.

She was gazing on me with eyes from which all fire, all meaning had flown, and a face colorless and apathetic.

"Is there a chill in the air, dear?" she said drowsily. "I almost shiver; have I been dreaming? Let us come in. Come; come; come in."

"You look ill, Carmilla; a little faint. You certainly must take some wine," I said.

"Yes. I will. I'm better now. I shall be quite well in a few minutes. Yes, do give me a little wine," answered Carmilla, as we approached the door.

"Let us look again for a moment; it is the last time, perhaps, I shall see the moonlight with you."

"How do you feel now, dear Carmilla? Are you really better?" I asked.

I was beginning to take alarm, lest she should have been stricken with the strange epidemic that they said had invaded the country about us.

"Papa would be grieved beyond measure," I added, "if he thought you were ever so little ill, without immediately letting us know. We have a very skilful doctor near us, the physician who was with papa today."

"I'm sure he is. I know how kind you all are; but, dear child, I am quite well again. There is nothing ever wrong with me, but a little weakness.

People say I am languid; I am incapable of exertion; I can scarcely walk as far as a child of three years old: and every now and then the little strength I have falters, and I become as you have just seen me. But after all I am very easily set up again; in a moment I am perfectly myself. See how I have recovered."

So, indeed, she had; and she and I talked a great deal, and very animated she was; and the remainder of that evening passed without any recurrence of what I called her infatuations. I mean her crazy talk and looks, which embarrassed, and even frightened me.

But there occurred that night an event which gave my thoughts quite a new turn, and seemed to startle even Carmilla's languid nature into momentary energy.

CHAPTER VI
A VERY STRANGE AGONY

When we got into the drawing room, and had sat down to our coffee and chocolate, although Carmilla did not take any, she seemed quite herself again, and Madame, and Mademoiselle De Lafontaine, joined us, and made a little card party, in the course of which papa came in for what he called his "dish of tea."

When the game was over he sat down beside Carmilla on the sofa, and asked her, a little anxiously, whether she had heard from her mother since her arrival.

She answered "No."

He then asked whether she knew where a letter would reach her at present.

"I cannot tell," she answered ambiguously, "but I have been thinking of leaving you; you have been already too hospitable and too kind to me. I have given you an infinity of trouble, and I should wish to take a carriage tomorrow, and post in pursuit of her; I know where I shall ultimately find her, although I dare not yet tell you."

"But you must not dream of any such thing," exclaimed my father, to my great relief. "We can't afford to lose you so, and I won't consent to your leaving us, except under the care of your mother, who was so good as to consent to your remaining with us till she should herself return. I should be quite happy if I knew that you heard from her: but this evening the accounts of the progress of the mysterious disease that has invaded our neighborhood, grow even more alarming; and my beautiful guest, I do feel the responsibility, unaided by advice from your mother, very much. But I shall do my best; and one thing is certain, that you must not think of leaving us without her distinct direction to that effect. We should suffer too much in parting from you to consent to it easily."

"Thank you, sir, a thousand times for your hospitality," she answered, smiling bashfully. "You have all been too kind to me; I have seldom been so happy in all my life before, as in your beautiful chateau, under your care, and in the society of your dear daughter."

So he gallantly, in his old-fashioned way, kissed her hand, smiling and pleased at her little speech.

I accompanied Carmilla as usual to her room, and sat and chatted with her while she was preparing for bed.

"Do you think," I said at length, "that you will ever confide fully in me?"

She turned round smiling, but made no answer, only continued to smile on me.

"You won't answer that?" I said. "You can't answer pleasantly; I ought not to have asked you."

"You were quite right to ask me that, or anything. You do not know how dear you are to me, or you could not think any confidence too great to look for.

But I am under vows, no nun half so awfully, and I dare not tell my story yet, even to you. The time is very near when you shall know everything. You will think me cruel, very selfish, but love is always selfish; the more ardent the more selfish. How jealous I am you cannot know. You must come with me, loving me, to death; or else hate me and still come with me. and _hating_ me through death and after. There is no such word as indifference in my apathetic nature."

"Now, Carmilla, you are going to talk your wild nonsense again," I said hastily.

"Not I, silly little fool as I am, and full of whims and fancies; for your sake I'll talk like a sage. Were you ever at a ball?"

"No; how you do run on. What is it like? How charming it must be."

"I almost forget, it is years ago."

I laughed.

"You are not so old. Your first ball can hardly be forgotten yet."

"I remember everything about it—with an effort. I see it all, as divers see what is going on above them, through a medium, dense, rippling, but transparent. There occurred that night what has confused the picture, and made its colours faint. I was all but assassinated in my bed, wounded here," she touched her breast, "and never was the same since."

"Were you near dying?"

"Yes, very—a cruel love—strange love, that would have taken my life. Love will have its sacrifices. No sacrifice without blood. Let us go to sleep now; I feel so lazy. How can I get up just now and lock my door?"

She was lying with her tiny hands buried in her rich wavy hair, under her cheek, her little head upon the pillow, and her glittering eyes followed me wherever I moved, with a kind of shy smile that I could not decipher.

I bid her good night, and crept from the room with an uncomfortable sensation.

I often wondered whether our pretty guest ever said her prayers. I certainly had never seen her upon her knees. In the morning she never came down until long after our family prayers were over, and at night she never left the drawing room to attend our brief evening prayers in the hall.

If it had not been that it had casually come out in one of our careless talks that she had been baptised, I should have doubted her being a Christian. Religion was a subject on which I had never heard her speak a word. If I had known the world better, this particular neglect or antipathy would not have so much surprised me.

The precautions of nervous people are infectious, and persons of a like temperament are pretty sure, after a time, to imitate them. I had adopted Carmilla's habit of locking her bedroom door, having taken into my head all her whimsical alarms about midnight invaders and prowling assassins. I had also adopted her precaution of making a brief search through her room, to satisfy herself that no lurking assassin or robber was "ensconced."

These wise measures taken, I got into my bed and fell asleep. A light was burning in my room. This was an old habit, of very early date, and which nothing could have tempted me to dispense with.

Thus fortifed I might take my rest in peace. But dreams come through stone walls, light up dark rooms, or darken light ones, and their persons make their exits and their entrances as they please, and laugh at locksmiths.

I had a dream that night that was the beginning of a very strange agony.

I cannot call it a nightmare, for I was quite conscious of being asleep.

But I was equally conscious of being in my room, and lying in bed, precisely as I actually was. I saw, or fancied I saw, the room and its furniture just as I had seen it last, except that it was very dark, and I saw something moving round the foot of the bed, which at first I could not accurately distinguish. But I soon saw that it was a sooty-black animal that resembled a monstrous cat. It appeared to me about four or five feet long for it measured fully the length of the hearthrug as it passed over it; and it continued to-ing and fro-ing with the lithe, sinister restlessness of a beast in a cage. I could not cry out, although as you may suppose, I was terrified. Its pace was growing faster, and the room rapidly darker and darker, and at length so dark that I could no longer see anything of it but its eyes. I felt it spring lightly on the bed. The two broad eyes approached my face, and suddenly I felt a stinging pain as if two large needles darted, an inch or two apart, deep into my breast. I waked with a scream. The room was lighted by the candle that burnt there all through the night, and I saw a female figure standing at the foot of the bed, a little at the right side. It was in a dark loose dress, and its hair was down and covered its shoulders. A block of stone could not have been more still. There was not the slightest stir of respiration. As I stared at it, the figure appeared to have changed its place, and was now nearer the door; then, close to it, the door opened, and it passed out.

I was now relieved, and able to breathe and move. My first thought was that Carmilla had been playing me a trick, and that I had forgotten to secure my door. I hastened to it, and found it locked as usual on the inside. I was afraid to open it—I was horrified. I sprang into my bed and covered my head up in the bedclothes, and lay there more dead than alive till morning.

CHAPTER VII

DESCENDING

It would be vain my attempting to tell you the horror with which, even now, I recall the occurrence of that night. It was no such transitory terror as a dream leaves behind it. It seemed to deepen by time, and communicated itself to the room and the very furniture that had encompassed the apparition.

I could not bear next day to be alone for a moment. I should have told papa, but for two opposite reasons. At one time I thought he would laugh at my story, and I could not bear its being treated as a jest; and at another I thought he might fancy that I had been attacked by the mysterious complaint which had invaded our neighborhood. I had myself no misgiving of the kind, and as he had been rather an invalid for some time, I was afraid of alarming him.

I was comfortable enough with my good-natured companions, Madame Perrodon, and the vivacious Mademoiselle Lafontaine. They both perceived that I was out of spirits and nervous, and at length I told them what lay so heavy at my heart.

Mademoiselle laughed, but I fancied that Madame Perrodon looked anxious.

"By-the-by," said Mademoiselle, laughing, "the long lime tree walk, behind Carmilla's bedroom window, is haunted!"

"Nonsense!" exclaimed Madame, who probably thought the theme rather inopportune, "and who tells that story, my dear?"

"Martin says that he came up twice, when the old yard gate was being repaired, before sunrise, and twice saw the same female figure walking down the lime tree avenue."

"So he well might, as long as there are cows to milk in the river fields," said Madame.

"I daresay; but Martin chooses to be frightened, and never did I see fool more frightened."

"You must not say a word about it to Carmilla, because she can see down that walk from her room window," I interposed, "and she is, if possible, a greater coward than I."

Carmilla came down rather later than usual that day.

"I was so frightened last night," she said, so soon as were together, "and I am sure I should have seen something dreadful if it had not been for that charm I bought from the poor little hunchback whom I called such hard names. I had a dream of something black coming round my bed, and I awoke in a perfect horror, and I really thought, for some seconds, I saw a dark figure near the chimneypiece, but I felt under my pillow for my charm, and the moment my fingers touched it, the figure disappeared, and I felt quite certain, only that I had it by me, that something frightful would have made its appearance, and, perhaps, throttled me, as it did those poor people we heard of.

"Well, listen to me," I began, and recounted my adventure, at the recital of which she appeared horrified.

"And had you the charm near you?" she asked, earnestly.

"No, I had dropped it into a china vase in the drawing room, but I shall certainly take it with me tonight, as you have so much faith in it."

At this distance of time I cannot tell you, or even understand, how I overcame my horror so effectually as to lie alone in my room that night. I remember distinctly that I pinned the charm to my pillow. I fell asleep almost immediately, and slept even more soundly than usual all night.

Next night I passed as well. My sleep was delightfully deep and dreamless.

But I wakened with a sense of lassitude and melancholy, which, however, did not exceed a degree that was almost luxurious.

"Well, I told you so," said Carmilla, when I described my quiet sleep, "I had such delightful sleep myself last night; I pinned the charm to the breast of my nightdress. It was too far away the night before. I am quite sure it was all fancy, except the dreams. I used to think that evil spirits made dreams, but our doctor told me it is no such thing. Only a fever passing by, or some other malady, as they often do, he said, knocks at the door, and not being able to get in, passes on, with that alarm."

"And what do you think the charm is?" said I.

"It has been fumigated or immersed in some drug, and is an antidote against the malaria," she answered.

"Then it acts only on the body?"

"Certainly; you don't suppose that evil spirits are frightened by bits of ribbon, or the perfumes of a druggist's shop? No, these complaints, wandering in the air, begin by trying the nerves, and so infect the brain, but before they can seize upon you, the antidote repels them. That I am sure is what the charm has done for us. It is nothing magical, it is simply natural."

I should have been happier if I could have quite agreed with Carmilla, but I did my best, and the impression was a little losing its force.

For some nights I slept profoundly; but still every morning I felt the same lassitude, and a languor weighed upon me all day. I felt myself a changed girl. A strange melancholy was stealing over me, a melancholy that I would not have interrupted. Dim thoughts of death began to open, and an idea that I was slowly sinking took gentle, and, somehow, not unwelcome, possession of me. If it was sad, the tone of mind which this induced was also sweet.

Whatever it might be, my soul acquiesced in it.

I would not admit that I was ill, I would not consent to tell my papa, or to have the doctor sent for.

Carmilla became more devoted to me than ever, and her strange paroxysms of languid adoration more frequent. She used to gloat on me with increasing ardor the more my strength and spirits waned. This always shocked me like a momentary glare of insanity.

Without knowing it, I was now in a pretty advanced stage of the strangest illness under which mortal ever suffered. There was an unaccountable fascination in its earlier symptoms that more than reconciled me to the incapacitating effect of that stage of the malady. This fascination increased for a time, until it reached a certain point, when gradually a sense of the horrible mingled itself with it, deepening, as you shall hear, until it discolored and perverted the whole state of my life.

The first change I experienced was rather agreeable. It was very near the turning point from which began the descent of Avernus.

Certain vague and strange sensations visited me in my sleep. The prevailing one was of that pleasant, peculiar cold thrill which we feel in bathing, when we move against the current of a river. This was soon accompanied by dreams that seemed interminable, and were so vague that I could never recollect their scenery and persons, or any one connected portion of their action. But they left an awful impression, and a sense of exhaustion, as if I had passed through a long period of great mental exertion and danger.

After all these dreams there remained on waking a remembrance of having been in a place very nearly dark, and of having spoken to people whom I could not see; and especially of one clear voice, of a female's, very deep, that spoke as if at a distance, slowly, and producing always the same sensation of indescribable solemnity and fear. Sometimes there came a sensation as if a hand was drawn softly along my cheek and neck. Sometimes it was as if warm lips kissed me, and longer and longer and more lovingly as they reached my throat, but there the caress fixed itself. My heart beat faster, my breathing rose and fell rapidly and full drawn; a sobbing, that rose into a sense of strangulation, supervened, and turned into a dreadful convulsion, in which my senses left me and I became unconscious.

It was now three weeks since the commencement of this unaccountable state.

My sufferings had, during the last week, told upon my appearance. I had grown pale, my eyes were dilated and darkened underneath, and the languor which I had long felt began to display itself in my countenance.

My father asked me often whether I was ill; but, with an obstinacy which now seems to me unaccountable, I persisted in assuring him that I was quite well.

In a sense this was true. I had no pain, I could complain of no bodily derangement. My complaint seemed to be one of the imagination, or the nerves, and, horrible as my sufferings were, I kept them, with a morbid reserve, very nearly to myself.

It could not be that terrible complaint which the peasants called the oupire, for I had now been suffering for three weeks, and they were seldom ill for much more than three days, when death put an end to their miseries.

Carmilla complained of dreams and feverish sensations, but by no means of so alarming a kind as mine. I say that mine were extremely alarming. Had I been capable of comprehending my condition, I would have invoked aid and advice on my knees. The narcotic of an unsuspected influence was acting upon me, and my perceptions were benumbed.

I am going to tell you now of a dream that led immediately to an odd discovery.

One night, instead of the voice I was accustomed to hear in the dark, I heard one, sweet and tender, and at the same time terrible, which said,

"Your mother warns you to beware of the assassin." At the same time a light unexpectedly sprang up, and I saw Carmilla, standing, near the foot of my bed, in her white nightdress, bathed, from her chin to her feet, in one great stain of blood.

I wakened with a shriek, possessed with the one idea that Carmilla was being murdered. I remember springing from my bed, and my next recollection is that of standing on the lobby, crying for help.

Madame and Mademoiselle came scurrying out of their rooms in alarm; a lamp burned always on the lobby, and seeing me, they soon learned the cause of my terror.

I insisted on our knocking at Carmilla's door. Our knocking was unanswered.

It soon became a pounding and an uproar. We shrieked her name, but all was vain.

We all grew frightened, for the door was locked. We hurried back, in panic, to my room. There we rang the bell long and furiously. If my father's room had been at that side of the house, we would have called him up at once to our aid. But, alas! he was quite out of hearing, and to reach him involved an excursion for which we none of us had courage.

Servants, however, soon came running up the stairs; I had got on my dressing gown and slippers meanwhile, and my companions were already similarly furnished. Recognizing the voices of the servants on the lobby, we sallied out together; and having renewed, as fruitlessly, our summons at Carmilla's door, I ordered the men to force the lock. They did so, and we stood, holding our lights aloft, in the doorway, and so stared into the room.

We called her by name; but there was still no reply. We looked round the room. Everything was undisturbed. It was exactly in the state in which I had left it on bidding her good night. But Carmilla was gone.

CHAPTER VIII

SEARCH

At sight of the room, perfectly undisturbed except for our violent entrance, we began to cool a little, and soon recovered our senses sufficiently to dismiss the men. It had struck Mademoiselle that possibly Carmilla had been wakened by the uproar at her door, and in her first panic had jumped from her bed, and hid herself in a press, or behind a curtain, from which she could not, of course, emerge until the majordomo and his myrmidons had withdrawn. We now recommenced our search, and began to call her name again.

It was all to no purpose. Our perplexity and agitation increased. We examined the windows, but they were secured. I implored of Carmilla, if she had concealed herself, to play this cruel trick no longer—to come out and to end our anxieties. It was all useless. I was by this time convinced that she was not in the room, nor in the dressing room, the door of which was still locked on this side. She could not have passed it. I was utterly puzzled. Had Carmilla discovered one of those secret passages which the old housekeeper said were known to exist in the schloss, although the tradition of their exact situation had been lost? A little time would, no doubt, explain all—utterly perplexed as, for the present, we were.

It was past four o'clock, and I preferred passing the remaining hours of darkness in Madame's room. Daylight brought no solution of the difficulty.

The whole household, with my father at its head, was in a state of agitation next morning. Every part of the chateau was searched. The grounds were explored. No trace of the missing lady could be discovered. The stream was about to be dragged; my father was in distraction; what a tale to have to tell the poor girl's mother on her return. I, too, was almost beside myself, though my grief was quite of a different kind.

The morning was passed in alarm and excitement. It was now one o'clock, and still no tidings. I ran up to Carmilla's room, and found her standing at her dressing table. I was astounded. I could not believe my eyes. She beckoned me to her with her pretty finger, in silence. Her face expressed extreme fear.

I ran to her in an ecstasy of joy; I kissed and embraced her again and again. I ran to the bell and rang it vehemently, to bring others to the spot who might at once relieve my father's anxiety.

"Dear Carmilla, what has become of you all this time? We have been in agonies of anxiety about you," I exclaimed. "Where have you been? How did you come back?"

"Last night has been a night of wonders," she said.

"For mercy's sake, explain all you can."

"It was past two last night," she said, "when I went to sleep as usual in my bed, with my doors locked, that of the dressing room, and that opening upon the gallery. My sleep was uninterrupted, and, so far as I know, dreamless; but I woke just now on the sofa in the dressing room there, and I found the door between the rooms open, and the other door forced. How could all this have happened without my being wakened? It must have been accompanied with a great deal of noise, and I am particularly easily wakened; and how could I have been carried out of my bed without my sleep having been interrupted, I whom the slightest stir startles?"

By this time, Madame, Mademoiselle, my father, and a number of the servants were in the room. Carmilla was, of course, overwhelmed with inquiries, congratulations, and welcomes. She had but one story to tell, and seemed the least able of all the party to suggest any way of accounting for what had happened.

My father took a turn up and down the room, thinking. I saw Carmilla's eye follow him for a moment with a sly, dark glance.

When my father had sent the servants away, Mademoiselle having gone in search of a little bottle of valerian and salvolatile, and there being no one now in the room with Carmilla, except my father, Madame, and myself, he came to her thoughtfully, took her hand very kindly, led her to the sofa, and sat down beside her.

"Will you forgive me, my dear, if I risk a conjecture, and ask a question?"

"Who can have a better right?" she said. "Ask what you please, and I will tell you everything. But my story is simply one of bewilderment and darkness. I know absolutely nothing. Put any question you please, but you know, of course, the limitations mamma has placed me under."

"Perfectly, my dear child. I need not approach the topics on which she desires our silence. Now, the marvel of last night consists in your having been removed from your bed and your room, without being wakened, and this removal having occurred apparently while the windows were still secured, and the two doors locked upon the inside. I will tell you my theory and ask you a question."

Carmilla was leaning on her hand dejectedly; Madame and I were listening breathlessly.

"Now, my question is this. Have you ever been suspected of walking in your sleep?"

"Never, since I was very young indeed."

"But you did walk in your sleep when you were young?"

"Yes; I know I did. I have been told so often by my old nurse."

My father smiled and nodded.

"Well, what has happened is this. You got up in your sleep, unlocked the door, not leaving the key, as usual, in the lock, but taking it out and locking it on the outside; you again took the key out, and carried it away with you to some one of the five-and-twenty rooms on this floor, or perhaps upstairs or downstairs. There are so many rooms and closets, so much heavy furniture, and such accumulations of lumber, that it would require a week to search this old house thoroughly. Do you see, now, what I mean?"

"I do, but not all," she answered.

"And how, papa, do you account for her finding herself on the sofa in the dressing room, which we had searched so carefully?"

"She came there after you had searched it, still in her sleep, and at last awoke spontaneously, and was as much surprised to find herself where she was as any one else. I wish all mysteries were as easily and innocently explained as yours, Carmilla," he said, laughing. "And so we may congratulate ourselves on the certainty that the most natural explanation of the occurrence is one that involves no drugging, no tampering with locks, no burglars, or poisoners, or witches—nothing that need alarm Carmilla, or anyone else, for our safety."

Carmilla was looking charmingly. Nothing could be more beautiful than her tints. Her beauty was, I think, enhanced by that graceful languor that was peculiar to her. I think my father was silently contrasting her looks with mine, for he said:

"I wish my poor Laura was looking more like herself"; and he sighed.

So our alarms were happily ended, and Carmilla restored to her friends.

CHAPTER IX
THE DOCTOR

As Carmilla would not hear of an attendant sleeping in her room, my father arranged that a servant should sleep outside her door, so that she would not attempt to make another such excursion without being arrested at her own door.

That night passed quietly; and next morning early, the doctor, whom my father had sent for without telling me a word about it, arrived to see me.

Madame accompanied me to the library; and there the grave little doctor, with white hair and spectacles, whom I mentioned before, was waiting to receive me.

I told him my story, and as I proceeded he grew graver and graver.

We were standing, he and I, in the recess of one of the windows, facing one another. When my statement was over, he leaned with his shoulders against the wall, and with his eyes fixed on me earnestly, with an interest in which was a dash of horror.

After a minute's reflection, he asked Madame if he could see my father.

He was sent for accordingly, and as he entered, smiling, he said:

"I dare say, doctor, you are going to tell me that I am an old fool for having brought you here; I hope I am."

But his smile faded into shadow as the doctor, with a very grave face, beckoned him to him.

He and the doctor talked for some time in the same recess where I had just conferred with the physician. It seemed an earnest and argumentative conversation. The room is very large, and I and Madame stood together, burning with curiosity, at the farther end. Not a word could we hear, however, for they spoke in a very low tone, and the deep recess of the window quite concealed the doctor from view, and very nearly my father, whose foot, arm, and shoulder only could we see; and the voices were, I suppose, all the less audible for the sort of closet which the thick wall and window formed.

After a time my father's face looked into the room; it was pale, thoughtful, and, I fancied, agitated.

"Laura, dear, come here for a moment. Madame, we shan't trouble you, the doctor says, at present."

Accordingly I approached, for the first time a little alarmed; for, although I felt very weak, I did not feel ill; and strength, one always fancies, is a thing that may be picked up when we please.

My father held out his hand to me, as I drew near, but he was looking at the doctor, and he said:

"It certainly is very odd; I don't understand it quite. Laura, come here, dear; now attend to Doctor Spielsberg, and recollect yourself."

"You mentioned a sensation like that of two needles piercing the skin, somewhere about your neck, on the night when you experienced your first horrible dream. Is there still any soreness?"

"None at all," I answered.

"Can you indicate with your finger about the point at which you think this occurred?"

"Very little below my throat—here," I answered.

I wore a morning dress, which covered the place I pointed to.

"Now you can satisfy yourself," said the doctor. "You won't mind your papa's lowering your dress a very little. It is necessary, to detect a symptom of the complaint under which you have been suffering."

I acquiesced. It was only an inch or two below the edge of my collar.

"God bless me!—so it is," exclaimed my father, growing pale.

"You see it now with your own eyes," said the doctor, with a gloomy triumph.

"What is it?" I exclaimed, beginning to be frightened.

"Nothing, my dear young lady, but a small blue spot, about the size of the tip of your little finger; and now," he continued, turning to papa, "the question is what is best to be done?"

Is there any danger?"I urged, in great trepidation.

"I trust not, my dear," answered the doctor. "I don't see why you should not recover. I don't see why you should not begin immediately to get better. That is the point at which the sense of strangulation begins?"

"Yes," I answered.

"And—recollect as well as you can—the same point was a kind of center of that thrill which you described just now, like the current of a cold stream running against you?"

"It may have been; I think it was."

"Ay, you see?" he added, turning to my father. "Shall I say a word to Madame?"

"Certainly," said my father.

He called Madame to him, and said:

"I find my young friend here far from well. It won't be of any great consequence, I hope; but it will be necessary that some steps be taken, which I will explain by-and-by; but in the meantime, Madame, you will be so good as not to let Miss Laura be alone for one moment. That is the only direction I need give for the present. It is indispensable."

"We may rely upon your kindness, Madame, I know," added my father.

Madame satisfied him eagerly.

"And you, dear Laura, I know you will observe the doctor's direction."

"I shall have to ask your opinion upon another patient, whose symptoms slightly resemble those of my daughter, that have just been detailed to you—very much milder in degree, but I believe quite of the same sort. She is a young lady—our guest; but as you say you will be passing this way again this evening, you can't do better than take your supper here, and you can then see her. She does not come down till the afternoon."

"I thank you," said the doctor. "I shall be with you, then, at about seven this evening."

And then they repeated their directions to me and to Madame, and with this parting charge my father left us, and walked out with the doctor; and I saw them pacing together up and down between the road and the moat, on the grassy platform in front of the castle, evidently absorbed in earnest conversation.

The doctor did not return. I saw him mount his horse there, take his leave, and ride away eastward through the forest.

Nearly at the same time I saw the man arrive from Dranfield with the letters, and dismount and hand the bag to my father.

In the meantime, Madame and I were both busy, lost in conjecture as to the reasons of the singular and earnest direction which the doctor and my father had concurred in imposing. Madame, as she afterwards told me, was afraid the doctor apprehended a sudden seizure, and that, without prompt assistance, I might either lose my life in a fit, or at least be seriously hurt.

The interpretation did not strike me; and I fancied, perhaps luckily for my nerves, that the arrangement was prescribed simply to secure a companion, who would prevent my taking too much exercise, or eating unripe fruit, or doing any of the fifty foolish things to which young people are supposed to be prone.

About half an hour after my father came in—he had a letter in his hand—and said:

"This letter had been delayed; it is from General Spielsdorf. He might have been here yesterday, he may not come till tomorrow or he may be here today."

He put the open letter into my hand; but he did not look pleased, as he used when a guest, especially one so much loved as the General, was coming.

On the contrary, he looked as if he wished him at the bottom of the Red Sea. There was plainly something on his mind which he did not choose to divulge.

"Papa, darling, will you tell me this?" said I, suddenly laying my hand on his arm, and looking, I am sure, imploringly in his face.

"Perhaps," he answered, smoothing my hair caressingly over my eyes.

"Does the doctor think me very ill?"

"No, dear; he thinks, if right steps are taken, you will be quite well again, at least, on the high road to a complete recovery, in a day or two," he answered, a little dryly. "I wish our good friend, the General, had chosen any other time; that is, I wish you had been perfectly well to receive him."

"But do tell me, papa," I insisted, "what does he think is the matter with me?"

"Nothing; you must not plague me with questions," he answered, with more irritation than I ever remember him to have displayed before; and seeing that I looked wounded, I suppose, he kissed me, and added, "You shall know all about it in a day or two; that is, all that I know. In the meantime you are not to trouble your head about it."

He turned and left the room, but came back before I had done wondering and puzzling over the oddity of all this; it was merely to say that he was going to Karnstein, and had ordered the carriage to be ready at twelve, and that I and Madame should accompany him; he was going to see the priest who lived near those picturesque grounds, upon business, and as Carmilla had never seen them, she could follow, when she came down, with Mademoiselle, who would bring materials for what you call a picnic, which might be laid for us in the ruined castle.

At twelve o'clock, accordingly, I was ready, and not long after, my father, Madame and I set out upon our projected drive.

Passing the drawbridge we turn to the right, and follow the road over the steep Gothic bridge, westward, to reach the deserted village and ruined castle of Karnstein.

No sylvan drive can be fancied prettier. The ground breaks into gentle hills and hollows, all clothed with beautiful wood, totally destitute of the comparative formality which artificial planting and early culture and pruning impart.

The irregularities of the ground often lead the road out of its course, and cause it to wind beautifully round the sides of broken hollows and the steeper sides of the hills, among varieties of ground almost inexhaustible.

Turning one of these points, we suddenly encountered our old friend, the General, riding towards us, attended by a mounted servant. His portmanteaus were following in a hired wagon, such as we term a cart.

The General dismounted as we pulled up, and, after the usual greetings, was easily persuaded to accept the vacant seat in the carriage and send his horse on with his servant to the schloss.

CHAPTER X
BEREAVED

It was about ten months since we had last seen him: but that time had sufficed to make an alteration of years in his appearance. He had grown thinner; something of gloom and anxiety had taken the place of that cordial serenity which used to characterize his features. His dark blue eyes, always penetrating, now gleamed with a sterner light from under his shaggy grey eyebrows. It was not such a change as grief alone usually induces, and angrier passions seemed to have had their share in bringing it about.

We had not long resumed our drive, when the General began to talk, with his usual soldierly directness, of the bereavement, as he termed it, which he had sustained in the death of his beloved niece and ward; and he then broke out in a tone of intense bitterness and fury, inveighing against the "hellish arts" to which she had fallen a victim, and expressing, with more exasperation than piety, his wonder that Heaven should tolerate so monstrous an indulgence of the lusts and malignity of hell.

My father, who saw at once that something very extraordinary had befallen, asked him, if not too painful to him, to detail the circumstances which he thought justified the strong terms in which he expressed himself.

"I should tell you all with pleasure," said the General, "but you would not believe me."

"Why should I not?" he asked.

"Because," he answered testily, "you believe in nothing but what consists with your own prejudices and illusions. I remember when I was like you, but I have learned better."

"Try me," said my father; "I am not such a dogmatist as you suppose. Besides which, I very well know that you generally require proof for what you believe, and am, therefore, very strongly predisposed to respect your conclusions."

"You are right in supposing that I have not been led lightly into a belief in the marvelous—for what I have experienced is marvelous—and I have been forced by extraordinary evidence to credit that which ran counter, diametrically, to all my theories. I have been made the dupe of a preternatural conspiracy."

Notwithstanding his professions of confidence in the General's penetration, I saw my father, at this point, glance at the General, with, as I thought, a marked suspicion of his sanity.

The General did not see it, luckily. He was looking gloomily and curiously into the glades and vistas of the woods that were opening before us.

"You are going to the Ruins of Karnstein?" he said. "Yes, it is a lucky coincidence; do you know I was going to ask you to bring me there to inspect them. I have a special object in exploring. There is a ruined chapel, ain't there, with a great many tombs of that extinct family?"

"So there are—highly interesting," said my father. "I hope you are thinking of claiming the title and estates?"

My father said this gaily, but the General did not recollect the laugh, or even the smile, which courtesy exacts for a friend's joke; on the contrary, he looked grave and even fierce, ruminating on a matter that stirred his anger and horror.

"Something very different," he said, gruffly. "I mean to unearth some of those fine people. I hope, by God's blessing, to accomplish a pious sacrilege here, which will relieve our earth of certain monsters, and enable honest people to sleep in their beds without being assailed by murderers. I have strange things to tell you, my dear friend, such as I myself would have scouted as incredible a few months since."

My father looked at him again, but this time not with a glance of suspicion—with an eye, rather, of keen intelligence and alarm.

"The house of Karnstein," he said, "has been long extinct: a hundred years at least. My dear wife was maternally descended from the Karnsteins. But the name and title have long ceased to exist. The castle is a ruin; the very village is deserted; it is fifty years since the smoke of a chimney was seen there; not a roof left."

"Quite true. I have heard a great deal about that since I last saw you; a great deal that will astonish you. But I had better relate everything in the order in which it occurred," said the General. "You saw my dear ward— my child, I may call her. No creature could have been more beautiful, and only three months ago none more blooming."

"Yes, poor thing! when I saw her last she certainly was quite lovely," said my father. "I was grieved and shocked more than I can tell you, my dear friend; I knew what a blow it was to you."

He took the General's hand, and they exchanged a kind pressure. Tears gathered in the old soldier's eyes. He did not seek to conceal them. He said:

"We have been very old friends; I knew you would feel for me, childless as I am. She had become an object of very near interest to me, and repaid my care by an affection that cheered my home and made my life happy. That is all gone. The years that remain to me on earth may not be very long; but by God's mercy I hope to accomplish a service to mankind before I die, and to subserve the vengeance of Heaven upon the fiends who have murdered my poor child in the spring of her hopes and beauty!"

"You said, just now, that you intended relating everything as it occurred," said my father. "Pray do; I assure you that it is not mere curiosity that prompts me."

By this time we had reached the point at which the Drunstall road, by which the General had come, diverges from the road which we were traveling to Karnstein.

"How far is it to the ruins?" inquired the General, looking anxiously forward.

"About half a league," answered my father. "Pray let us hear the story you were so good as to promise."

CHAPTER XI
THE STORY

With all my heart," said the General, with an effort; and after a short pause in which to arrange his subject, he commenced one of the strangest narratives I ever heard.

"My dear child was looking forward with great pleasure to the visit you had been so good as to arrange for her to your charming daughter." Here he made me a gallant but melancholy bow. "In the meantime we had an invitation to my old friend the Count Carlsfeld, whose schloss is about six leagues to the other side of Karnstein. It was to attend the series of fetes which, you remember, were given by him in honor of his illustrious visitor, the Grand Duke Charles."

"Yes; and very splendid, I believe, they were," said my father.

"Princely! But then his hospitalities are quite regal. He has Aladdin's lamp. The night from which my sorrow dates was devoted to a magnificent masquerade. The grounds were thrown open, the trees hung with colored lamps. There was such a display of fireworks as Paris itself had never witnessed. And such music—music, you know, is my weakness—such ravishing music! The finest instrumental band, perhaps, in the world, and the finest singers who could be collected from all the great operas in Europe. As you wandered through these fantastically illuminated grounds, the moon-lighted chateau throwing a rosy light from its long rows of windows, you would suddenly hear these ravishing voices stealing from the silence of some grove, or rising from boats upon the lake. I felt myself, as I looked and listened, carried back into the romance and poetry of my early youth.

"When the fireworks were ended, and the ball beginning, we returned to the noble suite of rooms that were thrown open to the dancers. A masked ball, you know, is a beautiful sight; but so brilliant a spectacle of the kind I never saw before.

"It was a very aristocratic assembly. I was myself almost the only 'nobody' present.

"My dear child was looking quite beautiful. She wore no mask. Her excitement and delight added an unspeakable charm to her features, always lovely. I remarked a young lady, dressed magnificently, but wearing a mask, who appeared to me to be observing my ward with extraordinary interest. I had seen her, earlier in the evening, in the great hall, and again, for a few minutes, walking near us, on the terrace under the castle windows, similarly employed. A lady, also masked, richly and gravely dressed, and with a stately air, like a person of rank, accompanied her as a chaperon.

Had the young lady not worn a mask, I could, of course, have been much more certain upon the question whether she was really watching my poor darling.

I am now well assured that she was.

"We were now in one of the salons. My poor dear child had been dancing, and was resting a little in one of the chairs near the door; I was standing near. The two ladies I have mentioned had approached and the younger took the chair next my ward; while her companion stood beside me, and for a little time addressed herself, in a low tone, to her charge.

"Availing herself of the privilege of her mask, she turned to me, and in the tone of an old friend, and calling me by my name, opened a conversation with me, which piqued my curiosity a good deal. She referred to many scenes where she had met me—at Court, and at distinguished houses. She alluded to little incidents which I had long ceased to think of, but which, I found, had only lain in abeyance in my memory, for they instantly started into life at her touch.

"I became more and more curious to ascertain who she was, every moment. She parried my attempts to discover very adroitly and pleasantly.

The knowledge she showed of many passages in my life seemed to me all but unaccountable; and she appeared to take a not unnatural pleasure in foiling my curiosity, and in seeing me flounder in my eager perplexity, from one conjecture to another.

"In the meantime the young lady, whom her mother called by the odd name of Millarca, when she once or twice addressed her, had, with the same ease and grace, got into conversation with my ward.

"She introduced herself by saying that her mother was a very old acquaintance of mine. She spoke of the agreeable audacity which a mask rendered practicable; she talked like a friend; she admired her dress, and insinuated very prettily her admiration of her beauty. She amused her with laughing criticisms upon the people who crowded the ballroom, and laughed at my poor child's fun. She was very witty and lively when she pleased, and after a time they had grown very good friends, and the young stranger lowered her mask, displaying a remarkably beautiful face. I had never seen it before, neither had my dear child. But though it was new to us, the features were so engaging, as well as lovely, that it was impossible not to feel the attraction powerfully. My poor girl did so. I never saw anyone more taken with another at first sight, unless, indeed, it was the stranger herself, who seemed quite to have lost her heart to her.

"In the meantime, availing myself of the license of a masquerade, I put not a few questions to the elder lady.

"'You have puzzled me utterly,' I said, laughing. 'Is that not enough?

"Won't you, now, consent to stand on equal terms, and do me the kindness to remove your mask?'

"'Can any request be more unreasonable?' she replied. 'Ask a lady to yield an advantage! Beside, how do you know you should recognize me? Years make changes.'

"'As you see,' I said, with a bow, and, I suppose, a rather melancholy little laugh.

"'As philosophers tell us,' she said; 'and how do you know that a sight of my face would help you?'

"'I should take chance for that,' I answered. 'It is vain trying to make yourself out an old woman; your figure betrays you.'

"'Years, nevertheless, have passed since I saw you, rather since you saw me, for that is what I am considering. Millarca, there, is my daughter;

I cannot then be young, even in the opinion of people whom time has taught to be indulgent, and I may not like to be compared with what you remember me.

You have no mask to remove. You can offer me nothing in exchange.'

"'My petition is to your pity, to remove it.'

"'And mine to yours, to let it stay where it is,' she replied.

"'Well, then, at least you will tell me whether you are French or German; you speak both languages so perfectly.'

"'I don't think I shall tell you that, General; you intend a surprise, and are meditating the particular point of attack.'

"'At all events, you won't deny this,' I said, 'that being honored by your permission to converse, I ought to know how to address you. Shall I say Madame la Comtesse?'

"She laughed, and she would, no doubt, have met me with another evasion—if, indeed, I can treat any occurrence in an interview every circumstance of which was prearranged, as I now believe, with the profoundest cunning, as liable to be modified by accident.

"'As to that,' she began; but she was interrupted, almost as she opened her lips, by a gentleman, dressed in black, who looked particularly elegant and distinguished, with this drawback, that his face was the most deadly pale I ever saw, except in death. He was in no masquerade—in the plain evening dress of a gentleman; and he said, without a smile, but with a courtly and unusually low bow:—

"'Will Madame la Comtesse permit me to say a very few words which may interest her?'

"The lady turned quickly to him, and touched her lip in token of silence; she then said to me, 'Keep my place for me, General; I shall return when I have said a few words.'

"And with this injunction, playfully given, she walked a little aside with the gentleman in black, and talked for some minutes, apparently very earnestly. They then walked away slowly together in the crowd, and I lost them for some minutes.

"I spent the interval in cudgeling my brains for a conjecture as to the identity of the lady who seemed to remember me so kindly, and I was thinking of turning about and joining in the conversation between my pretty ward and the Countess's daughter, and trying whether, by the time she returned, I might not have a surprise in store for her, by having her name, title, chateau, and estates at my fingers' ends. But at this moment she returned, accompanied by the pale man in black, who said:

"'I shall return and inform Madame la Comtesse when her carriage is at the door.'

"He withdrew with a bow."

CHAPTER XII

A PETITION

"'Then we are to lose Madame la Comtesse, but I hope only for a few hours,' I said, with a low bow.

"'It may be that only, or it may be a few weeks. It was very unlucky his speaking to me just now as he did. Do you now know me?'

"I assured her I did not.

"'You shall know me,' she said, 'but not at present. We are older and better friends than, perhaps, you suspect. I cannot yet declare myself. I shall in three weeks pass your beautiful schloss, about which I have been making enquiries. I shall then look in upon you for an hour or two, and renew a friendship which I never think of without a thousand pleasant recollections. This moment a piece of news has reached me like a thunderbolt. I must set out now, and travel by a devious route, nearly a hundred miles, with all the dispatch I can possibly make. My perplexities multiply. I am only deterred by the compulsory reserve I practice as to my name from making a very singular request of you. My poor child has not quite recovered her strength. Her horse fell with her, at a hunt which she had ridden out to witness, her nerves have not yet recovered the shock, and our physician says that she must on no account exert herself for some time to come. We came here, in consequence, by very easy stages—hardly six leagues a day. I must now travel day and night, on a mission of life and death—a mission

"

the critical and momentous nature of which I shall be able to explain to you when we meet, as I hope we shall, in a few weeks, without the necessity of any concealment.'

"She went on to make her petition, and it was in the tone of a person from whom such a request amounted to conferring, rather than seeking a favor.

"This was only in manner, and, as it seemed, quite unconsciously. Than the terms in which it was expressed, nothing could be more deprecatory. It was simply that I would consent to take charge of her daughter during her absence.

"This was, all things considered, a strange, not to say, an audacious request. She in some sort disarmed me, by stating and admitting everything that could be urged against it, and throwing herself entirely upon my chivalry. At the same moment, by a fatality that seems to have predetermined all that happened, my poor child came to my side, and, in an undertone, besought me to invite her new friend, Millarca, to pay us a visit. She had just been sounding her, and thought, if her mamma would allow her, she would like it extremely.

"At another time I should have told her to wait a little, until, at least, we knew who they were. But I had not a moment to think in. The two ladies assailed me together, and I must confess the refined and beautiful face of the young lady, about which there was something extremely engaging, as well as the elegance and fire of high birth, determined me; and, quite overpowered, I submitted, and undertook, too easily, the care of the young lady, whom her mother called Millarca.

"The Countess beckoned to her daughter, who listened with grave attention while she told her, in general terms, how suddenly and peremptorily she had been summoned, and also of the arrangement she had made for her under my care, adding that I was one of her earliest and most valued friends.

"I made, of course, such speeches as the case seemed to call for, and found myself, on reflection, in a position which I did not half like.

"The gentleman in black returned, and very ceremoniously conducted the lady from the room.

"The demeanor of this gentleman was such as to impress me with the conviction that the Countess was a lady of very much more importance than her modest title alone might have led me to assume.

"Her last charge to me was that no attempt was to be made to learn more about her than I might have already guessed, until her return. Our distinguished host, whose guest she was, knew her reasons.

"'But here,' she said, 'neither I nor my daughter could safely remain for more than a day. I removed my mask imprudently for a moment, about an hour ago, and, too late, I fancied you saw me. So I resolved to seek an opportunity of talking a little to you. Had I found that you had seen me, I would have thrown myself on your high sense of honor to keep my secret some weeks. As it is, I am satisfied that you did not see me; but if you now suspect, or, on reflection, should suspect, who I am, I commit myself, in like manner, entirely to your honor. My daughter will observe the same secrecy, and I well know that you will, from time to time, remind her, lest she should thoughtlessly disclose it.'

"She whispered a few words to her daughter, kissed her hurriedly twice, and went away, accompanied by the pale gentleman in black, and disappeared in the crowd.

"'In the next room,' said Millarca, 'there is a window that looks upon the hall door. I should like to see the last of mamma, and to kiss my hand to her.'

"We assented, of course, and accompanied her to the window. We looked out, and saw a handsome old-fashioned carriage, with a troop of couriers and footmen. We saw the slim figure of the pale gentleman in black, as he held a thick velvet cloak, and placed it about her shoulders and threw the hood over her head. She nodded to him, and just touched his hand with hers. He bowed low repeatedly as the door closed, and the carriage began to move.

"'She is gone,' said Millarca, with a sigh.

"'She is gone,' I repeated to myself, for the first time—in the hurried moments that had elapsed since my consent—reflecting upon the folly of my act.

"'She did not look up,' said the young lady, plaintively.

"'The Countess had taken off her mask, perhaps, and did not care to show her face,' I said; 'and she could not know that you were in the window.'

"She sighed, and looked in my face. She was so beautiful that I relented. I was sorry I had for a moment repented of my hospitality, and I determined to make her amends for the unavowed churlishness of my reception.

"The young lady, replacing her mask, joined my ward in persuading me to return to the grounds, where the concert was soon to be renewed. We did so, and walked up and down the terrace that lies under the castle windows.

"Millarca became very intimate with us, and amused us with lively descriptions and stories of most of the great people whom we saw upon the terrace. I liked her more and more every minute. Her gossip without being ill-natured, was extremely diverting to me, who had been so long out of the great world. I thought what life she would give to our sometimes lonely evenings at home.

"This ball was not over until the morning sun had almost reached the horizon. It pleased the Grand Duke to dance till then, so loyal people could not go away, or think of bed.

"We had just got through a crowded saloon, when my ward asked me what had become of Millarca. I thought she had been by her side, and she fancied she was by mine. The fact was, we had lost her.

"All my efforts to find her were vain. I feared that she had mistaken, in the confusion of a momentary separation from us, other people for her new friends, and had, possibly, pursued and lost them in the extensive grounds which were thrown open to us.

"Now, in its full force, I recognized a new folly in my having undertaken the charge of a young lady without so much as knowing her name; and fettered as I was by promises, of the reasons for imposing which I knew nothing, I could not even point my inquiries by saying that the missing young lady was the daughter of the Countess who had taken her departure a few hours before.

"Morning broke. It was clear daylight before I gave up my search. It was not till near two o'clock next day that we heard anything of my missing charge.

"At about that time a servant knocked at my niece's door, to say that he had been earnestly requested by a young lady, who appeared to be in great distress, to make out where she could find the General Baron Spielsdorf and the young lady his daughter, in whose charge she had been left by her mother.

"There could be no doubt, notwithstanding the slight inaccuracy, that our young friend had turned up; and so she had. Would to heaven we had lost her!

"She told my poor child a story to account for her having failed to recover us for so long. Very late, she said, she had got to the housekeeper's bedroom in despair of finding us, and had then fallen into a deep sleep which, long as it was, had hardly sufficed to recruit her strength after the fatigues of the ball.

"That day Millarca came home with us. I was only too happy, after all, to have secured so charming a companion for my dear girl."

CHAPTER XIII

THE WOODMAN

"There soon, however, appeared some drawbacks. In the first place, Millarca complained of extreme languor—the weakness that remained after her late illness—and she never emerged from her room till the afternoon was pretty far advanced. In the next place, it was accidentally discovered, although she always locked her door on the inside, and never disturbed the key from its place till she admitted the maid to assist at her toilet, that she was undoubtedly sometimes absent from her room in the very early morning, and at various times later in the day, before she wished it to be understood that she was stirring. She was repeatedly seen from the windows of the schloss, in the first faint grey of the morning, walking through the trees, in an easterly direction, and looking like a person in a trance. This convinced me that she walked in her sleep. But this hypothesis did not solve the puzzle. How did she pass out from her room, leaving the door locked on the inside? How did she escape from the house without unbarring door or window?

"In the midst of my perplexities, an anxiety of a far more urgent kind presented itself.

"My dear child began to lose her looks and health, and that in a manner so mysterious, and even horrible, that I became thoroughly frightened.

"She was at first visited by appalling dreams; then, as she fancied, by a specter, sometimes resembling Millarca, sometimes in the shape of a beast, indistinctly seen, walking round the foot of her bed, from side to side.

Lastly came sensations. One, not unpleasant, but very peculiar, she said, resembled the flow of an icy stream against her breast. At a later time, she felt something like a pair of large needles pierce her, a little below the throat, with a very sharp pain. A few nights after, followed a gradual and convulsive sense of strangulation; then came unconsciousness."

I could hear distinctly every word the kind old General was saying, because by this time we were driving upon the short grass that spreads on either side of the road as you approach the roofless village which had not shown the smoke of a chimney for more than half a century.

You may guess how strangely I felt as I heard my own symptoms so exactly described in those which had been experienced by the poor girl who, but for the catastrophe which followed, would have been at that moment a visitor at my father's chateau. You may suppose, also, how I felt as I heard him detail habits and mysterious peculiarities which were, in fact, those of our beautiful guest, Carmilla!

A vista opened in the forest; we were on a sudden under the chimneys and gables of the ruined village, and the towers and battlements of the dismantled castle, round which gigantic trees are grouped, overhung us from a slight eminence.

In a frightened dream I got down from the carriage, and in silence, for we had each abundant matter for thinking; we soon mounted the ascent, and were among the spacious chambers, winding stairs, and dark corridors of the castle.

"And this was once the palatial residence of the Karnsteins!" said the old General at length, as from a great window he looked out across the village, and saw the wide, undulating expanse of forest. "It was a bad family, and here its bloodstained annals were written," he continued. "It is hard that they should, after death, continue to plague the human race with their atrocious lusts. That is the chapel of the Karnsteins, down there."

He pointed down to the grey walls of the Gothic building partly visible through the foliage, a little way down the steep. "And I hear the axe of a woodman," he added, "busy among the trees that surround it; he possibly may give us the information of which I am in search, and point out the grave of Mircalla, Countess of Karnstein. These rustics preserve the local traditions of great families, whose stories die out among the rich and titled so soon as the families themselves become extinct."

"We have a portrait, at home, of Mircalla, the Countess Karnstein; should you like to see it?" asked my father.

"Time enough, dear friend," replied the General. "I believe that I have seen the original; and one motive which has led me to you earlier than I at first intended, was to explore the chapel which we are now approaching."

"What! see the Countess Mircalla," exclaimed my father; "why, she has been dead more than a century!"

"Not so dead as you fancy, I am told," answered the General.

"I confess, General, you puzzle me utterly," replied my father, looking at him, I fancied, for a moment with a return of the suspicion I detected before. But although there was anger and detestation, at times, in the old General's manner, there was nothing flighty.

"There remains to me," he said, as we passed under the heavy arch of the Gothic church—for its dimensions would have justified its being so styled—"but one object which can interest me during the few years that remain to me on earth, and that is to wreak on her the vengeance which, I thank God, may still be accomplished by a mortal arm."

"What vengeance can you mean?" asked my father, in increasing amazement.

"I mean, to decapitate the monster," he answered, with a fierce flush, and a stamp that echoed mournfully through the hollow ruin, and his clenched hand was at the same moment raised, as if it grasped the handle of an axe, while he shook it ferociously in the air.

"What?" exclaimed my father, more than ever bewildered.

"To strike her head off."

"Cut her head off!"

"Aye, with a hatchet, with a spade, or with anything that can cleave through her murderous throat. You shall hear," he answered, trembling with rage. And hurrying forward he said:

"That beam will answer for a seat; your dear child is fatigued; let her be seated, and I will, in a few sentences, close my dreadful story."

The squared block of wood, which lay on the grass-grown pavement of the chapel, formed a bench on which I was very glad to seat myself, and in the meantime the General called to the woodman, who had been removing some boughs which leaned upon the old walls; and, axe in hand, the hardy old fellow stood before us.

He could not tell us anything of these monuments; but there was an old man, he said, a ranger of this forest, at present sojourning in the house of the priest, about two miles away, who could point out every monument of the old Karnstein family; and, for a trifle, he undertook to bring him back with him, if we would lend him one of our horses, in little more than half an hour.

"Have you been long employed about this forest?" asked my father of the old man.

"I have been a woodman here," he answered in his patois, "under the forester, all my days; so has my father before me, and so on, as many generations as I can count up. I could show you the very house in the village here, in which my ancestors lived."

"How came the village to be deserted?" asked the General.

"It was troubled by revenants, sir; several were tracked to their graves, there detected by the usual tests, and extinguished in the usual way, by decapitation, by the stake, and by burning; but not until many of the villagers were killed.

"But after all these proceedings according to law," he continued—"so many graves opened, and so many vampires deprived of their horrible animation—the village was not relieved. But a Moravian nobleman, who happened to be traveling this way, heard how matters were, and being skilled—as many people are in his country—in such affairs, he offered to deliver the village from its tormentor. He did so thus: There being a bright moon that night, he ascended, shortly after sunset, the towers of the chapel here, from whence he could distinctly see the churchyard beneath him; you can see it from that window. From this point he watched until he saw the vampire come out of his grave, and place near it the linen clothes in which he had been folded, and then glide away towards the village to plague its inhabitants.

"The stranger, having seen all this, came down from the steeple, took the linen wrappings of the vampire, and carried them up to the top of the tower, which he again mounted. When the vampire returned from his prowlings and missed his clothes, he cried furiously to the Moravian, whom he saw at the summit of the tower, and who, in reply, beckoned him to ascend and take them. Whereupon the vampire, accepting his invitation, began to climb the steeple, and so soon as he had reached the battlements, the Moravian, with a stroke of his sword, clove his skull in twain, hurling him down to the churchyard, whither, descending by the winding stairs, the stranger followed and cut his head off, and next day delivered it and the body to the villagers, who duly impaled and burnt them.

"This Moravian nobleman had authority from the then head of the family to remove the tomb of Mircalla, Countess Karnstein, which he did effectually, so that in a little while its site was quite forgotten."

"Can you point out where it stood?" asked the General, eagerly.

The forester shook his head, and smiled.

"Not a soul living could tell you that now," he said; "besides, they say her body was removed; but no one is sure of that either."

Having thus spoken, as time pressed, he dropped his axe and departed, leaving us to hear the remainder of the General's strange story.

CHAPTER XIV
THE MEETING

"My beloved child," he resumed, "was now growing rapidly worse. The physician who attended her had failed to produce the slightest impression on her disease, for such I then supposed it to be. He saw my alarm, and suggested a consultation. I called in an abler physician, from Gratz.

Several days elapsed before he arrived. He was a good and pious, as well as a learned man. Having seen my poor ward together, they withdrew to my library to confer and discuss. I, from the adjoining room, where I awaited their summons, heard these two gentlemen's voices raised in something sharper than a strictly philosophical discussion. I knocked at the door and entered. I found the old physician from Gratz maintaining his theory. His rival was combating it with undisguised ridicule, accompanied with bursts of laughter. This unseemly manifestation subsided and the altercation ended on my entrance.

"'Sir,' said my first physician, 'my learned brother seems to think that you want a conjuror, and not a doctor.'

"'Pardon me,' said the old physician from Gratz, looking displeased, 'I shall state my own view of the case in my own way another time. I grieve, Monsieur le General, that by my skill and science I can be of no use.

Before I go I shall do myself the honor to suggest something to you.'

"He seemed thoughtful, and sat down at a table and began to write.

Profoundly disappointed, I made my bow, and as I turned to go, the other doctor pointed over his shoulder to his companion who was writing, and then, with a shrug, significantly touched his forehead.

"This consultation, then, left me precisely where I was. I walked out into the grounds, all but distracted. The doctor from Gratz, in ten or fifteen minutes, overtook me. He apologized for having followed me, but said that he could not conscientiously take his leave without a few words more. He told me that he could not be mistaken; no natural disease exhibited the same symptoms; and that death was already very near. There remained, however, a day, or possibly two, of life. If the fatal seizure were at once arrested, with great care and skill her strength might possibly return. But all hung now upon the confines of the irrevocable. One more assault might extinguish the last spark of vitality which is, every moment, ready to die.

"'And what is the nature of the seizure you speak of?' I entreated.

"'I have stated all fully in this note, which I place in your hands upon the distinct condition that you send for the nearest clergyman, and open my letter in his presence, and on no account read it till he is with you; you would despise it else, and it is a matter of life and death. Should the priest fail you, then, indeed, you may read it.'

"He asked me, before taking his leave finally, whether I would wish to see a man curiously learned upon the very subject, which, after I had read his letter, would probably interest me above all others, and he urged me earnestly to invite him to visit him there; and so took his leave.

"The ecclesiastic was absent, and I read the letter by myself. At another time, or in another case, it might have excited my ridicule. But into what quackeries will not people rush for a last chance, where all accustomed means have failed, and the life of a beloved object is at stake?

"Nothing, you will say, could be more absurd than the learned man's letter.

It was monstrous enough to have consigned him to a madhouse. He said that the patient was suffering from the visits of a vampire! The punctures which she described as having occurred near the throat, were, he insisted, the insertion of those two long, thin, and sharp teeth which, it is well known, are peculiar to vampires; and there could be no doubt, he added, as to the well-defined presence of the small livid mark which all concurred in describing as that induced by the demon's lips, and every symptom described by the sufferer was in exact conformity with those recorded in every case of a similar visitation.

"Being myself wholly skeptical as to the existence of any such portent as the vampire, the supernatural theory of the good doctor furnished, in my opinion, but another instance of learning and intelligence oddly associated with some one hallucination. I was so miserable, however, that, rather than try nothing, I acted upon the instructions of the letter.

"I concealed myself in the dark dressing room, that opened upon the poor patient's room, in which a candle was burning, and watched there till she was fast asleep. I stood at the door, peeping through the small crevice, my sword laid on the table beside me, as my directions prescribed, until, a little after one, I saw a large black object, very ill-defined, crawl, as it seemed to me, over the foot of the bed, and swiftly spread itself up to the poor girl's throat, where it swelled, in a moment, into a great, palpitating mass.

"For a few moments I had stood petrified. I now sprang forward, with my sword in my hand. The black creature suddenly contracted towards the foot of the bed, glided over it, and, standing on the floor about a yard below the foot of the bed, with a glare of skulking ferocity and horror fixed on me, I saw Millarca. Speculating I know not what, I struck at her instantly with my sword; but I saw her standing near the door, unscathed. Horrified, I pursued, and struck again. She was gone; and my sword flew to shivers against the door.

"I can't describe to you all that passed on that horrible night. The whole house was up and stirring. The specter Millarca was gone. But her victim was sinking fast, and before the morning dawned, she died."

The old General was agitated. We did not speak to him. My father walked to some little distance, and began reading the inscriptions on the tombstones; and thus occupied, he strolled into the door of a side chapel to prosecute his researches. The General leaned against the wall, dried his eyes, and sighed heavily. I was relieved on hearing the voices of Carmilla and Madame, who were at that moment approaching. The voices died away.

In this solitude, having just listened to so strange a story, connected, as it was, with the great and titled dead, whose monuments were moldering among the dust and ivy round us, and every incident of which bore so awfully upon my own mysterious case—in this haunted spot, darkened by the towering foliage that rose on every side, dense and high above its noiseless walls—a horror began to steal over me, and my heart sank as I thought that my friends were, after all, not about to enter and disturb this triste and ominous scene.

The old General's eyes were fixed on the ground, as he leaned with his hand upon the basement of a shattered monument.

Under a narrow, arched doorway, surmounted by one of those demoniacal grotesques in which the cynical and ghastly fancy of old Gothic carving delights, I saw very gladly the beautiful face and figure of Carmilla enter the shadowy chapel.

I was just about to rise and speak, and nodded smiling, in answer to her peculiarly engaging smile; when with a cry, the old man by my side caught up the woodman's hatchet, and started forward. On seeing him a brutalized change came over her features. It was an instantaneous and horrible transformation, as she made a crouching step backwards. Before I could utter a scream, he struck at her with all his force, but she dived under his blow, and unscathed, caught him in her tiny grasp by the wrist. He struggled for a moment to release his arm, but his hand opened, the axe fell to the ground, and the girl was gone.

He staggered against the wall. His grey hair stood upon his head, and a moisture shone over his face, as if he were at the point of death.

The frightful scene had passed in a moment. The first thing I recollect after, is Madame standing before me, and impatiently repeating again and again, the question, "Where is Mademoiselle Carmilla?"

I answered at length, "I don't know—I can't tell—she went there," and I pointed to the door through which Madame had just entered; "only a minute or two since."

"But I have been standing there, in the passage, ever since Mademoiselle Carmilla entered; and she did not return."

She then began to call "Carmilla," through every door and passage and from the windows, but no answer came.

"She called herself Carmilla?" asked the General, still agitated.

"Carmilla, yes," I answered.

"Aye," he said; "that is Millarca. That is the same person who long ago was called Mircalla, Countess Karnstein. Depart from this accursed ground, my poor child, as quickly as you can. Drive to the clergyman's house, and stay there till we come. Begone! May you never behold Carmilla more; you will not find her here."

CHAPTER XV
ORDEAL AND EXECUTION

As he spoke one of the strangest looking men I ever beheld entered the chapel at the door through which Carmilla had made her entrance and her exit. He was tall, narrow-chested, stooping, with high shoulders, and dressed in black. His face was brown and dried in with deep furrows; he wore an oddly-shaped hat with a broad leaf. His hair, long and grizzled, hung on his shoulders. He wore a pair of gold spectacles, and walked slowly, with an odd shambling gait, with his face sometimes turned up to the sky, and sometimes bowed down towards the ground, seemed to wear a perpetual smile; his long thin arms were swinging, and his lank hands, in old black gloves ever so much too wide for them, waving and gesticulating in utter abstraction.

"The very man!" exclaimed the General, advancing with manifest delight. "My dear Baron, how happy I am to see you, I had no hope of meeting you so soon." He signed to my father, who had by this time returned, and leading the fantastic old gentleman, whom he called the Baron to meet him. He introduced him formally, and they at once entered into earnest conversation. The stranger took a roll of paper from his pocket, and spread it on the worn surface of a tomb that stood by. He had a pencil case in his fingers, with which he traced imaginary lines from point to point on the paper, which from their often glancing from it, together, at certain points of the building, I concluded to be a plan of the chapel. He accompanied, what I may term, his lecture, with occasional readings from a dirty little book, whose yellow leaves were closely written over.

They sauntered together down the side aisle, opposite to the spot where I was standing, conversing as they went; then they began measuring distances by paces, and finally they all stood together, facing a piece of the sidewall, which they began to examine with great minuteness; pulling off the ivy that clung over it, and rapping the plaster with the ends of their sticks, scraping here, and knocking there. At length they ascertained the existence of a broad marble tablet, with letters carved in relief upon it.

With the assistance of the woodman, who soon returned, a monumental inscription, and carved escutcheon, were disclosed. They proved to be those of the long lost monument of Mircalla, Countess Karnstein.

The old General, though not I fear given to the praying mood, raised his hands and eyes to heaven, in mute thanksgiving for some moments.

"Tomorrow," I heard him say; "the commissioner will be here, and the Inquisition will be held according to law."

Then turning to the old man with the gold spectacles, whom I have described, he shook him warmly by both hands and said:

"Baron, how can I thank you? How can we all thank you? You will have delivered this region from a plague that has scourged its inhabitants for more than a century. The horrible enemy, thank God, is at last tracked."

My father led the stranger aside, and the General followed. I know that he had led them out of hearing, that he might relate my case, and I saw them glance often quickly at me, as the discussion proceeded.

My father came to me, kissed me again and again, and leading me from the chapel, said:

"It is time to return, but before we go home, we must add to our party the good priest, who lives but a little way from this; and persuade him to accompany us to the schloss."

In this quest we were successful: and I was glad, being unspeakably fatigued when we reached home. But my satisfaction was changed to dismay, on discovering that there were no tidings of Carmilla. Of the scene that had occurred in the ruined chapel, no explanation was offered to me, and it was clear that it was a secret which my father for the present determined to keep from me.

The sinister absence of Carmilla made the remembrance of the scene more horrible to me. The arrangements for the night were singular. Two servants, and Madame were to sit up in my room that night; and the ecclesiastic with my father kept watch in the adjoining dressing room.

The priest had performed certain solemn rites that night, the purport of which I did not understand any more than I comprehended the reason of this extraordinary precaution taken for my safety during sleep.

I saw all clearly a few days later.

The disappearance of Carmilla was followed by the discontinuance of my nightly sufferings.

You have heard, no doubt, of the appalling superstition that prevails in Upper and Lower Styria, in Moravia, Silesia, in Turkish Serbia, in Poland, even in Russia; the superstition, so we must call it, of the Vampire.

If human testimony, taken with every care and solemnity, judicially, before commissions innumerable, each consisting of many members, all chosen for integrity and intelligence, and constituting reports more voluminous perhaps than exist upon any one other class of cases, is worth anything, it is difficult to deny, or even to doubt the existence of such a phenomenon as the Vampire.

For my part I have heard no theory by which to explain what I myself have witnessed and experienced, other than that supplied by the ancient and well-attested belief of the country.

The next day the formal proceedings took place in the Chapel of Karnstein.

The grave of the Countess Mircalla was opened; and the General and my father recognized each his perfidious and beautiful guest, in the face now disclosed to view. The features, though a hundred and fifty years had passed since her funeral, were tinted with the warmth of life. Her eyes were open; no cadaverous smell exhaled from the coffin. The two medical men, one officially present, the other on the part of the promoter of the inquiry, attested the marvelous fact that there was a faint but appreciable respiration, and a corresponding action of the heart. The limbs were perfectly flexible, the flesh elastic; and the leaden coffin floated with blood, in which to a depth of seven inches, the body lay immersed.

Here then, were all the admitted signs and proofs of vampirism. The body, therefore, in accordance with the ancient practice, was raised, and a sharp stake driven through the heart of the vampire, who uttered a piercing shriek at the moment, in all respects such as might escape from a living person in the last agony. Then the head was struck off, and a torrent of blood flowed from the severed neck. The body and head was next placed on a pile of wood, and reduced to ashes, which were thrown upon the river and borne away, and that territory has never since been plagued by the visits of a vampire.

My father has a copy of the report of the Imperial Commission, with the signatures of all who were present at these proceedings, attached in verification of the statement. It is from this official paper that I have summarized my account of this last shocking scene.

CHAPTER XVI
CONCLUSION

I write all this you suppose with composure. But far from it; I cannot think of it without agitation. Nothing but your earnest desire so repeatedly expressed, could have induced me to sit down to a task that has unstrung my nerves for months to come, and reinduced a shadow of the unspeakable horror which years after my deliverance continued to make my days and nights dreadful, and solitude insupportably terrific.

Let me add a word or two about that quaint Baron Vordenburg, to whose curious lore we were indebted for the discovery of the Countess Mircalla's grave.

He had taken up his abode in Gratz, where, living upon a mere pittance, which was all that remained to him of the once princely estates of his family, in Upper Styria, he devoted himself to the minute and laborious investigation of the marvelously authenticated tradition of Vampirism. He had at his fingers' ends all the great and little works upon the subject.

"Magia Posthuma," "Phlegon de Mirabilibus," "Augustinus de cura pro Mortuis," "Philosophicae et Christianae Cogitationes de Vampiris," by John Christofer Herenberg; and a thousand others, among which I remember only a few of those which he lent to my father. He had a voluminous digest of all the judicial cases, from which he had extracted a system of principles that appear to govern—some always, and others occasionally only—the condition of the vampire. I may mention, in passing, that the deadly pallor attributed to that sort of revenants, is a mere melodramatic fiction. They present, in the grave, and when they show themselves in human society, the appearance of healthy life. When disclosed to light in their coffins, they exhibit all the symptoms that are enumerated as those which proved the vampire-life of the long-dead Countess Karnstein.

How they escape from their graves and return to them for certain hours every day, without displacing the clay or leaving any trace of disturbance in the state of the coffin or the cerements, has always been admitted to be utterly inexplicable. The amphibious existence of the vampire is sustained by daily renewed slumber in the grave. Its horrible lust for living blood supplies the vigor of its waking existence. The vampire is prone to be fascinated with an engrossing vehemence, resembling the passion of love, by particular persons. In pursuit of these it will exercise inexhaustible patience and stratagem, for access to a particular object may be obstructed in a hundred ways. It will never desist until it has satiated its passion, and drained the very life of its coveted victim. But it will, in these cases, husband and protract its murderous enjoyment with the refinement of an epicure, and heighten it by the gradual approaches of an artful courtship. In these cases it seems to yearn for something like sympathy and consent. In ordinary ones it goes direct to its object, overpowers with violence, and strangles and exhausts often at a single feast.

The vampire is, apparently, subject, in certain situations, to special conditions. In the particular instance of which I have given you a relation, Mircalla seemed to be limited to a name which, if not her real one, should at least reproduce, without the omission or addition of a single letter, those, as we say, anagrammatically, which compose it.

Carmilla did this; so did Millarca.

My father related to the Baron Vordenburg, who remained with us for two or three weeks after the expulsion of Carmilla, the story about the Moravian nobleman and the vampire at Karnstein churchyard, and then he asked the Baron how he had discovered the exact position of the long-concealed tomb of the Countess Mircalla? The Baron's grotesque features puckered up into a mysterious smile; he looked down, still smiling on his worn spectacle case and fumbled with it. Then looking up, he said:

"I have many journals, and other papers, written by that remarkable man; the most curious among them is one treating of the visit of which you speak, to Karnstein. The tradition, of course, discolors and distorts a little. He might have been termed a Moravian nobleman, for he had changed his abode to that territory, and was, beside, a noble. But he was, in truth, a native of Upper Styria. It is enough to say that in very early youth he had been a passionate and favored lover of the beautiful Mircalla, Countess Karnstein. Her early death plunged him into inconsolable grief. It is the nature of vampires to increase and multiply, but according to an ascertained and ghostly law.

"Assume, at starting, a territory perfectly free from that pest. How does it begin, and how does it multiply itself? I will tell you. A person, more or less wicked, puts an end to himself. A suicide, under certain circumstances, becomes a vampire. That specter visits living people in their slumbers; they die, and almost invariably, in the grave, develop into vampires. This happened in the case of the beautiful Mircalla, who was haunted by one of those demons. My ancestor, Vordenburg, whose title I still bear, soon discovered this, and in the course of the studies to which he devoted himself, learned a great deal more.

"Among other things, he concluded that suspicion of vampirism would probably fall, sooner or later, upon the dead Countess, who in life had been his idol. He conceived a horror, be she what she might, of her remains being profaned by the outrage of a posthumous execution. He has left a curious paper to prove that the vampire, on its expulsion from its amphibious existence, is projected into a far more horrible life; and he resolved to save his once beloved Mircalla from this.

"He adopted the stratagem of a journey here, a pretended removal of her remains, and a real obliteration of her monument. When age had stolen upon him, and from the vale of years, he looked back on the scenes he was leaving, he considered, in a different spirit, what he had done, and a horror took possession of him. He made the tracings and notes which have guided me to the very spot, and drew up a confession of the deception that he had practiced. If he had intended any further action in this matter, death prevented him; and the hand of a remote descendant has, too late for many, directed the pursuit to the lair of the beast."

We talked a little more, and among other things he said was this:

"One sign of the vampire is the power of the hand. The slender hand of Mircalla closed like a vice of steel on the General's wrist when he raised the hatchet to strike. But its power is not confined to its grasp; it leaves a numbness in the limb it seizes, which is slowly, if ever, recovered from."

The following Spring my father took me a tour through Italy. We remained away for more than a year. It was long before the terror of recent events subsided; and to this hour the image of Carmilla returns to memory with ambiguous alternations—sometimes the playful, languid, beautiful girl; sometimes the writhing fiend I saw in the ruined church; and often from a reverie I have started, fancying I heard the light step of Carmilla at the drawing room door.

THE END

MRS DALLOWAY IN BOND STREET

BY VIRGINIA WOOLF

Mrs Dalloway said she would buy the gloves herself.

Big Ben was striking as she stepped out into the street. It was eleven o'clock and the unused hour was fresh as if issued to children on a beach. But there was something solemn in the deliberate swing of the repeated strokes; something stirring in the murmur of wheels and the shuffle of footsteps.

No doubt they were not all bound on errands of happiness. There is much more to be said about us than that we walk the streets of Westminster. Big Ben too is nothing but steel rods consumed by rust were it not for the care of H. M.'s Office of Works. Only for Mrs Dalloway the moment was complete; for Mrs Dalloway June was fresh. A happy childhood--and it was not to his daughters only that Justin Parry had seemed a fine fellow (weak of course on the Bench); flowers at evening, smoke rising; the caw of rooks falling from ever so high, down down through the October air--there is nothing to take the place of childhood. A leaf of mint brings it back; or a cup with a blue ring.

Poor little wretches, she sighed, and pressed forward. Oh, right under the horses' noses, you little demon! and there she was left on the kerb stretching her hand out, while Jimmy Dawes grinned on the further side.

A charming woman, poised, eager, strangely white-haired for her pink cheeks, so Scope Purvis, C. B., saw her as he hurried to his office. She stiffened a little, waiting for Durtnall's van to pass. Big Ben struck the tenth; struck the eleventh stroke. The leaden circles dissolved in the air. Pride held her erect, inheriting, handing on, acquainted with discipline and with suffering. How people suffered, how they suffered, she thought, thinking of Mrs Foxcroft at the Embassy last night decked with jewels, eating her heart out, because that nice boy was dead, and now the old Manor House (Durtnall's van passed) must go to a cousin.

"Good morning to you!" said Hugh Whitbread raising his hat rather extravagantly by the china shop, for they had known each other as children. "Where are you off to?"

"I love walking in London" said Mrs Dalloway. "Really it's better than walking in the country!"

"We've just come up" said Hugh Whitbread. "Unfortunately to see doctors."

"Milly?" said Mrs Dalloway, instantly compassionate.

"Out of sorts," said Hugh Whitbread. "That sort of thing. Dick all right?"

"First rate!" said Clarissa.

Of course, she thought, walking on, Milly is about my age--fifty--fifty-two. So it is probably _that_, Hugh's manner had said so, said it perfectly--dear old Hugh, thought Mrs Dalloway, remembering with amusement, with gratitude, with emotion, how shy, like a brother--one would rather die than speak to one's brother--Hugh had always been, when he was at Oxford, and came over, and perhaps one of them (drat the thing!) couldn't ride. How then could women sit in Parliament? How could they do things with men? For there is this extraordinarily deep instinct, something inside one; you can't get over it; it's no use trying; and men like Hugh respect it without our saying it, which is what one loves, thought Clarissa, in dear old Hugh.

She had passed through the Admiralty Arch and saw at the end of the empty road with its thin trees Victoria's white mound, Victoria's billowing motherliness, amplitude and homeliness, always ridiculous, yet how sublime, thought Mrs Dalloway, remembering Kensington Gardens and the old lady in horn spectacles and being told by Nanny to stop dead still and bow to the Queen. The flag flew above the Palace. The King and Queen were back then. Dick had met her at lunch the other day--a thoroughly nice woman. It matters so much to the poor, thought Clarissa, and to the soldiers. A man in bronze stood heroically on a pedestal with a gun on her left hand side--the South African war. It matters, thought Mrs Dalloway walking towards Buckingham Palace. There it stood four-square, in the broad sunshine, uncompromising, plain. But it was character she thought; something inborn in the race; what Indians respected. The Queen went to hospitals, opened bazaars--the Queen of England, thought Clarissa, looking at the Palace. Already at this hour a motor car passed out at the gates; soldiers saluted; the gates were shut. And Clarissa, crossing the road, entered the Park, holding herself upright.

June had drawn out every leaf on the trees. The mothers of Westminster with mottled breasts gave suck to their young. Quite respectable girls lay stretched on the grass. An elderly man, stooping very stiffly, picked up a crumpled paper, spread it out flat and flung it away. How horrible! Last night at the Embassy Sir Dighton had said "If I want a fellow to hold my horse, I have only to put up my hand." But the religious question is far more serious than the economic, Sir Dighton had said, which she thought extraordinarily interesting, from a man like Sir Dighton. "Oh, the country will never know what it has lost" he had said, talking, of his own accord, about dear Jack Stewart.

She mounted the little hill lightly. The air stirred with energy. Messages were passing from the Fleet to the Admiralty. Piccadilly and Arlington Street and the Mall seemed to chafe the very air in the Park and lift its leaves hotly, brilliantly, upon waves of that divine vitality which Clarissa loved. To ride; to dance; she had adored all that. Or going long walks in the country, talking, about books, what to do with one's life, for young people were amazingly priggish--oh, the things one had said! But one had conviction. Middle age is the devil. People like Jack'll never know that, she thought; for he never once thought of death, never, they said, knew he was dying. And now can never mourn--how did it go?--a head grown grey. . . . From the contagion of the world's slow stain . . . have drunk their cup a round or two before. . . . From the contagion of the world's slow stain! She held herself upright.

But how Jack would have shouted! Quoting Shelley, in Piccadilly! "You want a pin," he would have said. He hated frumps. "My God Clarissa! My God Clarissa!"--she could hear him now at the Devonshire House party, about poor Sylvia Hunt in her amber necklace and that dowdy old silk. Clarissa held herself upright for she had spoken aloud and now she was in Piccadilly, passing the house with the slender green columns, and the balconies; passing club windows full of newspapers; passing old Lady Burdett Coutts' house where the glazed white parrot used to hang; and Devonshire House, without its gilt leopards; and Claridge's, where she must remember Dick wanted her to leave a card on Mrs Jepson or she would be gone. Rich Americans can be very charming. There was St James palace; like a child's game with bricks; and now--she had passed Bond Street--she was by Hatchard's book shop. The stream was endless--endless--endless. Lords, Ascot, Hurlingham--what was it? What a duck, she thought, looking at the frontispiece of some book of memoirs spread wide in the bow window, Sir Joshua perhaps or Romney; arch, bright, demure; the sort of girl--like her own Elizabeth--the only _real_ sort of girl. And there was that absurd book, Soapy Sponge, which Jim used to quote by the yard; and Shakespeare's Sonnets. She knew them by heart. Phil and she had argued all day about the Dark Lady, and Dick had said straight out at dinner that night that he had never heard of her. Really, she had married him for that! He had never read Shakespeare! There must be some little cheap book she could buy for Milly--Cranford of course! Was there ever anything so enchanting as the cow in petticoats? If only people had that sort of humour, that sort of self-respect now, thought Clarissa, for she remembered the broad pages; the sentences ending; the characters-- how one talked about them as if they were real. For all the great things one must go to the past, she thought. From the contagion of the world's slow stain. . . . Fear no more the heat o' the sun. . . . And now can never mourn, can never mourn, she repeated, her eyes straying over the window; for it ran in her head; the test of great poetry; the moderns had never written anything one wanted to read about death, she thought; and turned.

Omnibuses joined motor cars; motor cars vans; vans taxicabs; taxicabs motor cars--here was an open motor car with a girl, alone. Up till four, her feet tingling, I know, thought Clarissa, for the girl looked washed out, half asleep, in the corner of the car after the dance. And another car came; and another. No! No! No! Clarissa smiled good-naturedly. The fat lady had taken every sort of trouble, but diamonds! orchids! at this hour of the morning! No! No! No! The excellent policeman would, when the time came, hold up his hand. Another motor car passed. How utterly unattractive! Why should a girl of that age paint black round her eyes? And a young man, with a girl, at this hour, when the country--The admirable policeman raised his hand and Clarissa acknowledging his sway, taking her time, crossed, walked towards Bond Street; saw the narrow crooked street, the yellow banners; the thick notched telegraph wires stretched across the sky.

A hundred years ago her great-great-grandfather, Seymour Parry, who ran away with Conway's daughter, had walked down Bond Street. Down Bond Street the Parrys had walked for a hundred years, and might have met the Dalloways (Leighs on the mother's side) going up. Her father got his clothes from Hill's. There was a roll of cloth in the window, and here just one jar on a black table, incredibly expensive; like the thick pink salmon on the ice block at the fishmonger's. The jewels were exquisite-- pink and orange stars, paste, Spanish, she thought, and chains of old gold;

starry buckles, little brooches which had been worn on sea green satin by ladies with high head-dresses. But no good looking! One must economize. She must go on past the picture dealer's where one of the odd French pictures hung, as if people had thrown confetti--pink and blue--for a joke. If you had lived with pictures (and it's the same with books and music) thought Clarissa, passing the Aeolian Hall, you can't be taken in by a joke.

The river of Bond Street was clogged. There, like a Queen at a tournament, raised, regal, was Lady Bexborough. She sat in her carriage, upright, alone, looking through her glasses. The white glove was loose at her wrist. She was in black, quite shabby, yet, thought Clarissa, how extraordinarily it tells, breeding, self-respect, never saying a word too much or letting people gossip; an astonishing friend; no one can pick a hole in her after all these years, and now, there she is, thought Clarissa, passing the Countess who waited powdered, perfectly still, and Clarissa would have given anything to be like that, the mistress of Clarefield, talking politics, like a man. But she never goes anywhere, thought Clarissa, and it's quite useless to ask her, and the carriage went on and Lady Bexborough was borne past like a Queen at a tournament, though she had nothing to live for and the old man is failing and they say she is sick of it all, thought Clarissa and the tears actually rose to her eyes as she entered the shop.

"Good morning" said Clarissa in her charming voice. "Gloves" she said with her exquisite friendliness and putting her bag on the counter began, very slowly, to undo the buttons. "White gloves" she said. "Above the elbow" and she looked straight into the shopwoman's face--but this was not the girl she remembered? She looked quite old. "These really don't fit" said Clarissa. The shop girl looked at them. "Madame wears bracelets?" Clarissa spread out her fingers. "Perhaps it's my rings." And the girl took the grey gloves with her to the end of the counter.

Yes, thought Clarissa, if it's the girl I remember she's twenty years older. . . . There was only one other customer, sitting sideways at the counter, her elbow poised, her bare hand drooping, vacant; like a figure on a Japanese fan, thought Clarissa, too vacant perhaps, yet some men would adore her. The lady shook her head sadly. Again the gloves were too large. She turned round the glass. "Above the wrist" she reproached the grey-headed woman; who looked and agreed.

They waited; a clock ticked; Bond Street hummed, dulled, distant; the woman went away holding gloves. "Above the wrist" said the lady, mournfully, raising her voice. And she would have to order chairs, ices, flowers, and cloak-room tickets, thought Clarissa. The people she didn't want would come; the others wouldn't. She would stand by the door. They sold stockings--silk stockings. A lady is known by her gloves and her shoes, old Uncle William used to say. And through the hanging silk stockings quivering silver she looked at the lady, sloping shouldered, her hand drooping, her bag slipping, her eyes vacantly on the floor. It would be intolerable if dowdy women came to her party! Would one have liked Keats if he had worn red socks? Oh, at last--she drew into the counter and it flashed into her mind:

"Do you remember before the war you had gloves with pearl buttons?"

"French gloves, Madame?"

"Yes, they were French" said Clarissa. The other lady rose very sadly and took her bag, and looked at the gloves on the counter. But they were all too large--always too large at the wrist.

"With pearl buttons" said the shop-girl, who looked ever so much older. She split the lengths of tissue paper apart on the counter. With pearl buttons, thought Clarissa, perfectly simple--how French!

"Madame's hands are so slender" said the shop girl, drawing the glove firmly, smoothly, down over her rings. And Clarissa looked at her arm in the looking glass. The glove hardly came to the elbow. Were there others half an inch longer? Still it seemed tiresome to bother her--perhaps the one day in the month, thought Clarissa, when it's an agony to stand. "Oh, don't bother" she said. But the gloves were brought.

"Don't you get fearfully tired" she said in her charming voice, "standing? When d'you get your holiday?"

"In September, Madame, when we're not so busy."

When we're in the country thought Clarissa. Or shooting. She has a fortnight at Brighton. In some stuffy lodging. The landlady takes the sugar. Nothing would be easier than to send her to Mrs Lumley's right in the country (and it was on the tip of her tongue). But then she remembered how on their honeymoon Dick had shown her the folly of giving impulsively. It was much more important, he said, to get trade with China. Of course he was right. And she could feel the girl wouldn't like to be given things.

There she was in her place. So was Dick. Selling gloves was her job. She had her own sorrows quite separate, "and now can never mourn, can never mourn" the words ran in her head, "From the contagion of the world's slow stain" thought Clarissa holding her arm stiff, for there are moments when it seems utterly futile (the glove was drawn off leaving her arm flecked with powder)--simply one doesn't believe, thought Clarissa, any more in God.

The traffic suddenly roared; the silk stockings brightened. A customer came in.

"White gloves," she said, with some ring in her voice that Clarissa remembered.

It used, thought Clarissa, to be so simple. Down down through the air came the caw of the rooks. When Sylvia died, hundreds of years ago, the yew hedges looked so lovely with the diamond webs in the mist before early church. But if Dick were to die to-morrow as for believing in God--no, she would let the children choose, but for herself, like Lady Bexborough, who opened the bazaar, they say, with the telegram in her hand--Roden, her favourite, killed--she would go on. But why, if one doesn't believe? For the sake of others, she thought, taking the glove in her hand. This girl would be much more unhappy if she didn't believe.

"Thirty shillings" said the shopwoman. "No, pardon me Madame, thirty-five. The French gloves are more."

For one doesn't live for oneself, thought Clarissa.

And then the other customer took a glove, tugged it, and it split.

"There!" she exclaimed.

"A fault of the skin," said the grey-headed woman hurriedly. "Sometimes a drop of acid in tanning. Try this pair, Madame."

"But it's an awful swindle to ask two pound ten!"

Clarissa looked at the lady; the lady looked at Clarissa.

"Gloves have never been quite so reliable since the war" said the shop-girl, apologizing, to Clarissa.

But where had she seen the other lady?--elderly, with a frill under her chin; wearing a black ribbon for gold eyeglasses; sensual, clever, like a Sargent drawing. How one can tell from a voice when people are in the habit, thought Clarissa, of making other people--"It's a shade too tight" she said--obey. The shopwoman went off again. Clarissa was left waiting.

Fear no more she repeated, playing her finger on the counter. Fear no more the heat o' the sun. Fear no more she repeated. There were little brown spots on her arm. And the girl crawled like a snail. Thou thy wordly task hast done. Thousands of young men had died that things might go on. At last! Half an inch above the elbow; pearl buttons; five and a quarter. My dear slow coach, thought Clarissa, do you think I can sit here the whole morning? Now you'll take twenty-five minutes to bring me my change!

There was a violent explosion in the street outside. The shopwomen cowered behind the counters. But Clarissa, sitting very up-right, smiled at the other lady. "Miss Anstruther!" she exclaimed.

THE END

GLOSSARY OF TERMS USED IN "A CALL TO SERVE":

- *Sedren*: a province/region. There are eight sedrens in Monsiel – Kantuo, Quobia, Imgoll, Maxan, Chadriac, Zorran, Belchar, and Euramdian.

- *Sond:* a geographical subdivision of a sedren. eg, there are three sonds in Belcar – Prackus, Manthean, and Bastoleg.

- *Strong:* the strongs of Monsiel are the powerful families of the continent. The Borinth strong = the Borinth family.

- *Halisant:* the ruling monarch of Belchar.

- *Seecher:* the ruling monarch of Quobia.

- *Dullun:* the ruling monarch of Euramdian.

- *Jakeram:* the ruling monarch of Zorran.

- *By the broken:* a mildly blasphemous exclamation. The "broken" are three gods of Monsiel - three siblings - two brothers and a sister. The brothers are Vanring and Sinlio while the sister is named Fronsas. The theory of the world among believers in these three gods is that Vanring, Sinlio and Fronsas got into a vicious fight that resulted in them breaking apart into tiny pieces. When the pieces re-assembled in the void of space, they formed into the stars and Domondais, the world on which the known continents of Monsiel, Amadast, Hondrint and the great isle of Madgans lie.

- *Thank the broken:* an expression of gratitude to the broken gods for some good fortune.

Thank you for reading!

3	6	8	7	4	9	2	5	1
4	5	1	6	8	2	3	7	9
9	2	7	5	3	1	4	8	6
7	1	3	8	2	6	9	4	5
5	8	2	3	9	4	6	1	7
6	9	4	1	7	5	8	2	3
8	7	5	2	6	3	1	9	4
1	3	9	4	5	8	7	6	2
2	4	6	9	1	7	5	3	8

Issue 18 is coming out this winter!

www.ingramcontent.com/pod-product-compliance
Lightning Source LLC
Chambersburg PA
CBHW011149190726
48288CB00010B/3246